BOOK ONE

A Question of Duty

CHLOE WILLOWFIELD

A QUESTION OF DUTY: WEATHERBYS REGENCY ROMANCE BOOK ONE
First published in Australia in 2024 by Chloe Willowfield

This is a work of fiction. Names, characters, places, and incidents either are the product of the author's imagination or are used fictitiously, and any resemblance to actual persons, living or dead, business establishments, events, or locales is entirely coincidental.

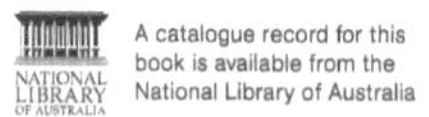
A catalogue record for this book is available from the National Library of Australia

ISBN: 9781763748002
ISBN: 9781763748019 (eBook)

Cover design by Miblart

To MD.

PROLOGUE

"Georgina," Ma said, "you need to go with Mrs Wilson."

The little girl crossed her arms and glared up at her mother. "But I want to stay here! It's not fair! Why can't I stay here with you and Bessie and Tobias and - and -"

With that, the girl broke down into sobs and rubbed furiously at her eyes.

Mrs Hartley glanced over at Mrs Wilson and their eyes met in silent conversation. Then, Mrs Wilson smiled kindly and said, "I'll go and check on the youngsters." She went out the back door to where the younger Hartley children were playing on the parched grass.

Inside the shack, Ma took her eldest daughter in her arms and sat with her in the rocking chair in front of the fireplace.

"Oh, my girl, whatever am I going to do with you?" Ma tutted gently as she rocked the chair back and forth. "I know it doesn't seem like it now, but this is the best opportunity you are ever going to have and, all going well, you won't have to labour your life away in the fields like generations of our family have had to. You'll learn singing and how to read your bible and you'll have a nice safe warm bed every night."

Georgina snuffled in a small voice. "But I won't be with you, ma."

"It won't be easy, but often worthwhile things aren't easy. You'll be my brave girl, I know you will Georgina." Ma fought to keep her voice one of even reassurance. "I'm so very proud of you, and I know your pa is looking down from heaven and he is very very proud of you too."

Ma kissed Georgina's forehead and rubbed her hair gently. "And don't forget, I'm not far away so we'll still see each other."

After what felt like the thousandth goodbye from ma, Georgina exited the Hartley family home for the last time as a resident. Now, thanks to her talent for singing, she would be moving in with the Reverend Wilson and his family. On many a Sunday, she had sung in the village church of St Cecilia's and the Wilsons had been very taken by her clear talent. So much so that they invited her to move in and be trained as a proper singer. Otherwise, they said it would be a shame to waste a voice such as hers.

Mrs Wilson took Georgina by the hand and together they walked down the lane towards the vicarage.

That first month at the Wilson's was a lesson in sheer disorientation. Almost everything Georgina thought she knew turned out to not be so at the Wilson's house. The hours the family kept were different, the table manners were different and the activities she was expected to perform were different.

When she lived with her family, she had helped with every task that needed a pair of hands. Be it cleaning, washing, picking crops or looking after her younger siblings, she had experience in it all. Yet the Wilsons had two maids and a cook and so Georgina's days had become a whirl of lessons in singing and all the requirements for life as a middle class wife.

She even had her own bedroom. Pokey though it was, and it was the smallest bedroom outside of the servants' quarters, it was hers and hers alone.

1790, GLOUCESTERSHIRE

Georgina sat on the bench directly beneath the window of the vicar's study. On this balmy summer's day, she was enjoying the warmth of the sun's rays while reading one of the comedic novels she so adored.

"It is of no use," Reverend Wilson sighed.

Georgina's ears pricked up as the sound of an unusually disgruntled vicar leaked out from the open windows directly above her head.

Reverend Wilson continued speaking. "I have gone through these account ledgers over and over again and what with the losses from that bad investment we can barely afford dowries for Lizzie and Anne."

Then the distressed tones of Mrs Wilson reverberated over Georgina's head. "Dearest, what do you mean we can barely afford dowries for our daughters?"

"I am afraid so. Nevertheless, I have done the numbers and we can still give Lizzie and Annie proper dowries," he said.

"Well that is a relief," Mrs Wilson said. "But what of Georgina?"

On the bench below the window, Georgina felt an uneasy tightness in her stomach. Whatever next came out of Reverend Wilson's mouth would define her life forever.

Reverend Wilson spoke again. "Ah now that is the most unfortunate business of it all. Try as I might, the only way I have been able to carve out sufficient dowries for Lizzie and Anne is by ensuring they are the only dowries that the estate will provide."

"Reverend Wilson! You mean to say that because of a shoddy investment in that sheep farm, Georgina will have no dowry at all? What is the poor girl to do?" Mrs Wilson sobbed.

Georgina could not sit and listen any longer. She put her book down on the bench, too distracted to consider what might happen to it, and stood up. Tears rolling down her cheeks, she walked through the small garden and into the wheat fields behind the house. Once she was sure she was out of sight of anyone in the nearby houses, she sat down on the ground and began to weep without abandon.

No dowry! No dowry! The thought was absolutely terrifying. Not since the passing of her father all those years ago had she felt so despondent. As though she had no direction in her life. For years, she and the Wilsons had operated under the belief that they would provide her with a dowry when she came of age and chose to marry. It went without saying that Georgina's dowry would be smaller than those of the Wilson's daughters but she would get something nonetheless. Enough for her to marry a tradesman, clerk or innkeeper. Now that plan had gone up in smoke. Whatever was she to do?

Had she never moved in with the Wilsons and had instead stayed with her mother, the question of a dowry would have been moot. She would have become an agricultural labourer and married one too. After all, dowries were not on the table for agricultural labourers. However, the respectable education that the Wilsons had provided for her would make it very hard for her to go back to the world of the poor rural folk. And she had seen too much of other lives and other possibilities to ever want to return even if it were a likely eventuality. She faced a true conundrum indeed.

August ebbed into September and, before anyone knew it, the leaves of autumn were upon the ground and the harvest was complete. The year kept racing ahead and Advent arrived. Christmas came and went and then 1790 gave way to the New Year of 1791.

Georgina was still at a loss for what her future might hold. Through it all she focused on her singing as her gift for it was the one thing of which she was certain.

Then February arrived and brought with it sheer tragedy.

Harsh winds swept through the village that fateful, icy night. The church bell clanged continuously against the background of creaking fences swaying in a precarious manner on what was the coldest February night in years. The two horses that slept in the vicarage stable whinnied and neighed in fright. Georgina tried to get to sleep and ignore the bedlam going on around her. After a while, sleep claimed her but it was a fitful night. She lost count of how many times she woke up what with the noise and worry.

Shortly after sunrise, she was awoken by a soft knocking at her door. Mrs Wilson entered the room wearing a dour expression.

"Georgina, there's no easy way for me to say this," the vicar's wife began. "The Lord has seen it fit to take your mother and siblings in the night. I am so sorry."

Georgina let forth an ear piercing scream.

Those first few weeks after that horrific night went by in a blur. Georgina got up every day, made her bed and ate with the Wilsons. Her singing tutors still came by but otherwise she ceased partaking in any instruction. She gave up reading books and pamphlets, finding her mind unable to focus on the words on the page and merely rereading the same word several dozen times. Instead, she went on long walks through the fields surrounding the village. Lost in her own mind, she screamed at whoever had created her for an explanation about what had happened to her mother and her siblings. Georgina would be eighteen in a couple of months and she could not see a path forward for her in this village.

Two weeks after her eighteenth birthday, when the earth had begun to dry after the earlier storms, she went on one of her regular walks and sat down at the edge of a field. Hedgerows surrounded her on one side and wheat stalks on the other. She herself sat on the patch of grass between them. She picked at the blades, pulling them with a strong roughness that her mind did not register.

Over and over, she considered the question of what she might do in the future. Until the horrific events of ten weeks ago, she had assumed she would stay at the Wilsons a while longer before moving somewhere else and becoming someone else. But her plans had never developed to anything beyond that nebulous notion.

She plucked at the grass some more and the city of Bath appeared in her mind's eye. She had visited that city every year since she moved in with the Wilsons and the annual trip had always been something she had looked forward to with great excitement. She loved the city for its general hustle and bustle, exposure to the latest fashions and variety of bookshops and pamphleteers. But most of all she loved it for the operas. On each trip to that city, the Reverend and Mrs Wilson had taken her and their children to the Old Orchard Street Theatre to see a performance. Every time, Georgina had been captivated. Now here was something she could see herself doing, performing onstage and using her vocal talents to their full effect. She was not naive to the realities for female opera singers in England during the reign of King George III. She had heard the stories about how they needed protectors to make ends meet and how that led them to become a type of courtesan.

With no dowry on the cards, her options were limited. Try and marry a man slightly above her on the class scale, not the level of a vicar but maybe an innkeeper like Mrs Wilson had suggested in excitement years ago, but even then he may be put off by her lack of dowry. She could try for a governess position but that was too long of a shot for her comfort. She wasn't middle class enough for a re-spectable middle class family to want to hire her, however many years she had spent at the Wilsons. Worse still, being a governess would mean she wasn't making real use of her vocal talents and would still be unable to pursue marriage given her lack of dowry. The other options for which she might be qualified, domestic service or agricultural labour, weren't viable either because they paid a pittance and would mean a hand to mouth existence far worse than that of a governess or a singer.

She picked at the grass and came to a decision. Opera singer and courtesan it would be. At least that way, if she played her cards right and had some luck come her way, she might be able to build up a nest egg for her dotage and may even find a gentleman who would be willing to support her as his mistress on an ongoing basis.

⁂

Little more than a month passed and she arrived in Bath courtesy of Mr Briar, a connection of one of her singing tutors.

A veritable mover and shaker of the West Country's operatic scene, Mr Briar knew everyone who was worth knowing in Bath.

He quickly placed her in a small supporting role at the opera.

Hardly the best standard, the opera was nonetheless a starting point for her singing career and journey to the better stages of London and Venice.

One summer afternoon soon after her arrival in Bath, she was studying her lines in the parlour at Mr Briar's residence where she was staying when there was a knock at the door.

"Who is it?" she called.

The maid opened the door and poked her head around. "Mr Briar and another gentleman are here to see you."

"Indeed," Georgina nodded.

The maid's head vanished and a few seconds later the door swung open to reveal Mr Briar and an elderly man whom Georgina did not recognise.

Georgina put down the booklet of lines she had been studying and looked at the pair with mild curiosity.

"Viscount," Mr Briar boomed, "May I present to you Miss Georgina Hartley." He then turned to Georgina. "Miss Hartley, this is the Viscount Redditch."

Georgina had never met a member of the peerage before and she was unsure precisely what she ought to do. Mrs Wilson had given her some training as part of her education in being a wife, back when everybody still thought Georgina would receive a passable dowry, so the young opera singer cast her mind back to that. A curtsey was what was required, yes that was it. Though since Mrs Wilson had herself rarely encountered members of the peerage, the instruction was somewhat hazy and confused.

Georgina rose from the settee and gave a slow curtsey to the viscount.

"My lord," she said in a deferential tone.

The viscount took stooping steps towards her.

"Miss Hartley, the pleasure is all mine." He reached for her hand and placed a gentle kiss upon it. "May I say that you are most charming on the stage. I saw you performing the night before last and thought to myself 'well, there is a beguiling young lady whom I would like to get to know better.'"

Before Georgina had a chance to reply, Mr Briar gave a loud cough and said, "His lordship seeks an arrangement with you, Miss Hartley."

Then before Georgina knew it, Mr Briar was bowing and departing the room, leaving her alone with the viscount.

And so she came to an agreement with Lord Redditch for him to be her protector until he left Bath in the winter.

Lord Redditch bid her farewell with the instruction to come to his townhouse at noon the following day for luncheon.

The front door of the house slammed.

Georgina wandered over to the window overlooking the street outside and peeped through the net curtains.

She saw Lord Redditch getting into his carriage, a sleek black contraption with a robin's egg blue coat of arms discretely adorning one of the doors.

Two footmen in matching pale blue liveries sat at the front of the carriage as it trundled its way down the street.

Georgina watched the carriage until it disappeared out of sight. Then she returned to the settee.

Now she was fully alone again, she felt a strange wave of emotion pass through her body. At first, she struggled to place it but on closer examination she realised it was a bewildering blend of apprehension and relief. On the one hand, she was nervous about what Lord Redditch would expect of her. She was new to this whole world, after all. But on the other hand, she had come to Bath with the goal of finding a protector close to the top of her mind and now she had achieved it. All going well, she had found some security that would see her through most of the remainder of the year.

The next day at the agreed time, Georgina sat on the settee in Lord Redditch's Bath townhouse. While she was awaiting the arrival of her protector, she cast her eye around the room. Everything was well kept and clean but it harkened back to the days of King George II. Even for his time, Lord Redditch was a man of old fashioned tastes and the influence of William Kent through the ornate, heavyset gilded furniture was most strong indeed. This was a house where the delicately refined influence of Thomas Chippendale had yet to raise its head.

There was a knock at the door and then Lord Redditch entered the room.

"Good afternoon, Miss Hartley," he said.

She raised herself from the settee and gave a curtsey. "Good afternoon, my lord."

As on the previous day, he reached for her hand and kissed it.

"Please, follow me to the dining room," he said.

He led her out of the room, his gait slow and shuffling, and across the hallway to a wood panelled room replete with oil paintings.

He gestured to a monumental mahogany table and set of chairs. "Please, have a seat."

She duly did so, taking a seat next to the head of the table.

The meal passed by pleasantly enough. As they ate and chatted, she looked around the room and reflected on its decor. While she had never been aboard a ship, the only vessels she had ever set foot on being rowing boats a few times on the River Avon with the Wilsons, she imagined that this was what a naval captain's quarters would look like. A medley of deep dark wood, stately furniture and stuffy paintings.

Once the servants had cleared the table, Lord Redditch raised himself from his chair and moved to stand behind her.

He placed his hands on her shoulders and bent over to give her forehead a kiss.

"Come upstairs, dearest Miss Hartley," he said.

And so she did.

As winter drew to a close, Georgina found herself wondering exactly when Lord Redditch would end their arrangement. His health seemed to be worsening week by week and she did not think he would be able to sustain their rendezvous for much longer.

Her suspicions were confirmed when he entered her apartment one day in a terribly frail state.

She cast her mind back to their first meeting, when he had walked with a stoop but still seemed to have a sprightliness in his spirit.

Now his stoop was more severe than ever and he was gaunt and drawn.

So she was not particularly surprised at what he told her next.

"Dearest Miss Hartley," he began as he looked her directly in the eyes. "My doctors have told me I have not much time left, likely only a month. So I am leaving Bath for my estate in Hampshire to set my affairs in order. And it pains me to tell you this, but I must bring our arrangement to a close. You may have the run of the apartment for the next couple of months, so you have a decent opportunity to come to an agreement with another protector but then my executors will want to take it over. My dear, may the Lord bless you."

Georgina opened her mouth to speak but struggled to find words appropriate to the situation.

Given his perceptive nature and many years of experience, Lord Redditch knew well what Georgina was struggling with. He knew she would be unable to find the words. "You have made an old man very happy indeed in his final days, Miss Hartley, and for that I will always thank you. It is my hope that down the years you will not look back too unkindly on me and on our time together. Rather instead that you will go forward with the blessing of Him on high so that one day you will find true contentment."

He reached for her dainty hand and kissed it with a gentle reverence.

Then he continued speaking. "If I were twenty years younger and had more time on this earth, I would have liked to have wed you."

"My lord -" she spluttered.

"I do not speak in jest, Miss Hartley."

"But that sort of thing isn't done."

"Not as a common course of practice, no. But it has happened before. The third Earl of Bolton, for instance."

She wrinkled her brows in thought at this bizarre turn of events.

"Alas it is too late for me, but one day you will make someone a very good wife indeed Miss Hartley, I do sincerely believe it," he said.

"Oh, um, thank you my lord," she replied for want of anything better to say.

He nodded sagely.

"Now please take this, my dear," he said before presenting a black leather box just a little bigger than the palm of Georgina's hand.

Curiosity overtook her facial features.

She took the box and opened it to reveal an ornate pair of ruby earrings. Never before had she had any object of such refinement and value.

"Thank you, my lord," she said with genuine sincerity.

"You are most welcome, my dear," he replied.

Later that afternoon, after they had parted ways for the final time and Georgina was back in the apartment Lord Redditch had given her the run of for the following couple of months, Georgina sat with her head in her hands.

The earring box sat wide open on the table next to her, its contents reassuring her that her decision to become a courtesan all those months ago had not been in vain.

Though she had not loved Lord Redditch, in fact she was still too inexperienced to have ever loved anyone at all, she felt regret that their rendezvous was over. On the most mercenary level, he had been a means of security for her and she a means of chasing the follies of his youth one final time for him. Yet he had also been kind and considerate. And she had heard too many tales of brutish lords to be unaware that kindness and consideration were by no means a given when it came to the men who dealt with courtesans.

After sitting lost in her thoughts for an hour, she looked across at the ruby earrings and focused her attentions on them. They were beautiful, it was true. But they were worth a pretty penny and she would need that money to get by if the worst ever came to the worst.

She resolved to sell the earrings and invest the proceeds, sentiment be damned.

Lord Redditch would not mind at all.

CHAPTER ONE

The carriage clattered around the square. It was midnight and most people in this part of town were indoors. Well, the respectable people, anyway.

Lord Weatherby wasn't entirely the respectable kind. For over a decade he had taken full advantage of the many hedonistic delights that England had to offer. He had spent many an evening at the gambling tables of Mayfair and St James's or at the gentlemen's clubs enjoying cigars and whisky. Not to mention his many escapades and entanglements with widows and courtesans. He prided himself on never getting involved with maidens, married women, ladies of the brothels or the streets, or any woman who was not interested in him. He had never taken a woman's maidenhead and he always obtained the full consent of any woman he had relations with. Still, his propensity for mistresses, tobacco, cards and the old amber liquid placed him within the ranks of London's rakes.

The carriage drew to a halt outside a three story black brick building and Lord Weatherby burst out of the wheeled contraption. He sauntered over to the building's fading red door and rapped on it four times in quick succession before making another three slow knocks.

In short order, the door swung open to reveal a candlelit hallway and pounding piano music coming from a side chamber.

"Weatherby!" someone roared with excitement from the top of the stairs.

Initially Edgar could not place the voice, but realised who it was as the speaker drew closer. "Tamworth, how have you been?"

The Baron Tamworth was always good for a laugh, thought Edgar. The two men had been at Oxford together back in the day, though saw little of one another now the baron spent most of the year on his estates in Cumbria and only came down to London a couple of times per year. Tamworth was a man who adored rural pursuits to the exclusion of almost anything else and so seldom saw a reason to pull himself away from the horses and deer.

Edgar, on the other hand, enjoyed shooting and horse riding but also liked the joys of town like the opera, theatre and gentlemen's clubs. A mix of city and country was best in his opinion. So it had become his custom to spend parts of the relevant seasons in London and Bath before visiting his rural estates the rest of the year.

The two men exchanged pleasantries before Tamworth gestured upstairs and said, "Fancy a game of commerce?

We're about to start a new one. Mowbrow and Yeovil are already up there."

Edgar acquiesced and followed the baron upstairs. Another long night of cards, cigars and whisky lay ahead of him.

Though Edgar was one of the ton's most eligible bachelors, not to mention a rake, his efforts to lose himself in a whisky-sodden haze of women and tobacco were not down to a mere lust for hedonism. Nights like these were instead an attempt to escape from the memories of the worst day of his life.

Yet, try as he might, Edgar would remember that horrendous day for the rest of his existence on this mortal plane.

Back in March 1790, he had returned home from Oxford for the break between the Hilary and Trinity terms.

He entered the hallway at the Weatherby's London home expecting to hear his parents in the drawing room, only to encounter a house of complete silence. The grandfather clock in the hallway at Weatherby House, the one with the constant ticking that had marked every day of Edgar's childhood in London, was still.

Then the most awful sight materialised before his very eyes. The family's longstanding London butler walked across the hallway towards him wearing a black armband.

The butler gave a deep bow. Much deeper than he would normally give to the son of an earl. In fact, it was the type of bow the butler would give to Edgar's father, not Edgar.

"My lord, I am deeply sorry -"

"No. Whatever you're about to say, it's not true, I'm afraid you've been misinformed," Edgar blurted.

The butler's face softened. He had been in the service of the Weatherby family for twenty summers now and had seen Edgar grow from a tiny baby to the refined gentleman he was today. "My lord, it is true. I would not lie about something so serious. The ship bringing the earl and countess home from Denmark was lost at sea."

Edgar's face was white.

"Do the others know...my brothers and sisters?" Edgar said.

"Not yet, my lord. They are all still at Yardley Manor and were not supposed to come to London for another week. It was thought best to inform you first and then leave the rest of the decisions with you."

"Oh...very well...quite so," Edgar said in a daze. "That will be all."

The butler gave a deep bow. "Yes, my Lord." Then he turned and left Edgar to his own devices.

If anyone were to ask Edgar what he did next, he would not have been able to give a clear response. Such was his trance-like state on that dreadful day.

The next memory that he was forever trying to evade was from later that same day. An hour could have passed since the butler delivered the awful news, or perhaps it was three hours or merely a quarter of an hour.

In that memory, he was sitting alone in his father's office at Weatherby House. Dread filled his stomach. In fact, he felt as though he had no stomach and that it had disappeared as soon as he realised he was now the earl. He didn't want to be there. He didn't want to be present. He didn't want to be this person.

He sat in his father's chair, keeled over so his face was on the desk and just sat there. He couldn't bring himself to find the strength to cry.

Time slipped away from him and he spent the remainder of the day in the chair. The sun set and the room was plunged into almost complete darkness and still Edgar did not move.

He was only roused from his otherworldly state by a knock on the door.

"Come in," Edgar called distractedly.

A footman wearing a black armband entered the room.

Shock briefly took over the footman's features before he schooled them into a pool of cool reserve. He gave a low bow.

"My lord," the footman said. "Is there anything I can get you? Would you care for something to eat or drink?"

"No, no thank you. Please light the candles and that will be all," Edgar said.

"Very good, my lord." The footman lit the candles and quickly exited the room.

The new Earl of Weatherby was alone again with his thoughts.

Tomorrow he would have to commence his duties as the earl.

Tomorrow he would have to set off for Yardley Manor to deliver the terrible news to his siblings. He could send a messenger and have them handle the task but he wanted to do it in person. It was only right that they hear the news from him as earl and eldest brother, after all.

Tomorrow he would have to be the rock the rest of his siblings would need to lean on.

Tomorrow he would have to assume his position as one of the leaders of British society.

But all of that could wait until tomorrow. For tonight, he would allow himself to take some time, just a little time, to bring his mind away from the situation at hand.

He stood up and headed towards the drinks cabinet where he knew his father had kept the best of the best. Reaching inside, he pulled out a bottle of the finest whisky money could buy and poured himself a generous glass.

Then he returned to the chair and began to imbibe with the intent of drinking until he could not feel anything at all.

So, dearest reader, this is where we will leave Edgar in the whisky-soaked world of his memories for the night. Rest assured, we will rejoin him when he is feeling somewhat better for wear.

Two days after the party and feeling miles better thank-you-very-much, Edgar sat in his chambers at his bachelor lodgings breakfasting on eggs and kippers. A pot of tea sat in front of him beyond his plate and to his left side he held the latest edition of the paper.

He glanced at it as he ate in an attempt to make the most efficient use of his time.

Skimming down the pages, he huffed internally as he came across an all too familiar name.

The Duke of Clarence.

That very name made Edgar's skin crawl.

Ever since that day in 1799 when the duke had had the audacity to stand up in the House of Lords and defend the vile slave trade, Edgar had loathed the swine with every part of his being. The duke was a toxic individual through and through, in Edgar's opinion, and seeing him first-hand give that disgraceful speech was an abomination. Clarence was definitely not a good representative of British high society or indeed Britons at all.

Edgar moved onto the next article and continued eating but now the food held an unpleasant tang. Everything was worse when the Duke of Clarence reared his diabolical head. And later today, he would likely have the misfortune of seeing him in the Lords. Confound it all!

He growled to himself and tried to turn his mind to other, hopefully less aggravating, matters.

The estates. Yes, that was a happier place for his mind to wander.

The earldom of Weatherby held several properties. There was Weatherby House on Grosvenor Square, the family's official residence when they were in the capital and where all of Edgar's unmarried siblings lived. Then there was Edgar's bachelor lodgings a few streets away where he spent most nights, including the last one. There were also smaller estates in Norfolk and Dorset that he visited from time to time.

But the undisputed diamond in the crown was the family seat, Renfregh.

Renfregh sat in Wiltshire, a still largely agricultural part of the country. There was the main house with its several dozen bedrooms, multiple drawing rooms and a spacious ballroom. Then the well manicured french style garden around the back of the house with its fountains and glistening pools, plus an orangery. And of course the sweeping lawns that led up to the lake, deer park and several follies dotted around the estate. Further afield lay the village where the agricultural labourers lived, all paying rent to the earldom.

Edgar didn't really know much about the lives of the villagers, he generally left day-to-day issues to his estate manager and handled the higher level things like rents when necessary.

Edgar loved living at Renfregh. It was the legacy of his father, grandfather and all the other generations before him, as it would be his legacy to his children and other descendents. That was the problem before him. He needed to sire descendents and secure the Weatherby line, yet had entered his third decade without getting anywhere near to doing so.

Just like his father before he wed Edgar's high-born mother, Edgar was focused on finding a bride from an appropriate station. If love came along to the party then that was all very well and good. However, Edgar's main concern was finding a suitable lady to become his bride and secure his legacy.

He berated himself. Try as he might, he could not stop his mind from wandering down morose paths. It was time to stop sitting around moping and get on with the business of the day.

❧❧❧❧❧ ❧❧❧❧❧

As the church bells chimed half past one, Edgar made his way into the Palace of Westminster.

He was here for yet another division. But he could not really complain. While some lords who shall remain nameless seldom showed up, Edgar took his responsibilities seriously and made sure he was a regular presence in the major debates and divisions.

His leather riding boots clacked on the floor. A man with a purpose. A gentleman with direction.

As he drew nearer to the division lobby, the groans and shouts from inside grew louder and louder. Any listener who was unaware that the leading peers of the land were the source of the noise would have been forgiven for instead thinking a rowdy rabble were responsible. But perhaps a rabble and the peerage are, in fact, one and the same.

Edgar entered the division lobby and joined a group of familiar faces. His oldest friend, the Earl of Mowbrow, stood proud in a smart emerald coat and de rigueur beige pantaloons. Next to him was the jovial Baron Yeovil, who greeted Edgar with a joy he struggled to fathom.

Their conversation was broken by a shout from the front of the room. "Order, order!" the Lord Chancellor cried. "The division for the National Excise Bill will now take place. Ayes to the left and nays to the right, my lords."

Having already made up his mind on the bill several weeks ago, Edgar took his place with the nays alongside Mowbrow, Yeovil and the majority of the men present.

At least this rigmarole would be over soon. Then he would have to get back to Grosvenor Square. He needed to meet with his little brother Lionel's tutor to discuss the youngster's progress.

❧❧❧❦❦❦

Night fell on Covent Garden. The moon cast a shimmering icy glow on the throngs of people promenading in the streets in search of entertainment, release and more specialised delights.

The day's duties attended to, now was the time for Edgar to pursue some pleasure.

Edgar entered the theatre lobby. He chatted amiably with his brother Xavier and the Earl of Mowbrow, an old prep school pal. The trio of gentlemen were regular attendees at theatres like this in London, sometimes seeing plays but more often the opera. Tonight, they were going to see *Don Giovanni* which was one Edgar had seen a couple of times previously.

But at this performance the main soprano would be played by a woman he had never seen perform before.

The three men took their seats in a box to the side of the stage and the curtain rose on a beautifully lit scene. The vision that was revealed took Edgar's breath away.

There upon the stage stood a stunning woman in a shimmering garnet dress and black opera gloves. She lifted her arms from her sides and began to sing.

Edgar was mesmerised. He had never heard a more beautiful sound in his entire life and the vision she created on the stage was glorious. Edgar knew he had to have her as his next mistress.

Enchanted by the beautiful soprano, Edgar watched the opera and before he knew it the interval was upon them.

As the curtain fell, the Earl of Mowbrow turned to Xavier and Edgar saying, "I'm going to get some fresh air. Want to join me?"

The other two men affirmed and they all made their way down the stairs, through the lobby and then onto the street outside.

Purchasing an orange from one of the orange sellers, Xavier peeled it and began eating.

"So, Weatherby, have you got a new mistress yet? I heard Miss Ashbury has gone up to Edinburgh," Mowbrow said.

"Not yet, she only left the other week!" Edgar chuckled. He had seldom been without a mistress since he had gone up to Oxford when he was eighteen but Hortensia Ashbury had barely left his bed and Mowbrow was already talking about a new mistress for Edgar. Nonetheless, thought Edgar wryly, his friend had a point. He always liked to have a courtesan on the go and the soprano starring in tonight's show could be just the ticket. "But that main soprano tonight, she could be a candidate."

Mowbrow and Xavier both laughed.

"Why am I not surprised?" Xavier said jovially between bites of orange.

"She is *exactly* your type, Weatherby," Mowbrow laughed. "Sweet voice, fantastic body, magnificent hair!"

"Indeed," Xavier said.

"That's true," Edgar smirked. "Do either of you know if she's already got a protector?"

"Last I heard no," Xavier said. "I think she had something going on with the Baron Hounslow but that's over now."

"And it didn't end well by all accounts, though if that curr is involved it's no surprise." Mowbrow gesticulated with his hand in frustration.

Edgar sighed. Hounslow had an abysmal reputation among the gentlemen of British high society, he really was one of the worst of the worst. "Well, I'm going to go and find her after this performance and see if she's looking for a protector."

"She could do much worse than you, brother!" Xavier chuckled as he finished his orange.

Shortly before the second act commenced, Edgar turned to his manservant and told him to speak to the head of house backstage and advise he wanted to talk with the main soprano after the performance.

Ten minutes later, the manservant returned with a positive answer and Edgar settled down to watch the remainder of the opera. Heavens, that soprano was absolutely enchanting, he thought! It was a real shame if the rumours about her being involved with the Baron Hounslow were true. Hopefully she'd find a better, kinder protector soon. Even if it did not turn out to be him, Edgar genuinely wanted that for the soprano. No woman deserved the treatment Hounslow was notorious for doling out.

As the final curtain fell, Edgar nodded at Xavier and Mowbrow and made a beeline for the backstage area, trailed by his manservant. When they approached the head of house's desk, he gave the man three shillings.

The head of house nodded in approval and bade them to follow him down a corridor.

The head of house stopped at a green wooden door and rapped on it smartly. "Backstage management," he cried.

"Come in!" was the response.

The head of house entered the dressing room and shut the door behind him, leaving Edgar waiting outside in the corridor.

After a minute, the head of house came back out the door and looked at Edgar. "She's all yours, my lord."

With that, the head of house walked back to his desk.

Edgar entered the room, leaving his manservant standing outside, and shut the door behind him. "Good evening, madam. You have such a pretty voice."

⊷❱ · ◆ · ❰⊶

CHAPTER TWO

Georgina exited the stage to rapturous applause. She loved singing but these performances were a means to an end for her. For a woman born into her position, this was about the best she could ever achieve. And she had achieved so much in her twenty-seven years on earth.

Since she was eighteen she had had a string of protectors to provide for her and keep her in comfort. But her recent experience with the dastardly Baron Hounslow had been horrific. It had finally ended three months ago and ever since she had been staying with her friend Jean Cookson above Jean's modiste shop. But she did not want to impose on the kindness of a friend.

Moreover, she also needed to find a new protector soon or else she would start running out of all the supplies, cosmetics and new dresses she needed to maintain her career on the stage here in England. Moving to the continent remained an option, but she was loathe to leave England again after having been away for so long.

In those final couple of months of hell with Hounslow, Georgina had cannily squirrelled away as many supplies and cosmetics as she could, ready for when she made her escape from his clutches and was her own woman again. But those supplies only went so far.

Here and there, when a protector had been particularly generous, she had received a gift of jewellery as a parting gift. Whenever this happened, she made sure to sell the jewellery and invest the proceeds in her retirement nest egg. The ruby earrings from Lord Redditch all those years ago had gone towards the first such investment. Her youthful looks would not last forever and should she receive the privilege of growing old she knew that she would not be able to continue as a courtesan all her days.

Alas, the investments were nowhere near enough to retire on yet and thus she could not bring herself to draw down on them even in times of strife. She always reminded herself that she had to be exceptionally careful with her money.

Making her way to her dressing room, she fretted about where she would be in a month. If she could not keep up with the latest trends in dress, she would stop getting parts in the operas. Though her voice was one of the sweetest in London, singers were expected to pay their own way in everything from costumes to rouge. It was a hand to mouth existence without a protector.

She sat on the settee in the dressing room and reached over to the coffee table to pour herself a glass of water. Sipping on it, she tried to relax and rest her weary feet.

After she had been sitting for several minutes, she heard a sharp rap at the door followed by the head of house calling out to her.

"Come in!" she called.

The head of house entered and closed the door behind him. "Miss Hartley, the Earl of Weatherby is here to see you. Says he wants to ask you if you would like an arrangement with him. Should I let him in?"

Georgina had heard the name Weatherby before but had never met anyone from that family. But he was the first gentleman to come calling since before she started with Hounslow, and she needed to find herself a protector. Fast. She stood up and walked towards the centre of the room. "Yes." Her voice was jaded.

"Very well," the head of house said before he left the room.

Georgina turned to face away from the door and await the Earl of Weatherby.

A moment later, she heard the sound of footsteps entering the room followed by the click of the door as it closed.

"Good evening, madam. You have such a pretty voice."

Georgina turned around to face her potential new protector and almost let out an audible gasp. He was absolutely smouldering with his dark brown hawk like eyes, black hair, handsomely chiselled face and imposingly fit body. She was in *trouble*.

Restraining herself, she said evenly, "Thank you, my lord. It's always a pleasure when a gentleman of your stature appreciates fine opera."

"The pleasure is all mine," Edgar smirked. "My name is Edgar, Earl of Weatherby. May I ask your name please?"

"Georgina Hartley," she said.

"Enchanted to make your acquaintance, Miss Hartley," he smiled. "So, am I correct in understanding you are seeking a protector?"

"Yes, my lord." Georgina's voice belied a note of caution beneath the sunny surface.

"Then I'd like to make you an offer."

Georgina smiled coquettishly. Finally, her luck seemed to be turning around! A new protector was exactly what she needed. And it did not hurt that he was as handsome as sin. "Tell me more, my lord."

Then Edgar explained how he would provide Georgina with a house in fashionable Fitzrovia as well as servants, access to a carriage whenever she wanted plus ample funds for supplies, clothes, food and all the rest. In return, she would be at his beck and call for pleasure whenever she was not working at the theatre. The standard arrangement.

"Is my offer acceptable to you, Miss Hartley?" Edgar asked.

"Yes, my Lord."

He walked towards Georgina and took her satin gloved left hand in his. Slowly rolling down the glove, he gently caressed his fingertips on her lower arm and it was all she could do to hold back a whimper of pleasure.

Hold yourself together, Georgina, she thought. He has barely even touched you and you are already losing control. But it felt wonderful, oh so wonderful, to be touched like this. She had not had it in such a long time, not since before that brute Hounslow.

Edgar removed the glove from Georgina's hand and placed it on the dressing table beside them. Then he bent down towards Georgina's hand and kissed it softly.

Oh, she was a goner, thought Georgina! What a gentleman!

"Then we are agreed," he said.

He claimed Georgina's mouth with his talented tongue. "When we leave here, I will take you straight to your new lodgings. And I'll have my servants come round to where you are staying now to move your things across. But now I want to have my prize. Do I have your consent?"

Georgina felt herself getting wetter between her legs. "Yes please, my lord. Take me now!"

"Very well."

With that, he turned Georgina around so she was facing the dressing table. "Bend over the table please."

She did as she was told.

"That's it, good girl," he cooed.

She looked at herself in the mirror of the dressing table. Right now, she still looked mostly put together in her stage makeup and rouge but soon that was going to change.

Then she felt strong, confident hands lifting her skirt and petticoats from behind followed by Edgar's cock pressing against her sopping slit.

She gasped excitedly.

Edgar chuckled warmly. "Oh we are going to have fun together, I can tell!"

Edgar thrust expertly inside her, in and out, in and out. As he built up a rhythm, he deftly reached around to her front and began to stroke her pleasure pearl with one finger.

Georgina whimpered with pleasure and closed her eyes. Edgar's cock felt so good inside her cunnyhole! So snug, so tight, so right!

"Come for me, Georgina," Edgar said soothingly.

Georgina felt herself move towards the precipice and she was hanging over the edge. Then, she let herself fall down and down and down into a bottomless pool of pleasure. All there was in the world right now were her and this man she had met less than a quarter of an hour ago. But the way he handled her body, it was as though he had known her for years.

"Keep coming Georgina, don't hold anything back," he urged.

It was all Georgina could do but obey his commands. She groaned in ecstasy as climax after climax rolled through her body.

"Look at yourself in the mirror," he said.

She lifted her head and met her own gaze. The sight looking back at her was truly a vision. Her cheeks were completely flushed, her makeup was running and her pupils intense. In short, she looked exactly how she felt. A woman well fucked.

"You're so pretty when you break," he growled.

Yet another burst of pleasure ran through her body at the earl's words.

Faster and faster he thrusted before he withdrew and finally released his seed.

She cleaned between her legs and then Edgar offered her a glass of water, rubbing her back gently as she took refreshing sips.

Then he took a cloth, wet it and began to clear the smeared makeup from her face.

Georgina was surprised at this last part. Not since her first protector, Lord Redditch, all those years ago had a gentleman taken such care of her.

And with Lord Redditch, it had been because he was a gentle older peer who was in his twilight years, Georgina being the last courtesan he ever had, and who understood that she was a young virgin of only eighteen years of age. Sex with him had always been very sweet and gentle and it had been the perfect introduction to the world of the courtesan for her.

But Edgar was different. He was rough and powerful when he fucked her but oh so sweet afterwards. Still, Georgina mused, the sweetness Edgar showed was its own kind of power as only a truly powerful man would be able to provide such care. A weak man, like the Baron Hounslow, only understood roughness and cruelty and had no comprehension of the power a man could wield when he channelled his rough side into protecting and defending those who needed it.

❧❧❧❧❧ ❦❦❦❦❦

Edgar sent round a carriage to the back of the theatre and Georgina hopped inside.

He followed her into the contraption and shut the door.

As they sat side by side, he could feel the sensation of her silken skirts and petticoats rustling against his legs. He turned to her and admired the way she looked in the candle-light. A true vision, her skin was magnificent and her countenance was most lovely. Atop her scarlet silken dress she wore a black velvet cloak and cream silken gloves covered her from fingertips to elbows.

He knocked on the roof and soon enough the horses began to pull the vehicle forwards.

She turned to him with a smile. "My lord, I am looking forward to our time together."

"Are you now?" he smirked. "Well, I am too. When a lady is as magnificent as you it is difficult not to, Miss Hartley."

He kissed her cheek before moving to claim her mouth with his own. As he did so, the velvet of her cloak softly rustled and brushed against his neck.

She moved her hands upwards to cup his face, stroking her fingers across his chin and around the backs of his ears, the silken material igniting a new flame within him.

And so the carriage travelled northbound through the streets of London while inside its two occupants were en-wrapped in one another's embrace.

A short while later, the carriage drew into a quiet square and pulled up outside a well appointed structure built around a hundred years before during the reign of Queen Anne.

Edgar jumped out and turned back to assist the soprano.

Then he drew a set of heavy keys from his pocket and handed them to her. "For you, Miss Hartley." He gestured to the biggest key and said, "This one is the front door, and the other is for the rear."

"Thank you, my Lord."

She made her way to the heavy navy blue painted door and turned the key in the lock, feeling the satisfying click as the gears did their work.

They walked through the door and Edgar rubbed his hand on Georgina's back.

"I'll give you a tour and then I'll leave you to it," he said.

He led her along the corridor into the parlour, then the kitchen before going up the stairs and pointing out the three bedrooms. Of most interest to Georgina was the piano in the parlour. She looked forward to playing it and performing for Edgar.

Once the tour was over, Edgar bade her farewell with a fierce kiss.

Later, after she had performed her evening ablutions, Georgina lay in the bed in the master bedroom and reflected on the events of the day. All in all, she felt at ease. These sorts of accommodations were familiar to her from her years as a courtesan. She had the whole run of the house to herself with its parlour, kitchen and several bedrooms. Combined with the house's location, it was most satisfactory to Georgina. She would not be disturbed by noise and would be able to discreetly come and go as she pleased.

She closed her eyes and dozed off in a contented spirit.

Soon after the church bells had chimed two o'clock the next day, Edgar knocked at the navy door of Georgina's house with a bouquet of posies in one hand.

The door swung open and Georgina greeted him.

Once the door closed behind the pair, Edgar took her dainty hand in his and brought it to his lips. "Good afternoon, my lady."

Georgina giggled internally. Lords did not call women of her kind 'lady' or the like. Perhaps this was a play her new protector liked to act out. In any case, she was happy to indulge him. "Good afternoon, my lord."

He rose from the kiss and handed her the posies. "A lady as stunning as you needs flowers to match her level of beauty,"

"Thank you, my lord," she trilled. "Would you like some tea?"

He agreed and a short while later they found themselves in the parlour and sipping on Bohea.

"Miss Hartley, you are enchanting," he said.

"Well, I must say you are rather easy on the eyes yourself, my lord."

Edgar smirked. He was good looking and he knew it. Despite his rakish reputation, he was one of the most in demand gentlemen at any society soiree and his name was on many a dance card. If he were to propose to any young lady of the ton, he would be able to expect a favourable response.

"Tell me, my lady, how you came to sing so exquisitely?" he asked.

"Well, I received training when I was younger from tutors. Then when I was eighteen I started professionally on the stage in Bath."

"So refined!" he sipped his tea and then said, "Say, I can't recall seeing you perform before. Are you new in town?"

She nodded. "I've been away performing in Italy and France for several years, doing the opera circuit over on the continent. So that's probably why you haven't seen me before. I did do some performances in Britain before that, mostly in London and Bath."

"I see. And what brings you back to these shores?"

"Homesickness for the most part. It's funny, you know, the weather down south is gorgeous but after so long there's only so much I can take. I must have imprinted too young or something."

He smiled. "Ah, so you grew up in Britain? Where?"

"Gloucestershire, near the border with Wiltshire."

"Quite close to the estate then!"

She gave a slightly quizzical look.

Edgar noticed and elaborated on his remark. "I mean my family's estate, Renfregh. It's near Devizes, a couple of hours by carriage from Bath if you put the horses to a moderate pace."

"Do you see much of the Moonrakers then?" Georgina quirked her lips. Edgar seemed like the kind of lord who would appreciate a joke. He had the right look in his eyes.

Just as Georgina had suspected, Edgar gave a small laugh. "Not that much to be honest. Smugglers who hang around by ponds and hack at the moon with their rakes don't like to associate with lords. I'm almost as bad as the exciseman for them, perhaps even worse."

"What a shame," Georgina laughed. "You'd rather hang around with the exciseman then?"

"Good grief, no! Can't stand all that rigmarole."

"And brandy is brandy, wherever it comes from."

"Miss Hartley!" Edgar feigned outrage.

Georgina dipped her chin coquettishly. "My lord, we all like to walk on the murky side of life from time to time, do we not?"

"That is -" Edgar reached forward and placed a kiss on Georgina's cheek - "Very true -" another kiss, this time on her other cheek - "you are most wise." Then Edgar pulled his lips away from Georgina and looked her directly in the eyes. "Now, Georgina, before we go any further I must find out from you your likes and dislikes and what you do and do not want to do," he said.

"In what regard, my lord?"

"Well, I was mostly thinking of in bed, but other things too if you've got something you think I ought to know."

"Hmmm...let me think." She took a sip of tea before continuing. "I do like having my cunny worshipped by a gentleman's tongue."

"I am very skilled at that, as you shall find out," Edgar said silkily.

"I look forward to it, my Lord. And I also like a good hard fucking from a caring gentleman, such as you delivered last night. I must commend you there."

"Glad to hear you enjoyed it, my lady," Edgar smirked.

"Oh and I am partial to being tied up sometimes. And tying you up too, if you're interested."

"That does sound intriguing."

"And one of my deepest loves is a gentleman in leather gloves."

He quirked an eyebrow. "Leather gloves, my lady? Pray tell me more."

"Well, I love to be touched by leather gloves, and I relish it when a gentleman wears them and puts his hand over my mouth so I am encased in the leather and must focus my attentions on what he is doing with his hand."

"Heavens, Miss Hartley! You are phenomenal," Edgar said.

"I look forward to showing you." She half-covered her smile with one of her hands.

She poked her left leg forward from underneath her skirts, her petticoats rustling as she did so.

She held Edgar's gaze with careful precision.

From where he sat in the armchair directly opposite her, Edgar let forth a small gulp. He dropped his eyes and admired her shapely lower leg. Though he could not see any higher than her calves, what little he could glimpse hinted at a feminine power.

Edgar raised his eyes to meet hers once more.

Then slowly oh so slowly she withdrew her left leg so it was nestled back beneath the layers of petticoat, taffeta and silk.

After the couple returned downstairs and had righted themselves again, Edgar sat in the armchair in only his breeches.

Georgina stood by the door and admired the delicious figure he cut. Unlike some of her previous protectors, Edgar was most pleasing on the eye and she enjoyed looking at him.

"Would you like a private concert, my lord?" she asked.

"I would love that, my lady."

"Then your wish shall be my command," she smiled.

She moved to sit at the piano and began to play.

Like Edgar's shirt and waistcoat, her petticoats and stays lay upstairs after their removal. All that remained of her earlier outfit was her velvet and silk black dress. The flamenco-style bottom half of the dress brushed against the base of the piano.

She began to sing:

"By dimpled brook and fountain brim,
The wood-nymphs deck'd with daisies,
Their merry, merry wakes and pastimes keep,
What has night to do with sleep!
What has night to do with sleep!
Night has other joys in store,
Skies with jewels studded o'er,
Tuneful voices, twinkling feet,
The cheering cup and converse sweet,
The cheering cup and converse sweet."

Edgar leant forward in his chair, his head resting on the palms of his hands. A man transfixed. Yes, not only was she alluring in the physical, she was also a lady of great musical talents who could captivate any listener willing to go on a journey with her.

As the honeyed tones of the music rose and swirled around the room, every crevice reverberated with the sweet warmth of Georgina's voice.

Edgar let the sounds transport him to another realm. Rarely did he get the opportunity to escape from the realities of his responsibilities. So he relished this quasi-otherworldly time with Georgina, where he could forget about being Lord Weatherby and instead be simply Edgar.

Georgina finished the song and switched to another piece. This time, one of the tunes she had sung with regularity when she was last on the Venetian stage.

Edgar was in heaven.

❧❧❧❧❧ ❧❧❧❧❧

The next day, in the early evening, Georgina sat at the vanity table in her dressing room and prepared herself for the night's performance.

Applying some rouge to her face, Georgina looked herself in the eyes in the mirror. A confident woman, she felt secure in her place in London society. She may be unmarried, but that gave her far more freedom than a wife could ever have, thought Georgina.

When she had been a little girl, she had dreamed of marrying a handsome husband and living a fairytale life. But it had been many years since she had allowed herself to have any dreams of romance. Any type of marriage available to her would be a trap, would only serve to pin her down to a man she could not trust. Her experiences over the past decade had taught her that lesson very well indeed.

No, not for her the life of a wife.

Certainly, protectors like Lord Weatherby offered her a measure of comfort and support. But it was only ever a mere measure and only ever fleeting.

The only person she could rely on was Georgina Hartley. A bleak truth, but not one she saw any point in trying to run away from.

Why waste time on dreams that will never come true?

Instead, she swore to herself that she would remain the independent woman that she was for the rest of her days.

Chapter Three

Four o'clock in the afternoon and the theatre was devoid of patrons. Finally some breathing space between the matinée masses and the distinguished evening crowd.

Georgina stood on the stage and practiced a scale. The current show had another fortnight left to run and already she had to prepare herself for the next production. Such was the competitive world of the opera.

"Fa la la la," she trilled.

Her voice reverberated around the theatre as she cast her eyes hither and thither.

Out of the corner of her eye, she spotted a flash of brilliant white fabric. A pair of very well cut pantaloons covering a pair of very well formed legs. She raised her eyes to confirm her happy suspicions. Yes, it was her protector. Lord Edgar Weatherby.

Georgina stopped singing.

Lord Weatherby gave her a rakish smile full of promise and began to walk towards her.

The pair's eyes locked. They held one another's gaze with fierce attention.

His black leather riding boots padded softly on the scarlet carpet of the theatre. A panther on the prowl. Not a sound could be heard in the entire theatre bar the gentle thud of his boots.

When Edgar reached the staircase that led to the stage, he stopped and held his breath in taut anticipation of what was to come. The vision in front of him was delectable. There was no other word for how entrancing she was. His eyes burned with desire as he drank in the sight of her in a copper-bronze dress and ivory satin opera gloves.

Then there was a rustle as Georgina hitched up her chiffon skirts. What a sweet sound. Music to his very ears indeed!

Georgina crossed the stage to the top of the steps. "My lord, so lovely to see you."

She took his proffered leather-clad hand and glided down the steps.

Then they walked, hand in hand, down the aisle. Georgina led Edgar through a discrete side door and they were into the backstage area.

He leaned forward and murmured in her ear. "So what do you want to do today, my lady?"

She turned back towards him. Her luscious lips formed a lascivious smile. "Well, I would adore it if you were to put those gloves of yours to good use, my lord. But first, let me have my way with you."

He raised her free, silken-covered hand, to his lips and punctuated each word with a reverent kiss. "That can be arranged."

She let forth a rippling laugh of enjoyment and they took off down the corridor. Georgina led the way the entire time through the twists and turns of the rabbit warren until they eventually arrived outside her dressing room door.

She opened the door and Edgar followed, shutting the door behind him as he did so.

Once they were safely ensconced in the room, Georgina could bear the wait no longer.

She reached upwards to Edgar's face and placed a gloved hand on each cheek. She stroked with gentle caresses before leaning forward and claiming his mouth with her tongue.

After she broke for air, Edgar reached behind her head and placed firm strokes on her scalp.

She let forth a moan of delight. The weight of his leather-clad hands was pure electricity. "You, Lord Weatherby, are simply delectable," she said.

Then, before he had a chance to utter even the most brief of replies, she claimed his mouth again and spun him towards the wall.

He was very happy to go along with what she had planned. She was a woman of many talents, after all.

In mere moments he had his back towards the wall. He could not wait to see what she would do next. She had him on tenterhooks and she knew it, that delectable woman.

She crashed her mouth against his and ran her tongue around and around. The flavour of bergamot mixed with something sweet filled every inch of her mouth.

He raised his arms above his head in wild abandon. The framed posters and paintings behind him rattled around as he did so.

Georgina giggled. "My lord," she murmured into his mouth.

She reached towards his uplifted arms and pinned his wrists in one place.

A moan of pleasure hummed from the man opposite her. "Georgina...please," Edgar said.

She writhed her hips about, back and forth and round and round, in a tantalising motion. Her skirts rustled against his riding boots and immaculately tailored pantaloons.

Edgar moaned again. He was on edge, with the fizzing of a thousand champagne bottles sparkling through his veins. He could hardly stand to wait any longer.

For her part, Georgina was alive with delight. When she was with Edgar, she felt more alive than she had in a long long time.

Finally, finally she pulled back for air. "My lord," she gasped. "I would adore it if you were to use your gloves now."

"Use them in what way?" He quirked an eyebrow and grinned the grin of a man who knows he has the power to please a woman. To make her forget that any other man has ever existed or will ever exist.

"In every which way, over all of me," she said.

"Very well, Georgina." His voice adopted the more authoritative tone that she had told him she liked. "But I must warn you, be careful what you wish for. Can you handle such pleasures?"

"Oh, I think I can," she said with confidence.

She released his wrists from her clutch.

He took her by the hand and twirled her across the room to stand in front of the scarlet velvet-covered settee. With deftness, he undid her chiffon gown and in rapid succession it was pooling around her ankles on the floor. Next, he untied her petticoats and stays. Finally, he removed her chemise.

Before he did anything else, Edgar took the time to drink in the magnificence of the vision before him. There she was, in only her ivory satin opera gloves. A more beautiful sight he had never seen.

He rubbed his leather-clad hands along her forearms with the most gentle of touches. "You, Georgina," he said, "are truly delectable."

She gasped at the sensation of his fingertips. "Please, my lord!"

He gave a soft chuckle. "All in good time, Georgina, all in good time."

"I may not be able to wait much longer!" she gasped again.

"Patience is a virtue, Georgina," he said.

He took her hands within his and then, with unmistakable deftness, worked his way up her arms to her elbows. One by one, he rolled down her satin gloves and placed them with the rest of her garments. After he removed each glove, he lifted the bare hand to his mouth and placed a reverent kiss atop it.

"You are truly beautiful," he said.

He took a step forward and drew her towards him in an enveloping embrace.

She let forth a sigh of pleasure and relaxed into his leather-clad hands.

They stood like that for several minutes, until Georgina tilted her lips upwards to Edgar's ear. "Are you not too clothed, my lord? I would love to see you in all your glory." she murmured.

He quirked his mouth. "What did I say about patience, Georgina? But, since I am a generous man, I would not want to refuse you entirely."

He placed a fierce kiss on her lips and then, with deftness, undid his shirt and discarded it on the floor.

"That's much better, my lord," she said.

"I endeavour to please," he said.

She brought a hand up to the centrepoint of his chest and delighted in the sensation of his smooth skin underneath her palm. Then she moved her hand a few centimetres to rest over his heart. The steady, slightly elevated pulse beneath her hand was strong and made her feel grounded. Yes, this was reality. This man, whatever else he may be, was someone with whom she could enjoy the moment and relish the realm of physical pleasures.

For his part, Edgar relaxed at her touch. This was a physical connection, but not in the most obvious of ways. Rather, Georgina's hand over his heart made him feel safe. The more obvious connection would no doubt come later.

After a while, Edgar leant down and murmured into Georgina's ear. "Come, sit with me," he said.

He lifted Georgina in his arms and walked over towards the plush scarlet settee. He sat down, all the while holding her with a secure yet gentle deftness.

"Let me take care of you properly," he murmured.

He settled back into the velvet sofa and held Georgina's back against his bare chest.

His leather-gloved hands massaged her shoulders, loosening the knots and easing the tension.

She moaned. "That feels good."

He leaned forward to murmur in her ear. "I'm very glad to hear it, my lady."

Then, he moved his hands downwards and began to glace his fingertips over and around her breasts.

Every inch of her was alight with a delicious tingling sensation.

She reached between her legs and increased the pleasure through her own control.

Edgar murmured in her ear again. "You are magnificent, simply magnificent. Come for me, Georgina." He kissed the back of her neck. "Come for me."

A wonderful climax built within Georgina, rising first from her core and then up and down throughout her entire body. She let forth a sigh of ecstasy.

The leather gloved-hands continued their worship, around her breasts and nipples and then sometimes up around her neck and shoulders and then teasing her sides. She loved it all. Oh, how she loved it all!

She let herself build up again, so she was standing on the precipice between reality and another realm. And when she had been teetering on the edge for as long as she desired, she let herself fall into that palace of wonders.

Three evenings later, at Landsdowne House, opposite Hyde Park, the most sought-after ball of the ton was in full swing. Well, the most sought-after ball for this week. No doubt there would be something else coming along soon that would be even grander and would itself become the hottest ticket in town.

Immaculately attired ladies and lords danced about the ballroom in a swirl of silk dresses and finely cut suits. The Landsdowne family's regular string quartet provided the musical accompaniment while seemingly every eligible young lady of the ton vied for the hand of some lord or other.

In the midst of it all stood Edgar. He cut a dashing figure in his three piece suit, replete with black waistcoat, black velvet jacket and matching pantaloons. Any mama of the ton would be overjoyed to have her daughter become the next Countess of Weatherby. And balls like this were the ton's preferred opportunity for its members to find prospective spouses. Edgar, however, was in no fit mood to do so. He had a family to lead and an earldom to run, so finding a suitable Countess of Weatherby ought to have been near the top of his list of priorities. But tonight he wanted nothing to do with the marriage mart and the search to find a bride.

He had come tonight with Xavier but his younger brother had since dissipated to God knows where to do God knows what with God knows whom. Such was the life of a second son. Free to stroll around and seek pleasure without responsibility, yet alas all too often struggling to find a purpose.

Edgar's heart hummed along at a rate his doctor would say was rather too high. Being at these balls and being obligated to play his part on the marriage mart created an unpleasant tension.

To one side of the room, right by the roaring fireplace, Belinda sat with her husband the Duke of Faversham and a selection of other members of the ton.

Edgar cast his eyes over the group and walked over to them.

He turned towards Belinda.

"Sister, would you like to take a turn about the room?" he asked.

"Alright," she said.

Faversham held a protective hand on the small of Belinda's back as he assisted her to her feet.

Then, Belinda and Edgar linked arms and began their steady stroll around the edges of the ballroom.

"So brother," Belinda said, "are there any ladies of the ton who have captured your eye this evening."

"No, not tonight."

"Ah, now that is a shame. Marriage would do you the world of good."

The pair walked a half a dozen steps in companionable silence until Belinda spoke again.

"Petunia Reynolds at ten o'clock," Belinda said.

Edgar turned his head ever so slightly to catch a glimpse of the ton's most prolific purveyor of insults and haughtiness. The sight that met his eyes confirmed that, yes, unfortunately Lady Petunia Reynolds was less than eight feet from them.

Lady Petunia Reynolds cast a disapproving sneer over the evening's proceedings. Nothing and nobody would ever please her. Instead, she took great joy from finding fault wherever she could find it. Even if no such fault existed. The Favershams and the Weatherbys knew this propensity all too well.

Edgar turned his head back towards Belinda. "Pay her no mind, dear sister."

Belinda let out a small laugh. "That's wise advice. You would do well to take it yourself." Belinda turned her head to look Edgar in the eye and her voice grew more grave. "She has some power, though not as much as she likes to think she does."

"I wish you were right."

"I *am* right."

Again, they walked in companionable silence until Belinda broke it with her words.

"Say, how are the estate incomes doing?" she asked.

Edgar smiled. "You always did have -"

"A head for figures, I know. You said as much to Alexander before we wed. But, I digress, how are the estates doing?"

"Better than ever. Renfregh's doing very well and the Norfolk and Dorset places are pulling their weight too. The earldom is in a good position."

"Glad to hear it. Now all you need to do is find a bride," Belinda said.

Edgar sighed and raised his eyebrows for a brief moment before replying. "Somehow I knew you were going to bring that topic up again. It's not as simple as finding a bride though. I've got the earldom to run, the family to lead, four siblings still to find spouses and the seat in parliament to represent."

"I meant it, when I said marriage would do you the world of good," she said.

He looked at her with scepticism and said nary a word. His heart was still beating at an elevated rate that his doctor would not appreciate.

Belinda continued. "It's not easy finding a spouse to whom one is suited, and I will be the first to admit that Alexander and I are unusually blessed in that regard, but it's worth it. With so much on your plate, with all your duties, wouldn't having someone at your side make it easier?"

He took in a big breath of air. The room wasn't cool enough to provide much relief but he would take what he could get nonetheless.

She rubbed his arm in a gesture of comfort.

His eyes were weary as he looked at her and replied, "It might make things easier, to have someone by my side. But the requirements for any future Countess of Weatherby necessitate that I marry a lady of good breeding, of refined taste, someone who can fulfil all the duties as though they were second nature."

A flash of concern overtook Belinda's features before she schooled her face into sheer neutrality. "Are those duties second nature to anyone though?"

"To you I think they are. You do it all so well."

"So often I felt like they weren't, when I first became duchess."

"You *do* do it well though," he said with an affectionate smile.

She returned it. "Thank you, dear brother. That means a lot, coming from you."

Their promenade about the room was complete.

Belinda returned to where Alexander sat by the fireplace, placing an affectionate hand on his knee as she did so.

Edgar felt a small pang of jealousy. But just as quickly as it bubbled up, he succeeded in suppressing it. It was true that his eldest sister had found genuine, committed love with Alexander despite the challenging start to their marriage. However, he was the Earl of Weatherby and he had to prioritise the earldom and leading the family above all things.

Around him, the music slowed and drew to a halt. A gap between dances. He might as well join in. It would be rude not to, after all. And, once he had performed that perfunctory social nicety, he would be free to seek his pleasures elsewhere.

Quickly, he cast an eye about the room and spied a suitable candidate. Miss Juliet Jones, second daughter of the Baron Aberystwyth. He made his way over to her.

He made a gracious bow. "Miss Jones, may I have the honour of the next dance?" he asked.

"Why yes, my lord," she said.

Behind Miss Jones, the Baroness Aberystwyth watched on with the gleaming eyes of anticipation so prevalent amongst society mamas with unmarried daughters.

Miss Jones and Edgar danced a hornpipe along with many other couples. She was nimble on her feet and conducted each move with grace and refinement.

Then the dance concluded and the pair bowed to one another before going their separate ways.

Almost immediately, Edgar cast his eyes about the room in search of his next dancing partner. In the interests of keeping up appearances, this couldn't simply be a one-and-done matter.

A couple of dances later and, with Xavier nowhere to be found, Edgar had had enough.

The string ensemble played on and on.

Edgar couldn't take any more of it. He was ready to leave. He turned on his heel and slunk away, through the ballroom doors and down the hallway and out through the main doors of the house. The evening air hit him like an arctic blast but he paid it no mind. It was rather refreshing. Then he was striding down the stairs, one two three, and into a loitering carriage.

He seated himself and gave two sharp raps on the roof. In short order, the horses trundled off northeast and he was on his way to Fitzrovia.

He leant back into the leather seat and felt his pulse begin to slow down. That blasted ballroom at Lansdowne House had been achingly, stiflingly hot. Situations like that, where the games of the marriage mart were in full swing, put him on edge. He was glad of the respite that Miss Hartley could provide.

The carriage pulled up outside the Fitzrovia house and Edgar darted from it.

He knocked on the door and, very quickly, the door swung open to reveal Miss Hartley.

She was positively splendid. A deep blush chiffon dress adorned her body while around her neck she wore a black and pink velvet pendant.

"Good evening, Miss Hartley. May I come in please?" Edgar asked.

"Of course, my lord," Georgina said.

Edgar stepped across the threshold and shut the door. He enwrapped Georgina in his arms. At first his hands met around her back, at the point where her gorgeous locks ended, before moving lower.

Georgina claimed Edgar's mouth in a fierce kiss, leading him to let forth a contented moan.

After several minutes, Edgar broke the kiss and inhaled the sweet air of Georgina's house. She was burning incense, he could tell, with the rich scent of cedarwood and jasmine swirling about them.

Georgina reached up and caressed Edgar's neck. "How was the ball, my lord?"

"The same old story," he said. "So many society mamas trying to get the best possible position on the marriage mart and secure a match for their daughter. I can't blame them really, I've two unmarried sisters myself, but it's unsettling to be in the middle of it after a while."

"Ah, so you are not one to be the centre of attention?" Georgina laid a kiss on Edgar's cheek. The flickering candles of the hallway bathed her face in shades of mandarin and amber.

"Not in the regular course of events," he said.

She widened her eyes theatrically before continuing to speak, punctuating each word with a kiss to his neck. "Well, my lord. Perhaps you will not want to be the centre of my attentions tonight then?"

"The centre of your attentions? Now, that does sound like something I'd enjoy." A broad smile erupted on his face.

She placed her arms around his upper back and relished the sensation of his taut muscles through the velvet of his jacket. "But first," she said, "we'd better remove this."

She ran her fingertips over his shoulders and down his arms.

He could barely feel her touch, but still he was aching for her.

Then she reached the cuffs of his jacket and reached underneath to the bare skin of his wrists. She ran her fingertips in delicate swirls around his wrists and onwards to his hands.

The backs of his hands being more sensitive than the palms, he moaned in pleasure when she focused her caresses on the rear of his hands.

"Please," he whimpered.

She quirked a smile. "All in good time, my lord. Almost there."

He let forth a huff of frustration.

And then at last at last at last, she ran her dainty fingertips along his masculine ones and entwined her fingers within his.

"Allow me, my lord," she said.

With that statement, she removed his jacket and hung it on the mahogany coat rack behind her.

She turned back to him and reached up to take his face betwixt her hands. She kissed him with her sweetly puckered lips.

He tasted like bergamot and molasses.

"Edgar," she mewed.

Now he could wait no longer. He ran his hands behind her back and, taking her posterior in his hands, lifted her up with her legs wrapped around his waist. He kissed her hungrily.

Together, like that, they remained in the hallway enjoying the sensation of one another.

And then at some point, which neither of them would have been able to determine if anyone were to ask, they must have made their way to the master bedroom because in the morning Georgina awoke enwrapped in Edgar's arms. She studied his still-sleeping form with curiosity. On the one hand he had the air of the devil-may-care rake about him, leaping from carriages and being so dashing, yet he had a strong sense of duty to his family and the earldom. And on another hand, if it were possible to even have three hands, he was a man who craved her touch and enjoyed her company. She did not know what to make of him yet.

CHAPTER FOUR

A week later, Georgina stood on the wooden measuring block at her friend Jean Cookson's modiste shop.

At her feet, Jean was busy pinning up the hem of Georgina's dress. It was a pink velvet number with a flamenco style ruffled skirt.

"So Georgina, how's it going with your new patron?" Jean asked.

"Oh better than the last one," Georgina wrinkled her nose in displeasure at the memory of her last paramour. The Baron Hounslow had turned out to be a real disappointment and a rake in all the worst ways.

Jean laughed sympathetically. "That's not a hard standard to beat."

"No, it's not. But Edgar is a real catch. I've got high hopes for this one."

"I'm glad to hear it," the modiste said with firmness.

Jean was one of Georgina's dearest friends in London and the opera singer regularly kept her appraised of the goings on in the turbulent world of the courtesans. Yet Jean herself was never tempted to partake and find her own protector.

Instead, Jean focused on running her small modiste and lacemaking business. Ever since she was a young girl growing up near Lulworth Castle in Dorset, she longed to be a successful woman of business more than anything and through years of hard work she had achieved her dream. She was financially comfortable and was one of the most sought after seamstresses in the whole of southern England.

Georgina turned her attention to her friend's affairs. "How's business going?"

"Rather well. What with the upcoming season, there are plenty of ladies putting in orders. I shall have to hire a couple more assistants at this rate," said Jean.

"Oh, that's wonderful," Georgina replied with sincerity.

Jean finished pinning the hem and stood up.

"There, that's done for today," the modiste said. "If you want to get changed, I'll get us some tea and then there's a story I think you'll enjoy hearing about a certain viscount who was caught somewhere he most definitely should not have been!"

Georgina giggled. "I look forward to hearing it."

Then she made her way to the small curtained changing room and drew the drapes across behind her. She removed the pink velvet dress and exchanged it for her own green one.

A quick readjustment of her hair in the mirror and then she was back out on the main floor of the modiste shop.

She carried the pink velvet dress over to where Jean stood in the back parlour. "Here, where should I put this one?"

"Ah yes, let me handle that," Jean replied.

Jean took the dress in both hands and draped it over the back of an armchair. Then she walked back over to Georgina and gestured to the kitchen table. "Have a seat, poppet."

Georgina duly did so and in short order the two were at the table sharing cups of strong Bohea tea.

"So," Georgina said, "what was this about a viscount who was caught in a place where he shouldn't have been?"

Jean gave a wicked smile. "So, you've heard how the Viscount Stafford and his wife have been having marital issues?"

"I have heard that, yes."

"Well, the word on the ton is that two days ago he was found in the boudoir of the Baroness Truro!"

Georgina raised her eyebrows and sipped her tea.

Jean continued. "Found in a most compromising position, by all accounts, as well."

"And who, pray tell, did the finding?"

"The Baron Truro his very self!"

Georgina gasped and brought her hand to her mouth before letting forth a few sharp laughs. "Heavens! I thought I'd seen and heard it all, well nearly almost all, in my years in this game. But to get caught by the lady's husband himself, how outrageous."

Both women sipped their tea and shared scandalised smiles.

Georgina leant forward towards her friend, such was her excitement. "Say, how did the baron react? Are he and the viscount to duel?"

"That's the thing," Jean said. "There's been some talk that they might be, but so far no challenge appears to have been laid. Or else I suppose we would have heard about one by now."

Georgina nodded. "True indeed."

"Perhaps the Baron is hoping if he keeps quiet, this whole scandal will go away," Jean said.

"That might work out. Provided there's another scandal that comes along in quick succession to distract everyone's attention."

"And knowing the ton, that's a likely proposition." Jean took a sip of tea and then continued. "Honestly, the way these denizens of the ton carry on as though they're the most moral and high and mighty of us all. When all the while, they are the ones carrying on salacious lifestyles. The hypocrisy!"

"It keeps me in work though," Georgina said with a wry grin.

"That's true, that's true," Jean said. "For each and every strange deviant of the ton there is a downtrodden member of the working class who is going through the world without malice and doing what they can to get by."

"I'll drink to that."

"Yes, let's."

The two women clinked their half-drunk tea cups together and laughed joyfully.

Across town, in the hallway at the Weatherby's London home, Edgar put on his navy blue jacket while a maid secured Philomena's stone grey capelet.

"Ready to go?" Edgar asked his second sister. She was still a few years away from her first season and entry into society.

"Yes," Philomena replied.

A footman opened the heavy front doors to reveal a brisk, cloudless day.

Edgar and Philomena made their way to the waiting carriage adorned with the deep purple family livery.

He assisted her inside before climbing in himself.

Then he gave a couple of short raps on the roof and the carriage rolled down the street.

Today's destination was somewhat unusual. Faversham House. It was not somewhere they normally went, but today Edgar was making an exception because Belinda's time in town for the fortnight was almost over.

Since her marriage to the duke, she had spent most of her time at Faversham Hall in Yorkshire and so all her siblings looked forward to her London visits with great anticipation.

The carriage headed down Grosvenor Street towards Park Lane.

Philomena huffed softly. "I can't believe we have to see Caroline today."

"She's your cousin, Philomena. Please try to be civil," Edgar said authoritatively.

Philomena crossed her arms. "I'll do my best."

"See to it that you do," Edgar said.

"But I must warn you, I make no guarantees -"

"Philomena!" Edgar growled. "You need to be civil with Caroline. If she annoys you, just rise above it."

Philomena tutted but ceased contradicting her brother. It wasn't worth the argument. Besides, she was more interested in the prospect of seeing her beloved sister Belinda than in having a spat with that pretentious ninny Caroline.

***

After a short journey of around ten minutes, the Weatherby carriage drew up outside Faversham House.

A green liveried footman opened the door.

Edgar stepped out and then turned around to assist his sister.

The front door opened and Belinda materialised. She wore a lilac dress accompanied by a deep purple capelet.

"Brother! Sister!" Belinda exclaimed in delight.

The three exchanged pleasantries.

Then a short while later, another figure appeared from the imposing oaken door. She was a girl of four and ten years and a brunette with luscious curls.

Belinda turned to the girl and gave a welcoming smile. "Caroline, come and join us!"

Caroline made her way over to the group with haughty steps. She wore a turquoise silk dress and a pale aqua capelet to match.

Edgar took Caroline's hand between his own and greeted her. "How goes the day?"

Caroline's proud features formed the hint of a smile.

"Most well, thank you," she said.

Then Caroline turned to Philomena and enquired after her cousin's wellbeing in a refined voice. Ordinarily, Caroline would not deign to ask such a question but she was always keen to ingratiate herself to her social betters. As the only child of the Ninth Baron Ilfracombe, who had himself succeeded Edgar's maternal grandfather to the title some sixteen years ago, Caroline had a secure place in the ton. However, any lower rank than a barony would mean being a mere commoner and she could never countenance the very idea!

Edgar assisted the three young ladies into the Weatherby carriage. Best to get this show on the road, after all.

A short while later, the Weatherby carriage made its way down Park Lane. Rows of verdant trees lay to the right of the carriage while on the left sat several imposing townhouses built in the same vein as Faversham House.

Inside the carriage, Caroline sat opposite Edgar and Belinda, while Philomena was at her side.

"So Caroline, did you enjoy visiting Bath last season?" Edgar asked politely.

"Oh yes, I loved being at the Pump Room and then I went to three different modistes," she replied.

"How splendid," Belinda said with a kind smile.

Caroline leaned forward in her seat in excitement. "It was truly wonderful! But I must say," she added with a confidential relish, "it was surprising to see how poorly so many in the provinces dress. Why, one would think one was at a village fair and not one of the nation's most salubrious cities."

Philomena began to roll her eyes but stopped when Edgar shot her a warning glance.

Meanwhile, Belinda sucked in her lips and did all she could to keep a neutral face. "Well, not everyone is fortunate enough to be in a position to afford the most up-to-date fashions. I'm sure they're doing the best they can."

Caroline sniffed in response. "I suppose they are."

At that moment, the carriage entered Rotten Row along the southern side of Hyde Park.

Riders of the ton trotted alongside the Weatherby carriage.

Caroline held her head high. She loved being here, in the very centre of London society, in the carriage of an earl and seated opposite a *duchess*. Yes, her cousin, a duchess! She hoped to reach such heights herself one day when she herself would have her own debut season.

Then, out of the corner of her eye, she spied a most pleasing sight. Mr Archibald, heir to the earldom of Portishead, on his mighty mahogany steed. A man of eight and ten years, he admittedly did cut a fine figure.

"Look, it's Mr Archibald! May we stop and talk with him?" Caroline asked.

Edgar's face grew stern. "No, we may not. We're here to enjoy a carriage ride as a family."

Caroline let forth a small huff but maintained her external composure.

Philomena rolled her eyes and this time Edgar did nothing to stop her.

He knew he had a level of responsibility to protect Caroline's reputation, but he was walking a fine line. He was not her head of household, after all, and so did not have the same level of authority in her life as he did when it came to Philomena and Genevieve. Or, for that matter, Belinda before she was married. He allowed himself to follow the inevitable train of thought. Whoever he married would be someone he himself would hold authority over, at least in the eyes of the law. He believed he had proven himself a capable figure through his stewardship of his sisters, but they had had no choice in the matter whereas a wife would be choosing to marry him of her own free will. A very different proposition indeed.

Belinda broke the silence inside the carriage. "Philomena, what have you been reading lately?"

Philomena began to talk about several pamphlets and the carriage ride continued.

⁂

After the Weatherby carriage had deposited Belinda and Caroline back at Faversham House, Edgar and Philomena made their way back to Grosvenor Square.

"I'm sick of Caroline. She's always the same," Philomena said.

"She hasn't had the best luck with parents," Edgar said.

Philomena scoffed. "She's a total snob."

"That's true," he said. "I'll grant you that. But her father is constantly absent. He takes no leadership role in that family and just spoils Caroline with expensive gifts out of guilt at not stepping up. And Aunt Thomosina, well she's awful to Caroline. Really ghastly the way she treats her."

"We haven't had easy lives, none of us have. I don't see why she's so special." Philomena crossed her arms and curled her lip.

Edgar let forth a sigh. "That's true, we haven't had the most straightforward of lives, despite all the privileges we enjoy. And Caroline is no more special than any of the rest of us. But she is living under a bad influence. A very bad influence indeed."

The pair sat in silence as Edgar's words settled into every nook and cranny of the carriage.

Philomena replayed them over and over in her mind.

Then, after a few minutes, she breached the void.

"After a week or so with Belinda, she seems to improve," she said.

"I agree. Being out of her father's house, even if only for a short while, seems to help her a great deal."

At that moment, the carriage pulled up outside the Weatherby's London home.

A purple-liveried footman opened the door, bringing the siblings' conversation to a close. Neither of them would ever have dreamt of discussing family disputes within earshot of a servant, after all.

The mist swirled around the Renfregh estate, clouding the deer park in an almost smoky haze that took on a grey lavender tone when the sun shone through it and at other points warm golden orange specks of light filtered through the haze. Scattered throughout the park were robust and strong oak trees, their leaves bare of all leaves and conkers now it was winter. The trees cast imposing figures on the landscape and to anyone standing from far away, they appeared completely black. One would have to get closer to the trees to realise they were in fact detailed living beings with shades of russet and maroon and slate.

Frost coated the grass. Whichever animal or person would be first to walk on it this morning would likely leave a trail of seemingly clear footprints, evidencing their pathway.

In the distance, up on the hill, to anyone who cared enough to look closely, the faint wisps of smoke would be visible. These smokelines came from the ramshackle homes of the labourers, trying to keep warm in the depths of the English winter. Unlike the Weatherbys, there was no one to light their fires before the occupants arose in the morning and keep them burning throughout the day while the occupants attended to their leisure activities. No! For the labourers life was hard and cruel and often all too short. They had to light their own fires, keep them burning with whatever wood they could find and try to make the best of the situation.

Meanwhile, in the entrance hall of Renfregh, Edgar stood and felt the weight of generations of history bearing down on him.

Portraits of his ancestors, both the accomplished and the less salubrious alike, stared down at him. The freshest portrait, painted only twenty-five years ago, featured his father standing confidently in the grounds of the estate as he surveyed the Weatherby lands. It was as though his father's eyes were boring at him accusingly, asking Edgar when he was going to take his responsibilities as the earl seriously and secure the Weatherby line.

Edgar felt a chill run through his body. He was doing all he could to keep the estates running, to represent the earldom in the House of Lords and within the ton. It wasn't his fault his father had died decades before his time was due and had thrust Edgar into a world of responsibility for which he was not ready. It had been a baptism of fire and for years afterwards he was drowning drowning drowning in the grief of that monumental loss.

I'm doing the best I can. I never asked for any of this, thought Edgar.

If one were to ask him back when he was seventeen about how he envisaged the course his life would take, he would have replied that on leaving school he would go up to Oxford or Cambridge for a few years, taking a mistress at that time. Then he would graduate and really begin sowing his wild oats. Of course, he would do the Grand Tour with all the traditional sights like Rome and Naples, before returning to England to learn more about running the earldom from his father with big swathes of time spent with mistresses and leisure activities. Eventually he would marry, probably in his late twenties, and produce a brood of children with his high born bride before ultimately becoming the earl when he was well over the age of forty.

But of course, reality had something different planned for Edgar. Both his parents were lost in a shipwreck and then he suddenly had an earldom to manage with hundreds of tenants and a seat in the House of Lords. Being the earl also meant taking responsibility for his two brothers and three sisters, not to mention producing an heir and a spare for the next generation to take the earldom in due course. All while he was enveloped in the grief at losing his beloved mother and father.

So many of his experiences over the past decade had left him feeling adrift and anxious about what might happen next. The weight of his responsibilities bore down heavily upon his shoulders.

In fact, the only thing he felt secure of was his position in the British aristocracy. That was unchallengeable.

He was pulled away from his train of thought by footsteps and squealing on the black and white chequered tiles behind him.

"Tag, you're it!" his youngest sister Genevieve cried.

Edgar turned around to see Genevieve laughing along with the youngest Weatherby brother, Lionel.

Lionel tilted his head sardonically. "Not for long, dear sister!"

Edgar stood with his hands behind his back and watched the proceedings with lightly concealed amusement.

It was at that point that the youngest Weatherby brother, fast approaching the age of thirteen, noticed Edgar's presence.

"Hello, Edgar," Lionel said with confidence.

"Hello, Lionel, Genevieve," Edgar replied.

Genevieve returned the greeting.

Edgar addressed his siblings. "Have you been keeping up with your studies?"

"Yes, Edgar," they chimed. As was the custom for children of the ton, Lionel's studies focused on Latin, Ancient Greek, French and mathematics while Genevieve's education was centred around music, dancing, French, Italian and needlework. Both also studied theology and, per Edgar's somewhat eccentric decision, bookkeeping.

Edgar gave his siblings a firm nod. "Very good. Make sure you maintain your progress."

The pair affirmed that they would and then ran off with joyous aplomb through the doors that led to the drawing room.

"Be careful," Edgar called after them.

❧❧❧❧❧ ❧❧❧❧❧❧

"Renfregh is my legacy," Edgar said with all the passion of a man who had had a couple too many whiskys.

His friend, the Earl of Mowbrow, pinched the spot where his nose and eyes met between his fingers. "I know. You say that almost every time we come here."

The pair were at one of the dining tables in the Lumley Club in fashionable Mayfair. When in London, men from the aristocratic set generally attended their club three or four times a week and the Earls of Weatherby and Mowbrow were no exception.

"I'm only a custodian of Renfregh, it's up to me to leave it to the next generation," Edgar said.

"As is true for all of us with earldoms and duchies, it's a big responsibility," Mowbrow said.

Edgar's mood took a turn, moving from passion to depression. "I'll never be able to fulfil that responsibility."

"Why not? Too busy sowing your wild oats?" Mowbrow joked.

"No! No!" Edgar was agitated in his drunken state. "I'll never find a wife."

"Aw, come on," Mowbrow cajoled, "You're one of the most eligible bachelors in all England, you could have your pick of the ladies."

"I mean it! None of them are suitable."

"How so?"

"None of them have captivated me."

Mowbrow wrinkled his brow. "Captivated you? I don't know if that's a requirement for a wife. Let your mistress captivate you if you must be captivated. When the time comes to marry, just find any lady of fine breeding who has a good reputation and make her your bride. There's no need to overcomplicate things."

Edgar took a sip of whisky and savoured the peaty taste. Yes, there was no need to overcomplicate things.

Georgina walked out onto the stage. In her pink and white dress with glistening beads, she was the very vision of a jewel. Relishing the applause from the audience, she smiled and prepared herself to deliver another performance.

Tonight it was *Atraxerxes*, a favourite of fashionable London society.

In the box closest to the left side of the stage, she could see Edgar with some of his friends.

He smiled in her direction, as he had on so many nights before. A promise of what was to come later on in the evening.

Attempting to turn those thoughts aside, Georgina began to sing.

But it was a struggle. Every time she looked in Edgar's direction, he was staring down at her watching her every move.

Finishing her final song, she curtsied and left the stage. Once in her dressing room, she began to unpin her bun. It wasn't long until she heard that familiar knock at the door.

"Hello, my sweet," Edgar said once she had opened the door and was standing facing him.

Edgar was a strange one for a patron. She had had rich men as patrons before, but they had always been transactional. Money for her time and attentions. A tit for tat exchange. Her liaison with Edgar had started out the same way, but had morphed into something else. Quite what, she did not know.

"Hello, my lord," Georgina said.

Edgar stepped inside the door, closing it behind him and wrapping Georgina in his arms. "You were exquisite as ever, the voice of an angel. I could listen to you all evening."

Georgina laughed coquettishly. "You do flatter me, my lord."

Leaning up to kiss Edgar, Georgina stroked his back and enjoyed feeling the strength of his muscles. This was a man who kept fit.

Edgar lifted Georgina from the ground and carried her towards the dressing table. Placing her atop the table, he slowly ran his left hand down the side of her leg before raising her skirt slightly and beginning to explore the inside of the space between her legs.

CHAPTER FIVE

One Saturday morning, Georgina and Edgar lay curled up on the bed at her house.

Edgar's breaches and shirt were folded on the back of a chair. Georgina's garments, meanwhile, had so far not left the wardrobe for the day.

The pair sat discussing this and that before conversation turned to the matter of Georgina's opera schedule.

"I won't have performances for the next couple of weekends, I'm doing the weekday ones instead," Georgina explained.

An idea germinated in Edgar's head.

"In that case, what do you say to coming with me on a trip to Renfregh the weekend after next?" Edgar said.

Georgina wrinkled her nose. "Isn't that going to expose the fact that you have a mistress to your family?"

"Sorry, I should have been clearer. The rest of my family will be in London."

She breathed a sigh of relief. "In that case, thank you for the invitation. I will accept."

He smiled and took her hands in his. "This is one decision you won't regret, my lady."

Georgina was not sure about that, but she was growing fond of Edgar and he was her protector after all.

⁕ ⁕ ⁕

The Weatherby carriage made its way off the turnpike and down a smaller road where sheep were chewing grass in verdant fields on either side. Then the carriage pulled up at a stone archway and turned through it.

"Welcome to Renfregh," Edgar said.

"Thank you my lord," Georgina replied.

Now they were moving down the main driveway. On either side were rolling lawns where deer lightly grazed. A groundskeeper rode a horse swiftly in the distance.

Georgina wrung her hands together. She gulped and brought a hand to her mouth in an attempt to hide her reaction from Edgar. But to no avail.

"Are you feeling alright, Georgina?" Edgar asked.

"Yes, yes, fine," she said.

He quirked an eyebrow. "Hmmm, are you sure you wouldn't like some water?" He reached underneath his seat. "I have some here -"

"No, no, it's quite alright."

"You are not going down with an illness?"

She bit her lip. "I don't believe so. It's just, well, this feels like me intruding on your family's private space."

"There's no intrusion, I assure you my darling. I am head of the family and I invited you."

She nodded. "As you command, my lord."

Their eyes met across the carriage.

He saw the mirth in her pupils as she battled to keep a straight face.

He kept staring directly into her eyes with an intense gaze.

"My lord," she spluttered, "please stop looking at me like that."

He quirked an eyebrow. "Looking at you how?"

"Like *that*."

"I am terribly sorry, Georgina, but you will need to be more specific. In what way would you like me to stop looking at your gorgeous visage?"

She emitted a harrumph of frustration. "Oh you know precisely what I mean! Like that, all commandingly."

A wolfish grin took over his features. "Well, you were the one who said I gave a command. I was merely attempting to meet your expectations. Who am I to try anything otherwise?"

He reached across to her and took one of her dainty hands in his own. Then he placed a gentle kiss on it before continuing speaking. "But if you would like me to issue commands, I would be more than happy to do so."

She raised his hand that had taken hers and brought it to her lips. As he had done to her, she kissed his hand with a smile on her face.

"I should like that, my lord," she replied.

"As you wish. I would hate to deny you a single thing, my darling," he cooed.

The carriage pulled up outside the main entrance to Renfregh house.

A footman opened the door and Edgar jumped out of the carriage, before turning around and assisting Georgina.

Georgina looked up to see a grand stone building formed in the Neo-Palladian style so popular during the first half of the eighteenth century. Its Bath stone walls cast a warm and inviting honeyed glow about the vicinity.

Once they were both on their feet on the gravel driveway, Edgar took her arm-in-arm and guided her up the steps and through the great oaken doors to the entrance hall.

"Welcome to Renfregh, Georgina," he said with proud flourish.

"Thank you, my lord," she replied.

This wasn't the first time Georgina had been inside a country house of a member of the aristocracy. Some gentlemen had a penchant for bringing back their mistresses when their wives and children were elsewhere. Georgina might have found it distasteful, for a married man to bring his mistress into the family home, but she couldn't afford to care about such matters when she had to worry about securing an income. That sort of morality was a luxury for the wealthy, after all. Besides, it wasn't like Edgar was even married so the situation was a peg or two more innocent than some others she had found herself in over the years.

And Edgar's smile was oh so charming. So often, she found him hard to resist.

"Come," he said with excitement. "Let me show you around the place."

Cynical and world weary though she ordinarily was, today she could not help but let herself get swept up by his boundless enthusiasm. "I would like that, my lord."

Edgar took a look at her and blinked. "How rude of me, I do apologise. Would you like some refreshments as we go around?"

She nodded. "That would be nice."

Edgar turned to a footman who was standing towards the back of the entrance hall with his eyes cast fastidiously ahead. "Mulwick, some biscuits and -" Edgar broke off and turned back to Georgina. "What beverage?"

"Lemonade if your cook has some, please," Georgina said.

Edgar pointlessly relayed the request to the footman, who gave a bow and made off for the kitchens.

Georgina reached out and took Edgar's hand. "Where would you like to show me first?"

"Oh, the drawing room," he said with a rakish smile.

There it was. Georgina was caught within his world hook, line and sinker. And she could not say she did not enjoy it.

The pair walked hand-in-hand through the doorway to the drawing room.

Almost immediately, Georgina's attention was piqued by the gigantic neoclassical windows lining the entire wall opposite the fireplace.

"That's some view," she said.

She led Edgar towards the windows and they stopped in front of one.

He stood right by her side as she looked through it and out onto the main lawns.

She pointed at the different sites, the pond, the heavy stone folly in the distance and the sweeping driveway that cut through the rolling lawns as he told her the story behind each of them.

Georgina's skirts and petticoats rustled against Edgar's leg. He relished the sensation; a promise of things to come. But he would not allow himself to lose his composure right then and there. He wanted to maintain the bounds of propriety here in the ancestral seat, where he had brought Georgina for the first time. He did not want to rush things. That would not do for a lady. No, good things come to those who wait and he would do well to wait.

His train of thought was interrupted by a brief knock at the door.

Two liveried footmen entered the room carrying silver trays laden with lemonade and biscuits. They placed them on the ornate mahogany coffee table close to the fireplace and then, almost as quickly as they had entered the room, made their exit.

Edgar rubbed gentle circles around Georgina's knuckles. "My lady, would you care for some refreshments?" he asked.

"Oh yes, let's," she said with a smile.

The pair walked towards the coffee table.

Edgar handed Georgina a glass of lemonade before taking one for himself.

Georgina helped herself to a biscuit and savoured the sweet taste of the gingernut treat.

As they imbibed and ate, Edgar pointed out several family portraits dotted around the canary yellow walls of the drawing room.

Georgina was struck by the close resemblance of the past earls to Edgar. They shared his hawk like brown eyes and dashingly symmetrical face. Those Weatherby genes were strong indeed!

After promenading down the length of the quasi-art gallery, Georgina and Edgar left the room via a white door and found themselves in a sweeping corridor. They made their way down the maroon carpet and Edgar pointed out the various rooms along the way.

All the while, they shared soft touches and achingly fleeting glances. Georgina enjoyed seeing the opulence of the house, a part of her always did in a place such as this, but she would much rather be with Edgar properly. Who wanted to look at antiques and Rococo furniture when such a handsome gentleman was standing right next to her?

Together, arm-in-arm, they walked down a corridor lined with scarlet damask silken wallpaper. Along the way, Edgar pointed out various rooms. Most of the corridor seemed to be guest bedrooms and offices.

Georgina had seen this sort of arrangement before and she was far more interested in Edgar than she was in the house. She rubbed his arm with her free hand.

At the end of the corridor, they came to an imposing set of cream doors, boarded by carved stone ionic columns. Carvings of Grecian vases stood atop the columns.

Edgar opened a door and held it open for Georgina. "Please, after you, my lady."

Georgina did as she was bid and walked forward into the as-yet unknown room.

"This is the ballroom," the voice behind her announced.

Georgina headed into the centre of the room and walked around in a small circle. Sage green walls with white stucco Grecian decorations greeted her eyes. The ceiling, too, was adorned with imagery of the gods and goddesses of Mount Olympus. On first glance, it was a typical ballroom of the ton. But then Georgina looked again. Here and there, layers of dust indicated that this was a ballroom that hadn't seen any dancers in a long long time.

Edgar joined Georgina in the centre of the room. He took both of her hands in his. "Yes, you're correct in what you're thinking. This ballroom hasn't been used in many years."

She nodded gently. There was a slightly pained look in his eyes and she had a fair idea as to the cause. "Since before you became the earl, my lord?"

"Yes, not since the days of my mother has there been a ball in here."

Georgina squeezed his hands in a gesture of comfort.

Edgar continued speaking. "Renfregh used to host some of the most talked about balls of every year. My mother was an excellent hostess. I, alas, am not a great host." He bit his lip.

Georgina squeezed his hands again. "Well, with no countess around, it can't all fall to you, my lord."

"That's true," he sighed. "But sometimes I still wish I could do more."

"There are only so many hours in the day."

"I know, I know, Miss Hartley. You're right. You speak sense," he replied.

"Sometimes sense is not enough."

He let forth another sigh. "Yes, that's precisely it."

"It's hard when the head and the heart do not align, my lord. Though I do think you could stand to be a little easier upon yourself." She gave his hands another squeeze.

He made a small smile. "I should try to follow that advice more often."

An idea germinated in Georgina's head. "Say, my lord, have you ever danced in here?"

"When I was a younger man, at a few of the balls straight after Eton and before I went up to Oxford." Edgar looked Georgina deep into her eyes. In that moment, he understood her train of thought completely. "My lady, shall we have a dance?"

"I would like that, my lord."

"Very well." Edgar let go of Georgina's hands. He took a step back and made a bow.

Georgina gave a curtsey in response.

Then they walked towards one another.

Edgar placed an arm around Georgina's waist. With his free hand, he met Georgina's dainty palm and intertwined his fingers with hers.

Together they began to move around the room.

Georgina nested her head on Edgar's shoulder and hummed a tune. Her sweet, melodic notes reverberated in Edgar's ear.

Dancing like this with a lady wasn't an uncommon occurrence for him. He attended the requisite balls as part of the social season each year, after all. But dancing with Georgina ignited a sensation within him that he couldn't quite put his finger on. Was it contentment? Peace? He wasn't sure what either of those words really meant. If he had ever felt either of them, it would have been before his parents died. But he had heard others talk of those sensations of peace and contentment with great rapture and maybe what he was feeling right now was the very same. It was pleasant, whatever it was.

They danced for a good quarter of an hour.

Then a side door burst open.

A maid, probably only about fourteen years of age, stood in the doorway holding a mop and a pail of water. Shock overtook her facial features.

"I beg your pardon, my lord," she stammered. "I-I-"

Edgar and Georgina drew apart.

Edgar turned to the maid and said kindly, "It's quite alright. You weren't to know. We'll be going now."

Then he took Georgina by the hand and led her through the colossal cream doors by which they had come into the room, leaving the maid standing confused in their wake.

***

Back in the scarlet corridor, Edgar said, "I've got somewhere else to show you."

"Please, do," said Georgina.

The moment between them in the ballroom, whatever it had been, had dissipated now. Nonetheless, Georgina still wanted to spend time with Edgar and find out more about him.

Edgar offered her his hand and together they walked down the corridor until Edgar brought them to a halt in front of an unassuming oaken door. This wasn't something Edgar had pointed out earlier, when Georgina had assumed it was merely the door to some sort of storeroom.

She was proven wrong, however, when Edgar opened the door to reveal a stunning orangery.

The pair entered the realm of greenery, white blossoms and vibrant fruits. A zesty aroma of oranges filled the air.

Georgina had seen her share of small orangeries in country houses before. And she had even seen them growing outdoors, on the terraces and in the *piazze* in southern Italy. But something on this scale was beyond her experience.

She could not help but be a little bit impressed. "This place is fantastical, my lord. The smell is incredible."

At the back of her mind, however, she could not help but wonder how much all this cost and if it was really the best use of funds. How did Edgar's tenants live?

Edgar smiled and wrapped his arm around Georgina's waist. "I am so glad you like it, my lady." He placed an affectionate kiss on her cheek.

"What do you do with the oranges? There must be so many of them," she said.

"Well, some we eat or drink here, some we give to the tenants and the rest we sell now and then in Bath and some of the nearby towns." He placed another kiss on Georgina's cheek. "Say, would you like to try one?"

"Go on then, yes please."

Edgar reached for a nearby orange, hanging from one of the abundant trees, and plucked it from its branch. He handed the fruit to Georgina.

Her dainty hands peeled it with deft poise. She tossed the peel into the terracotta planter behind her. Soon enough it would be mulch to support the growth of new life. She broke the fruit in half and tore off a segment.

A spray of juices filled the air, bringing with them a strong citrus perfume.

Popping the segment into her mouth, she savoured the tangy flavour as the juice erupted and engulfed her taste buds. Once she had finished chewing, she said, "Now my lord, that was delicious." She tore off another segment. "Would you like to try some?"

"Go on then, my lady." His eyes were wide, enraptured by her presence.

She dropped the segment into his well-shaped mouth.

He closed his eyes and let the flavoursome juices wash through him. After he had finished the segment, he opened his eyes. "Yes, my lady. You are correct. That orange is delicious."

"Isn't it so?" she said with a slight grin.

"But," Edgar said, "I do believe that it is not quite as delicious as you."

"My lord, you do flatter me."

"Ah, it's not flattery if it's true." He leant forward and placed a kiss on her neck.

She let forth a moan of pleasure.

Then she peeled off another segment of orange and fed it to Edgar, before taking another piece for herself.

Like that, they shared the orange until every segment was gone.

Edgar brought Georgina's dainty hand to his lips and place a passionate kiss atop it. "You are most delectable, my lady," he said.

And so they spent the next hour touring the delights of Renfregh before retiring to Edgar's chambers.

Georgina held her candle and looked out of the window. Not that she could see much of the Renfregh landscape given the turbulent night sky that cast a dark pall over the entire county of Wiltshire.

She jumped. A blurry figure in shades of blue and cream appeared reflected in the window. She turned around to see it was Edgar.

"Darling, what are you doing up at this hour? Do you feel alright?" Deep concern filled his entire face.

She sighed. "I'm not ill, but I'm having trouble sleeping. Sometimes I get this insomnia. I didn't want to wake you up with my tossing and turning, so I came in here."

He walked towards her. "My darling, would you like me to keep you company? I could read to you if you wish."

"It's worth a try," she said with a small smile.

"Your wish is my command, my lady." He gestured to the bookshelves around the room. "Have you a particular book in mind? We've got about every genre going here."

"Oh something comic if it's there."

"I know just the thing." He turned and plucked a thin red tome from the bookshelves.

Together, they sat on one of the window seats and Georgina curled up against Edgar as he put his arm around her and began to read.

The next day, Edgar sat in the drawing room reading a pamphlet and drinking some tea.

Feminine footsteps filled the air and he looked up to see his sweet Georgina.

She seemed somewhat tired, but alert.

"How are you feeling today, sweetheart?" he asked.

"Better, thank you," she said.

She moved to sit next to him and reached for his hand.

He stroked her hand gently and brought it to his lips in a protective kiss.

"The insomnia, last night, thank you for being there," she said with a small smile.

"It was my privilege, Georgina." He said resolutely. "Though I am sorry that it's something that causes you strife. I must admit I had no idea."

"Yes, until last night it had not afflicted me while we were together. It can be so intermittent and I usually find it better to focus on happier things."

"Well, I'm here if you ever want to talk about it, Georgina," Edgar said. He kissed her on the forehead.

"Thank you, my lord."

CHAPTER SIX

Days turned into weeks and weeks turned into months. Aside from his family and Mowbrow, Georgina had become the person with whom Edgar spent most of his time.

This time around, Georgina was due to come to his bachelor lodgings to spend the weekend together.

Edgar shuffled through some papers he had been working on at his desk at the side of what was essentially a glorified parlour. Though he had his own office at the family home a short walk away, he often preferred to take his paperwork back to his bachelor house. Better chance of focusing and getting work done that way.

A footman entered the room and bowed. "Miss Hartley is here to see you, my lord."

"Very good," Edgar said. "Send her in please."

The footman exited the room and a short while later Georgina stood in his place.

Edgar walked over to where she stood. With deftness, he removed her silken glove and kissed her bare hand.

Georgina giggled. "Good afternoon, my lord. You are looking in fine form as always."

"As are you, my Lady."

He moved to claim her mouth with his own in a passionate kiss.

She moaned and wrapped her arms around his toned waist.

⁓⁓⁓⁓⁓ ⁓⁓⁓⁓⁓

Enwrapped in one another's arms as they lay on Edgar's bed, the couple basked in the warm afterglow of sex.

Georgina scanned her eyes around the room in an effort to learn more about the man she called her protector. His innermost sanctum.

Directly opposite the bed was a magnificent oil painting of the English countryside. It put her in mind of a Gainsborough. She would have to ask him about it later. Fine arts were not an area she had heard him discuss much before and she was keen to learn more about this side of him.

In the corner closest to the windows stood a sturdy oaken chest of drawers. Atop was a small collection of half full cologne bottles. Georgina wagered with confidence that those bottles would contain the leathery scent with a slight hint of forest floor that she so adored to breathe in when she was close to Edgar.

The corner closest to the door played host to a combined hat and coat stand. A couple of silken top hats sat near the top and underneath was the navy velvet jacket he so often wore when he called on her in Fitzrovia.

Almost matching the jacket were heavy navy velvet curtains at each window. Every wall was panelled in a dark walnut. The floorboards too were a deep colour, though covered in a large part of the centre by an intricate Persian rug.

Here was a room that simply oozed refined masculinity from every nook, cranny and crevice.

Later that day, when they were sitting side-by-side in the room that could not make up its mind whether it wanted to be a drawing room or a parlour, Georgina turned to Edgar and asked. "Say my Lord, I noticed you have a very striking landscape in your bedroom. Is it a Gainsborough?"

"Oh you have a good eye," he said. "Yes, it's one of his."

"Then you've excellent taste."

A smile graced his lips. "I do hear that quite often."

"How did you come by it?"

"It was my grandfather's. He was a great collector of British landscape art. When he died, most of his collection was mothballed at Renfregh, my father much preferred portraiture you see. And while I'm fond of a portrait myself, I came across my grandfather's collection about five years ago and realised what gems we had simply gathering dust in a store room somewhere."

"Did you know your grandfather then?"

"Alas no, not too well at all. He died when I was four. I have extremely hazy memories of him, of when we went shooting at Renfregh mostly, but sometimes it's hard to tell what's a genuine memory and what's something I've subconsciously concocted based on information other people have given to me."

Edgar stroked Georgina's head affectionately.

"Genuine memories can be hard to determine, I find. But sometimes it's nice to reminisce nonetheless," Georgina said.

"That's true," Edgar replied.

"Say, what was your father like?" Georgina asked.

"He was a great leader of our family," Edgar said. "Someone I always looked up to, and still try my best to emulate to this very day."

"And your mother?"

"Ah now she was a most excellent countess in every way. A phenomenal society hostess."

Georgina looked straight ahead in thought before turning back to Edgar. "My lord, please don't take this the wrong way, but do you look back on them with fondness?"

"Of course, they were my parents," he stated bluntly.

"Quite so my lord," she said.

Despite her verbal agreement, Georgina struggled to shake off the sensation that Edgar's parents may not have been the idyll that he claimed. It was probably easier for him to revere and quasi-canonise them rather than face the reality that mere mortals are never without flaws.

After Georgina exited the stage to rapturous applause, she made her way backstage to her dressing room.

Unsurprisingly, Edgar was waiting outside her dressing room door with a bouquet of posies in his hand.

She stopped outside her dressing room door and smiled at her protector.

"Good evening, Georgina," he said before he kissed her.

He relished the sensation of her soft lips between his own. She tasted like strawberries with a hint of a spice he could not quite place.

She broke the kiss. "Good evening, my lord."

Then he handed her the bouquet. "For you. Congratulations on another wonderful performance."

"Thank you my lord." She took the flowers in her hand and sniffed them. The aroma of honeysuckle and rose was a true delight!

She opened her dressing room door and beckoned him inside, before shutting the door behind the pair.

She placed the bouquet on her dressing table and turned towards Edgar.

"Ah, I need to get out of this costume and change into something more comfortable. Could you give me a hand please?" she said.

"Of course," he grinned.

Atop her head she wore a faux gold tiara adorned with an intricate design of gleaming small leaves. It looked beautiful to those in the back row of the Gods, but heavens its cheap construction made it hurt like hell to wear for any significant length of time. Thankfully, Georgina only had to wear it for the final two songs of the performance.

With a gentle touch, Edgar deftly removed the tiara and placed it on the table next to the bouquet.

Georgina stood still with her hands hanging loosely at her sides.

He returned to her and walked in a slow circle around her, eyeing her as though she were a specimen for his exclusive examination as he did so.

Her pulse began to increase as she felt his penetrating gaze on her body and the warmth of his presence mere inches from her skin.

Then hands reached at the fastening hooks on the back of her dress and oh, it was like pure electricity ghosting over her skin and through her very core.

One by one he undid the hooks down to where they finished at her lower back.

"Hold your arms out in front of you," he said.

She duly did so.

Then he rolled down the sleeves of her dress and extricated her torso from the garment.

"Step out," he said.

Again, she did as he bid.

He bent down to the floor and picked up the dress, leaving her standing in her stays, chemise and drawers.

He went over to the wardrobe and placed the dress on a hanger. Then he removed her own dress, a pale pink satin piece, and brought it over to her.

"Step in," he said.

She did so and pulled the sleeves over her shoulders.

Edgar made nimble work of the fastening hooks before he removed her black velvet cloak from where it hang near the door.

He placed it gently over her shoulders before doing up the fastening ties. He stepped back to admire her, the glorious vision that stood before him.

"You look beautiful, sweetheart," he said with a soft smile.

"Thank you my lord."

"Now. Come with me."

He held out his hand and she took it in hers.

The pair headed towards the door and she picked up the bouquet from the table on the way.

As the pair exited the theatre, they bumped into a rowdy crowd who were watching a preacher standing on a crate in the square.

The booming voice of the preacher drifted towards Edgar and Georgina. "For as Satan will take away the murderers and the idolaters, so too shall he take into his realm all the whores and prostitutes. And let it be known, yes let it be known, that any woman who follows the ways of Jezebel will find herself in the pits of fire come Judgement Day."

Edgar quickly hustled Georgina into a waiting Weatherby carriage.

"Pay that preacher no mind, darling," said Edgar as the horses trotted off towards his bachelor lodgings.

"Thank you, Edgar. But you should know I don't feel any shame in doing what I do," Georgina said.

"I'm not saying you should, but -" Edgar said.

"Besides, you're the one who's paying for me, not the other way around."

He guffawed in surprise. "That's true. Few would be so blunt about it."

"It's the truth of the situation though." A ghost of a smile graced her lips. "I do think he was wasting his time too, even preaching there in the first place."

"Why?"

"It's Covent Garden at eleven o'clock on a Friday night. The only people around are either ladies of the night, mollyboys, johns or people whose incomes rely on the selling of sex. Even the lowliest orange seller knows they'd be out of work in a flash if it weren't for people like me willing to sell themselves on the stage and between the sheets."

Edgar bit his lip and sat in a moment of brief contemplation.

Georgina caught his gaze and gave him a wry smile.

"You are far wiser than I am," he said.

Georgina gave a happy laugh and rubbed his arm.

Yet despite Georgina's outward gaiety, Egdar could not shake the unsettled sensation in his stomach. He hated seeing that preacher and hearing those sermons insulting Georgina and other people like her, while all the while knowing that he himself was pushing Georgina into such a situation. A bitter taste clung to the inside of his mouth.

⁂

A few days later and Georgina and Edgar were in his bedroom at his bachelor lodgings. Late morning sunlight shone through the windows, the blinds drawn three quarters of the way up, casting a green-golden haze across the interior.

The pair lay in a close embrace on top of the bed.

Georgina wore only her thin ivory chemise while Edgar wore even less.

She ghosted her fingertips up and down his bare back and buttocks, delighting in the goose pimples that formed just underneath the surface of his skin.

He let forth a satisfied moan as the tingling sensation of electricity burst from underneath his skin. "Geo…Georgina—"

"Hmm…do you like that, darling?" she giggled.

"You know it." He closed his eyes and let the pleasant sensations wash through him.

She continued her attentions in silence for several minutes.

After a while, she said, "So, what have you got on for the week?"

"Well, there's a ball on Saturday night. Xavier and I are both attending, but there's not much point now that Belinda is married," he said.

"Oh, why is that my lord?" she asked, continuing her attentions with her talented fingers.

He scoffed lightly. "It's hardly as though Xavier or I are candidates for the marriage mart any time soon. He is more than content to sow his wild oats and I am far to busy with all the duties of being the earl."

She giggled. "So you are not sowing your wild oats with me?"

His voice lost its mirth and adopted a far more serious tone. "You know it's not like that between us, Georgina. I want to protect you, always."

A funny feeling built within her. Was Edgar saying these things for his benefit or her own? It *seemed* as though she was more than wild oats to him, but for a man to make claims to a woman who was not his wife that he would always want to protect her was very far fetched indeed. Still, it did not do to dwell on uncomfortable thoughts. She brushed off the sensation and let herself fall into the moment with him.

"Quite so, my lord," she smiled by way of reply.

He hummed in agreement.

"Say, what do you do at these balls? With the fine ladies?" Georgina asked.

"Allow me to show you." Edgar climbed up off the bed and offered his hand to Georgina.

She accepted it and then they were both standing on their feet facing one another.

"May I have this dance, my lady?" Edgar bowed and kissed Georgina's hand, before taking hers in his hand and putting his arm around her waist.

The pair began to waltz around the room. Georgina hummed a rhythm before she burst out into giggles.

Edgar lifted Georgina up off the floor and she wrapped her legs around his waist.

"I hate going to balls without you there," Edgar grumbled. "Everything is so dull without you, Georgina."

"Then it's a good thing you're not at a ball now, my lord," she said airily.

"How I wish I could take you to balls with me, you would be the prettiest, most admirable lady in all the room."

Georgina giggled. "I'm no lady, my lord."

"You are to me," Edgar said.

***

Georgina and Edgar lay together on the settee in her Fitzrovia house, the fire roaring away in the behind them. Georgina sat with her back against the arm of the settee and her legs pointing straight ahead while Edgar dozed with his arms wrapped around her waist.

Turning the pages of the pamphlet she was reading, Georgina became lost in the words in front of her. So she was taken by surprise when Edgar roused from his slumber and blurted, "What are you reading?"

"The latest letter from the editor in *The Trumpet*," she said.

"A radical piece!" He smiled. "I've not read that one, though Philomena I know would have. What do you think of it?"

"There are some good points. It puts me in mind of Sayer's newest piece, one can see where the author developed some of the ideas."

"Oh I read that. Reminded me of Paine's Common Sense," he said sleepily.

"I can see how that would be so. Say, what did you think of Common Sense?"

"Some good points, though it doesn't work entirely for me."

"Why not? Too egalitarian?" She smirked.

"I don't want to put it like that. More, what would someone like me do in such a society? I have duties to fulfil and without those duties, who am I?"

Georgina sat on the settee in her parlour sipping on a cup of tea with the newspaper on her lap.

The rain pattered against the windows but despite the dismal day she was safe and cosy inside.

The logs lit up the roaring fire.

Turning the pages of the newspaper, she read about the latest goings on around Britain as well as the word from Europe and beyond. Some days she could not believe her luck, that God had blessed her with the gift of her voice and that the vicar had noticed that gift all those years ago, yet other days she wished the world were different. Today, however, she was very glad to be a long way away from the Gloucestershire village she grew up in and to instead be here in this lovely terraced house by a warm fire relaxing and safe from the elements. She wiggled her stockinged feet in the air in the direction of the fire, basking at the warm sensation that touched her toes and the soles of her feet.

Later that day, Georgina made her way along Fleet Street and turned into Wine Office Court. It was coming up for eight o'clock in the evening and many of the printers and journalists that frequented this part of the city were spending a few hours in the inns. She herself was headed to Ye Olde Cheshire Cheese.

She came up to the lowly, stubby wooden door and entered the establishment.

At a booth near the door sat a bespectacled man in a green waistcoat and navy cravat. He was engaged in intense conversation with two other men, one in a brown greatcoat and the other in a black waistcoat.

"The position of the poor in this country is reprehensible," said the man in the green waistcoat. "Something must be done and the wealthy and the aristocracy can no longer afford to stand by or, worse still, take action that harms the poor. They have a duty to do all they can to help their fellow man."

Georgina did not know who the speaker was. Nonetheless, she smiled internally at his tirade. He was bang on the money in her opinion. She continued walking through the pub, looking for the familiar faces she had come to meet.

"Georgina!" cried a female voice above the din of the pub.

Georgina turned her head in the direction of the voice and her face lit up in recognition. It was her friend and fellow opera singer Chloe Thorne.

Next to Chloe sat two of Fleet Street's finest. Journalists and muckrakers that Georgina knew in passing from her time in the capital. Though really they were more Chloe's friends than Georgina's.

"How do you do?" said the first journalist. Georgina remembered his name was Martin Cliveden.

"I'm well, thank you, Mr Cliveden," Georgina said.

The other man introduced himself as Mr Hatt.

Georgina and Chloe talked shop a little.

Then Mr Hatt waved across to a group on a nearby table behind Georgina.

"I didn't expect you three to be here tonight, come on over!" Mr Hatt exclaimed merrily.

Georgina turned around and realised that Mr Hatt was addressing the man in the green waistcoat who had been talking about the position of the poor, plus his two comrades in the black waistcoat and brown greatcoat.

The three men made their way over to Georgina's table, bringing their stools behind them.

"Ah, Miss Hartley, Miss Thorne, may I present to you Justice Brazier, Peter Ridgeway and Walter Cole," said Mr Hatt, gesturing to each individual as he mentioned them in turn.

Mr Ridgeway and Mr Cole were both in the printing trade.

However, it was Justice Brazier that most caught Georgina's attention. He was the man in the green waistcoat and blue cravat who she had earlier overheard railing against the treatment of the poor. From time to time, Georgina had encountered men of the law. It came with the territory of living and working on the fringes of high society, after all. Yet there were not many of that profession who were willing to so vocally state a point of view in opposition to the current state of affairs. It was refreshing to hear.

Mr Cliveden hailed over a barmaid. "Another two pitchers of ale, please."

The barmaid nodded and sauntered over to the pumps.

Georgina turned to Justice Brazier and said, "Say Justice, what brings a man of the law like you to a situation such as this?"

"To Fleet Street, Miss Hartley?" he said.

She gave a small smile. "To this whole evening, to sharing a table with journalists and printers and opera singers. I did overhear you as I came into the place, when you were setting the world to rights, and that's not normally the type of talk one would expect from a man of the law. Too revolutionary, some might say."

"You have a point, Miss Hartley. Many of my peers would avoid places and situations such as this. But, if there's one thing I've come to learn since becoming a justice is that it serves no one but the most privileged wrongdoers and miscreants if men of the law surround themselves with only those of the highest echelons of society," Justice Brazier said.

"How did you come to that realisation?" Georgina asked.

"Through practising the law and seeing the cases that come up before me in the courts and how those miscreants from the higher classes usually think they can buy my agreement or scare me off because they were born to a higher station than I -"

Justice Brazier broke off as the barmaid placed a tray with two pitchers of ale and seven mugs on top of the table.

He poured himself and Georgina a mug each and then said, "I had enough of dealing with gentlemen who think they can set the terms of everything. So that's how I ended up here, on a night such as this."

Both Georgina and Justice Brazier took a sip from their mugs.

Justice Brazier gave a small smile. "I'm not one for revolution though. Rather, what I seek is reform."

"It was a bloody business, what happened in France, and I'd hate to see the like here. But things can't go on as they are," Georgina said. "Something has to change. The aristocracy, they have to change."

"And the rest of us? Are we to change too?"

"Well, now you've got me on a roll sir! The middle classes, those of them that chase after the ways of the aristocracy in every way will need to end that. The reformers, though, they need to keep on as they are. And the workers and the labourers and the poor, they should keep on with it too."

"You should be in parliament, Miss Hartley," smiled Justice Brazier. "You make more sense than several members of my acquaintance."

She returned the smile. "That's kind of you to say, though it seems a far off proposition even if I were ever able to stand. I think I'll stick to the opera."

"Ah, so that's how you know Miss Thorne." Justice Brazier gestured to where Chloe sat in conversation with the journalists and printers.

"Yes, we've worked together on and off for several years." She took a sip of ale before continuing. "I take it you've not seen me perform?"

"No, I seldom go to the opera. Or, for that matter, the theatre or anything else on the stage."

"That makes sense. You would've been sure to remember me if you'd ever seen me perform," she laughed.

He spluttered in surprise. "Quite so, Miss Hartley."

Georgina took another sip of her ale. "I do wish our society were different though. That it were easier to get on if one is willing to put the work in."

"I concur, Miss Hartley. I must say my life so far in the law has been an exercise in developing an all too close appreciation of the low expectations our betters have of us," Justice Brazier said.

"Many of us aren't willing to sink to the expectations of our so-called betters," Georgina said.

"That's very true. I for one have never been prepared to do so."

"Nor I," Georgina smiled.

"I'll drink to that!" Justice Brazier said.

The pair clinked their glasses together.

It wasn't everyday courtesans and judges met and it was intellectual, not sexual. A true breath of fresh air for everyone.

***

Genevieve plucked cautiously on the harp. This was so dull, she thought. Why could she not be outside playing on the lawn at Weatherby House with the family pets? Instead, she had to sit in the drawing room and practice this stupid instrument. Life was so unfair!

As she was lost in her train of thought, there was a loud barking from the hallway followed by thumping paws. Brydon, the family's beloved basset hound, entered the room. He wagged his tail and made his clumsy way towards Genevieve.

Brydon was so cute, thought Genevieve. She would much rather spend the afternoon playing with him than practicing the boring old harp. She stepped away from the instrument and bent down to pat the dog.

"Good boy," she said happily.

Brydon wagged his tail and barked.

"Let's go outside, I'll throw your ball," she said and picked up the ball from the sideboard.

Then she lead Brydon through the French doors and out onto the patio.

No one else was around. Perfect, she thought. Really she should not be doing this.

Edgar would be cross if he found out she had neglected her musical practice to play with the dog. He was forever going on to her about the need to learn the skills required to be a lady of the ton and how she needed to invest in her future rather than spending time on frivolous things.

She scoffed at the memories of Edgar's lectures. Brydon was not frivolous in the least!

She threw his ball a short way away onto the grass and the hound bounded after it. What a great way to spend an afternoon!

❧❧❧❧❧❦ ❦❦❦❦❦❦

After she had been playing with Brydon for around twenty minutes, she heard a coughing behind her and turned around. There stood Edgar, his arms crossed and a stern look on his face.

"This doesn't look like practicing your harp," he said.

"It's not." She stuck her tongue out at him. "It's so much more fun."

"Genevieve," he said with a warning tone.

She huffed. "I know. I know. Practicing the harp is important for my future, it's important I invest in myself and prepare myself for the marriage mart."

"There's no need to be impertinent about it," Edgar said. Heavens, he loved his sister dearly but she could be so exasperating at times. "Please take this seriously." He sat down on the edge of the patio.

Brydon made his way over to Edgar and the earl stretched out his hand to give the dog a pat. "Good boy," he said.

Genevieve made her way towards the family patriarch and sat down next to him. She crossed her arms and looked away from him.

"Genevieve, dear," his voice became gentler. "I understand that the marriage mart probably doesn't seem important to you now, but in eight or nine years you'll be debuting into society and it will matter a lot to you then. More than you realise. I am aware you don't enjoy playing the harp, but sometimes everyone has to learn things they don't enjoy because it's better for them in the long run. Not many young men want to learn Ancient Greek, for instance, but everyone does."

"Hmph! Well maybe I'd like to learn Ancient Greek too!." said Genevieve, looking into the distant landscape at the woodland and the church on the hill.

"That can be arranged if you wish. But you'll still have to keep up with the harp."

Genevieve stroked Brydon's smooth coat and he barked happily. "Alright, brother. I still don't see why I need to worry about the marriage mart. Say, are you on the marriage mart?"

"Kind of," Edgar replied.

She turned her head towards him and threw him a quizzical look. "What do you mean kind of?"

"Well, gentlemen don't strictly go on the marriage mart. They look for a lady who is herself on the marriage mart," he explained.

"And are you looking for a lady?"

"Yes."

Genevieve clasped her hands together in excitement, her sour mood dissipated now she could quiz her brother on his marriage plans. "So will we be seeing a Countess of Weatherby soon? Will I get to be a bridesmaid?"

"Maybe and maybe." Edgar was non-committal.

"What does that mean?" Genevieve laughed.

"I hope to get married, but there's nothing on the cards anytime soon."

Byron began to bark loudly and chase his own tail in circles. Both sibling's attentions switched to the basset hound.

"What a fool," laughed Edgar, gesturing towards the dog.

Genevieve giggled.

Chapter Seven

"Come away with me." Edgar stroked Georgina's hair as she lay in his arms in his bachelor pad bed.

"Pardon?" Georgina said with surprise.

"Come away with me for the winter. For the season in Bath."

Georgina blinked with wide eyes. "The season in Bath? Isn't that for ladies?"

"I'm serious, Georgina my sweet. It would be so dull without you, and I think you'd really enjoy it."

Georgina sighed inwardly. Bath was a place she knew better than Edgar likely realised. Earlier on in her singing career, she'd been a regular figure in the theatres of the city where she had been renowned for her vocal talents. It was in Bath that she'd met her first protector, kindly Lord Redditch, and though she hadn't been attracted to him at all he'd always been respectful of her. Unusual for a protector, as she'd learnt through experience in the subsequent years. But Edgar was her protector now, so it would be a really silly decision financially if she turned down his suggestion of going to Bath.

"Alright, my lord," Georgina said.

"Then it's settled." Edgar kissed Georgina's neck before continuing, "We'll leave for Bath two weeks from today."

Georgina sat in the parlour, her trunk packed and waiting by the door. Any minute now, Edgar's coach would be around to take her to Bath. She had agreed to visit that ancient city because to refuse would have been an insult to her protector. Yet, she had a history in the city that, though she looked back on with some fondness, she had moved on from years ago.

Then there was the clatter of hooves and horses neighing outside. Georgina looked out of the window and saw one of the Weatherby coaches pull up. Her protector disembarked the vehicle and before she knew it, there was a rapping at the door.

"Hello, my darling," Edgar smiled at her wolfishly. "Are you ready to go?"

Georgina assented and two of the Weatherby coachmen retrieved her trunk. Edgar took her by the hand and assisted her into the coach.

"You look radiant as always, sweetheart," Edgar said. He kissed her hand and then rubbed her knuckles gently.

"Thank you my Lord."

Edgar put his hand on Georgina's knee and the coach made its way through London's crowded streets. The hurly burly of London life, with its beggars, merchants and streams of carriages, made for slow progress. But once they reached the green gardens of Hammersmith, the traffic thinned out and the horses picked up the pace.

❧❧❧❧❧❧ ❧❧❧❧❧❧

The carriage clattered ever onwards towards Bath.

The night would soon be drawing in and the agricultural labourers were already making their way home after a long day of drudgery in the fields.

Georgina looked out of the carriage window at a landscape that had changed little since the days of her youth. The same wheat fields, the same hedgerows, the same trees almost bare now autumn was upon this corner of England, the same churches, the same small cottages, the same inns.

Visiting the English countryside was like visiting a world that had never changed, although Georgina knew that the globe still spun day in and day out.

But Georgina had changed.

On one small level, she felt a pang of wistful nostalgia for the childhood she'd spent in a village very much like the ones they'd been passing throughout the late afternoon. She would never be ashamed of where she came from. Yet there was a bigger part of her that was glad that life was behind her.

❧❧❧❧❧❧ ❧❧❧❧❧❧

With the last vestiges of the late afternoon light, the sky was a mix of burnt peach and gunmetal, wrapped in a lavender haze. The trees behind the hedgerows made for imposing figures against the horizon. These ancient figures had seen many a person come and go. Since before the days of the Romans, lives had been lived along and near these arbours. Underneath their boughs had passed monarchs and nobles, the middling sort and the peasantry alike.

Dusk drew nearer now. The carriage pulled into Marlborough's high street and stopped outside the Marlborough Arms coaching inn.

Georgina pulled the hood of her black velvet cloak over her head.

Edgar leapt from the vehicle and turned back to assist Georgina out of the carriage.

Once her feet were on the cobblestones, Edgar offered her his arm and she took it with a soft smile.

⁂

After arriving in Bath, Edgar set Georgina up in one of the Weatherby houses. It was a secluded townhouse constructed in the city's characteristic limestone with three rooms upstairs and another three downstairs.

Edgar had to sort out a staffing dispute at the family home in the Circus, so the pair agreed to meet in the evening outside the Pump Room.

Before he exited the building, Edgar took Georgina's face gently between his hands and claimed her mouth with a kiss.

Her petticoats rustled as they brushed against his legs.

Edgar relished the sensation. "Goodbye, darling," he said.

"Goodbye my lord, until we meet again," she replied coquettishly.

Standing outside the Pump Room in the square by the Abbey, Georgina reflected on how much she'd changed since she was first in Bath for a season ten years ago. Back then, she'd been far more naive to the world of men. Certainly, she'd understood the nature of creation from growing up in an agricultural environment. The lambs in spring, the foals and calves and all the other farm animals that labourers like her parents had a hand in raising and in turn brought much needed income through the door and bread on the table. But how fickle so many of the aristocratic men could be was unknown to her back then. Also unknown to that naive eighteen year old was how strangely respectful some men could be, like her first patron the far older Lord Redditch, and how pleasurable other men could be. Georgina blushed at that latter thought, as images of Edgar sprung into her head.

The vision materialised as Edgar strode across the square towards her. Wearing those black leather riding boots she adored, he was by the far the most gorgeous patron she had ever had. Combined with his tight beige breeches, blue frock coat and black top hat, he was a fantasy personified. And oh, one of her favourite parts completed the look, he was carrying that Weatherby family heirloom, a silver-topped obsidian cane. Ostensibly the cane was to assist with walking, but a man of Edgar's youth and vigour had no need of that sort of help. Instead, in Edgar's hands the cane was a sign of authority and his high position in society.

"Georgina!" Edgar was joyous to see his lover.

"My lord, how lovely to see you," Georgina said through the heavy veil she wore for privacy. Not many people were around in Bath at this time of night, but she wished to retain as much anonymity as she could. She would never dare go out in public with him in London, such was the risk of scandal there. However, a provincial city in the dark was a little more acceptable. So long as she guarded her identity with great care.

Taking Georgina by the arm, Edgar led her across the square towards the haberdasher's shop windows.

"Pray, my lady, does anything here catch your eye?"

"Oh you do flatter me when you call me *my lady*," Georgina said coquettishly.

"Well, why not? I'm a lord, so does that not make you my lady?"

This was getting awkward, thought Georgina. Her previous protectors hadn't wanted to mess around and call her by these aristocratic titles, not least of all in public! Trying to change the subject, she pointed at a ribbon in the haberdasher's window. "That's a pretty ribbon, my lord."

"Then you shall have it."

After purchasing the ribbon, the pair headed towards the weir. The air was somewhat brisk and they were the only couple strolling arm-in-arm along the riverbank. Indeed, there was hardly another soul around.

"How are you going getting parts?" Edgar asked as he rubbed his arm on Georgina's back.

"Well my Lord, when we come back from Bath I've got a part in *The Mouth of the Nile*. That should run for a couple of months," Georgina said.

"That's good, I'm glad to hear it. Tell me, my darling, do you always want to stay on the stage?"

Georgina turned her head towards Edgar's and plastered on a chirpy smile through her veil. "Yes, for as long as I can."

Such was the life of a courtesan, always having to twist and contort herself to suit the whims of her protectors so she could keep bread on the table and a roof over her head.

One afternoon, after luncheon, Georgina sat at the piano and played a tune of her own devising. As her fingers moved up and down the ivories, she began to sing.

Oh, when the sun cometh,
In the morning,
With the sparrow and the lark,
The sparrow and the lark.

She sang a few more verses, her mind and her voice wandering through memories and snippets of conversation she could half-recall from down the years.

She carried on playing until a strong, masculine hand began to stroke her shoulders.

A tension she had not realised she was holding began to ease away.

She let forth a purr of pleasure and turned around to tilt her head towards Edgar.

He lent down and claimed her mouth in a passionate kiss.

The murmur of his low voice rumbled like molasses in her ear. "How are you feeling, my Lady?"

"Good, my lord," she replied with a smile.

She reached her dainty hands towards his face and ran her fingertips teasingly along his jawline.

He moaned in delight.

She giggled a little. Then she said, "Let me have you, my Lord."

She pulled his face towards hers and returned his earlier passionate claiming of her mouth.

A flash of lust darted across Edgar's eyes. "Upstairs. Now," he growled.

"Yes, let's," she said.

He offered her his hand and they made their way through the door and out into the hallway. Georgina's satin skirts rustled against his leg. A tantalising promise of what was to come.

Then they galloped up the stairs, their laughter ringing throughout the house all the while.

Edgar led Georgina to the master bedroom they had been sharing throughout their stay in Bath.

Once they were inside, he took her face between his hands and kissed her hungrily. He relished the way she tasted of sweet dried currant and sugar.

He pulled away from her mouth. "Allow me to undress you," he said.

She gave a nod of assent. "Please," she breathed.

With exquisite deftness, he removed her satin dress and stays. Next, he took off her layers of cream petticoats. Finally, he unlaced her chemise and, in mere moments, it was on the floor.

He took the time to admire the sight that stood before him. "I love to see you like this, in all your glory," he said wolfishly.

She took a confident step towards him. "And what will you do now, my lord?"

He placed his hands behind her neck and brought her face towards his own. He claimed her mouth greedily in a kiss, before placing his mouth by her ear and murmuring, "Why, my lady, I am going to pleasure you. That's what I'm going to do."

Goosebumps of sheer excitement arose on Georgina's skin.

Then Edgar lifted her in his powerful arms and carried her to the plush bed with its sage green sheets. Georgina enjoyed the way the damask felt against her body, the silken material rubbing against her back and limbs and sending sparks of delight through her.

Before she fell fully into the sensations, Edgar appeared at the foot of the bed.

She looked at him through hooded eyes, the space between her legs wet with anticipation.

He climbed on the bed and crawled towards her like a panther on the prowl. He rubbed firm circles on the soles of her feet.

She let forth a moan of pleasure. Edgar was well on his way to making good on his promise!

Edgar chuckled and moved his hands to her shapely calves. He ran his fingers delicately up and down and then teased those sensitive spots behind her knees.

Georgina yelped in delight.

Edgar smirked in response. "Oh, you like that my lady, do you?"

"I do indeed," she said.

"I'm very glad to hear it. But I think you will like what I am going to do in a moment even more."

With that, he spread her legs apart and moved up to the place where her dark curls met the tops of her thighs.

Then, before she had even an instant to think, Edgar buried his face between her legs.

She was slick with desire. How she wanted him, wanted him, wanted him!

His tongue lapped around her folds. Then moved to tease her pearl in slow circles.

Georgina felt herself on the precipice of release. She was teetering on the edge in a beautiful dance.

All the while, Edgar continued nuzzling between her legs.

One focused flick of his tongue across her clit and she was falling down down down into a cocoon of pleasure. Her climax ripped through her body, her nipples hard and erect buds and her skin a sea of goosebumps, and the only thought running through her mind was how good she felt.

Edgar toyed with her clit again and again and again as she writhed in ecstasy.

After some time, when Georgina was spent from countless climaxes and her forehead was shining with sweat, Edgar moved onto his knees and removed his shirt and pantaloons.

Then, oh then, he moved in and out of her sweet cunny. Being within her was absolute bliss.

And as for Georgina, she had not thought it was possible for her to climax again after the many attentions she had received from Edgar's talented mouth. But the wonderful sensation of his cock moving in and out of her was too much to resist. And so she once again fell off that delicate precipice and into that ocean of delicious delight.

❦❦❦❦❦ ❦❦❦❦❦

A fortnight later and Georgina and Edgar were curled up together on the settee at her Fitzrovia house.

"Tell me about your childhood," Edgar said.

"My lord, it's not much to tell," Georgina replied coquettishly.

Edgar sighed. "Why are you so closed off about it?"

"Have you ever been to one to see how your tenants live, on your estates?" Georgina stilled in Edgar's arms, agitation evident in her voice.

Sensing where this was heading, Edgar replied cautiously. "I have, as a matter of fact."

"Then you know what my childhood was like."

"Not many from the estates would end up opera singers though," Edgar said. "How did you end up here?"

"The vicar noticed me, when I was only nine or so. He could hear I was a good singer, could hear the potential in my voice. So I was trained up, trained as a singer. If I had been a boy, I would've been sent to one of the cathedral schools to join a choir. But that of course wasn't available to me. So Reverend Wilson schooled me with his own children. That was really a massive step up from how things were in my family home. My ma and pa tried, God rest their souls, but we were often hungry. We had enclosure to thank for that sad state of affairs."

Georgina gave Edgar a steely glare and he averted his eyes briefly at the mention of the word 'enclosure'. Oh he knew what the word meant, how his own family had benefited very well indeed from it and continued to benefit from it, while thousands of people up and down the country suffered from the loss of access to their traditional community agricultural lands.

Edgar returned his gaze to meet hers.

She spoke again. "I'll always remember the bitterly cold winter we had when I was seventeen. That winter that took ma and my remaining siblings. Three brothers and a sister. It was the year before I went up to Bath for my first season on the stage. My father had already passed in a harvest accident eleven years before, and my mother had lost two children to sickness. I only survived because I was still living at the vicarage, where there were better supplies. And it was a proper house, rather than the dilapidated wooden shack my family lived in."

Edgar's mouth hung open in shock. The bitter, draining loss of his parents that he had experienced ten years ago was bad enough. But his sweet Georgina had lost even more than he had, with not even any siblings left alive to speak of.

"After that," she continued, "I decided it wasn't worth me hanging around in the village any longer than I had to. I had no dowry to speak of, that had all been lost in a bad investment. A sheep farm of all things, would you believe. So when I was eighteen I attended my first season in Bath."

Edgar felt his heart take a painful jump. What Georgina was alluding to was a story he already knew deep down must be true, but it wounded him deeply to think about. And yes, he knew he was a massive hypocrite to get concerned about these stories when year in and year out they happened to women who grew up in poverty in England with clockwork regularity. But putting a face to the anguish made it all that much more real.

The way she called the experience her "first season" as though she was a noble debutante going out to a ball made him think back to when his sister Belinda had her first and ultimately only season a couple of years ago. His discomfort was palpable. The sick comparison between the two experiences was stark.

"Georgina, I'm so sorry about what happened to you," he said, letting the words fall from his mouth based on raw emotion rather than his usual careful, measured speech.

Georgina gulped. What was Edgar saying? "Which part? The poverty? Becoming a courtesan? Hounslow?"

Edgar sighed. "All of it. None of it should have happened."

"To me or to anyone?"

"To anyone," he said with conviction. "But least of all to you."

Georgina felt tears prick at the corners of her eyes. Don't cry, she willed herself, whatever you do don't let him see you cry. Try as she might, she lost the battle and soon let out an ugly sob as the ghosts of difficult situations from the past reared their awful heads. And before she knew it, she was weeping openly.

Edgar felt even worse. How could he have been so callous to broach the subject of Georgina's past in the first place? A dam had burst and the past was flooding into the present.

Yet Edgar was no coward. He saw his role as one of leading and protecting, at all levels from his family to his employees to those on his estates to those he represented in the House of Lords. This experience with Georgina had shown him he needed to make changes regarding how those on his estates were treated, and he needed to advocate more broadly for those in poverty through his privileged political position. What use was power and authority, he asked himself, if you don't use it to do good?

But before all of that, he had a weeping woman in front of him who needed taking care of.

Everything looked different to Edgar now as he rode around the Renfregh estate with fresh eyes. Before he met

Georgina, it had always been the idyllic heritage of generations of Weatherbys. It was the place where they rode, they shot, they hunted, sharing family joys as well as tragedies.

The Weatherbys took income from the estates though much of that income only ever crossed their minds as mere numbers on a balance sheet without any real consideration for how the money was made or whose labour and rents produced that income.

Certainly, the tenants had been a constant presence but they had been pinpricks in the distance. Easy enough for Edgar to ignore and leave to his estate managers.

Not so now Georgina had entered his life and opened his eyes to some of the realities of life for the rural poor in England during the reign of George III.

As the eldest Weatherby son, he had been destined to be earl. Had Georgina and the millions of people living in poverty up and down the country been destined to their situations too?

The thought did not sit well with him at all. Surely, no one was fated to live such a wretched existence.

Looking across the horizon, he could see the village church perched on the hill. St Anne's was surrounded by a hodgepodge collection of labourers' shacks, a few shops barely worthy of the name and an inn.

The church reminded him again of darling Georgina, of how her life's trajectory had changed dramatically when the vicar of her local village had spotted her superb vocal talents at the tender age of nine and had taken her under his wing. There she had thrived but she had been obliged to live apart from her family.

Edgar resolved to go and speak with the vicar to find out what, if anything, was being done by the church to improve the lot of the labourers and how he could support this endeavour.

Riding past the sheep grazing in the upper fields, he reflected on how different his upbringing had been to Georgina's.

The life of an agricultural labourer had been the pathway the world expected her to take, until one day the vicar had noticed her vocal talents. Had she never have been born with such a beautiful voice, or if by chance the vicar had never noticed her singing abilities, the trajectory of her life would have turned out very differently indeed. She would have spent her days tending to livestock like these sheep, harvesting, threshing, picking berries and all the rest of it.

Edgar, on the other hand, had never been destined for a life like that. From birth, all pathways in his life pointed to him ascending to the earldom. From the awful prep boarding school to the illustrious heights of Eton and Oxford, his education had put him right in the midst of his peer group. The creme de la creme of British society. The future leaders of the land. Like generations of his forefathers, his elite education had been the making of him. He reached the edge of the village. The hooves of his horse clattered on the dry mud of the road.

The mare moved at an easy trot through the heart of the village. She whinnied and neighed when she encountered others of her equine kind being tethered to posts outside the inn. Some kind of ruckus was going on whereby some of the horses were unwilling to stay in one spot after a morning on the road taking goods to or from the market town four miles to the north of Renfregh.

Edgar rubbed his horse's neck and bent forward to whisper in her ear. "Steady girl, it's alright."

At her rider's soothing touch, the horse grew calmer and by the time the pair had reached the end of the main street any onlooker would have been hard pressed to guess that the horse had been grossly unsettled only mere minutes before. Such was Edgar's way with horses. He found them easier to deal with than humans at times.

Edgar surveyed the bunches of small houses dotted around the village. Well, houses was a stretch of description because really they were rough wooden shacks and wattle and daub constructions built and rebuilt from centuries past. They were terribly out of date and not fit for human habitation. Edgar remembered how Georgina's family had suffered to the point of death in a freezing winter in a shack very similar to the ones on his estate. Another family was at risk of meeting the same fate if the weather turned bad.

Pangs of horrendous guilt brewed within Edgar's stomach. How could he have been so blind to the suffering of people right on his own doorstep, on his land?

He had already vowed to do better, so he could truly live up to the duties of an earl. Not that most earls in the nation did a better job than he had done, but that was no excuse. He needed to set things right and lead the way so that others would be encouraged to make similar improvements on their own estates.

He reached the church itself and dismounted his horse. He headed inside to seek out the vicar.

The day after his ride through the village and meeting with the vicar, Edgar sat at his desk in the grand study at Renfregh.

Resolute as to what course of action he should take, he reached to the servant bell pull on the side of the desk and rang it.

A footman entered the room, saying, "You rang, my lord?"

"Send for my estate manager," Edgar said.

"Very good, my lord." The footman bowed and exited the room.

About five minutes later, the estate manager entered the room.

"Good afternoon, Mr Payne," Edgar said.

"My lord, you asked to speak with me?" replied the estate manager. He was a thin and reedy man with balding hair, small spectacles and a dour countenance.

"Yes, Payne, please have a seat."

Mr Payne was, on the surface, a timid man. However, Edgar knew that beneath Mr Payne's seemingly milquetoast exterior lay a man of terrific talent, intellect and strong drive for action. Exactly the sort of man Edgar wanted in the role of estate manager.

Mr Payne sat down and looked at Edgar with great expectation in his eyes.

"Going forward I will be taking a more active role and pushing forward improvements to the estate, in particular regarding the village and the tenancies," Edgar said.

"My lord, if I may be impertinent -"

"Please do be, I need to hear it," Edgar said.

"The thing is, in all your years as earl and during your late Father's time as well, the estate has essentially run without any input from the earl beyond a 'keep a steady ship and don't make any changes' approach. Is this no longer to be the approach we are to take?"

"That's correct," Edgar said. "I want to make necessary changes to keep the estate up-to-date and improve the lot of the tenants."

"Not that this isn't a very welcome development, my lord, but what's brought about this change?"

"It's not that I'm dissatisfied with the work you or anyone else on the estate have been doing, don't for a moment think I'm unhappy in that regard. Rather, I haven't been providing the right direction for the estate these past eleven years and that's my issue not yours. I can see what is happening across the Channel, the discontent, and I don't like what happened in France back when I was a young boy. I view it as a cautionary tale, if lords neglect their tenants to such an absurd degree then the lords can hardly be surprised when those tenants make at best a paltry effort or at worst go so far as to rise up against them."

Mr Payne blinked several times before saying. "Very good, sir. Where should I start on improvements?"

"First off, those wooden shacks that the tenants live in need a complete overhaul. I want every shack reviewed for leakage and mould and rectified where appropriate. Then the main street needs repaving. And sort out the issues of the water supply once and for all."

Mr Payne nodded at each command. All of this made sense to him, and had he himself have been the earl then much of it would have already been done years ago. However, it was not his place to question the desires of the Earl of Weatherby. They paid his salary, after all, and without it he and his family could quickly find themselves in hard times. He was glad, nonetheless, that the earl was finally taking action. Better late than never, supposed the estate manager.

CHAPTER EIGHT

Georgina and Edgar walked hand in hand round the lake at Renfregh.

No one else from the Weatherby family was on the estate at all this week, with everyone else staying in London. Aside from the servants, the Weatherby-only parts of the estate were completely empty.

At Edgar's suggestion, Georgina had agreed to come up to Renfregh for five days to get away from the hustle and bustle of the city.

Georgina tilted her head towards Edgar.

"Being an earl, is it what you wanted for your life?" she asked.

"Heavens, no!" Edgar replied.

"But surely on some level you must enjoy the power?"

Edgar pinched his nose between thumb and forefinger and briefly bent his head towards the ground, before raising his gaze to face Georgina. "I will admit I have it easier than most."

"Oh really, my Lord," the soprano smirked.

"Yes, really."

"So if you could be anyone, who would you be?" Georgina said.

Edgar sighed. "Sometimes I'd like to be a country squire, forget all this earldom and peerage. It would be so much easier to settle down near a village somewhere, have a manor house and some farmland, a wife and children and be done with all the rest of it."

Then he laughed at himself derisively. "But who am I to complain about my position, really. I've got no right when thousands are starving in this country."

He turned to Georgina. "What about you? Who would you be if you had the choice?"

"I wish I'd been born in a different time, maybe the future will be different. A world where it's easier to get on if you're willing to put the work in," Georgina said.

The ducks quacked happily in the pond and dragonflies hovered around the edges near the reeds.

Edgar squeezed Georgina's hand. "Would be it so here."

Georgina sighed. "I wish."

She turned her head towards Edgar's. "Do you really wish you weren't the earl?"

"Often I do, yes. Ever since I became the earl when I was nineteen, I wished it wasn't me or at least that my parents had lived longer. I felt so unprepared and had I have had a couple more decades to ease into the role, I may well not have given you the answer I did when you asked me who I would be if I could."

Georgina mulled over Edgar's words. She understood his position carried with it a lot of responsibility. However, she doubted that when push came to shove he would give it up. In the time she had known him, he had maintained a constant focus on his duties to the title and to his family. It seemed unlikely that he would ever change course.

⁕ ⁕

"I've got an idea," grinned Edgar wolfishly.

Georgina giggled. "And what's that, my lord?"

"Well it's just you and me on the estate today, so we should take advantage of that. There's a very nice lake that's just begging for me to tie you up and fuck you by it."

"I like your thinking," Georgina said. "Let's go."

⁕ ⁕

The pair made their way across the black and white chequered floor of the rear hall, Edgar carrying a large wicker basket in his right hand and holding Georgina's hand in his left. They exited through the French doors and out onto the patio.

The splendour of Renfregh lay before them.

They climbed down the steps and onto the gravel path that led to the well-manicured Italianate garden.

Hand-in-hand, they ran down the path, past the neat rows of shrubbery and the ornate fountain.

Edgar looked across at Georgina. Truly, she was magnificent in this light. Well, she would always be magnificent in any light, he corrected himself.

Georgina's skirts and petticoats billowed in the gusts as she ran along. She was a lady, not wholly unrestrained, but someone who was willing to stake a claim on her freedom. And Edgar found that fact most beguiling.

They reached the row of Mediterranean cypresses and then the garden wall. They ran through the open green smoke door and then they were out on the unbridled freedom of the rolling lawns of Renfregh.

Edgar called out to Georgina. "You are so beautiful, you know that."

"And you are most handsome," she replied.

She laughed as they ran down towards the lake. Being out here with Edgar, in the warm sunshine, felt wonderful.

In the distance she could see a couple of Renfregh's follies, a stone temple dedicated to Venus and a gnarled tower like something out of a fairytale. They were nestled amongst the trees, on the cusp of turning orange and red in the coming autumn days. She and Edgar had spent several happy afternoons in those follies, enjoying each other and the sensation of being together as one. Today, however, the lake would be the scene of their pleasure and delight.

When they reached the lake they came to a halt.

"Here's the spot." Edgar put the wicker basket down and then laid out the tartan blanket on the soft grass near the lake. "Please sit my darling."

Edgar was enchanted by how Georgina looked in the light, her sweet puckered lips being perfectly formed and the sun's rays shining through her hair. What a woman, he thought!

After Georgina had sat down, Edgar rummaged through the wicker basket and pulled out a small box and two scarves.

"Now, my lady, are you ready to obey your lord?"

"Oh yes please!" Georgina loved these sorts of games and Edgar knew exactly what she liked.

"Very well," Edgar said. "Hands behind your back, my lady."

Doing as she was told, Georgina felt herself begin to slip into that glorious subspace. She adored journeying there with Edgar. He made her feel so safe and cared for, the perfect dominant gentleman.

Reaching behind Georgina, Edgar deftly tied her arms together with the muslin scarf. Then he tied the other scarf around her head, covering her eyes as he formed a blindfold. He kissed her on the cheek. "Good girl."

Georgina beamed at the praise.

Edgar picked up the small box. "Would you like some strawberries? They're fresh from the greenhouses."

"Yes please, my lord."

"My pretty girl, bite on this." Edgar held a large strawberry up to Georgina's waiting lips and she opened them with eagerness.

She bit down on the strawberry and relished the sweet juices of the fruit. Rarely did she ever get to eat strawberries so it was a real treat to have an opportunity like today.

"Tastes sweet, yes?" Edgar murmured.

Georgina nodded and continued to eat the strawberry.

"You know," Edgar's voice grew gruffer. "That's exactly how sweet your glorious cunny tastes."

Georgina felt herself wetten at Edgar's filthy words. Though it was a comfortably warm day, goosebumps began to form on her skin as she contemplated the situation and what might happen next. She loved it when Edgar put her on edge in the *best* way!

She finished the strawberry and before she knew it, another one was in front of her lips.

"Have a taste," Edgar said.

Georgina obliged and again the sweet strawberry juices engulfed her mouth.

"You are so beautiful like this, my lady," Edgar said happily. "If I could, I would have you by my side like this at all times, ready and willing for me but prim and proper in public. Because we know that you're a little harlot deep down, aren't you my darling? And no one else needs to know that, it's our secret for just the two of us."

Georgina nodded and said softly, "Yes, my lord."

"Good girl." Edgar stroked Georgina's hair and put another strawberry to her lips.

As the box of strawberries became emptier, Edgar leaned in towards Georgina and claimed her mouth with a ravenous kiss. "Now, my Lady. I'm going to change the position of your hands so I can pleasure you properly."

Georgina hummed happily as Edgar undid the scarf around her arms and then lifted her arms above her head before tying them together in that fashion.

Again, Georgina felt herself get wetter and wetter between her legs.

There was a delightful contrast between Edgar's dominant control of the situation and the tender and affectionate way he was caring for her as part of the very same scenario. Deep down, the combination of dominance and tenderness was within Edgar's nature and befitted his role as an earl well indeed.

Yet, if anyone ever asked him, Edgar would have denied the blend of dominance and tenderness that he was so skilled at.

Society said that it would not do for a gentleman to dominate his wife like this. Why should she be interested in life's sensual pleasures, was society's belief. Those sort of delights were for mistresses and courtesans, not ladies of the ton, went the common refrain. How could a man like Edgar ever hope to find true happiness in such a situation where he would be forced to repress his true desires?

"Lie down, my darling," Edgar said.

Georgina complied as Edgar assisted her in getting positioned on the blanket. She was flat on her back with her arms above her head, held securely by the muslin scarf, and her legs outstretched on the floor.

"You are absolutely delectable and don't you ever forget it," Edgar said. "Are you ready to give yourself to me?"

"Yes, my Lord," Georgina mewed.

Delicate fingers began to touch her thighs, ghosting along so she could barely feel them. They felt oh so good, sending frissons of delight through her entire body and straight to her core. Then the fingers went behind her right knee and began to pay special attention to the spot where she was helplessly ticklish. Edgar knew exactly what would happen if he tickled her there. That wonderful bastard!

Georgina squealed, part in shock and part in pleasure, and her joyous giggles rang around the lake. "Edg...Edgar, oh Heavens!"

The hands stopped.

Edgar's warm chuckles ran through Georgina's ears like burnt caramel. "That was *quite* a reaction, my lady! Let's see how you respond to this!" And with that, Edgar resumed the tickles with an even greater intensity than ever before.

Georgina's cries and squeals continued. Then, all of a sudden, she felt the hands grow gentler again and they moved up to her thighs, stroking them as though they were soft velvet.

"Spread your legs for me, darling," Edgar commanded in his rich, deep tone.

Georgina obeyed and placed the sole of each foot on the floor so Edgar had a glorious view of her most intimate places.

"Good girl," he cooed.

A gentle finger found its way to Georgina's pleasure pearl, running delicate circles over the tender flesh. Then, almost as quickly as the finger had arrived, it went away again.

"Heavens, Georgina, you are absolutely sopping!" Edgar chuckled.

"Touch me, touch me please," she whimpered, bucking her hips up in desperate desire.

"Not until you're good and ready," he said.

Georgina mewed. "But I'm good and ready now!"

"You know the rules, I need to prepare you first." Edgar's gentle voice allowed for no disobedience.

"Yes, my lord," Georgina replied softly. "It's just so hard to wait, it feels so good."

"I know, sweetheart, I know. But it just wouldn't do for me to give you something before you're ready." Edgar returned his hands to Georgina's thighs, petting them delicately and enjoying the sensation of her goosebumped skin beneath his strong hands.

"You are so beautiful," he said.

He leant beneath her legs and nuzzled his nose into her folds. Sucking greedily, his tongue explored the depths of her crevices.

Georgina moaned and thumped her arms against the blanket.

Hearing her wanton reaction, Edgar smirked into her cunny and continued his explorations. Kissing her labia, he made his way inwards towards her pleasure pearl and moved his tongue up and down slowly oh so slowly.

"Oh Edgar," she mewed.

As his attentions continued, Georgina felt herself grow warm at her core as the anticipation of journeying up that mountain of ecstasy built within her. She writhed against the blanket.

Edgar ran his hands along her thighs as he continued to lick and kiss and suckle. She felt like glass, like she was an ornament being brought to life under Edgar's touch. He was leading her to a whole new dimension of existence. And then, oh! She could not help herself but let herself fall off that cliff of control and propriety and into the depths of deepest pleasure. She rode out her climax on Edgar's handsome face, her hips bucking wildly as he never ceased his unrelenting attentions. How good it felt to be under Edgar's control, under his command! Here was a man who knew what she wanted and had made it his mission to deliver exactly that.

Then, Edgar pulled away from between her legs and pushed two fingers deep into her cunnyhole. He brought those fingers to Georgina's lips. "Taste yourself."

She obeyed and suckled on his fingers with relish.

"That's it, good girl. You. Are. Absolutely. Delicious." Edgar beamed with pride at his Georgina. "You are one of God's most exquisite creations and don't you ever ever forget that, darling."

Then Georgina felt Edgar pressing against her entrance. He pushed in with vigour and then withdrew almost as suddenly.

She gasped in delight. "Please, my lord!"

Edgar did as he was bid and entered her again, before pulling out once more.

"My lord, you tease me!" Georgina mewed.

Edgar gave a devilish laugh. "All in good time, my darling Georgina. All in good time."

Then and oh, what blessed joy, Edgar entered her and pumped in and out, filling her up with his wonderful cock. How Georgina loved to be full of *his* cock. It was an absolutely delectable sensation.

As Edgar's rhythm built, Georgina could feel the need growing within her again. She brought her legs up around Edgar's back and crossed them together, bringing him closer and closer to her so they were in perfect unity.

"Oh, Georgina, you are absolutely stunning! How I adore you!" Edgar cried as he moved in and out with intense passion. "Your cunnyhole is just divine, you're absolutely soaking for me."

Georgina felt yet again that she was on the edge of a cliff, with no choice other than to let go and give herself over to the waves of pleasure she knew would be awaiting her at the bottom. Her breath began to speed up and her cheeks grew redder and redder.

Edgar couldn't help but notice his lover's reactions and murmured, "That's it, come for me my pretty Georgina, come for me."

And it was all Georgina could do but comply with her Lord's command. Oh it felt delightful! The cliff crumbled away beneath her and she fell down and down and down into the pool of pleasure, hitting the bottom with a splash and then she was kicking in the water, feeling so new and alive. More alive than ever before!

Edgar could see the pleasure in Georgina's eyes and he was so so proud of his sweetheart. The pride he felt enhanced his own pleasure, he was in control of the delight she was experiencing, he did this! He continued to pump in and out of her cunny as she moaned and giggled beneath him. Then he himself felt pleasure building in his core and the urge to release. He shot his seed into her tight cunnyhole.

Georgina relished the sensation of Edgar's warm seed entering her most secret place in all the world. This is what it truly meant to be united with a man. Oh, how she wished she could be with Edgar always and forever!

Edgar pulled away from Georgina and reached behind into the wicker basket. He pulled out a small cloth and a bottle of water. He poured some of the water onto the cloth and wiped between Georgina's legs with it.

Georgina moaned happily at Edgar's caring administrations. Not since Lord Redditch had a protector taken the time to do this for her. It was a sign of Edgar's understanding of responsibility and his true status as a gentleman. Whoever married Edgar would be a very lucky woman, thought Georgina wistfully.

Edgar untied Georgina's arms and helped her to sit up. Then he untied the blindfolding scarf and brought the water bottle to her lips. "Drink, darling," he said.

Rubbing Georgina's back gently, Edgar cooed. "You did so well, Georgina sweetheart, so so well. You truly are the most amazing lady."

After Georgina had had her fill of water, she handed the half empty bottle to Edgar. He took a few gulps and resealed the cork. Then he took Georgina in his arms and stroked her hair, murmuring in her ear as he did so.

As the ducks quacked around them, the couple hardly heard. For they were bathed in a cocoon of just their two souls merging together as one entity until not even the most brilliant minds in all the universe would be able to tell the difference between Georgina's being and Edgar's.

CHAPTER NINE

T he carriage crossed under the archway. With no lighting, it was pitch black beneath the archway's brick construction.

On an autumnal night like this with the chill in the air, the London streets were devoid of people.

Inside, Georgina sat naked in Edgar's lap with her legs spread and her back resting against his chest. She giggled as he stroked his leather-clad fingers up and down her arms with a feather-light touch.

Edgar, on the other hand, was fully clothed.

He placed his right hand over her mouth and pressed hard. "Just breathe, darling, focus on your breathing. You're safe in my hands, these hands of mine."

Georgina inhaled the smell of the leather glove and relaxed. It made her feel so secure and cared for to be beneath Edgar's strong hand. Stop that! She told herself. He is your protector, not your husband, and this is a commercial arrangement only. A member of the peerage like him will never truly care for a woman like you, however accomplished and intelligent you are. But heavens it felt good to be with Edgar!

Edgar pulled out his cock from his breeches and rubbed it against Georgina's back.

Then, he moved his left leather-clad hand towards Georgina's breasts and tweaked at her nipples. "Focus on your breathing, my sweet Georgina. I'll count for you to get you into a rhythm. One-and-two-and-three-and-four. One-and-two-and-three-and-four."

Georgina began to breathe time to the rhythm Edgar had set and Edgar smiled at her compliance. "That's it, good girl. I've got you."

Edgar then moved his left hand downwards towards Georgina's slit. Entering her sopping folds, he found her most sensitive place and began to stroke her pleasure pearl with feather-light touches.

Georgina tried her hardest to keep breathing in the rhythm Edgar had commanded, but as the pleasure between her legs grew and spread towards her belly she could not help but speed up her breaths.

Edgar immediately removed his hand from her special place and said sternly, "Georgina, darling, you need to focus on your breathing. Breathe like this - one-and-two-and-three-and-four. One-and-two-and-three-and-four."

Georgina grew even wetter at Edgar's authoritative tone and resumed the one-and-two-and-three-and-four breathing pattern her protector required.

"Good girl," Edgar cooed.

The leather-clad finger returned to Georgina's pleasure pearl and this time she kept perfectly to the breathing rhythm as the finger moved around and around creating deliciously exquisite circles of pleasure.

"That's it, come for me my girl," said Edgar as the carriage rattled along through London's streets.

Obeying her protector's order, Georgina felt a wave of ecstasy spread from her core through to her belly. Oh, she could do this for hours and hours, she thought! What delicious bliss!

After Georgina came down from her climax, Edgar lifted his cock into her slit with his left hand. Slowly, oh so slowly at first, he pumped in and out of Georgina. "Keep to your breathing, sweetheart. You're doing so well."

The gloved finger returned to Georgina's pleasure pearl. She was a very lucky girl, thought Georgina! To be fucked like this, with such precision and care.

Edgar sped up his rhythm as the carriage rattled along. It felt fantastic to be filled with Edgar's massive cock, so snug, so tight, so right!

Georgina felt herself reach another precipice and the only choice she had was to let herself fall off it into the exquisite pool of ecstasy below. Edgar chuckled darkly. "I love it when you're so wanton, Georgina. So wanton, willing and wet for me!"

One-and-two-and-three-and-four, thought Georgina, one-and-two-and-three-and-four. She tried her hardest to focus on Edgar's breathing orders even though she felt oh so full of his cock!

Edgar groaned. "You are a filthy woman! So filthy and all mine, all mine!"

Edgar pulled out of Georgina, shooting his seed into his handkerchief, and then slowed down his hips.

Removing his hand from her mouth, Edgar noticed the glove was now covered in her slobber. What a good girl, he thought! She'd done so so well at obeying his breathing commands. They had already discussed her passion for hands over her mouth and for leather more generally and he was delighted to be able to incorporate them into their encounters. Anything for his darling Georgina!

Then he removed his hand from between Georgina's legs and examined the glove. It was slick with her juices. Clearly, she'd enjoyed herself.

He smiled at the thought and lifted the glove to this mouth, lapping up the juices from the index and middle fingers. Heavens, Georgina tasted absolutely delicious! He was so proud of her, she was a real woman who knew what pleasure she wanted and was not afraid to take it.

Then, he lifted the ring and little fingers of the glove to Georgina's mouth and said, "Taste yourself."

Georgina obeyed and hummed happily as she slurped on her juices.

❦

Mowbrow sipped on his glass of whisky, as Edgar leaned back in the armchair facing him. It was eight o'clock in the evening on a Friday night and the two men were in their usual haunt. The Lumley Club.

"Any ladies you're seeing lately?" Edgar said.

"Well," Mowbrow chuckled. "I wouldn't call them ladies. But you know me, I've usually got someone on the go."

"Do you think you'll settle down anytime soon?" Edgar said.

"Ah, we'll see how that goes. I'm in no rush." Mowbrow was completely at ease.

Unlike Edgar, Mowbrow did not consider passing thirty years of age to be a sign that he needed to hurry up and find a bride. On the contrary. Mowbrow intended to continue sowing his wild oats for most of the rest of the coming decade. One day he might sire an heir, he thought, but if he never got round to it then there would be bound to be an heir from some other branch of the family tree. What did he care? He was enjoying the life of pleasure his station afforded him. He wasn't about to give up the fun anytime soon for anything as trivial as finding a bride, he mused.

"Quite so," Edgar said.

Edgar sipped on his whisky and thought about his friend's lack of urgency in finding a bride. He struggled to identify with it. Certainly, he had enjoyed some hedonism during his twenties but now he was the other side of thirty he wanted to get serious about marriage and siring an heir. Deep down, on those dark nights when Georgina was not at his side, he felt a wave of loneliness wash over him. All the mistresses and parties in the world could not make up for the fact that he was without a companion to travel through life with. There was no one with whom he could share his hopes, his fears, his joys and all the daily rigmarole that comes with living and running an earldom.

The streets of Fitzrovia were almost deserted at this late hour. That was not going to stop Edgar, however.

Jumping down from the carriage, he turned to the coachman. "Don't wait up, Michelhome."

"Very good, sir," Michelhome replied. He was one of the Weatherby family's longest standing servants and someone whom Edgar knew he could count on for reliability and discretion.

Edgar walked up to the door of the Fitzrovia house and banged the knocker. Behind him, he heard Michelhome mush the horses and the carriage begin to move off.

A couple of minutes later and the door swung open to reveal his sweet Georgina.

"Good evening, my lady," he said with a bow.

"Good evening, my lord," she replied. "Please, come in."

Edgar entered the familiar hallway.

"Fifteen hours a day?" Edgar was incredulous. "That's ridiculous! They're working you far too hard."

"That's what you need to do to keep competitive as a singer here in London. If you want to succeed, then you need to be prepared to contort yourself to the producers' demands," Georgina said.

Edgar reached his arm behind where Georgina sat next to him on the parlour settee and kissed her on the forehead.

She gave him a small smile in return.

Then she tried and failed to stifle a yawn.

Edgar frowned. This wasn't right at all. Those producers at the theatres were working Georgina and other performers like her to the bone. He laughed mirthlessly on an internal level and reflected how no Countess of Weatherby would be working her fingers to the bone and would have a life where she was provided for and protected and able to pursue her charitable interests as much or as little as she wanted. How he longed to provide that for Georgina.

"Georgina, have you got to be up for anything tomorrow?" He asked.

"No, fortunately not." She yawned again. "It's a rest day."

"I'm glad to hear it. You should get some rest now though too."

"But my lord, you made the effort to come all this way, I'd hate for it all to be for naught. The night is still young!"

Edgar stroked her forearm and bore a deep gaze into her sagging eyes. "Georgina, it's quite alright I assure you. I'd rather you get some rest, and then God willing you'll feel better tomorrow."

"My lord, I couldn't possibly -"

"You can and you will, Georgina. Am I not your protector?"

He awaited her response before she nodded in affirmation.

He continued sternly, "Then let me protect you tonight. Get some sleep, sweetheart. There will be other nights for us to fuck, but if you don't get enough sleep regularly it's going to escalate and be a real detriment to your health. And I will not stand for it, do you understand me?"

"Yes, Edgar," she said.

"Very good. I will make sure things are settled down here and then I will come up and we can chat for a little bit."

She stepped forward and claimed his mouth in a passionate kiss before she made her way out of the room and climbed the stairs.

Edgar set to work drawing the curtains and snuffing out the candles that were dotted around the parlour.

⁂

Upstairs in her master bedroom, Georgina performed her nighttime ablutions. She changed into her lacey white nightdress, a gift from Edgar, pulled back the bed sheets and blankets and then clambered onto the bed.

So tired was she that she was fast asleep within mere moments.

⁂

Edgar entered the room a short while later, intending to talk with Georgina a little as they had agreed. But the sight which greeted his eyes was rather different.

Georgina lay on her side on the bed, letting out soft grunts and sniffles. The sheets and blanket were pooled around her ankles and so Edgar worried she would become too cold during the night.

Edgar tucked in the sheets and then placed a blanket across her.

She always looked beautiful, he reflected, but tonight in all her feminine vulnerability she was the most beautiful he had ever seen her.

Wanting to leave her to her rest, he turned and made his way down the stairs and out onto the street. Looking at his pocket watch, he saw it was already gone one in the morning and he resolved that he would do well to follow his beloved into the land of dreams. He made his way back towards his bachelor lodgings.

While the night has not turned out exactly as he had planned, Edgar was not unhappy. What had started out as a lord engaging the services of an opera singer had turned into so much more.

It wasn't mere lust anymore, it was love.

CHAPTER TEN

Bang! Bang! Bang!

Georgina awoke from where she was dozing on the sofa. Another night with her insomnia plaguing her.

The sound repeated. Bang! Bang! Bang!

She realised it was someone or something banging on the front door. Groggily, she stood up and made her way to the door and opened it. Edgar was the sight that greeted her. And he looked rather the worse for wear for drink, Georgina thought as she wrinkled her nose in distaste.

"Miss Hartley, may I come in please?" Edgar said.

Georgina sighed internally. "Alright, but stay in the parlour."

Edgar strode into the parlour and sat down on the settee.

Georgina offered him a glass of water and he sipped on it ponderously.

"I've been thinking a lot about you and I these past few weeks," Edgar began.

"Oh have you?" She replied.

"I have indeed. And all that thinking has made it more and more evident that there's something I need to tell you."

"And that something would be?"

"The thing is," he said cautiously through his drunken haze. "I've become very fond of you, Miss Hartley. To the point that I know I am in love with you."

Georgina blinked at Edgar, her eyelids fluttering in rapid succession. "My lord, are you quite well?"

"I know what I'm saying. I love you, Georgina."

This was not the first time a lord had professed love to his mistress, of course. It was a quotidian, stupid event. So why were her eyes beginning to feel damp, thought Georgina.

She chose her words carefully. "That's sweet of you to say."

"It's true, Miss Hartley, I assure you. I love you and I desire nothing else than to have you by my side as my lawful wedded wife." Edgar's eyes burned with a fiery intensity the likes of which Georgina very rarely ever saw.

Funny, she thought, Edgar was completely and utterly in his cups yet the words he had just confessed to her were more profound than many of those he uttered when sober. In vino veritas, after all.

"My lord, it's getting late." Georgina took the reins of the situation. Someone needed to be in control and Edgar was in no fit state for that. "I'll fetch you some water."

She left Edgar on the sofa staring into her fireplace, his eyes boring into a fixed point, the significance of which only he might know.

* * *

Despite his claret-sodden haze, Edgar felt a clarity of mind that when sober he refused to allow himself to experience.

Georgina was everything to him and he wished she would be by his side forevermore. Not as a woman he paid, but as his lawful wedded wife. She was the only woman he had ever loved. Before he met Georgina, he had not thought himself capable of love.

Certainly, he knew that love existed elsewhere. For Belinda and Alexander, for his cousins and of course for his parents, the greatest example of love he had ever known.

Yet for him, love had seemed impossible.

Once Georgina had entered his life, he had surprised himself with how deeply and intensely he was capable of loving someone. At first he had found her absolutely gorgeous, a very talented and beautiful woman but merely someone who would help him pass the time between his duties. Slowly, ever so slowly, however, the sensation of love had grown within him and he had tried to pluck it out at the root so it would wither long before it ever bloomed. Yet that had proved to be a fool's errand.

Now his love for Georgina was undeniable.

The question was, what was he going to do about it?

Lost in his thoughts, he jumped internally when Georgina reentered the room. She placed the glass of water on the coffee table in front of Edgar along with a blanket.

"Goodnight my lord," she said softly before taking her leave.

Georgina trudged upstairs and shook her head.

Edgar's confession had taken her by surprise. Yet it had forced her to admit her own feelings.

The fact was, if she were honest with herself, her sentiments of affection for Edgar had turned to love months ago.

She was not a fool, however, and so she resolved to forget that Edgar had ever said anything of love. It would not do for a mistress to let herself get swept up in romantic, impossible dreams of her protector. Besides, Edgar was in his cups and likely would not remember a word of their conversation come morning. No, he would leave in the morning and go back to his home with nary a thought about the words that had passed his lips. That was how lords always operated.

❧❧❧❧❧ ❦❦❦❦❦

Edgar opened his eyes and blinked. Unfamiliar surroundings greeted him and his head felt full of pieces of hessian and leather rubbing against each other. He sat up slowly and tried to recall how he had ended up here.

Flashes of the night before began to appear before his eyes. He had begun the night with other gentlemen of the ton at Lumley's where he had enjoyed several rounds of cards and more rounds of claret and cigars. Then, as the night entered the small hours, he had made what on reflection was an exceptionally foolish decision, even by his dire rakish standards. Full to the brim of oenological courage, he had adopted the highly intelligent notion to pay a visit to Miss Hartley and tell her precisely how he felt about her.

And hadn't that gone well? Selfish fool that he was, he had roused her from her blessed rest at an obscene hour and had then proceeded to impose on her hospitality with his drunken declarations of love. What on earth would she be able to do with those?

He berated himself and held his head in his hands, partly in shame and partly as an attempt to massage his now pounding headache. One way or another, he was going to pay for the events of the night before.

He lifted himself off the sofa and ambled towards the kitchen. As he approached the room, he felt his cheeks redden at the sight that greeted him through the open door to the kitchen. Darling Georgina was busily making tea.

She heard his footsteps and turned towards him with a wry smile on her face. "Good morning, my lord. How are you feeling?"

Edgar walked through the doorway and rubbed the back of his neck with his hand. "Like a complete fool. I am truly sorry about last night, Miss Hartley. It was unreasonable of me to burden you like that, both with what I said and did."

"But was what you said untrue?"

"No, it was the truth."

Georgina sighed internally and said, "Then we need to talk."

Edgar nodded sheepishly as his cheeks tightened.

"Please, have a seat." She gestured towards the kitchen table.

He obliged and once they were both seated with a cup of tea in front of each of them, she continued to speak. "It doesn't do to dwell on fantasies, as you well know. You're not a stupid man, my lord. I don't begrudge you your feelings, but you're hardly the first lord to declare his love for a whore."

"Don't call yourself that!" blurted Edgar.

"Whyever not? It's the truth of the situation."

Edgar rubbed the back of his neck again in an attempt to gain comfort. "It's, well, to me you're more than that."

"But to the rest of the ton, that's all I'll ever be. My lord, you and I both know it so please don't delude yourself."

He pinched his nose between thumb and forefinger. "It's not a delusion though, the way I feel."

"I know. Because I feel the same way."

He stared at her and blinked. The whole axis of his world tilted in that moment before the globe froze and then started moving in reverse.

"I love you Edgar," she said. "I can't deny it. But this can't go any further than it already has."

Edgar sighed. Deep down, he knew Georgina was right but it didn't make facing the facts of the matter any easier. "You're right, you're absolutely right, Georgina. It vexes me so that everything is like this, that I can't change things to make it possible for us to be together properly, as man and wife."

"You can't reorder a whole society, Edgar. No matter how much you might want to," she said.

The pair sat in silence.

Georgina willed herself not to cry but she could feel the tears building up in her eyes nevertheless. She looked over to Edgar and saw his face had become oddly sickly in its colour, so much so that he seemed haunted.

Then, after what felt like an age, Edgar found some words. "I love you and you love me. It should be simple, really."

"But it's not."

"No, it's not."

Tears fell from Georgina's eyes and she began to sob.

Edgar noticed immediately and wrapped his arms around her. It was not long before he too lost his composure. He kissed the top of Georgina's head as silent tears fell down his cheeks.

They sat like that together for several minutes before Georgina broke the silence. "Look at us, we are a right pair."

"You can say that again."

She snorted between her tears, unable to hold back her laughter at the dark humour of the situation.

"Charming, my lady!" Edgar chuckled softly.

"I aim to please."

"And you achieve that so well," he said before releasing a sigh. "I understand completely if you wish to end this arrangement. I know this isn't what you signed up for, to have some fool of a lord bothering with you with his fantastical notions."

Georgina bit her lip before responding. "We can continue, my lord. So long as we both swear to admit to ourselves that we can never be to each other anything more than protector and courtesan."

"I can swear to that."

"Then so can I."

Several more cups of tea later and Edgar was pulling out his pocket watch, curling his lip briefly at the time that greeted him. "I'm sorry, Georgina, I have to get going. My duties, they await. I've got to get to the Lords for a division."

"Of course, my lord," she replied.

He kissed Georgina and hurried out of the kitchen, down the hallway and through the front door.

Georgina rolled her eyes and made to clear up the remains of the tea. Edgar had revealed his true feelings last night and it had been so hard this morning to bring herself to do the responsible thing and remind him that their involvement could only ever be that of protector and courtesan. The class differences and the very nature of her position as a courtesan made it an impossibility. Turning her mind to more pleasant matters, she thought ahead to the new opera she would soon be starring in and resolved to spend the rest of the morning rehearsing her lines.

❧❦

One cloudy Wednesday afternoon, Georgina and Edgar lay in bed at his bachelor lodgings.

Edgar held Georgina in his arms and kissed her on the forehead.

"There's a ball the Saturday after next. At Heywood House. Would you like to come with me?" asked Edgar.

"This is fantastical, my lord," Georgina giggled. "Ridiculous even!"

Edgar punctuated each word with a kiss. "There is nothing ridiculous about you."

"But me going to a ball? With high society? It's not done," said Georgina.

"Well, maybe not many people do it, but why should we let it stop us?" Edgar gave a wolfish grin.

Georgina turned serious. "I mean it, my lord. For you, bringing me to a ball is a fun way to subvert convention. But for me, well, it's putting me in the firing line to be a laughing stock."

"No one will laugh at you so long as you're with me," Edgar said.

"That's exactly it. No one will laugh at me when I'm with you. But the minute we're apart, or the day after in the street, the ladies of the ton will be sneering at me, mocking me, the whispers of 'whore at the ball', 'the earl's whore' and all the rest of it will be going around for months."

Edgar sighed. Georgina had a point. So long as he brought Georgina to balls as his mistress and nothing more, then he would always be putting her in harm's way. And other than his family, she was the most important person in the world to him and he had a *duty* to protect her. "You're right, I'm sorry my love. Please forget I ever suggested it."

Georgina snuggled closer into Edgar's strong arms. "As you so desire, my Lord."

As he held Georgina in his arms, Edgar felt a deep pang of regret. He wished more than anything to be able to bring Georgina to balls, to parties, to have her by his side every day and have no one in society say a word. But would that dream ever be possible?

CHAPTER ELEVEN

Georgina took a sip of champagne from the flute as she sauntered across the dance floor. Tonight there was not a member of the ton in sight. This was a party strictly for the ladies of the stage and all those who worked in the theatre, including the back of house staff, the composers and the playwrights.

"Coo-eee, Georgina!" A friendly face, Deborah Tamworth, lept in front of Georgina, did a careless pirouette and turned again to face her before giving a curtsey.

Georgina laughed so hard that champagne bubbles entered her nose and threatened to exit with a sneeze. "Deborah, darling, you weirdo! How are you doll?"

"Oh I am very well, Miss Hartley. Come on, let's dance!"

The pair began to dance facing one another in something that bore a slight resemblance to a rustic jig but did not really fit easily into any category. A dance of their own devising.

"But seriously, Georgina, I can see there's a sadness in your eyes," Deborah said through her tipsy haze.

Georgina bit her lip and said nothing.

"I don't know what's caused it. You having trouble getting parts?"

"Parts are going great, no problems there," Georgina said.

"Oh, it's not the anniversary of something? Your parents' passing, God rest their souls?"

Georgina shook her head.

"Some problem with a man? What's your protector's name, Lord Weatherby, are things alright with him?"

Georgina said nothing.

Deborah put her hands on her friend's shoulders. "Oh, Georgina, so it *is* him. What's he gone and done, because if he's broken your heart I'll fight him, I'll fight him I will and make no mistake!"

"You don't need to fight him," Georgina. sighed. "No one needs to fight him."

"So what's the matter? You're not in love with him, are you? 'Cause you know how that's only playing with fire. These lords, they never go for the likes of us, not as a serious prospect anyway." Deborah blinked her eyes in rapid succession and took Georgina into her gaze as though she were looking at her for the first time, really seeing her rather than the bonne vivante she saw at parties and on the stage. "Oh heavens, you are!"

Georgina cast her eyes at the floor.

"Georgina, doll, you're only going to break your own heart. And the world needs you on the stage, with your beautiful voice singing your heart out, not as the wife of some lord popping out babies and vowing herself to obey him."

Georgina stayed as a statue.

Around the pair, revellers continued to dance and swirl their way around the room in all manner of waltzes, jigs and reels.

"Has he told you he's in love with you?" Deborah asked.

"Yes," Georgina nodded.

"What a mess."

Georgina sighed. "You can say that again. Listen, I came here tonight to forget Lord Weatherby. Can we just forget about him and have a good time?"

"That we most certainly can," Deborah said. She turned behind her and cried, "Meredith! Chloe! Get yourselves over here at once!"

A few beats later and Meredith and Chloe joined the dancing circle. The band in the centre of the room began to play *The Lass of Richmond Hill*, a standard of the streets and stage, and the four young women began to sing along as they danced.

On Richmond Hill there lives a lass,
More bright than May-day morn,
Whose charms all other maids' surpass,
A rose without a thorn.

This lass so neat,
With smiles so sweet,
Has won my right good will.
I'd crowns resign

To call her mine,
Sweet lass of Richmond Hill!

Sweet lass of Richmond Hill,
Sweet lass of Richmond Hill,
I'd crowns resign to call thee mine,
Sweet lass of Richmond Hill.

❧ ❦

Edgar knocked at the door to Georgina's Fitzrovia accommodation, flowers in hand.

After a minute, the door swung open and Georgina stood facing him. She was a vision in her garnet silk dress, ruby necklace and black silk stockings, thought Edgar.

"Good afternoon, my lord," she said.

"My lady, how lovely to see you." Edgar reached for her hand and bent to kiss it. "Are you keeping well?"

"As well as ever. Please, come in."

Edgar crossed the threshold and shut the door behind himself. "These are for you," he said as he handed Georgina the bouquet.

"Thank you my Lord, how thoughtful of you." Georgina kissed Edgar on the cheek and they made their way into the parlour.

Georgina placed the flowers in a vase on the sideboard and turned to Edgar. "Would you like some tea?"

Edgar assented and Georgina made her way towards the kitchen, Edgar following behind her.

Georgina filled the kettle and placed it on the stove. "How are things going with Philomena?"

Edgar sighed. "About as well as they always do with her. I struggle to understand her, I really do. Belinda was never like this."

"They have different personalities, yes?" Georgina had never met any of Edgar's siblings but he spoke about them enough that she had garnered a basic outline of who was who and what drove each family member. At least, according to Edgar's view of things!

"They do indeed. And on one level it makes sense why they react to things differently, but I still for the life of me cannot understand why Philomena doesn't seem to want to make a good marriage and settle down with a family."

Georgina filled the tea infuser with a special bergamot blend of leaves and placed it in the teapot. "Maybe she does really, but the loss of freedom terrifies her."

"Loss of freedom? But she'll gain so much from making a good match," said Edgar with a note of bemusement in his voice.

"She might, but at the moment it doesn't sound like she sees it that way. I can't pretend to understand fully what your sister thinks though I suspect she doesn't really see the benefits of marriage, however great they may be. Thinking back to when I was her age, wanting to settle down and start a family was so far out of my realm of comprehension that I would have been very unlikely to pursue marriage at that point. I wanted to sing."

"Philomena though, she can't sing," Edgar said. "I'm not really sure what talents she has, if any."

"Maybe she doesn't really have any, maybe she does," Georgina replied. "But I'll bet she has interests beyond marriage."

"She's forever reading, radical pamphlets and such," Edgar said.

"Oh a radical!" Georgina laughed. "Dreaming of changing the world, of righting all its wrongs? Well at least her heart is in the right place. There's a lot that needs changing." She turned to Edgar. "She can still read, be involved in those pamphlets once she's married. But she probably doesn't understand that and, dare I be impertinent, my lord?"

"Be my guest, be as impertinent as you like," Edgar guffawed.

"Has anyone ever sat down and talked about the benefits of marriage, shown her what a healthy marriage can be like? Or is it a case of people telling her she needs to get married?"

Edgar sighed. "The latter."

Georgina nodded. "And Philomena is four years younger than Belinda. Your older sister would probably have formed a lot of her beliefs about marriage based on the example of your parents. Philomena, on the other hand, is likely too young to remember much from when your parents were alive so she is forming her opinions based on what she sees going on outside your family. And there are a lot of bad examples, especially those that churn through the rumour mill. Who is going to gossip about a happy marriage?"

"That's a fair point."

"Is there anyone in the family who could talk with Philomena about it?"

By now the tea had finished brewing.

Georgina reached for the pot and poured two cups. She passed one to Edgar and held the other in her right hand.

Edgar thanked her and then said, "Belinda could, I suppose. There are also some older cousins to whom I'll make enquiries. You've given me a lot to think about, it's been really helpful sweetheart."

He meant what he said. For so many years, he had tried to do it all on his own. Now he was learning, however, that sometimes speaking with someone else helps one to see the wood for the trees.

"You're welcome, my lord," she said with a smile.

She took a sip of tea and savoured the bergamot taste.

Then she asked, "And how are you other siblings getting along? Who's the next youngest after Philomena, Lionel?"

"Yes, Lionel's still being educated at home with tutors and a governess," said Edgar.

"Was it similar for you at his age?" Georgina asked.

"No, he's twelve now and I was packed off to prep boarding school when I was nine," Edgar said.

"But you didn't want the same for Lionel?"

"I most definitely did not!" Edgar rubbed the back of his neck. "I absolutely hated it at that blasted prep school. There was, of course, the usual homesickness for the first few months."

That was an understatement. If he were to be completely honest with himself, he doubted whether he had ever totally gotten over the harsh separation from his family at such a tender young age.

He sipped his tea. "But the conditions were roundly terrible, as were the masters. I couldn't bring myself to put Lionel through that. About the only good thing to come out of my time there was becoming friends with Mowbrow."

Georgina gave a sympathetic smile. Her own life had featured loss and separation and she knew well what it was to be taken away from one's childhood home too soon.

Edgar's voice grew nostalgic. "Leaving that prep school and moving up to Eton when I was thirteen was a breath of fresh air."

"And Lionel, are you planning to send him on to Eton?" Georgina said.

"Yes, it will be the making of him. As it was for me," Edgar replied.

Georgina smiled internally. In her experience, gentlemen of the ton always referred to their time at Eton, Harrow or one of Britain's other elite public schools with phrases such as 'it was the making of me'. Never having had the opportunity to attend such a school herself, she could not say if they really were the making of the men of the ton. However, she knew full well that they offered all the essential academic requirements for noblemen during the reign of George III.

"Indeed, my lord," Georgina said.

Edgar leant forward over the table and rested his head on his left hand. He looked into Georgina's eyes with keenness.

"What sort of education did you receive, Georgina?" he asked.

"The same as the Reverend Wilson's daughters. Reading and writing and arithmetic. French and Italian too, and history. And theology, a *lot* of theology," she said.

"Probably more theology than me," Edgar smiled.

"Yes, knowing the Reverend Wilson that's a fair statement. And then piano, dancing and of course singing. How to run a middle class household too, Mrs Wilson taught me that."

"That sounds a bit like the education my sisters receive." He smiled. "Genevieve came to me recently and mentioned she wanted to learn Ancient Greek."

"Good for her," Georgina said.

"She's been having lessons for several months now, with the same tutor I engage for Lionel. I was surprised at first, I thought it was a jest on her part. But she seems to be taking a genuine interest in the lessons. More fool me for jumping to hasty conclusions, I suppose."

He gave a wry smile at his initial assumption being proven wrong.

Another evening and another ball. Edgar stood at the side of the elegant room and watched with dispassion as gentlemen twirled ladies about the floor. Every step of those refined dances was intimately familiar to him. He had danced them at many a ball over the past decade, after all. Yet so seldom did he feel himself making a real connection with any of the ladies he danced with. In fact, come to think of it, he had not felt a genuine connection with any other soul for many years. Until his recent arrangement with Miss Hartley.

Edgar shook his head at himself. Here he was getting lost in his own thoughts, fruitless as they were. He could dislike these sorts of events as much as he wanted, but it did not negate the necessity of finding a society bride. And balls were some of the best places to find such a lady.

As he turned his focus towards the here and now, an all too familiar female figure entered his line of sight. Lady Petunia Reynolds. Dressed in a pale sunshine gown and cream gloves, at first glance to the untrained observer she may have seemed jovial and good natured. A true belle of the ball. Edgar, however, knew from bitter experience that she was anything but.

She was less than a foot away from him now. Too close for Edgar to dash off in silence. Not unless he wanted to come across as highly rude and, dislike Lady Petunia as he did, he had no desire to break the bounds of social propriety this evening and risk causing a scene by giving her the cut direct.

"Good evening, my lord," Lady Petunia began.

Edgar inclined his head towards her. "Good evening, my lady."

She smirked and stood directly in front of him. So close that they were mere inches apart.

Then she twittered with gleeful malice. "I saw you with her again."

Edgar eyed her steadily. "I don't know who you're talking about, my lady."

"Oh I know you know," Lady Petunia fluttered her fan in front of her face, "and if you're not careful, the whole of English society is going to know about your little singing sparrow soon as well." She leant towards Edgar's ear and whispered, "I know you *love* her. I know you want to *be* with her."

"You forget yourself, my lady. Please excuse me." Edgar bowed quickly at Lady Petunia and walked away.

Damn, damn, damn, thought Edgar. Blast it all to hell! He knew he needed to clear his head. Making his way towards the gardens, he replayed Lady Petunia's words again. *I know you* love *her. I know you want to* be *with her.* It was true, but it didn't make it something that could ever be reality. The thought of being with Georgina as man and wife was a pretty picture, for sure, but it could only ever be that. A picture and nothing more.

Stepping out onto the terrace, Edgar was relieved that the crowds were thinning. He was alone at last. Alone to process his feelings, for all the good he was at that. There were burning torches in the garden, creating a romantic atmosphere. But Edgar could never have true romance, he knew that. His priority first and foremost had to be to the family and to carrying on the Wetherby line. Romance might be possible for some of his younger siblings, but as the eldest son he could not afford to let it be a factor in his choice of spouse.

***

Edgar had been with Georgina in her house for three hours.

After they had shared tea in the parlour, they had made their way upstairs and were in the second bedroom.

"Hold me close, my Lord!" Georgina embraced Edgar and kissed him on the cheek. "Our time is running out."

Edgar looked at his pocket watch. "Georgina, it's almost half past ten."

Rolling her eyes internally, Georgina put on a coquettish carefree expression. "Just start the time, put it in your pocket and come with me."

"You know I cannot stay, my duties await." He kissed her cheek. "So I'll see you on Thursday?"

"Alright," Georgina replied resignedly.

Edgar strode out of the room, casting Georgina a parting smile full of promise as he did so.

Georgina sat down on the firm green velvet settee and gripped the seat with each hand, trying to give her tense muscles something to focus on.

Chapter Twelve

The fleetingly golden dust particles floated past the shafts of light coming through the french windows that led onto a balcony overlooking the square.

Georgina lay face down on the bed, not bothering to cover her modesty with a sheet, with one leg elegantly raised in the air as she bent her knee.

Heavens, she looked gorgeous, thought Edgar.

Georgina scrutinised the novella she was reading, a light piece from Italy.

"You are absolutely delectable," Edgar growled.

With that, Georgina smirked and turned her head towards where he stood in the corner of the room, shirtless and in those black breeches she so loved.

"Then you should come over here," Georgina laughed.

Edgar strode towards the bed where his paramour was discarding the novella on the floor. "Hmmm, that's a careless way to treat a book," said Edgar as he gave her left cheek a smack and climbed onto the bed.

"Oh, is it now?" Georgina smoothly replied.

"I do believe so." Then, Edgar kissed her and she reached towards his waist to undo the ties around the top of his breeches. Sometimes, thought Edgar, the woman had a one track mind. But then again, so did he. He wasn't known as a real rake for nothing.

Edgar intensified the kissing as Georgina giggled. Claiming her mouth, he quietened the sounds until they turned into soft moans. Yes, thought Edgar, that's exactly what my Georgina likes.

Reaching his hands down to that glorious spot between her legs, Edgar could feel her wetness already building.

He'd never known a woman to be so eager, yet so controlled in public. Yes, that's exactly how he liked his woman. His Georgina. Wanton and willing at all times in private, but prim and proper in public. Of course, when they were alone on the estate he'd fuck her wherever it pleased them both. And he'd done that oh so many times. Against the garden wall. In the old hayloft. And many many times on the tartan blankets by the side of the lake. The lake was his favourite place to lay her down on the rug, tie her hands together above her head with one of the muslin scarves and then bury his face between her legs. He loved to taste her and be in complete control of her pleasure. He couldn't think of a time when she was spread before him when she wasn't absolutely soaking wet. The naughty little harlot. Exactly how she was behaving right now.

A couple of hours later, the couple lay together in Edgar's bed.

He was sitting propped up against the headboard while Georgina lay with her head across his chest.

"Would you ever marry, Georgina?" asked Edgar.

"Well I don't have a dowry, so that rules it out rather quickly," she said.

"But supposing you did have a comfortable dowry, what then?"

"Maybe," Georgina said, choosing her words with care. "It would mean giving up the stage though."

Edgar raised an eyebrow. "Really?"

"Yes, really. Can you think of any married women on the London stage?"

"You've got a point."

She giggled. "Of course I've got a point. But coming back to your question about whether or not I would ever marry, it would mean an inevitable loss of independence. And I might gain some benefits in return, but it's risky. What if my husband turned out to be a brute?"

"That's fair. But what if he wasn't a brute?"

"I sincerely hope he wouldn't be but some men are brilliant actors. The stages of a thousand Theatre Royals couldn't contain all the men who speak false in England."

Edgar sighed and nodded.

Georgina continued. "I would have to be absolutely certain of a man before I married him, and I don't see how it is possible to even be certain of someone's character in the first place."

"But say you could be certain of a man's character? What if you could know without a doubt that he was a man of honour who would be faithful and true and would protect and provide for you always? What then?"

"Well then, if he were truly able to prove himself as such a man of honour then I would strongly consider him." Georgina kissed Edgar's cheek. "But that's only speaking in fantasies and hypotheticals. I doubt such a man would wish to marry me."

Mrs Buppetts Team Rooms were busy on this particular Tuesday. Not an uncommon occurrence. In the booth by the window sat four members of one of the ton's most distinguished families. There being no parliamentary sittings today, Edgar saw a good opportunity to take the three youngest Weatherbys out for afternoon tea.

Edgar sat next to Lionel while Philomena and Genevieve directly faced their brothers.

Philomena addressed the group. "Have you heard about *A Midsummer Night's Dream*?"

"Yes," Lionel replied. "I've been reviewing it with my tutor."

The three youngest Weatherby siblings continued laughing and chatting.

Edgar excused himself and went to take some air in the powder room. He weaved his way through the maze of tables, careful not to bump into any lady or gentleman present. That sort of thing would not do at all.

As he entered the courtyard that led to the powder rooms, his heart sunk at the sight that met his eyes.

Lady Petunia Reynolds.

Blast! Would there ever be any escape from her? Could anyone of the ton ever find such an escape.

"Lord Weatherby, how goes the day?" Lady Reynolds simpered.

Edgar would really rather not have had this conversation, thank you very much, but the interests of propriety demanded he take part. And so he did.

"Most well, my lady. And yourself?" he asked.

"Oh, quite splendidly." She gave a little casual chuckle before continuing. "I find days like this most amusing. Seeing everyone out and about, the bright sparks of the ton, everybody dressed in the fineries of the latest fashions. But there's something else I find even more amusing. Do you know what that is, Lord Weatherby?"

Edgar stared at Lady Reynolds with a hard glare. "I haven't the foggiest idea what you are talking about, my lady. But whatever your point is, I urge you to carefully consider the appropriateness of making it."

Lady Reynolds let forth a laugh of derision. When she spoke again, her voice was harsh and cold. "Lord Weatherby, I don't need to consider any questions of appropriateness. In fact, the matter of what is and is not appropriate is far more relevant to your dalliance with your little singing sparrow. Oh, won't the ton be amused when they find out that you love her and wish to be with her."

Edgar did all he could to bite his tongue. Nothing good could come of a hasty reply to the utter balderdash coming from her mouth.

Lady Reynolds continued. "If you're not careful, everyone will know and then who will want to associate themselves with the great and the glorious Weatherby family? Why, your sisters will struggle to find a good match on the marriage mart."

"Lady Reynolds, you forget yourself," Edgar said. He gave her daggers, which she returned before averting her eyes and withdrawing through the door to the tearooms.

⁘ ⁘

Later, once Edgar had crossed the courtyard and was reentering the tearooms, he cast his eyes over to where Genevieve, Philomena and Lionel sat. The trio were engaged in lively conversation, laughing and joking.

Lionel bit into a small pastry and strawberry jam oozed out onto his cheek.

The boy and his sisters laughed. Then he picked up a napkin to wipe the jam and sugary traces from his cheek.

Lady Petunia Reynolds' words swirled around Edgar's head. He couldn't do anything that would harm his siblings. Least of all his unwed sisters who were relying on him to secure their futures through excellent marriages.

His heart ached. He was the closest thing to a father figure they had ever known. And Philomena, though she was old enough to have some memories of their father, she too had come to rely upon Edgar in many ways.

He walked through the tearoom to rejoin his siblings.

Each of them gave him an excited smile.

He forced himself to return it. He didn't want to let them down, after all.

In his office at the Weatherby's London townhouse, Edgar sat at his desk and scratched the final total for the family's monthly expenditures into the ledger. He dropped his quill and slumped back in his chair.

After a shared family dinner, he had recused himself in the office for the remainder of the evening. The ledgers needed attending to and he needed a distraction from that unfortunate encounter with Lady Reynolds the other day. Ever since had suffered the bad luck of running into her in the courtyard at Mrs Buppetts, his mind had been engulfed by thoughts of how he might hurt his siblings through his involvement with Georgina.

But he also did not want to hurt dear, sweet, beloved Georgina. She was the other half of his soul and he could not stand the thought of no longer having her in his life.

Such was his fragile mental state that he had stayed away from darling Georgina in recent days because he didn't wish to expose her to any more of his nonsense. He had put her through more than enough already.

So it was that Edgar found himself at one in the morning with the candle burnt halfway down and a complete ledger. Now he was at a loss for what to do.

He arose from his chair and strode over towards the imposing bookshelves. Perhaps some reading material would prove a distraction from the worries that plagued his mind.

Without much thought, he grabbed a heavy leather tome and took it with him to his chair.

He cracked the book open and began to read.

His eyes skimmed through the first few pages and the more he read, the more his spirits flagged. Out of all the books in his office, he had ended up somehow selecting the official account of his family history.

He sighed and slammed the book shut. Then he got up and put it back on the shelf.

There was a growing tightness within his stomach. Choosing another book right now likely wasn't going to relive it. What might have helped, if this were a night before he had ever met Georgina, would have been a glass or five of the old amber liquid to dull the ancient sorrows. The situation facing him tonight was far too sharp for that approach, however.

There was nothing else for it. A long night with his thoughts chasing themselves around and around inside his head lay ahead of him.

Carriages and carts clattered across Westminster Bridge, carrying all manner of people and cargo. On the northern banks of the Thames the Palace of Westminster stood as it had for centuries. Inside sat the gentry in Commons while the Lords were in their namesake chamber. One of the festering power centres of the British Empire, Parliament was at the heart of decisions that impacted the lives of millions of souls across the globe.

Inside the Lords, Edgar sat on one of the benches dedicated for peers such as himself. Like generations of Earls of Weatherby before him, he took part in votes and listened to speeches from the great and the not so good.

When Parliament was sitting, Edgar ordinarily attended several times a week and voted in most divisions. He spoke on the major issues and represented the interests of the Weatherbys and his tenants and employees as best he knew how. While he had little ambitions of being in cabinet or on the front benches, he nonetheless took his role seriously and never wanted to be the sort of lord who spent all his time at leisure neglecting his responsibilities.

He leaned back on the red leather seat and tried to focus on the debate at hand. Something or other to do with taxes, though he had no idea of any of the specifics.

Failing in his attempt to turn his mind to the taxation question, he could not help but feel a tight knot in his stomach. Thoughts of sweet Georgina erupted in his mind. Usually this was a pleasing occurrence, yet today it just brewed more guilt within him. Then Petunia Reynolds burst into his head, with her sneering face at the party saying that she knew Edgar loved his mistress. And then the spectre of every Earl of Weatherby who had ever gone before him flew into his head. What would they think about his love for Georgina?

The air around him felt stuffy. How he wished someone would open a window!

The voice of whichever lord was speaking reverberated around the chamber. But Edgar was oblivious. So wrapped up was he in his own mind.

Clamminess rose within Edgar. Then, there was a searing heat within his chest. The seconds drew by and he began to feel worse and worse.

He needed to get out. Leave the chamber and find somewhere to calm himself down and edge away from the precipice of danger.

He stood up abruptly. The row of benches thumped in response.

The baron seated next to Edgar cast him a look of annoyance at the interruption.

Edgar, however, was in such a single-minded hurry that he missed the baron's dirty glare entirely. Instead, Edgar stumbled towards the doors and out into the hallway.

He navigated through the rabbit warren of corridors and doors until he got to the water closet. He darted inside and braced his hands on a sink. The cool porcelain between his hands came as a relief.

Hunched over, he focused his gaze on the sink and tried to combat the thoughts rushing through his mind. He thanked the powers that be that no one else was in the room and so he could suffer this breakdown alone.

He hated himself for what he was about to do. This decision was not one he wanted to make. At all. However, he could not see any way forward that would allow him to fulfil his duties.

His heart raced.

He forced himself to take deep breaths. The sharpness of the air shocked his lungs.

Slowly, he raised his head towards the mirror so he was staring himself in the eye. The face that greeted him bore a strong resemblance to himself. Yet something was off. He could not quite place his finger on it. Probably it was just nerves, he reasoned.

He looked at his grey, pallid visage and made a vow to himself. He would do what he had to do for the sake of duty, regardless of the cost to his own heart.

Love was a luxury for other men. A luxury he could ill afford.

❧❧❧❧❧ ❧❧❧❧❧

Georgina walked through the door from the hallway to the quasi-parlour at Edgar's London bachelor apartment. Her pale mint green overcoat rustled against the petticoats concealed beneath. The intense fir green braided cords that decorated the back of her coat cut a striking image against the paler hessian fabric that formed the majority of the garment. In her hand she carried a fawn reticule embellished with green embroidery and tassels.

Edgar arose from his position on the settee as she entered the room. He placed his hands behind his back and bowed his head in greeting before meeting her eyes.

"Georgina, I'm so sorry but this needs to end," he said.

Bemusement took over Georgina's dainty face. "My lord, what do you mean?"

"This. Us. I can't do this anymore. I have my duty to my family and the earldom."

"But you said you'd always want to protect me," Georgina's voice was quiet and cold.

"I know...I'm sorry,"Edgar stumbled over his words. "But I have...have to do my duty."

Tears fell down Georgina's cheeks. Why was she getting like this? All arrangements like the one she had with Edgar came to an end eventually. Women like her would stay with a protector for a season or two, maybe three at the most before the protector would get bored of her and would pay her off with jewellery and then it was back on the market trying to find another. Trying to find another to provide bed and board, clothes and a carriage.

Walking over to the bureau, Edgar opened one of the drawers and pulled out an emerald necklace that had been in his family for fifty years. He went back to the dejected Georgina and placed it in her hands. "Please, this is for you," he said, looking intensely into Georgina's eyes.

Georgina nodded. "Very well, thank you my Lord. I'll leave you to your duties."

She placed the necklace in her reticule and closed the bag.

With that final action, she turned and left the room.

Edgar could hear her footsteps in the hallway before the main door of the house slammed and his sweet Georgina was gone. He needed to stop thinking of her as his sweet Georgina. She was gone now, thought Edgar wistfully.

He made his way to his desk and sat down. Head in his hands, he let the wave of emotions roll over him. Georgina wouldn't be the only one in tears today.

Chapter Thirteen

A week later, London

Georgina rolled the pink silken gloves up her arms to where they ended slightly above the top of her elbows. Then she affixed the feather headdress to her hair. The outfit complete, she headed out of her dressing room door and down the winding maze of corridors to the wings.

Applause greeted her before she even stepped foot on stage. Despite everything that had gone sour in her personal life of late, at least she could still count on her professional reputation as an opera singer. She took a deep breath, made her way out onto the stage and began to sing.

In a box to the side of the stage, well within Georgina's initial line of sight, sat Philomena and Belinda. To Belinda's left hand side sat Edgar. He had been loathe to come this evening given that he knew his now former mistress would be performing. But Belinda and Philomena had insisted and who was he to deny his sisters?

He sat with his head tilted away from the stage and towards the floor, hoping to God that Georgina would not look up at the Weatherby box and notice her former protector was in attendance.

One small blessing was how engrossed both his sisters were in the performance. No one would suspect a thing, he told himself.

***

Unbeknownst to Edgar, Belinda turned her head to her left and noticed her brother's curious line of sight. Whatever could be on the floor that was of greater interest to him than the soprano on the stage? Oh, how she hoped it was not a rat or a mouse! She did not have the stomach for small rodents at the best of times.

"Edgar," Belinda hissed in his ear, "are you feeling quite well?"

Jolted from his trance, he mumbled a reply. "Yes, yes, sister."

"Alright then," she said.

Belinda kept her eyes on her brother as he returned to his own world of distraction. Curiously, he had returned his gaze towards the floor. This was most odd.

She cast her mind back to when Philomena had raised the idea of going to the opera. At first, Edgar had looked impassive. Yet when Philomena had waved the programme in front of his face with its prominent headline feature of

'Miss Georgina Hartley', his face had briefly turned sour before returning to its previous impassive state. At the time, Belinda had thought little of the fleeting change in her brother's countenance, almost imperceptible as it had been, but on reflection she suspected it held greater meaning than she had initially understood.

What could be the cause of her brother's disdain for the concert and subsequent odd behaviour. Was her brother unwell? Possible, thought Belinda. Then again, it was highly curious that his face adopted that briefly funny expression only when Miss Hartley's name was mentioned and not at another point in time. Belinda surmised that her brother's conduct related directly to the soprano in some way.

Did he dislike Miss Hartley's singing? Belinda thought that notion unlikely. After all, Miss Hartley was a genuine crowd pleaser and could always be relied upon to put in a good performance when she took to the stage.

Was there something else about Miss Hartley that was bothersome for Edgar? He seemed so eager to avoid even looking at Miss Hartley, after all. So keen to avoid the kind of eye contact that opera singers so often made with audience members seated in the boxes closest to the stage.

Belinda sucked her cheeks inwards. This was a most troubling conundrum. If she did not know any better, she would surmise that her brother somehow knew Miss Hartley and that something bad had happened between the two of them. Dire enough that Edgar was unwilling to even look at the soprano, let alone meet her eyes.

Belinda looked down upon Georgina. Curious, thought the duchess. Georgina was steadfastly avoiding directing her gaze at the Weatherby box. She was looking in every other direction within the theatre other than their own box.

The singing went on.

Belinda came to a realisation. Yes, something had gone on between her brother and Miss Hartley. But what?

The duchess wracked her brains for an explanation.

She thought about how her brother and Miss Hartley may have come into contact in the first place.

As a woman two years wed and the wife of one of the most illustrious dukes in Britain, Belinda was not some missish young girl who saw sweetness and light wherever she went. She was not naive to the ways of the world and the ways of the men of the ton.

An explanation developed in her mind. A very likely explanation indeed.

Belinda knew that many gentlemen of the ton entered into arrangements with actresses, singers and other ladies of the stage. Arrangements where the gentleman acted as a protector and funded the lady. In return, the lady was his courtesan and was expected to provide the gentleman with all manner of pleasures.

Considering this arrangement made Belinda very conflicted inside. On the one hand, did people not have the right to make what arrangements and associations they wanted of their own free will? But on the other hand, she knew full well that men like her brother held the levers of power while women held very little. Who was Belinda to say how a woman should use what little agency she had in an effort to support herself and make her own way in the world?

One thing that did enrage Belinda's sense of justice was the use of the word 'protector' to describe the behaviour of the men of the ton towards courtesans. It didn't strike her as any real kind of protection at all, given that the man could withdraw it on a mere whim and leave the woman high and dry. Conversely, a husband took sacred vows to protect his wife and owed that protection to her until the grave. While that duty to protect could sometimes misfire, as it had in the case of her husband during the first year of their marriage, Belinda nonetheless believed that it mattered immensely. She could not imagine her marriage without her husband protecting her.

So it saddened her to think of her brother treating any woman poorly, no matter the circumstances of their arrangement. If he had offered his protection to Miss Hartley and then withdrawn it in such a way that he could not even bring himself to look at Miss Hartley, then he had decreased in Belinda's eyes.

Then again, maybe she had misread the situation and Miss Hartley had chosen to leave her brother of her own accord. Perhaps she had obtained a better offer from elsewhere.

In truth, Belinda didn't know what she thought about the morality of it all.

But something funny had gone on with her brother and she was determined to keep a close watch on him.

Georgina had stayed at the Fitzrovia house for several days after Edgar had ended their arrangement. After all, he had never specified a date that she should leave by so she had seen fit to take her time in clearing her effects from the place. But she did not want to hang around there indefinitely and so, in short order, she moved into a spare room at Jean Cookson's.

As ever, Jean had proven a solid and reliable friend. She had given Georgina space to focus her efforts on her stage career for a while. Both women knew, however, that Georgina would ultimately have to find another protector. It was the only feasible way for someone like her to survive.

Nonetheless, there was still time before the need to secure a protector would become a pressing priority. Until then, Georgina filled her days with performing and rehearsing as well as outings with friends. Alongside Jean, she took in the entertaining delights of art exhibitions and the Tower of London and, as a larger group with Jean and the opera crowd, she went to Astley's Amphitheatre. With so many activities, Georgina had little time to wallow in the sorrows of her disappointment over Edgar. Ever the realist through it all, she accepted that they would never work out. It was better this way. For everyone.

Across town it was a different story, however.

Every day since he had made that gut-wrenching decision to end his arrangement with Georgina, Edgar had replayed that moment in his mind again and again and again. He could hardly bear to think of the devastated look on Georgina's face. But whenever he tried to think of something else, of anything else at all, there she was haunting him.

He grew more snappish and short with Lionel and Xavier in particular. He knew he was being unfair and, after several days, withdrew to his bachelor lodgings away from the Weatherby townhouse. They didn't need him around. Grouching and griping. They were better off without him and his blasted melancholy.

He told himself that ending things with Georgina was the right decision. The best decision in the long run. It was what duty required, after all.

From sunrise to sunset, he did his utmost to lose himself in paperwork and account ledgers. Yet night after night at his bachelor apartments he thought of Georgina and nothing else. His heart panged with regrets.

When Belinda and Philomena had broached the idea of a night at the opera, he had acquiesced in the hope that anything, anything would take his mind off Miss Hartley. But confound it all, when he looked at the programme he realised she would be performing onstage that very night! Seeing Georgina perform had sent him into an even worse spiral.

He would spend hours at his desk in his bachelor lodgings, staring into the fire grate and achieving two-fifths of sweet nothing whatsoever. Or else he would pace around the apartments, his arms behind his ramrod straight back as the tension in his shoulders grew and grew with no release in sight.

And the nights, oh the nights, they were without sleep, without rest, without succour. Either he lay in his bed in a futile attempt at sleep or he would give up the battle entirely and end up sitting in an armchair in the parlour as the darkness wrapped itself around him.

Two weeks after the night at the opera, he was sitting as usual in his office and again the face of sweet Georgina filled his mind's eye. This motionless existence could go on no longer. He hatched a plan for what he would do next. Yes, this was sure to work. Success was guaranteed.

The bouquet of flowers in his hand was comically over-sized. Edgar had not intended it to appear so when he had purchased the posies earlier on in the evening, but the visual effect was unmistakable to any passers by. Even so, Edgar himself did not realise the odd figure he cut as he marched intently down London's streets and over to the house where Georgina was staying.

It was the house of her friend Jean Cookson, who had gone away on business for a couple of weeks. Jean had a modest house in Soho with two bedrooms upstairs and a few rooms downstairs. Georgina regularly stayed with her when she was in between protectors.

Rounding the corner into the street where Jean lived, Edgar tried to screw up every ounce of courage within his guts.

He hated himself for telling Georgina things were over. He wanted to be with her again in every way. Of course, he told himself, they could never be together in every way that mattered. They would never be man and wife. Georgina would never be the Countess of Weatherby. But were not there many men who maintained a mistress outside of their loveless marriages? Why could that not be him too? He could marry a lady of the ton, do his duty towards her and provide for her for life, sire some heirs and then enjoy love with Georgina on the side. It was a win-win situation, he told himself.

At this time of the evening, Edgar was the only soul around on Georgina's street. On the main road a few minutes away, horses' hoofbeats would still be clattering and the night watchmen would be doing their patrols, but not so in this part of the city.

He stopped outside Jean's house and knocked on the door.

A couple of minutes later, the door opened slightly to reveal the peeping face of his beloved Georgina.

"My lord, what is the meaning of this?" she said.

"Miss Hartley, are you still without a protector?" Edgar held up the bouquet to Georgina's line of sight.

Georgina bit her lip briefly before responding. "Perhaps I am. Not that it's any of your concern."

"I am so so sorry for ending things, Miss Hartley, and I have come to you tonight to ask if you would like to give things another go, with me as your protector?"

Georgina felt torn. On the one hand, she wanted to forget Edgar Weatherby and start afresh with someone new. He had hurt her really badly when he ended things with her and capriciousness did not suit him. Yet on the other hand she still loved him and any chance to get close to him was worth it in her opinion. Moreover, she had yet to secure another protector and she did not want to wear out Jean's hospitality.

Quickly making a decision, she replied, "Come in my Lord and we'll talk."

Edgar's face lit up.

"I'm not guaranteeing anything though," she said. She wanted to make him sweat a bit.

Edgar's face took on a studied impassivity.

Georgina opened the door wider and gestured for Edgar to follow her.

He entered the house.

She closed the door. She made her way towards the stairs and stood on the third step before she turned around to face Edgar. He was standing on the grey flagstones of the hallway.

"Why did you end our arrangement in the first place?" asked Georgina.

"I know I've been unfair to you. I foolishly thought it best to end things because I have duties to my family and to the Weatherby legacy."

Georgina rolled her eyes. Not this talk of his duties yet again. "Then why come back to me now saying you want to be my protector again, if your *duties* are so important?"

"Because I love you and I can't bear to be apart from you," he said in earnest. "That's why I want to be your protector again."

"I warn you my lord, I will never be anyone's possession." Georgina spat. She looked down at Edgar from where she stood three steps above him.

"Oh for crying out loud," Edgar growled before his voice grew gentler. "I don't want to possess you, I want to *marry* you."

She crossed her arms. "I grant you that you have conviction in what you say, but ultimately it's folly. You'll never marry me, much as I may want you to. I'm not some lady of the ton, who your high society would welcome with open arms and open minds."

Edgar knew she had a point. But it still didn't change what his heart wanted more than anything else in all the world. He sighed. "You're right, you're completely right. We can never marry. But it doesn't change the way I feel and the depth of my love for you, Miss Hartley."

Damn, damn, damn! Edgar had gotten her hook, line and sinker, thought Georgina. She uncrossed her arms and stepped down from the stairs, she kissed him on the cheek and took the bouquet from his outstretched hands. "These are beautiful flowers, thank you my lord. I accept your offer."

Edgar's smile returned. "Miss Hartley, I will send a carriage round tomorrow for your things."

Edgar was joyous. Everything could go back to how it was before, to the happy carefree times with Georgina as his mistress. He would again be able to spend time with her in the evenings and at all the other times of day he so pleased, and still maintain his duties to the Weatherby title. Down the track he would also be able to keep Georgina on as his mistress once he got married to a lady of high society. Certainly, it would be a loveless marriage but having Georgina as his mistress on the side would make it much easier to bear.

"Very well," she said. Then she offered her hand to Edgar. "Come with me my lord."

He took her proffered hand and let her lead him up the stairs to her chamber.

Georgina awoke yet again. Heavens, this was frustrating! Why couldn't she get to sleep properly, no matter how hard she tried? Her protector was sleeping soundly beside her, so why couldn't she be blessed with the same rest?

She felt a tight knot in her stomach, the same as she had felt when Edgar ended their arrangement a month ago. In the intervening weeks, she had begun to feel better in herself and had been sleeping properly. She loved Edgar deeply and intensely and she had always enjoyed their time together, so why now she had him back in her life was she tossing and turning at night?

She sighed and rolled over, willing herself to fall asleep. It was going to be a long night.

Edgar woke up the next morning with a new vigour in his step. He rolled over to find the bed empty of his companion. Getting out of bed, he went to perform his morning ablutions, dressed and then made his way downstairs.

He walked along the flagstone hallway and entered the kitchen. There he found Georgina sitting at the table sipping on a cup of tea with a newspaper in front of her. She turned to him with a seductive smile on her face.

"Good morning, my lord. I trust you slept well?" she said.

"All the better for having you by my side." He leaned down to where she was sitting and kissed her on the cheek. "How was your rest, my darling?"

"Good, thank you my lord," she lied.

He quirked an eyebrow but said nothing. She probably just did not want to bother him, he thought, but there were unmistakable bags beneath her eyes.

Chapter Fourteen

A few weeks later, Georgina was walking along the ramshackle boardwalk at Greenwich. This part of the city was not normally part of her stomping ground, but she needed to get away and clear her head and this was the first place that had sprung to her head when the hackney carriage driver had asked her where she would like to go.

So now she found herself on this moonless March night wrapped in her black velvet cloak walking outside the inns that dotted the banks of the Thames.

Strains of sea shanties played on the fiddle and accordion made their way from the pubs to her ears.

Brightly light windows highlighted the shadows of the revellers inside.

This was never Georgina's world. Though she had lived in London off-and-on all her adult life, at her core she was a daughter of the countryside. And she enjoyed city life but her idea of a good time was around Covent Garden, the centre and the West End. Not here near the docks. This wasn't her patch at all.

She resolved that she needed to find somewhere she could go to clear her head and think through what had happened with Edgar. In the distance, she saw the spire of a church. That will do, she thought, and made her way towards it.

A short walk later and she was outside the church.

Saint Alfege's read the sign outside. Unusual name, she thought.

She made her way through the columned entrance and up the aisle towards the altar. Not a single other soul was inside the building. Good, she thought. Likely no one in this part of London would know who I am anyway, but I would rather not run into a familiar face at a time like this all the same.

She sat down in a pew near the front and fixed her gaze on the sanctuary lamp. Peering into the golden flame, she focused her thoughts on what path she should take with Edgar.

After sitting in the church for almost two hours, Georgina got up from the pew and made her way down the aisle and out onto the quiet street outside. She drew her black and purple shawl tighter around herself. The cold chill of the night was closing in.

She was resolved now in what she had to do. For her future and for Edgar's.

She retraced her footsteps to the point where the hansom cab had dropped her off and hailed another to take her back to Fitzrovia.

Lord Weatherby exited the carriage. Darting quickly across to the building, he was ready for another night with Georgina.

He opened the front door anticipating Georgina's sweet face would be awaiting him inside. He could feel the warmth of the candles she would surely have lit, like she always did, before he even set foot inside. He could hear her angelic singing voice as she passionately played the keys of the piano.

But once he entered the parlour, all of these visions and sensations disappeared.

Georgina wasn't there.

She'd left a note.

Picking it up, he read in disbelief, her familiar hand taunting him from the page.

My Lord,

Please do not try to find me as I have gone far away and it is better for you to focus your efforts on finding a suitable wife to your station. I have loved you and a part of my being will always love you. But for both of our sakes I need to leave your life. I have come to realise that I will never be happy being the other woman once you are married to the rightful Countess of Weatherby. I will not be able to withstand the pain of seeing you with her and while it pains me greatly to leave, staying here to be your mistress would be even harder. In a better world, in a fairer world, one where we could be together truly and fully then I would give my whole heart to you and be yours forever. But we do not live in that world. So this is goodbye my love.

Love,

Georgina

Edgar read and reread Georgina's letter again and again, standing frozen on the spot.

His stomach felt as though it had disappeared from his body and his face at first felt cold like a tombstone before his cheeks began to burn up and hot tears ran down his face. Willing himself to stop weeping, he tried to focus on what he needed to do next and where he needed to go.

But it was all to no avail.

He was mired in the here and now, stuck with the horrible realisation that Georgina had chosen to leave him for good and that her heart would never be his.

He threw the letter down on the table. How could Georgina do this? Did she not love him? Why would she want to go away? Did she not realise that she was the woman that made him happy, not some high society lady? And though he would never be able to marry her, he could have her in his life as his mistress for decades to come, if she wanted it. So why did she not want it?

Edgar stopped his train of thought.

His heart sank.

He knew full well that had been, and was still continuing to be, completely and utterly selfish. Of course Georgina would not be content to spend the rest of her life as his mistress. She would not play second fiddle to anyone. What woman in the world would?

But the one thing that would make her want to stay with him would be for her to become his lawful wedded wife. She had every right to expect nothing less. He wanted her to have nothing less!

But it could not be with him, he told himself harshly. She was beneath his station by far too many levels. And there was the inconvenient matter of her having been his mistress and not a 'respectable' maiden. The two together were a deadly combination for any hope of a marriage between them, he mused.

For want of anything better to do, he made his way to the drinks cabinet and poured himself a generous serve of whisky.

Then he carried the bottle and glass to the settee, slamming them down on the coffee table, and downed the glass in one hit.

He poured himself another drink.

It was going to be a long night.

The next morning, Edgar awoke with a cricked neck.

His throat felt dry like sandpaper and his eyes were groggy.

Looking at the scene in front of him, he remembered the devastation of the night before when he had found Georgina's letter. That blasted letter telling him she was leaving his life forever, for allegedly his own good.

So now he was free, he pondered, free to pursue a high born society lady of the ton and not to have to take into account the feelings of his mistress.

Yet he didn't want that freedom. He wanted to be with Georgina forever, to have her in his life and to always take into account what she wanted and what her feelings were. He wanted to always look after Georgina's best interests, to care for her, to protect her and to provide for her...*That sounds awfully like the responsibilities of a husband. And a man in my position can never take a woman like Georgina as a wife.*

I must do my duty to the Weatherby name. I must forget Georgina completely and, like she wrote, focus my efforts on finding a wife of a suitable station.

Rising from the sofa, he padded down the hallway into the kitchen and poured himself a cup of water.

He drank it greedily, like a man who had not seen water for days after crossing the desert.

CHAPTER FIFTEEN

The carriage clattered along through the French countryside. Inside, Georgina kept her head down behind her brown hat and beige veil. Making eye contact with others was the last thing she wanted to do right now.

In the row of seats opposite sat a man and a woman in their early twenties. The man was bellowing and guffawing stupid jokes and the woman was alternating between laughing along with him and trying to shush him.

Behind her veil, Georgina rolled her eyes. Why oh why could other passengers not be more considerate of those around them?

The hours rolled by and after a morning sat across from that irritating couple, Georgina was relieved when they disembarked in a dusty village and the coachman unloaded the pair's luggage.

"Goodbye everyone," hollered the woman as she exited the carriage and walked off down the road with her beau.

Then the coachman's head appeared at the carriage door. "Right, we'll set down here for luncheon. The inn over the road does a decent feed. We'll head off again at half past one.

I won't stay behind to wait for any stragglers so be sure you are not late."

Georgina joined the small group headed towards the inn, her arms folded and her veil still drawn across her face.

After luncheon, they were back on the road and a new cast of fellow travellers had assembled inside the carriage.

The wheels trundled round and round.

A baby wailed on the lap of a woman in the seat opposite Georgina.

The opera singer sat back in her seat and willed herself to get through the journey to Paris in one piece.

As day broke, the carriage pulled up outside the Wall of the Ferme générale of Paris. It joined the queue of carriages, carts, horses, livestock, and people on foot awaiting entry to the City of Love. After what felt like an age, the vehicle cleared the toll gate and was on its way to the heart of Paris.

Finally, thought Georgina, as she stepped out onto Parisienne soil. She was here at last and was on the road to putting England and Edgar behind her. She took her bag from the coachman. Recalling the residence of her long-standing friends the Renoirs, she left the square and made her way to their home.

Paris had changed little since she was last here, she mused as she strutted with small steps down the medieval cobbled streets. Though it had officially been a republic for well over a decade, much of the city seemed as tired and as unequal as ever. Some things seldom change, mused Georgina.

Ah yes, now she was on familiar territory. Her old stomping ground of Rue du Bac came into view and with it the home of the Renoirs. She walked up to the door and knocked.

Less than thirty seconds later and the door swang open to reveal a stylishly liveried footman. "Oui, Madame?"

"Good day, my name is Georgina Hartley and I have come from England to visit Monsieur and Madame Renoir," she said.

"Oh, Mademoiselle Hartley," the footman said. "Monsieur and Madame Renoir have spoken of you a lot these past few weeks. Please, come in and follow me."

Georgina did as she was told and followed the footman into a well appointed drawing room.

A short while later and footsteps creaked along the floorboards. Georgina looked up from the settee to see the face of her old friend, Madame Renoir.

"Ma cherie, you look like a deer caught in a crossbow," Madame Renoir began.

Georgina was tired, oh so tired. Tired of running away from thoughts of Edgar. Tired of her life as a courtesan. And tired of being in that blasted carriage clattering around Northern France with all manner of annoying individuals. Tears began to fill her eyes as she looked up at Madame Renoir. "I feel like one too."

"That Lord Weatherby has certainly done a number on you, I'll say," said Madame Renoir before she turned and called to her maid to bring in some refreshments.

"I'm so sorry to impose on your hospitality," wept Georgina. "I'll be on my way soon."

"Mademoiselle Hartley, you have nothing to apologise for. And you can stay here as long as you like until you decide what to do next."

"That's very kind of you to say," said Georgina between sobs.

Madame Renoir nodded sagely and handed the Englishwoman a handkerchief.

"There, there," Madame Renoir said. "Things may seem difficult now, but you will get through this and it will be brighter later."

The pair sat in silence for several minutes as Madame Renoir rubbed gentle, soothing circles on Georgina's back.

Then a knock at the door.

"Come in," Madame Renoir cried.

The maid reappeared and laid down a metal tray of sandwiches, tarts and tea.

Madame Renoir poured tea for the pair.

Georgina took the cup gratefully.

"Have something to eat too, ma cherie," Madame Renoir said. "You need to keep your energy up."

Not one to turn down a good meal given the hungry memories from her early childhood, Georigna obliged and reached forward for a sandwich. Madame Renoir was right; she did need to keep her energy up. Especially as she needed to make her own way in the world and stand on her own two feet again.

Eventually she would need to find another protector but she wanted to delay that for as long as possible. She knew was a broken woman and she needed time to heal.

Lining up at the opera house were a gaggle of young singers eager to find work.

"I hope I'll get a named part this time," said one young ingenue to another.

"Me too! We both will this time, I can feel it in my bones," her friend replied.

Georgina smiled wryly at the eagerness of the young singers. This had been her all those years ago when she went for her first season in Bath. But the years had worn away at her youthful exuberance and excitement for the game of the stage. She had been a bright talent right from the start, with named roles coming her way thick and fast right from her early years on the stage.

Yet what had it gotten her?

Today she found herself here in Paris with a broken heart, reliant yet again on her vocal and stage talents as well as her ability to secure a protector.

Marinating in these thoughts, she did not pay attention at first as a jovial voice cried behind her. "Signorina Hartley! It's been too long!"

Then a familiar face met hers and Georgina was jolted to attention.

"How are you, Signorina?" It was her old contact from the Venetian Opera House, Signore Giovinazzo.

The pair chatted about old times and what they had been up to, before Signore Giovinazzo said, "What are you doing in Paris, Signorina?"

"Ah well the London scene was getting a bit stale and since the treaty's made travel to the continent easier, I thought I'd see what work I could get in Paris," she said.

"I can get you work in Venice if you want," he said. "We're in need of an experienced soprano such as yourself. And besides, this city is a real hole. You know it and I know it, now don't deny it Signorina."

Georgina gave a small smile.

"Come to Venice instead," he expanded his arms in a gesture of jovial welcome, "it's so much better!"

"You do make an intriguing offer," she said. "Pray, tell me more?"

"It would be for four months, performing in our summer season of works. The Opera Company would give you full accommodation during that time, an apartment of your own for the duration of your contact. And you remember Teatro di San Carlo, no?"

Georgina nodded.

"Yes, it would all be performances at Teatro di San Carlo. It's the main theatre we're using these days, the other two smaller ones are closed for renovations so it's San Carlo all the way."

"I remember San Carlo. And what sort of works are the Company planning for the season?"

"The usual ones, you've probably done them before. Piccinni, Gluck and Salieri. You're an experienced hand at it all and I have no doubt you'd rise to the occasion. So, how about it Signorina Hartley?"

"Yes, let's do it! In boca al lupo!"

Signore Giovanazzo beamed. "Crepe! It's always so good to be working with such an experienced performer of your calibre, Signorina. The whole Company will be delighted when they hear the news. Now, I must dash off to Venice tomorrow, I need to get things going for the coming season. I'll send round a boy with the funds for your trip tomorrow, then if you set off in a couple of weeks, tie up whatever you need to here, and I'll see you on the first of June."

"Pleasure doing business with you, Signore," Georgina said.

"Likewise, Signorina."

The pair shook hands and went about their separate ways.

Chapter Sixteen

"You can't carry on like this, for God's sake!" Xavier paced around his eldest brother's study.

Edgar sighed from his seat behind his desk. "I have to. It's my duty."

"You keep saying that, brother, but what duty are you performing when you're forcing yourself to play the martyr?"

Rubbing the crux of his nose and forehead between his thumb and forefinger, Edgar was grave. "I *love* this family, don't you ever forget that! What I do, the choices I make will have a direct effect on the choices of each of you. The girls, they need to make a good match. I need a wife of good background so you all, especially the girls, can make good matches for yourselves."

"You misread the situation," Xavier said, "you're an earl. You can make your own decisions."

"Oh come on -"

Xavier continued, as though Edgar hadn't uttered a word. "The rest of us will be *fine*. We're Weatherbys. This is an earldom. We're not some group of social climbers who need to worry about who we're marrying and who we're associating with at every turn."

"It's not that simple though," Edgar muttered, "if you were in my position, you wouldn't be saying things like this."

"Maybe not, maybe there's a lot I'm not seeing," Xavier made his way towards the door before turning back to face his eldest brother, "but all I'm saying is don't make yourself into a martyr."

With that final comment, Xavier exited the room and left his brother alone in the study to contemplate the future.

Upstairs, Philomena entered the library. Deep mahogany bookshelves lined the walls on three sides, their varied leather and cloth tomes encompassing every subject of interest to at least one Weatherby. A grand set of lead lattice windows adorned the bookless-wall. In the centre of the library stood a large table and comfortable set of chairs. Atop the table was a sepia-toned globe which every Weatherby child of her generation had used as part of their geography studies at one time or another.

She loved it in here, as did her younger siblings, and so had Belinda back before she was married. Xavier too spent many happy hours in this room, though most of these these days seemed with the aim of instructing the younger Weatherbys rather than for his own reading entertainment.

The only sibling who did not visit the library much was the family patriarch himself. Philomena mused as to why this might be. Casting her mind back to before Edgar became the earl, she could not recall a time when he had a great passion for reading. While he had done well in his studies at Eton and at Oxford, they always seemed a means to an end for him and he was far more interested in hunting and horses from a tender age.

Shrugging internally, Philomena picked *The Mysteries of Udolpho* off the shelves and smiled to herself. Perfect reading for a winter's day.

Belinda sat at the small amber wooden table awaiting her brother's entrance. Compared with the Faversham's London residence, it was of equal luxury and similar size despite the differences in degree of rank of their respective owners.

The door swing open to reveal Edgar himself, replete in a blue waistcoat, beige pantaloons and white shirt.

"Brother, how are you this afternoon?" Belinda said.

The pair began to exchange pleasantries before Edgar made his way to where Belinda sat and joined her at the table.

A maidservant placed a pot of tea on the table and Edgar poured for the pair.

"So, how goes the marriage mart this season?" Belinda asked. "I hear you have been meeting with quite a few ladies and their mamas."

"About as well as can be expected," Edgar said.

Belinda sipped her tea and eyed him thoughtfully. "Anyone to whom you might ask for her hand in marriage?"

"Not yet."

"That's a shame. It would be nice to have a Countess of Weatherby again."

Edgar gave a wry smile. "To go with your position as duchess, Your Grace?"

"Something like that," she said. "But in all seriousness, maybe it's worth your while to consider a bride from beyond the usual suspects of the ton."

"Belinda, there's a family reputation to uphold."

She smiled softly. "Of course. But I do not think the ton is the only place to find a bride who will preserve the family reputation and strengthen the Weatherby line. And I say this as the only married Weatherby of our generation, but what I have seen really matters in a marriage is the commitment the couple make to their vows and to each other." She took a sip of her tea. "If the bride and the groom both mean their vows, really sincerely mean them, and they are both committed to the family and to each other then that is what matters most of all. Not both being from the ton."

Edgar looked at his sister with eyes anew. It was as though he was seeing her, really truly seeing her for the first time. For the past two decades he had always been the older brother to her younger sister and from when she was nine to the day she married, he had been her head household and she had been his responsibility. She had always fulfilled the role of obedient younger sister so well. Yet in the past eighteen months since her marriage to the duke, she had changed. And he had known on one level that that would be the case the moment he gave her away at her wedding but now he was seeing it and it was really sinking in. She was a woman who knew more than she let on. A matriarch of society, she was a duchess and had crossed a boundary into a whole new level of society.

"There's no way it could work," he said. "I must marry a bride from the ton."

"Oh, Edgar." Sympathy shone in her eyes. "It can work. If you want to fight for it. If you want to fight for her."

Edgar tried to maintain some dignity but it was a struggle. "Sister, I do not know of whom you speak."

"Oh please do not insult my intelligence. You know full well exactly who I mean. Miss Hartley," she replied.

Edgar pinched the top of his nose between thumb and forefinger and looked at the floor. He sighed.

Belinda sat in silence and watched the expressions change on her brother's face.

The pair sat like that for several minutes until Edgar looked at his sister and said, "I have already caused enough hurt, I cannot allow myself to be the cause of any more."

"Who would you hurt if you married Miss Hartley?" asked Belinda.

"The family and Miss Hartley herself."

"Well on your first point, it would not really hurt us. We, all of us, want nothing more than for you to be happy."

"And happiness is what I want for each of you," Edgar said. "But my being the earl means I cannot put my happiness above yours. I have to put all of your interests first and foremost. Your marriage prospects matter."

Belinda gave a wry glance and met her brother's eyes.

Edgar let out a surprised chuckle before continuing. "Well, not your own marriage prospects, sister. I am well aware of your most fortuitous and excellently suited match. But the prospects for all of our younger siblings."

"I think it is not as complex as you might believe," Belinda said. "Xavier will be able to have almost any bride he wants. Philomena and Genevieve, yes they will end up on the marriage mart at some point, but they have an earl for a brother and a duchess for a sister. And Lionel too, when the time comes, he will be fine. The ton is hardly going to turn its back on four such well connected young people. And on your second point, how do you fear hurting Miss Hartley?"

"By placing her in a situation for which she is grossly ill prepared," Edgar said.

Belinda took a sip of tea before she spoke. "Becoming a duchess, that was hard. Granted, the preparation I had through my education, especially being able to read my way around a ledger, made for a somewhat easier time. But there was still so much to learn, and it was from trusted ladies and later my husband that I gained my instruction. Should you marry Miss Hartley, I am happy to return the favour from those ladies and pass along what I know."

He scrunched his brow together and blinked several times. What his eldest, beloved sister was proposing made sense on one hand. Yet would Georgina even be interested? Would she want to retain her status as an independent woman of the stage for the rest of her days?

He schooled his facial features into the expression of the serious, considered Earl of Weatherby and gave a brisk nod. "Thank you sister, you have given me much to ponder. Your most kind offer shall not go unacknowledged."

Belinda stifled an internal laugh. Heavens, at times like this her brother bore a more than striking resemblance to her husband! Both men could be so serious when they were nervous, after all. And from experience of living with the Earl of Weatherby for the bulk of her life, she knew that beneath Edgar's outwardly poised and authoritative demeanour lay a foundation of insecurity and fear. Fear of letting the family down, fear of disgracing the Weatherby name and fear of being a disappointment.

❧❧❧❧❧❧ ❧❧❧❧❧

As the musicians began to play a hornpipe, the ball's attendees formed two lines, the women on one side of the room and the men on the other.

Edgar stood between the Viscount Malmesbury, that insufferable bore, and the much more tolerable Baron Durham. A very practical and down to earth man, someone with whom he had common ground, thought Edgar.

Knowing the moves by heart, the men stepped forward towards the line of women opposite them, each bowing at the woman directly facing him before offering her their right hand.

Edgar took the hand of a sweet faced brunette. He'd met her once before. Miss Catherine Chevalier. A pleasant enough young lady, exactly the sort his parents would have wanted him to wed.

Catherine smiled at Edgar as they danced together. Raised to be every inch the lady, she said demurely, "my lord, don't you just love this piece? Bach is one of my favourites."

"Quite so, he is very talented," Edgar replied. "Tell me, what do you think of Beethoven?"

"Ah, I never could enjoy his music," Catherine giggled, "far too serious for me!"

With that, she laughed and jumped with vigour at the most energetic part of the piece.

Well, what are common interests really worth, thought Edgar. Someone like Catherine Chevalier could be the right choice for his future and the continuation of the Weatherby line. Catherine had been raised from birth in the same world as Edgar; she understood implicitly the rules, regulations and standards of the aristocracy. With a wife like Catherine, there would never be any need to explain how society social events ran, how to run a dinner party, how to manage a large household with dozens of servants. All of that was the role Catherine had been primed to play to perfection.

As the piece drew to an end, Catherine and Edgar bowed to one another.

"Miss Chevalier," Edgar said, "would you care for another dance?"

"Oh why yes!" Catherine was still young, this being her very first season out in society, and she was not yet jaded like so many of the twenty-somethings that surrounded them.

The pair continued to dance as the string quartet struck up another tune.

❧ ⸱ ◆ ⸱ ❧

CHAPTER SEVENTEEN

The boat bobbed roughly as it pulled up at the shore of Venice. Georgina twitched the curtain aside, peeping out at life in all its many variants. She could see a juggler entertaining a crowd of visitors and mothers carrying young children, hurrying them away from the distractions of the street performers.

Georgina gave a wry smile. It always seemed to be the way that visitors let themselves get sucked in by all the distractions a place had to offer while the locals themselves had long ago learnt to ignore them and carry on about their business.

Burly men tied the ropes of the boat to the dock and the vessel began to stabilise.

Passengers began filing off the boat and Georgina joined them.

Once on the dock, she was immediately met by Signore Giovanazzo, a representative of the Venetian Opera Company who she knew well from her days on the London stage.

"Ah, Miss Hartley! It is so good to see you." He bowed and kissed her hand.

"You too, Signore Giovanazzo. I trust you have been keeping well?" she replied.

After going through the usual pleasantries, Signore Giovanazzo said, "Come this way, please, signora. I'll have my boys take your trunk to your new accommodation."

The pair made their way along the shore and Signore Giovanazzo directed Georgina through the maze of streets until they arrived at a pretty eggshell building, adorned with maroon shutters on every window.

"This is it, Miss Hartley." He unlocked the door and held it open for her.

She entered a hall with a black and white chequered floor, pale orange walls and mirrors placed intermittently along the sides. A maid appeared from a door off the hall and curtsied to Georgina.

"I'll leave you to get settled here, the boys will be along with your trunk soon. Then I'll be round tomorrow morning," Signore Giovanazzo said.

✦✦✦ ✦✦✦

Georgina sat on the bed in her new room. For the next four months, this would be home. And unlike in England, she had no need of a protector while she was here. The wages on the Venetian stages were far higher than those in London and, unlike in England, opera companies in the City of Canals put on accommodation for their performers.

It was a shame on some levels to be away from England relatively soon after returning, but financially being back in Southern Europe made so much sense. She hoped she would get used to it.

A blessing of the whole situation was that she would not have to come face to face with Edgar anytime soon.

She still loved him, deeply and intensely, but it was not healthy for her to stay in a city where a man she could never truly have resided.

Better for everyone that she be hundreds of miles away, ready to start anew.

She was good at starting over, at reinventing herself. Ever since she had been spotted by the vicar all those years ago, she had constantly been the fish out of water who had to recreate herself to survive.

First she want from rural poverty as the daughter of agricultural labourers, someone who was never expected to amount to anything beyond farm work and raising children, to being part of the vicar's middle class household where she learnt to read and write and honed her vocal talent with regular visits from singing masters the vicar knew.

And, alongside the vicar's daughters, she learnt the basics of how to run a middle class household. Not that she'd ever need to know that, she thought, but the vicar insisted in case she ever decided she didn't want to be a singer.

Who knows, the vicar's wife had said, she may even end up an innkeeper's wife one day!

Georgina scoffed at that. As if she'd ever be anyone's wife, innkeeper or otherwise.

She grew wistful. Though she would not change the education she had received thanks to the vicar for all the world, the day she stepped foot inside that vicarage as a resident and not as a visitor marked the dividing line between one world and another. Between one future and another.

Because no matter how hard she tried, once she left the world of the agricultural labourers she could never ever go back. She knew too much about the outside world, and was too educated. Whoever heard of an agricultural labourer who could speak French and Italian, dance the cotillion and sing an aria by Mozart?

Yet, she never truly belonged in the middle class world of the vicar and his family either. For all their kindnesses, she ultimately was only there as a charity case. A highly talented and promising young woman, but a charity case nonetheless. And a charity case to whom no one could afford to give a dowry of any note once the vicar's investments fell through.

So at eighteen, when the vicar's wife and the tutors had nothing more to teach her, she had decided to up sticks and try her luck in Bath. She soon found work on the stage and found her first protector too.

For the past seven years, she had flitted from city to city across England, France and Italy, in each place trying to find somewhere to belong.

But she was a misfit everywhere.

Life on the road was fun for the first few years, and it granted her more freedoms than many other English-women, but it was also a tiring, rootless existence. The more and more she travelled, the more and more she came to learn that the lot of women was essentially the same throughout Western Europe. She didn't know much about the world beyond, but from her personal experience leaving England had not meant a whole new world of opportunity and equality for a woman like her.

For a brief time when she was with Edgar, she had let herself dream of spending the rest of her life with him. He loved her and she loved him. It should have been simple.

But love is never simple.

However much he loved her, his duty would always be to his title and to the Weatherby legacy. His focus had to be on finding a suitable bride from the ton.

Regardless of what Lord Redditch had told her all those years ago, about the rare occasions when noblemen marry for love and marry their mistresses, such a situation was outlandish.

If she knew nothing else, she knew that when push came to shove Edgar would choose duty every time.

Yes, she told herself. She had made the right decision. Venice was the place for her to start over and move on from Edgar.

CHAPTER EIGHTEEN

Clouds hung low over the Renfregh estate, casting patches of grubby shadow hither and thither.

Edgar picked up the rifle and aimed it at the flock of birds. Pulling the trigger with expert precision, several of the birds fell from the sky shortly after his action.

"Good shot," Xavier called.

Edgar gave a courteous nod in his brother's direction and then aimed the gun at the sky again. Time for round two.

Bang! Bang! Bang!

From boyhood, hunting had been one of his favourite pastimes. As a very young boy his father had taught him the art and as an adult he enjoyed partaking either alone or with his siblings or friends. But now he was barely paying attention to what he was doing, getting no enjoyment from it at all. It was merely a distraction. A distraction from the thoughts of Georgina that ran through his mind at all hours of the day and night. He could not get her out of his mind, try as he might. He was losing the battle.

Bang! Bang! Bang!

More birds fell from the sky, the gamekeepers running onto the field to collect the carcases. Most would find the way into a stew or pie, a few might even take a starring role on Edgar's dinner table as a roast.

Xavier took his turn and pointed his own rifle at the sky.

After another quarter of an hour of shooting, Xavier turned in Edgar's direction and said, "That's enough for me, I'm going to head back in. Are you coming?"

Edgar growled. "No, I'll stay out here for a while."

"Alright," Xavier said. "Well I'll see you at dinner then."

With that, Xavier made his way towards the patio and the french doors of the house, leaving Edgar to continue endlessly shooting the birds.

Xavier had organised the shooting as a way to calm his brother down and get him out of his own head. After all, Edgar had been a keen marksman for as long as the second son could remember and he had hoped an afternoon's shooting would bring Edgar back to the happy memories of their shared childhood when they would regularly go hunting with their father.

Yet today Edgar had seemed to merely shoot on autopilot, his head nowhere near the reality on the ground of a shooting party.

Xavier had a sneaking suspicion that Edgar was still wrapped up in thoughts of Miss Hartley.

Dejected that his plan had not worked and deeply concerned about his brother, Xavier entered the doors and made his way to his chambers to change out of his hunting attire into something more suitable for a dinner in a stately home.

Dinner that evening was an awkward affair. At half past seven, the mealtime gong rang and those family members present at Renfregh assembled at the dining table with Edgar seated in his usual position at the head, Philomena to his left and Xavier on his right.

Edgar stared resolutely into the candle flame at the centre of the table, as though transfixed by it. His siblings shared a worried glance into one another's eyes.

The butler began to fill their glasses with white wine. Edgar picked up his glass and supped keenly.

"So, Philomena, what have you been reading lately?" Xavier said. He knew it was a lost cause to try to engage in conversation with his oldest brother tonight.

Philomena began to speak about the latest pamphlets she had acquired. Xavier nodded politely while Edgar let the conversation wash over him, barely hearing a single word his siblings uttered.

A footman entered the room, carrying a large silver tureen.

"My lords, my lady, may I present to you the first course. Celery soup," said the butler.

The footman placed the tureen on the table and began to serve each family member.

Xavier and Philomena began to eat the dish but Edgar's spoon lay untouched on the table.

"What's wrong, brother?" Philomena turned her head to Edgar. "Are you feeling unwell?"

Edgar sighed internally and picked up his spoon. "No, no, I'm distracted, that's all."

His two siblings shared another concerned look across the table.

The meal continued through each course in the same stilted fashion, with Edgar almost completely disconnected from what was going on and his sister and brother trying to keep up a polite discourse.

⁂

After dinner was finished and the footmen had cleared the table, Edgar excused himself and slunk away to his chambers.

Philomena and Xavier, meanwhile, sat together on a settee in the blue drawing room. The lights of the candles flickered as they cast a warm glow around the edges of the room.

"So, brother, what *is* going on with Edgar?" said Philomena.

Xavier smiled wryly. Trust his sister to get straight to the point and not bother with social niceties. "This isn't completely my story to tell, but I'm going to share what I can with you because after his behaviour at dinner this evening, you deserve to have some understanding of what's happened."

"Go on."

"It's a matter of the heart. Edgar had an involvement with a woman that didn't turn out well. He's in large part to blame and he admits that himself, but it's also because the woman isn't from our strata of society," said Xavier.

Philomena's mouth was wide open.

"And because she wasn't from our station, Edgar didn't believe marriage could ever work between the two of them, so he broke it off. Then they were back together for a short while, before she left him."

Philomena's hand was on her mouth, such was her level of surprise.

Xavier continued with his explanation. "Edgar hasn't been coping at all with what happened. I haven't seen him struggle like this in years, not since mama and papa passed. It's really affected him more than I or I think even he thought that it would. He really does love her, but the stubborn fool won't admit it to himself and is too caught up in what he thinks the ton want -"

"To hell with the ton!" Philomena cried.

Xavier chuckled. "I knew you'd say that."

"Well, it's true," she said. "The whole concept is rotten to the core. The whispers, the gossip. Why is the ton so elite, why do we even have elites at all?"

"You're sounding awfully radical, sister," Xavier said with mirth.

"That I am, but I'm beyond caring. If a group of so-called elites, the crème de la crème of society, includes such dregs as the Reynolds family then what does it all stand for? Just snobbery and pointless innuendo to the exclusion of people who might actually have something more worthwhile to contribute than many of the members of the ton. I love Edgar, I really do, but sometimes he can be so pigheaded."

"That's true," Xavier said.

She sighed. "I don't know how to help him."

"Nor do I. He's his own man, he needs to make the decisions for himself."

"I agree. But thank you for telling me what's been going on. I'll think on it."

Philomena entered the modiste's shop, the bell jangling softly behind her. From the depths of the shop, she could hear Jean Cookson's trill voice in conversation with what sounded like a delivery boy.

"I heard about the Earl of Weatherby and Georgina Hartley. Good for her, giving him the boot," said the boy.

"Yes, he really messed her around. She made the right choice," Jean replied.

The conversation raised Philomena's interest. The Earl of Weatherby was *her* brother, so why on earth were a delivery boy and a modiste talking about him in the same sentence as Georgina Hartley? The only Georgina Hartley she had ever heard of was the soprano who often graced the floorboards of the stages in Covent Garden. Moreover, what was all this about the earl messing Georgina Hartley around, and Georgina making a choice that Jean thought was the right one? The mind boggled.

"Well, farewell Miss Cookson," said the delivery boy.

Curses! Jean would come into the main part of the shop and see the sister of the man she had just been gossiping about. How awkward for everyone! Resolving she needed to carry out further investigation before making any moves, Philomena quickly turned on her heel and exited the building.

The carriage rattled westwards.

"Faster man!" Edgar banged on the ceiling of the carriage with the metal head of his obsidian walking cane. Turning to Xavier, he was clearly exasperated. "We need to be in Bath by nightfall, what the devil are they playing at?"

"Brother, do not worry," Xavier said, "we are making good time as it is."

Edgar practically growled in frustration. Nothing today was going his way. Nothing had felt right since the day Georgina left him that note. That blasted note telling him she was walking out of his life for good, to leave him to find a suitable wife of good background to become the next Countess of Weatherby.

"How can you be so calm?" Edgar snapped.

Not this old performance, thought Xavier. I'm not going to put up with this cantankerousness all the way to Bath, elder brother or not. "Well, I'm not the one who's been pining for the same woman for weeks, who left him because she seems to have her head screwed on far better than him!"

"You don't know what you're talking about."

"Oh don't I? Brother, I've seen you play the martyr for months and months over not being able to have Miss Hartley, all in the name of some wildly misplaced perception of what it means to fulfil your duty as earl. Then she finally tires of your martyrdom and now you're an angry snarling bear who is lost to reason."

The carriage pulled up outside the Weatherby family's home on The Circus.

Thank Heavens this journey has finally finished, thought Xavier. Spending another minute sitting opposite to his oldest brother was hardly an appealing proposition. Xavier respected and admired his eldest brother greatly, but his behaviour over the past few weeks had been nothing short of a nightmare.

A footman opened the carriage door and Edgar stormed out.

Xavier watched his brother bound into the house with an agitated step.

Sighing to himself, Xavier got out of the carriage and made his way into the property.

The usual servants were awaiting him, the butler at the head of the line giving a bow, next to the housekeeper who smiled and curtsied followed by several footmen and maids.

Nodding to them, Xavier said a few words to the butler and housekeeper and excused himself to head upstairs.

Walking past his brother's room, he was not too surprised to see the door was already slammed shut. Clearly Edgar shared Xavier's desire to be alone after their disastrous carriage ride.

Yes, thank you Edgar, thought Xavier, for making that journey so pleasant. What a privilege and delight it had been. He rolled his eyes internally and entered the room he called his own while in Bath.

In his own room, Edgar paced up and down, up and down. He berated himself for losing his composure in the carriage. Definitely *not* the behaviour of a gentleman. He held himself to higher standards than that, he wanted to lead not lose his head. Xavier didn't deserve to be spoken to like that, after all, and Edgar knew he'd been terrible company the whole way. If someone had said Edgar had to spend the journey with a copy of himself, he would most certainly have refused.

Running his hands through his hair, he felt his waves of anger begin to roll into despair. How could he have lost Georgina? She was the best thing in his life and he hadn't realised it until it was too late!

But what choice did he have?

Like Xavier had said earlier, Georgina had a lot more sense than Edgar because she had realised their dalliance needed to be over once and for all as their two stations in life were completely incompatible. Irreconcilable, even.

Kicking off his boots, Edgar lay flat on his back in the centre of the bed and wrapped his arms behind his head. He stared at the ceiling and ruminated on what to do next.

He really did not feel like talking to anyone else. Besides, he would hardly be the best company right now.

He sat up and rang the servants bell.

A minute later, there was a knock on the door.

"Enter!" called Edgar.

The door swung open and a footman stepped in.

"Run me a bath please," Edgar said wearily.

"Very good, my Lord." The footman bowed and then left the room.

Edgar pinched the top of his nose between his thumb and forefinger and tried to get his head straight. Georgina had made her decision, and it was the logical one, the best one for her to make given what he had to offer her. The life of a mistress for years and years! What sort of a life was that?

No, she had made the right choice.

So why did his heart still ache?

Why had the situation made him so furious with himself?

Surely if it were the right choice, he would be at peace with her decision rather than feeling as he did at this moment.

Another knock at the door. The footman had returned to advise Edgar his bath was ready.

Edgar rose from the bed and made his way down the corridor to the bathroom. He shut the door behind himself and began to remove his clothing, first his waistcoat, then his shirt, undershirt and finally his breeches.

He looked across to the chair at the edge of the room and, as anticipated, the footman had left fresh clothes there ready for him.

Well, if nothing else, he had good staff he could rely on so that made life a little easier.

Edgar stepped into the bath and submerged himself in the warm, clear water. He lay still for several minutes, letting the water soothe his aching muscles. Then he reached over to the bath table and grabbed the soap, sudding it up in the water, and cleansed himself.

The grime and the dirt from the carriage ride came away from his skin and he felt a smidgen calmer.

He dipped his head under the bathwater for a few seconds.

Then he took the shampoo and rubbed it through his dark black hair, massaging his scalp as he did so.

For a second time, he put his head under the water and then resurfaced.

Worn out from the journey and his experiences of the past few weeks, Edgar lay still in the bath for several more minutes.

Then he stepped out to dry himself off and get dressed.

⁕⁕⁕

Edgar headed down the staircase to the main hallway.

As he turned to leave the house, he said to the butler, "I won't be back for a while, so please don't wait up."

"Very good, my lord." The butler gave a bow.

Edgar affixed his top hat to his head and took his favourite cane in hand.

Striding down the path and onto the street, he appeared the very picture of a man in command and in control of himself. But he was anything but. This was one of the lowest points of his life, he had been rejected by the person he loved most in all the world and it was essentially his own fault. His own stubbornness had gotten him into this situation.

After about an hour, he found himself outside Bath Abbey near the Pump Room. How he had ended up here, he did not know because his head had been preoccupied with thoughts of Georgina ever since he left the house in The Circus earlier on.

This was not a good place to be for a man who was trying to let go of his desire for one Miss Georgina Hartley. It was flooded with the memories of the two of them together in happier times, when he had purchased ribbons and trinkets for her, when they had strolled contentedly through the hilly streets of the city and when he had spent many joyous nights with her at one of the Weatherby family houses.

It would not do to dwell on the past, to ruminate on past mistakes, Edgar told himself sternly.

He needed to focus on more practical, pressing matters.

He needed to find himself a high society wife and he needed to get serious about it.

Later that day, as the dying strains of sunlight shone weakly through the window, Edgar sat at the desk in his study with fresh resolve and picked up his quill. So poor was the light in the room that he had already lit several candles. Their flames flicked and danced, casting a warm amber glow about the room.

Edgar rested a hand on the top corner of the parchment and proceeded to write his checklist.

"Requirements for a wife:

1. She must be of noble or gentle birth.

2. She must be of childbearing age.

3. She must desire a Christian marriage according to the rites of the Church of England.

4. She must want to have children.

5. She must want to be a countess.

6. She must be trained, or be prepared to be trained in the ways of being a countess, such as being a society hostess.

7. She must be intelligent."

He put down his quill and keenly reviewed the seven requirements he had jotted down. Yes, those would serve very well indeed, he told himself.

All he needed to do now was find a lady who met those seven stipulations and he would be set for a life of respectable responsibility. He would be able to carry on the Weatherby line and secure a countess who would guide his two youngest sisters in the ways of being a good wife while he guarded the family. He would fulfil the duties in exactly the way he was born to do. In every way.

And as for love, it had brought him nothing but trouble and pain. An ocean of heartbreak and heartache. It was a dangerous, frivolous concept. Love could go to the devil for all he cared.

$$\text{❧} \cdot \text{✦} \cdot \text{❧}$$

CHAPTER NINETEEN

Back in London a fortnight later and newly resolved to find himself a society bride, Edgar set himself forth on the marriage mart.

Thus he found himself inside the drawing room of the Baron Chevalier's London townhouse, taking tea with the baroness and discussing her eldest unmarried daughter.

"Oh yes, Catherine as you will see is very accomplished on the piano," said the Baroness Chevalier, as she leant forwards to where Edgar was sitting on the white settee.

"I should like to hear her play." Edgar picked up his teacup and drank from it.

"Would you?" The Baroness Chevalier clasped her hands together. "That's wonderful. I'll send for her." The matriarch turned to where the maid stood and nodded to her. The maid curtsied and left the room.

A minute later, Miss Catherine Chevalier entered the room. Still in the midst of her first season, her face was the picture of innocence and naivety.

"Catherine, dear, give Lord Weatherby a demonstration of your skills on the piano," her mother said with a smile.

Catherine went over to the piano and began to play. A lilting piece by Mozart. One thing was for certain, the Baroness Chevalier had not lied when she said her daughter was very accomplished on the piano. Technically she was highly proficient and she added an emotional verve that made her playing stand out.

Edgar was impressed. "Bravo," he said and applauded when Catherine finished the short piece.

The following day, Edgar sat in his study ruminating on his meeting with Catherine Chevalier.

What benefit was piano playing to a countess? Not much, thought Edgar ruefully. Catherine was a sweet young woman who one day would make an excellent wife for a member of the ton, but deep down in his heart of hearts he knew that Catherine was not the one for him. She was far too inexperienced in all manner of life matters to be able to keep up with a rake who was trying to reform, such as himself.

He crossed her name off his list and began to pen her mother a quick, polite note to advise he would not be pursuing courtship with her daughter.

Walking around the Serpentine with his hands in his pockets, Edgar cut a solitary figure. He made for a curious sight.

One of England's most eligible bachelors but a man who seemed to not have a fixed destination in life. He stopped to watch the ducks swimming on the pond. How simple their lives seemed, with their life of swimming in the water, laying eggs and raising young. No concerns about social class or the expectations of the ton for them!

A gentleman he recognised, the Baron Yeovil, approached him. "Good day, Weatherby," the baron said. He tipped his hat at Edgar and Edgar returned the courteous gesture.

"Good day, Yeovil," Edgar said.

"How goes the search for a bride? Are you having much joy on the marriage mart?" Yeovil's voice was far too chipper, thought Edgar.

"Nothing as of yet," the earl sighed.

Yeovil patted Edgar on the shoulder. "Never mind, old chap, something will come up soon! And you know, I've got a most enchanting cousin I would love to introduce you too. She's very witty and really the heart and soul of our family."

Edgar was intrigued. "Who is she may I ask? Have we met before?"

"I don't think you have. Her name is Lady Leonora Young-Hughes. Her father is a baron down in Dorset, very old established family. Came over with the Conqueror way back when," Yeovil chortled. "I really should introduce the two of you sometime."

Edgar nodded. "Yes, please do. I'm in London for the next couple of weeks, then I'll be heading up to Renfregh for a while."

"You won't regret it, old chap!" Yeovil's moonlike face beamed.

The ducks quacked almost like a chorus of approval. Maybe a Weatherby and Young-Hughes match was on the cards.

❧❧❧❧❧ ❧❧❧❧❧

A week later, Edgar found himself in Mrs Buppett's Tea Rooms sitting across from Lady Leonora Young-Hughes herself.

Mrs Buppett's Tea Rooms was one of the most popular eateries in London. As ladies from the upper and middle classes could rarely attend the bars and clubs frequented by their menfolk, establishments like Mrs Buppett's provided a refreshing spot for social conversation and community.

Lady Leonara laughed raucously. "And then Aunt Sally said to Cousin Mary, 'Well, why don't you just do it yourself?' And I simply could not believe it! Simply could not believe it!"

Edgar leaned forward in his seat. "Oh, and -"

"It reminds me of the time when Cousin Mary was trying to climb a tree and Cousin Jack tried to follow after her! He wasn't successful at all!" Lady Leonara let out another chortle.

"So then-"

"You know our Jack, he's always one to follow the leader," she continued, as though she had not heard Edgar's attempts to get a word in.

Edgar had never met Lady Leonara's Cousin Jack. As he was an eight year old boy, he and the earl had never had a reason to cross paths and very likely would not for at least another ten years.

While her passion and love for her family were to her credit, her complete self-absorption was something Edgar could not afford to overlook.

The Countess of Weatherby would need to be an excellent conversationalist if she was to host the parties and soirees he hoped she one day would. Part of her hostess duties would include making polite small talk to guests wherever they came from and being able to do that was as reliant on her being a good listener as on her knowing how to string a witty sentence together.

And Edgar himself did not fancy spending decades with a woman who never let him get a word in edgewise. He was a man of strong opinions and wanted a wife who had her own views. Certainly, they might debate their respective points of view, but he wanted an equal when it came to conversations.

He sighed internally.

Yes, Lady Leonora Young-Hughes was not a viable prospect for the future Countess of Weatherby. For the sake of politeness, he would have to sit through the rest of this excruciating rendezvous and then cross Lady Leonora off his list of potential brides.

The following week and Edgar was back again in Mrs Buppett's Tea Rooms, this time seated opposite a young woman in a deep purple silk day dress.

"So Miss Vardon, do you have a preference for town or country living?" Edgar said to his companion.

"Whatever you want, my lord." Miss Cordelia Vardon batted her eyelashes and tilted her head downwards before angling her eyes up towards him.

"Right," Edgar said, "And what about recreation? How do you see yourself at leisure once you are wed?"

Miss Vardon smiled into her cup of tea. "Oh I don't know my Lord, whatever you want."

Edgar growled internally.

Did this woman have no opinions? Did she stand for nothing?

All she seemed to do was smile coyly and give noncommittal answers that turned every question he asked her straight back onto him, as though she had no desire to make any decisions.

He definitely did *not* want a marriage where his wife deferred to him on every tiny thing.

He wanted a wife with personality, with her own views and thinking.

Yes, he wanted to be in alignment with her on the big issues but he strongly hoped she would come to agreement with him because she had come to that conclusion independently, rather than presenting herself as a blank piece of clay he could mould to his will. Some men might like that, but not Edgar.

This conversation is painful, thought Edgar. Another rendezvous he would have to sit through as a gentleman of good manners before leaving and cutting his losses.

❧ ❦

Edgar sighed and crossed Miss Cordelia Vardon's name off his list. She had been the final name on his list of several dozen candidates, across England and Wales, and not for want of trying had he come up empty handed with no fiancee to speak of. So many of them were lovely ladies who would doubtless make a fine wife for another man, but none of them were right for him.

None of them could hold a candle to Miss Georgina Hartley.

He groaned and held his head in his hands.

What was he going to do now?

❧ ❦

Philomena stormed into her eldest brother's office with a face like thunder. "I can't believe that you would get involved in something like this, brother!"

Edgar had been engrossed in paperwork and his sister's sudden entry made him jolt internally. However, on the surface he maintained his composure and looked up at her coolly. "It wouldn't hurt you to knock first, instead of coming in here screaming at me for a reason I do not understand."

"It's about Miss Hartley," Philomena said with a tone that insinuated an iceberg lurking beneath.

Edgar fought to maintain his composure. "Then you had better shut the door, sister."

Philomena did so and then turned again to her brother. She crossed her arms and said, "Well? Care to explain yourself?"

"I don't know what you mean. And besides, even if I did, I don't have to explain myself to you." Edgar fiddled with the quill between his fingers.

"Miss Hartley, you were using her like a - well I don't want to say the word, but you know what I mean. She's one of the best sopranos in England, we've all been to see her perform, what are you playing at?" Philomena gesticulated with her hands forming staccato points in the air.

"Philomena, I'm sorry you found out about my arrangement with Miss Hartley. But really it's none of your business. It was a completely consensual arrangement between two adults." Edgar pinched the top of his nose between his thumb and forefinger. "And besides, it's over now."

"What demon ran through you to even give you the idea to have such an arrangement? Normal gentlemen don't do that!" Philomena's voice was ice.

Edgar sighed. "Sister, I had hoped you would never find out about anything like this. Ever. In your whole entire life -"

"Well, now I have! Now I know my eldest brother, who need I remind you is supposed to be the *leader* of this family, has been cavorting around half of southern England with a soprano who he has tricked into his bed!"

"I never tricked her," Edgar said evenly.

"You must have!" Philomena held her hands in clenched fists at her sides, "Why else would any woman agree to that without marriage! How can you do that? Don't you have a conscience?"

"I do have a conscience. And I'm not the only gentleman who engages in such arrangements with singers, actresses and the like. How do you think those performing ladies afford the costumes they wear, the homes they live in, the carriages they travel in?"

"The theatres charge us enough for the tickets, surely they pass that along to the performers." Philomena's voice was quieter now as she grew more subdued at the horrific realisation.

Edgar shook his head sadly. "No, they pay the performers hardly a pittance."

"Then how can we all be expected to go to those theatres in good conscience?" Philomena said. "They're houses of sheer exploitation."

Edgar felt his cheeks burn in shame. His sister was absolutely right, but it was as though she had stepped in from another planet. It simply wasn't how things were done in England during the reign of George III. "You are correct, Philomena. But it's beyond the power of you or I to change it. Most gentlemen in London participate in it. You'd need to get almost all of them on side, to change their ways, before the system could even have a hope of changing."

"Then I shall make it my life's work to end that exploitative system," Philomena said resolutely.

"And I commend you for it." Edgar held his quill between forefinger and thumb.

"But brother, I cannot but ask - why did you partake in that system?" Philomena said, her hands now flat at her sides.

"Like I said, it was a consensual agreement between adults. And better a gentleman like me than a brute. Because there are brutes around." Hounslow and all the stories he had heard about him immediately sprung to Edgar's mind.

"It still doesn't make it right," Philomena said.

"Maybe it does, maybe it doesn't," Edgar said.

"But did you ever feel anything for her? Anything at all?" Philomena asked.

"Yes, yes I did. With more intensity than I have ever known, in fact," he replied.

"Then why did you let her go?"

"I ask myself that question dozens of times a day," Edgar said wistfully. "But it always comes down to a question of duty. Ultimately, my duty is to you and the rest of the Weatherby family, to do what is right for your interests."

"And what is right for *my* interests," Philomena said.

Oh Heavens, not this again, thought Edgar. Love her as he did, Philomena could infuriate him no end sometimes. "Your interests are for me to help you find a suitable husband who will treat you well, a gentleman who is befitted to your station in life."

"And that is all I am to expect out of life? All I am to experience?" Philomena's voice began to rise in volume.

"That is the main area for you, yes," Edgar said slowly.

"So it's alright for gentlemen to cavort with mistresses, as part of an exploitative theatre system, but all I can ever hope for is to find a husband fitted to my station?"

"Like I said, it's the main area for you to find a suitable husband. Not necessarily the only area, but the main area."

"And who are you a suitable husband for?"

"Sister, you forget yourself," Edgar said.

"I'm serious, brother. You talk of me finding a suitable husband. But who are you suited for? Surely you must marry at some point and produce an heir, so who will your wife be?" Philomena's voice was calmer now.

Edgar sighed. "I don't know. Some high born lady from the ton."

"You don't sound too enthralled about that prospect," Philomena laughed wryly.

"I'm not," Edgar nodded. "But it's my duty. What choice do I have?"

"Maybe you have more choices than you think. Why not try for someone who you have a real connection with, and forget about whether or not she's a high born lady from the ton?"

"That's very radical of you, Philomena," Edgar said.

"It goes with the territory," she said with a smile.

❦

CHAPTER TWENTY

Yardley Manor was the Weatherby estate's smallest country home. Located an hour's horse ride north of London, most of the family used it as an occasional bolthole to get away from the stresses of the city. With a relatively compact layout, it was more of a glorified Jacobean vicarage than a full blown stately home.

On this particular Tuesday, Edgar was the only member of the family present at Yardley Manor. He had chosen to come here to get away from the rest of the Weatherby clan, especially after his disastrous conduct in Bath and at Renfregh. He knew he had been thoroughly unpleasant company these past couple of months and needed space to think through what had transpired ever since he asked one Miss Georgina Hartley if he could be her protector.

He stood on the small wooden bridge that divided the pond in two. All around, the wind whistled gently through the willow trees as the refraction of the sunlight through their leaves cast an icy shimmering silver glow around the gardens. Willing himself to imbibe some of the serenity of the garden, he leant over the bridge and pondered the situation.

When he was young, before the death of his parents in that cruel shipwreck, he had imagined himself marrying a lady from the ton when he was around thirty years of age. He would have still been in the middle of receiving his training on how to be an earl from his father and would have had far more energy for matters of the heart than he had had over the past dozen or so years.

He had spent so long trying to do precisely what he thought his parents would have wanted, to live up to the Weatherby legacy, that he had completely lost sight of himself. Thinking back to his conversations with Xavier, he accepted now that there was more than one side to the Weatherby legacy. Certainly, the earl had a duty to run the estates well, to look after the rest of the family and to be loyal to the crown. Had he not performed those duties impeccably well? Done everything his parents could have ever wanted?

The one thing he had not done was marry and secure an heir. For years, years now, he had assumed he would marry a high born lady whom he did not love and who did not love him, secure some heirs through her and then they would live their separate lives. That was safest, after all, and hardly uncommon in the ton. Better to protect one's heart and find one's pleasures elsewhere. However, Georgina coming into his life had blown apart that assumption and he longed to have her as his wife. To be exclusively, to be with her forever and always, to be with her as man and wife in *every* sense of the word. He scoffed, thinking of the marriage vows almost the entire ton took and that he would one day take when he married as a baptised and confirmed member of the Church of England. What an irony. There it was in the marriage vows, *To love.* Both the husband and the wife vowed that to one another in every single Church of England wedding ceremony, as per the 1662 Book of Common Prayer. It was staring him right in the face and he had been blind to it all along. What was the first marriage vow a husband made? *To love. To love. To love.* A husband did not vow to concern himself with the background of his wife, or with keeping up with the Joneses. He first and foremost vowed to love. And that love extended to loving his wife as Christ loved the Church, loving his wife as he loved his own flesh, as it said in the Book of Common Prayer. And if he could not keep the first vow, *To Love*, if he only did it as a way to go through the motions of societal expectations then what good were the rest of his vows? He would also vow *To Comfort* his wife, *To Honour* her, *To Keep* her, and *forsaking all others keep only to her.*

What a farce it would be to go into a marriage already planning to keep a mistress, to have every intention of breaking the vow about forsaking all others and keeping only to his wife. Edgar's cheeks reddened in shame as he thought back to his earlier plan to marry a high born woman and keep Georgina on the side as his mistress. That was an absolutely appalling plan, one he could not ever envision himself carrying out now. Moreover, it would have made a disgraceful mockery of one of the founding reasons for marriage, as outlined by the Church of England, that of being a way to avoid fornication. Why on earth would someone marry with the full intent of fornicating? He was flabbergasted that he ever thought that was an acceptable, even advisable, course of action. Whoever he married deserved him to genuinely mean every single word of his wedding vows. He had a duty to his future wife to mean his wedding vows wholeheartedly, to fulfil them with every ounce of his being for the rest of their lives together. He could not take wedding vows that he did not sincerely, wholeheartedly and reverently mean.

He had to marry a woman who he loved and who he could comfort, honour, provide for and be faithful to for the rest of their lives. There was only one woman who he had ever loved in his whole life. Miss Georgina Hartley. And though he had tried to find a lady of the ton whom he could love, it was all in vain. No one else could ever compare to Georgina. If he were to marry, it would be to Georgina or he would not marry at all.

Deep down in his heart, he realised he had come to this conclusion a while ago but only now had the courage to admit it to himself.

All of his adult life, he had prided himself on being a man who stood for values that really mattered. To the crown, to the earldom, to duty, to courage, to the Weatherby line. Yet so far he had been a master of disaster when it came to matters of the heart and of marriage. He berated himself.

For over a decade it was as though he had a rigid iron rod running vertically down his back. The rod dictated how he stood and how he sat and how he moved through the world. It provided support, made him have the perfect posture so anyone who saw him would think "there goes a man in control of himself, a well bred gentleman."

But the rod was built on a false premise, the premise that he had to marry a high born woman of the ton and it did not matter whether or not he was faithful to her or loved her, but only that she was high born.

Once upon a time, that rod had provided him support in a situation where he had really needed its rigour, back when the grief of the death of his parents was still freshly raw. It had allowed him to stay strong for his siblings and to run the estates as best he knew, for his family and for the tenants.

As the years wore on, however, it had become more and more of a burden. The rod constrained him, unflinchingly demanding he remain upright at all times as the very definition of English nobility. With the rod on his back, he could not deviate from the one and only direction it required of him. He had no freedom, no ability to do anything but perform the rigid role of the Earl of Weatherby, when he was wearing the rod.

And the rod had grown to hurt. Hurt. Hurt. Hurt. For something that had originally been intended to guard him from drowning in the pain of losing his parents, and hadn't it failed at that, it had instead grown into a source of agony in and of itself.

Now it was time to cast off the rod. It served him no longer.

If you stand for nothing, then what really are you worth, Edgar thought to himself. It was time to stop living according to what other people wanted and decide for himself for a change. Certainly, Edgar never wanted to hurt his family. But forcing himself into decades of unhappiness benefitted no one in the long run.

He knew he'd never be truly happy unless he was with Georgina.

So Georgina it had to be.

His future was her.

He had no idea where she might be now. She disappeared into the night leaving only the note telling him that she was choosing to exit his life.

Ruminating on where Georgina might be or who at least might have information, he recalled her friend Jean Cookson. A tenuous lead, but as good as anything he had to go on given his current situation of knowing nothing.

He made his way to the stables and set off on horseback to the city.

Clattering along the cobblestones of London, Edgar's horse gave one last push as he rode it towards the stables of Weatherby House. Dismounting, he handed care of the horse to the stableboys and immediately left the grounds. The stableboys looked at each other in confusion.

Edgar strode across the square and towards Jean Cookson's shop in Covent Garden. As he walked the familiar streets, he thought of all the happy times he had spent there with Georgina. How many times he had seen her performing at the opera! How many hours they had spent at his bachelor house, or at the house in Fitzrovia he provided for her as her protector! The late night séjours, talking about everything and experiencing a connection he had never felt before with another human being!

If only, if only, if only, he had often thought during those encounters with Georgina. If only she had been born a lady. If only I were not born into the aristocracy. If only society didn't care about class.

Well, vowed Edgar, he was not going to let any of those things get in the way of him being with Georgina any longer. The only thing that would stop him fighting for her was if she turned him down herself out of her own free will, and not because she thought it was best for him if she leave. Damn the class system!

He had reached Jean Cookson's modiste shop. Looking discreetly through the windows, it appeared she was the only person currently in there so he entered, the bell on the door jangling tinnily as he did so.

Jean had been engrossed in sorting through some fabric samples on her desk in the back storeroom. On hearing the jangling bell, she called, "Just a moment, madam!"

Making her way to the main part of her shop, she gaped in surprise at the person awaiting her. "My lord, what is the meaning of this?"

Edgar bowed his head. "Madam, please forgive my intrusion. I know I have no right to ask but I am hoping you know Miss Hartley's whereabouts?"

"I may and then again I may not. Not that it is any business of yours, my lord."

"I know I have no right to ask," Edgar said.

"No, you don't have that right," Jean said. "But you're doing so anyway."

"This is probably hard to believe, Madam, but I love Miss Hartley."

Jean scoffed. "You're hardly the first lord to say he loves a mistress, and you won't be the last."

"I mean it though." Edgar was earnest.

"Oh ho ho," Jean laughed derisively. "I know your kind. All you lords are the same. You declare great love to your mistresses, but a mistress is only ever a thing to men like you. A thing to use as you see fit and discard when you're finished with her. Tell me, my lord, how many mistresses have you had before?"

"What's that got to do with it?"

"Miss Hartley is certainly not the first mistress you've had. So, how. Many. Mistresses. Have. You. Had. Before?"

"Eight." Edgar tried to keep his voice even, but Jean was getting under his skin.

Jean raised an eyebrow. "And what makes Miss Hartley different from all the others?"

"I love Miss Hartley, genuinely and completely. With every fibre of my being. This isn't some young rake's obsession, I know what it might look like. But this is serious. I'm in my thirtieth year, I don't have time to mess around on youthful obsessions anymore!"

Jean's voice was even and emotionless. "So, what is this? Trying to get one last fling out of your system before you settle down and marry your high born wife? Because if it is, you've got no right going anywhere near Miss Hartley. She chose to leave you, need I remind you."

"I don't want a high born wife," Edgar said in exasperation.

A brief flash of realisation crossed Jean's features, before she regained control and her visage again became impassive. "I tell you where she is, you go, and then what?"

"I ask Miss Hartley for her hand in marriage. And if she says yes, she will become the Countess of Weatherby," said Edgar with an intensity of conviction Jean had rarely ever heard, not least of all from a lord in his dealings with low born commoners like herself or Georgina.

Jean laughed in disbelief. "My lord, that's absurd -"

"No it's not," Edgar said gruffly. "If Miss Hartley accepts, then she *will* become the Countess of Weatherby."

"Really, you mean it?" Jean's voice was softer now.

"More than anything. Miss Hartley will become the Countess of Weatherby if she wants to be, and I will stop at nothing for her to have everything in the world," Edgar said with conviction.

Jean shook her head in wonder. "I'll tell you what I know of where she's gone. God help me, if this doesn't work out, if you're *lying* to me then she'll have my guts for garters. She told me she was going to Paris, to stay with some people she knows over there and hopefully find some work. She said she'd stay with the Renoir family on Rue du Bac."

"Miss Cookson, thank you, sincerely."

"You're welcome, my lord."

And with that, Edgar strode out of Jean Cookson's modiste shop and headed towards the Weatherby mansion. So Paris it would be, he thought.

Edgar strode into the mansion and made his way up the stairs.

The servants he had passed on the way looked at one another in bemusement. First, the earl had rode in, left the horse in the stables and departed as quickly as he had arrived. Then, less than an hour later, he was in the mansion striding around like a man on a mission with a focus in his eyes that the servants had rarely ever seen before.

Edgar made his way to the library, a favourite haunt of the second eldest Weatherby son, and pushed open the door.

Just as Edgar expected, Xavier was inside conversing with Lionel and Genevieve about books.

"Xavier, brother, can I have a word?" Edgar said.

Xavier murmured a few words to his younger siblings and headed out into the corridor to meet the head of the family.

"Come into my study," Edgar said.

The pair crossed the corridor and Xavier entered his brother's study. Edgar followed and closed the door behind him, before making his way to the whisky decanter on his desk and pouring out two glasses of the amber liquid.

Handing a glass to his brother, Edgar said, "You were right all along, you know."

"Ah, so you've finally come to your senses," Xavier smirked. "We're to have a new Countess of Weatherby at last."

"Well, only if she agrees," Edgar said cautiously. "I haven't actually asked her yet. I found out from Miss Cookson that she went to Paris, though whether she's still there I have no clue."

"When are you leaving for France?"

"As soon as possible. I can make the evening coach to Dover if I leave within the next couple of hours," Edgar said.

"That's what I like to hear, being the martyr never suited you. If you pull this one off, this is going to be a story for the ages."

Xavier was developing a new level of admiration for his brother. Certainly he had long respected the role Edgar played in the family. They had both lost their parents when they were still of tender years but Edgar had drawn the short straw on top of that as he had the responsibilities of being an earl immediately thrust upon him many years earlier than he, and their parents, had anticipated. Edgar had risen to the challenge in the most admirable way, yet Xavier could see that internally his brother was struggling. So he was overjoyed to hear that for once in his life, Edgar was making a decision that best suited *him* rather than only thinking about what societal standards expected.

The two men spoke about arrangements for running the households and estates while Edgar was on the continent. The earl knew his brother was a capable deputy so his main concern was instead how the very youngest Weatherbys would cope with his sudden absence. But again, he knew Xavier had what it took to look after the family while he was away.

Finishing his whisky, Edgar looked at his pocket watch. Half an hour had elapsed since he had entered his study so he needed to get moving if he were to make tonight's Dover coach on time. He started for the door. "I'll take my leave now, but thank you for everything Xavier. Truly I mean it."

"I know. Now go and get your lady, brother."

CHAPTER TWENTY-ONE

Edgar was off. He couldn't quite believe it, but it was really happening. In twenty generations, no Earl of Weatherby had done what he was about to try to do. Marry a commoner. And his former mistress to boot. He had fought against taking this course of action for so long, bound as he was by the constraints of the society in which he lived, but he was giving up that fight now and was taking on a new one. The fight for Georgina's heart and for her forgiveness. He only hoped he would win.

Settling down into the carriage seats, he reflected on how he would be in Dover by this time tomorrow and from there it was a matter of finding a boat to take him to the continent.

After an uneventful journey through Kent, the carriage at last pulled into the Dover docks. Edgar had made this journey once before, when he went to the continent with his father when he was fifteen. With all his responsibilities as earl, he really had no time for unnecessary travel and instead left that to his younger brothers. But this trip was very necessary indeed. The entire future of his heart was at stake.

Disembarking the carriage, Edgar was hit by the putrid smell of seaweed and salt water. He wrinkled his nose. There were many reasons why he rarely went to the coast, and the foul odour was close to the top of the list.

Having brought no trunk with him and with only the canvas bag he was carrying, he had no need to organise a porter. What he needed to do was find a boat.

The boat rocked forward and back. Forward and back. Forward and back.

Edgar could feel himself growing queasy. Willing himself to maintain his composure, he made his way up to the deck and tried to keep his eyes focused on the horizon.

Gulls circled overhead in menacing circles, their cawing cries echoing down on the boat deck and drumming themselves through Edgar's brain. Most of the other passengers were still below deck, with Edgar and a couple of others being the only ones out in daylight.

"What shall we do with the drunken sailor, what shall we do with the drunken sailor," sang the sailors who were out on deck, attending to the needs of the boat.

Oh Heavens, thought Edgar, That singing was making everything worse. This sea was making him feel as though he were drunk and it was all he could do to stop himself from emptying his stomach. But as his head grew dizzier and dizzier he lost the battle.

The gulls continued their mocking cries overhead and the sailors carried on with their sea shanties. A lord who lacked his sea legs was not an uncommon sight on the English Channel, after all.

Finally landing in Calais after the journey from what felt like hell, Edgar was mightily relieved to be back on dry land. However, when he was on land it still felt like he was at sea, such was the sorry strength of his seasickness. Looking around the port, he could see the town centre was a short walk away so he made his way there. Just like in Dover, there was that wretched smell of salt and seaweed. Some things England and France regrettably had in common, thought Edgar.

Walking up the street, he pondered his next moves. First, he'd have to recover from this blasted seasickness. And wouldn't that be fun to deal with on the way back to England! Something to really look forward to. But once he'd gotten over the malady, he would need to make his way to Paris and find the Renoirs that Miss Cookson had mentioned when he saw her last. Then darling Georgina might, if he was very lucky, still be staying with them and he could ask her for her hand then and there. If not, he would have to make other plans.

After ten minutes, he found himself in the town centre. He vaguely remembered Calais from his time here coming and going on his trip with his father when he was fifteen, and recalled staying at a decent hotel in the town. Wracking his brain, he looked around the street and had an inkling that the hotel was a little way up the hill. He headed in that direction and after five minutes he was outside the dimly familiar building.

Laying down on the hotel bed, it was all he could do to try to rest. The trip so far had been exhausting and the seasickness had not helped matters one iota.

Sipping from the glass of water on the bedside table, he reflected on what it would take to give himself a chance of winning Georgina back and earning her hand in marriage. He understood now what it would take for her to become the Countess of Weatherby and he was committed to making it happen. Nothing would make him happier in life than to have her by his side as his lawful wedded wife.

He let thoughts of Georgina wash over him and drifted off to the land of dreams.

After a deep sleep, Edgar awoke the next morning in a state of confusion.

He was in oddly familiar surroundings.

Was he dreaming that he was back on that trip with his father, in that hotel in where was it again - Calais?

Then recalled that he really *was* in that hotel in Calais. And this time it was not because he was travelling with his father. This time around, he was on a mission to win back the woman he loved most of all in the entire world.

Sitting up in the bed, he was relieved to discover that the seasickness had passed. He got out of bed and prepared himself to face the day with a new spring in his step and a resolve to do better for Georgina.

❧ ❧

At around midday, he went for a walk around the town.

Along the way, he considered the best way to get to Paris. Taking a coach to Amiens and then another to Paris itself would be the most efficient way. So now it was a matter of finding a coach to take him on the first leg of this French journey.

❧ ❧

The coach rattled off through the French countryside.

The skies here looked fairly similar to those in England, thought Edgar.

What was different was that France was a republic now, and his position as a peer meant absolutely nothing here. In some ways, it was freeing to be just another common man. But in other ways it shook Edgar to the very core of his being, the core of how he defined himself.

He thought what it would have been like, less than twenty years ago, when the Revolution and the Terror were in full swing. His French equivalents, whoever they were, would most likely not have survived unless they had been fortunate enough to be able to find safe passage to a country like England.

Edgar himself had known some boys of French noble descent during his days at Eton, but the horrors of the preceding years were never discussed. Edgar assumed this was because those who had suffered during that time did not want to draw attention to themselves or endure the pain of digging through the past.

It was so stuffy inside the coach, thought Edgar. He wished someone could turn the temperature of the world down ten degrees. That would be so much better.

***

"Monsieur, monsieur," a woman's voice drifted through the air.

Edgar opened his eyes groggily.

They were met by a pair of watery blue ones.

Blinking hard several times, Edgar brought the vision in front of him into sharper focus. Now he could see the eyes were not watery at all but were the eyes of a kindly older woman, he would guess in her early sixties, who had her grey hair peeking out from beneath her white bonet, a relic of fashions from thirty years before.

"Where...where am I?" Edgar said groggily.

"Saint-Marie," replied the woman. "You were travelling on the Amiens coach but the coachman had you taken off here because of your illness."

"Illness? Wh...what illness?" Edgar said.

"Ah, it is a terrible fever. Combined with the stress of travel, your body couldn't handle it. But you are over the worst of it now."

"Oh," Edgar said weakly. "How long have I been here?"

"Two weeks."

"Two weeks?" Startled, Edgar tried to sit up but he was too weak to do so.

"Please lie down, monsieur, it's better for your recovery."

Edgar complied with a groan.

The woman dabbed at his forehead with a wet cloth before holding a cup of water to his lips.

Edgar stared up at the ceiling, trying to piece together the events that had led him to this predicament. He remembered the journey across the Channel and how horrendously seasick he had been. Had that been where the trouble started? Knowing him, it was highly likely. He hadn't felt right since Dover, after all.

"Thank you, Madame - I'm sorry, I didn't catch your name?" Edgar said.

"You can call me Madame Toussaint," she replied.

"Well, thank you Madame Toussaint. For everything," he smiled with sincerity. "I'll be out of your way before you know it."

She chuckled. "Ah, monsieur, you still have some way to go on your road to recovery. I'm afraid we're stuck together for a couple more weeks at least, so the doctors say."

Edgar sighed. Not only had he fallen ill, he was now delayed in reaching Paris and finding Georgina, not to mention the hassle he had caused Madame Toussaint. "I am sorry about that. I hate to be a burden. Please be assured that you will be compensated most handsomely for your efforts."

"Monsieur, it is the duty of any decent person. Who would I be if I had not assisted you? Please, forget about any compensation."

Madame Toussaint dabbed again at his forehead before taking her leave, making the sign of the cross and shutting the door behind her.

Before too long, Edgar was dozing and comatose to the world.

A week went by and Edgar's health gradually improved with each passing day.

He was still confined mostly to the bed in the sparse room with nary a piece of decoration save for a small oil painting of a bowl of fruit on the wall to his right. To his left was a simple fireplace with a mirror hanging above it. However, what he could see when he looked directly ahead was most pleasing.

A few steps away from the foot of his bed was a large set of windows that overlooked a cottage garden filled with all manner of flowers and herbs. Beyond the garden lay rows and rows of verdant vineyards and in the distance there were stately cyprus trees.

One afternoon, Madame Toussaint entered the room carrying a wooden tray. Atop the tray was a plate of roast chicken, carrots and potatoes alongside a glass of apple juice.

She smiled at Edgar and placed the tray on the bedside table next to him. "There you go, monsieur."

"Thank you, madame," he replied.

"Say, what brings you to these parts?" she asked.

"It's a long story."

"Well, I don't have anywhere I need to be this afternoon, so why don't you tell me the tale of how a British gentleman came to be in this little corner of France. I know our two countries are now at peace, thanks to the treaty, but we don't get many of your kind here."

He nodded slowly and then picked up the glass of apple juice. He took a swig and put it back down.

"This story, the truth, it does not paint me in the best light," he said. "So I pray you will not judge me more harshly than I deserve. Though I do deserve your recrimination nonetheless."

Madame Toussaint pulled a chair over from by the fireplace and placed it next to Edgar's bed. She smoothed her skirts and sat down.

"You had better tell me more," she said. "Let me be the judge of who does and does not deserve my recriminations."

And so between bites of food, Edgar told her the whole sorry story. He spoke of how he had met Georgina, of how he had treated her appallingly and ended their arrangement, of how she had briefly taken him back before vanishing into the ether and how he had come to the realisation that she was the only woman for him and that now he was seeking to find her and ask her for her hand in marriage. Through it all, he spurned no opportunity to tell the complete truth about how he had behaved so poorly.

When he finished his explanation, he glanced down at the bedsheets before looking up again at Madame Toussaint.

"That's how I came to be here," he said.

She sighed. "Well, I never thought I would meet a British earl, that's one thing. But it's also not every day that one meets a man so devoted to love. And perhaps she will choose to take you back, perhaps she will not, but at least you tried to fight for her."

She gave him a small smile which he returned.

He yawned. Speaking at such length had expounded so much of his energy.

"You should get some rest," Madame Toussaint said.

Edgar murmured in agreement before shutting his eyes and drifting off to sleep.

Madame Toussaint made the sign of the cross before leaving the room and heading downstairs.

A fortnight later and Edgar was back in full health.

He stood across the threshold of Madame Toussaint's cottage, his bag on his shoulder and his hat in his hand.

"Thank you madame, most sincerely, for everything," he said.

"Oh monsieur, it was nothing," she replied with her usual modesty.

"Without you, I would have faced a terrible fate."

She shook his hand with a firmness that surprised him.

Then he pulled five gleaming gold guineas from his pocket.

"I know you said you did not want any compensation, so please put these in the poor box if you wish. But it did not sit right with me to leave without giving something, for the charity you have shown me," he said.

"Thank you monsieur, may the Lord bless you."

"And may he bless you as well."

They shook hands for a final time and then Edgar turned and walked down the garden path.

He turned and waved as he stepped out onto the main road.

Madam Toussaint returned the greeting before shutting her front door and going about her business.

Now Edgar was back on the road, he sauntered to the town square and stood outside the inn awaiting the coach to Paris. It would be along within a quarter of an hour.

❧ ☙

Here it was, number 10, Rue du Bac. It was a three story townhouse on a side street off the Champs-Élysées. Paris retained much of its medieval architecture and Edgar would guess the house was from the seventeenth century. Screwing up his courage, Edgar walked up to the door and banged the knocker against it three times.

A footman opened it and looked at him quizzically. "Oui, Monsieur?"

Edgar explained how he was there to speak with Miss Georgina Hartley as he had known her in England and the footman's eyes widened at the word 'Weatherby'.

The footman bade him to enter and wait in the drawing room.

❧❧❧❧❧❧ ❧❧❧❧❧❧

Edgar sat on the plush settee, running through his head again and again all he wanted to say to Georgina. How he wished she would forgive him and take him back! Then, footsteps across the floorboards but they did not sound like Georgina's. He looked up and was dismayed to see a man and a woman he did not recognise. He stood up to greet them.

"Good afternoon, Lord Weatherby," began the man. "My name is Maurice Renoir and this is my wife Ludivine."

Both men bowed to each other, then Madame Renoir offered her hand to Edgar and he bent down to kiss it.

"A pleasure," Edgar said.

"Come, let us sit." Mr Renoir gestured to the settees.

Once they were all seated, Mr Renoir continued. "I understand you have come looking for Miss Georgina Hartley, correct?"

"Yes, that is so," Edgar said.

"Well, you won't find her here. She was staying with us for a good while, but she left three weeks ago," Mr Renoir said.

Edgar's heart sank to the pits of despair. He had come all this way, endured so much with his recent illness, only to have missed Georgina by a mere three weeks. Was this a sign from the heavens that he and Georgina were never meant to be together? Should he give up the fight now? No! Edgar would not give up trying to make things right with Georgina, not unless she refused his hand in marriage once and for all! Edgar may be many things in life, but if there was one thing he was not, it was a *coward*, he resolved.

"Do you know where she went?" Edgar asked.

The Renoirs exchanged a meaningful look, before Madame Renoir began to speak.

"She has explained her side of the story to me. Lord Weatherby, I must say your behaviour towards Miss Hartley was disgraceful much of the time. She thought she would never see you again, but the fact you have turned up on our doorstep looking for her shows me that there must be some depth of genuine feeling on your end. I am not one to pry into matters of the heart, so I shall not ask any questions of you. But if you want to find Georgina, you should head to Venice," the Renoir matriarch said.

"To Venice? Where in Venice?" Edgar asked.

"She had taken up a contract at the Teatro di San Carlo," provided Mr Renoir.

"Do you know for how long?" Edgar said.

"Ah no, she did not say." Madame Renoir shook her head with regret.

Edgar walked out of the Renoir home somewhat disappointed but not totally dejected. While he had not been able to meet with Georgina today as he had hoped, all was not lost. He had a new lead to follow. Venice, city of gondolas, operas and masquerade. He would head south tomorrow, but first some planning was required.

With every mile the carriage trundled through the continent, Edgar felt a growing mix of relief and apprehension. Relief because he was getting ever closer to Georgina. Apprehension because his endeavour could all be in vain and he could forever be without the lady he truly loved. What if she were not in Venice or, worse still, turned him down?

After his disastrous crossing of the Channel and journey through northern France, the road had fortuitously grown easier for Edgar. From Paris onwards, it had been a fairly straightforward ride through eastern France and into northern Italy.

Once he got past Milan, he was on the final push towards Venice. He would be in the City of Masks within four mere days, everything going well, and he hoped with all his heart that he would meet Georgina there. Not long to go until he would learn how the rest of his romantic life would pan out. Not long at all.

CHAPTER TWENTY-TWO

The lagoon glistened like it was sprinkled with sapphires as the gondola made its way towards the mooring.

Paying the gondolier, Edgar disembarked and placed his feet on Venetian soil for the first time since his trip fifteen years before. It didn't look like the place had changed much in the interim. At least that was one blessing, he thought.

But it was going to be a real challenge to find Georgina. If she was even still here.

The information he'd received from the Renoirs in Paris had been three months out of date, after all. But it was the only lead Edgar had to go on and he knew he'd wasted too much time without his beloved Georgina already.

He needed to find her at any cost. He would never be happy otherwise.

Striding across the square, Edgar stood out with his restrained English clothing. He had always been a man to take great pride in his looks and by English standards he was quite the dandy. But Venice took it to another level.

Some street urchins squealed and laughed as he walked by, no doubt thinking it was highly amusing to see an English aristocrat so out of place.

But Edgar paid them little mind. Georgina was why he was here.

Thinking back to his conversation with Renoirs, he focused his mind on remembering where the Teatro di San Carlo was located. He had been to see a few operas there when he was last in Venice. With the route now becoming clearer in his mind, Edgar walked past the duomo on the right side of the square and entered one of the side streets. Following the general direction of the crowd, he heard the bells from the duomo chime that it was two o'clock in the afternoon. Still hopefully some time to catch Georgina before she'd be taking to the stage tonight, thought Edgar.

After taking some familiar twists and turns down the narrow streets, he came to a small square where the Teatro di San Carlo stood. Its pale yellow walls were inviting, but Edgar couldn't be certain that what lay inside would be a happy outcome. All he had to go on was a thread of hope. Hope that his plan would work and that his long journey from London all those weeks ago would pay off.

Walking up to the main doors, he could see that entry wasn't going to be as easy as simply striding in. An elderly attendant sat dozing in a wooden chair underneath the veranda by the large wooden doors, the large key dangling from a chain around his waist.

Nothing for it, thought Edgar. If Georgina was inside the theatre, he wanted to get in and talk to her as soon as he possibly could. Edgar cleared his throat loudly, waking the attendant.

Glaring up at Edgar, the attendant raised an eyebrow giving the unspoken command for Edgar to quickly state his business.

Making use of his limited Italian, Edgar said, "Excuse me, sir. A friend of mine is performing inside and I'm trying to get in to see her. Would you let me in please?"

The attendant just glared at Edgar in irritation. Nothing comes for free in this world, why can't this rich Englishman understand that, thought the attendant to himself.

As if he'd read the attendant's mind, Edgar hastily continued. "I'll make it worth your while if you'd be so kind to let me in."

Reaching into his pocket for two gold coins, Edgar smiled at the attendant and tried to show his intentions were good. Edgar presented the coins to the attendant, who nodded gruffly and raised himself from the chair.

The attendant walked towards the door and unlocked it.

Edgar entered the cool lobby of the theatre, the flagstones giving welcome respite from the stifling heat outside. Through the glass paned doors in front of him he could see into the main hall of the theatre. A small group of women sat talking on the edge of the stage. Could one of them be Georgina? He was too far away to say for sure. He needed to get closer.

Striding towards the doors to the theatre, his riding boots clacked on the flagstones. He opened the doors and stepped onto the carpeted floor of the theatre. Surrounding him on the left and the right were rows and rows of red velvet covered chairs. But his main focus was straight ahead, where he could see the group of women sat on the edge of the stage.

Now he was closer, he had a better view of the women and realised that one of them was indeed Georgina. His efforts, his whole journey across half a continent had not been in vain after all. Well, it had not been in vain in the sense that he had found Georgina. She still could turn him down. And she'd be well within her rights to do so, of course. Reflecting on how he'd behaved in the past, Edgar knew Georgina had every reason to do so. He'd treated her poorly at points in their liaison. But he wanted to turn that all around. He wanted to commit. Would it be too little, too late?

⚜

"Where on earth is this new pianist?" tutted Maria, an experienced alto with the company.

"He should have been here half an hour ago," said Dominique, another alto. "It's getting a bit ridiculous."

There was a creaking noise as the back door of the theatre swung open, followed by the sound of footsteps as someone entered the room.

"Ah, our pianist has graced us with his presence at last!" Maria said. "Nice of him to be punctual."

Georgina turned her head forwards and spied a familiar figure standing at the back of the theatre. Her eyes widened for a few seconds before she regained her composure. "That's not the pianist."

"Well then who is it?" Maria hissed.

In her own head, Georgina's voice sounded as though she were far, far away. "Someone I used to know." She rose to her feet. "Please excuse me, ladies."

❧❦

She said something to the other women and headed towards where Edgar stood in the theatre aisle.

Edgar felt his heart beat faster and faster with every step Georgina took in his direction. All sound disappeared from his ears so the only thing he could hear was the racing of his own pulse. Time slowed down so that he had the sensation of every second that passed feeling as though it were a minute. Terror seeped through his veins. Oh God, oh God, oh God. What if she rejected him? What if she was disappointed in him?

And then, Georgina was standing right in front of him and time began to speed up and adopt to its usual pace again. This was it. The moment he had been waiting for for so many long weeks. It was now or never.

"Lord Weatherby," Georgina began cautiously, "what are you doing here? Why are you in Venice?"

Edgar looked at Georgina, his eyes full of hesitant hope. "I came because I can't bear a single day without you by my side, Miss Hartley. Not prioritising you was the worst mistake I ever made, and for that I am truly sorry."

"Go on," said Georgina.

"I want the whole world to know that you are the woman I love, Miss Hartley. I love you more than anything and

I will always love you." Edgar declared with a ferocity of passion that Georgina had never heard before from a man. "When I wake up, you are the first thing in my mind, and when I sleep at night you haunt my dreams. I've tried so many times to not love you, but I cannot. I can never ever stop loving you."

Georgina looked at Edgar in disbelief. This was the last thing she had been expecting to hear when she awoke earlier that day.

Edgar continued. "You have captured my heart, Miss Hartley. And I'm through with pretending that you aren't my soulmate, that you wouldn't make an outstanding countess."

"Edgar, it does not do to dwell on fantasies," Georgina said softly.

"I mean it, Miss Hartley. I know you are my soulmate. There is no other woman on earth or who will ever be on earth who could make me as happy as you make me. And I know you would make an excellent Countess of Weatherby."

Georgina shook her head.

Edgar could feel his heart breaking, if it were even possible for an already twice shattered heart to break yet another time.

"I'd be terrible, Edgar. I know nothing about being a countess and I'd just be fumbling the whole time," she said.

"You'd be better than you think," Edgar said. "If you're willing to learn, I can teach you what I know of it and a duchess is willing to help you too."

"But all those parties, organising the balls...I don't know how I'd do it."

"Miss Hartley, I can't pretend to truly understand what your life has been like and the hardships you've faced, but I love you with all my heart and I know you have what it takes within you to be a great Countess of Weatherby. And for your first few years you wouldn't have to organise balls or parties at all. There hasn't been a Countess of Weatherby in a decade and so there have been no balls or parties hosted through the earldom in many years. A few more years without them won't do anyone any harm. And if anyone were to dare ask why not, the simple answer would be that I didn't want them to happen. I'm the earl, after all, so at the end of the day the buck stops with me on all decisions."

Georgina felt a little relieved at what Edgar had said, but still her mind was brimming with questions.

"But what about managing the household? I don't know much that would be helpful for managing something as big as Renfregh," she said.

"That's no bother, I'd teach you what you needed to know. I've done it myself for years and years. I won't pretend it's an easy job but you're intelligent and with the right training you'd handle it really well. I know you would. It's an important role no doubt, but ultimately I'd still be the final person accountable for what goes on over and above your role."

To hear Edgar speak so clearly about the countess' position in relation to the earl made Georgina blush. But, she rued, this was just pie in the sky talk. She sighed internally. She needed to be the one to bring them both back down to reality, for both their sakes. "Edgar, why are you here? Really, why did you come all this way?" she asked.

"I'm here because you wrote to me that in a better world, in a fairer world we could be together properly," Edgar said.

"I did, yes," Georgina said cautiously.

"Well, what if I could work to make that world real, real for you at least?"

Edgar's earnestness pulled Georgina towards him. But still her doubts nagged at the back of her mind. "That's a beautiful picture Edgar, but how would it work?"

"I would *make* it work. I've never wanted anything more in my life than I want you, Miss Hartley and I will never be satisfied unless we are man and wife. I can't promise you it will always be easy, but I swear to you that I will always protect you as your husband. As only a husband can."

"But what of your title? Your family? Your duties?" Georgina said.

"I've talked it over with my eldest brother and I have his full support in coming here to ask you for your hand in marriage."

"Wait, your *brother* supports you in this endeavour?" Georgina's mouth was wide in wonderment. It was one thing for a lovestruck lord to let himself get carried away and make grandiose declarations to his courtesan. It was quite another for a senior member of the lord's family to support him in those declarations. Unheard of, really.

"Yes, he does," Edgar said with a smile. "He understands that I will have no one but you. I will be happy with no one but you. You are the only one for me, Miss Hartley. If we can produce an heir, then I will be glad, but if we cannot then there are always other routes the title could go. And as for duties, I've been giving them a lot of thought." Edgar's hawklike eyes bore deeply into Georgina's with such intensity that she almost wanted to look away from his gaze. It was as though he could see into the depths of her very soul. "There is more than one type of duty in the world, not just to titles and estates and family. But also to love and to the heart. And I would not be doing my duty to you if I did not come here today. I want to make it work with you, Miss Hartley, more than anything else in the world. What good are titles and abiding by rigid societal rules if the heart ceases feeling, ceases honour, ceases conviction? I cannot separate love and duty any longer, they are two sides of the same whole for me, and so that is why I come before you today."

"But I left," she said.

"You had *every* right. I came here today because you deserve to hear a proper proposal of marriage and if you decline then I can do nothing but respect your will. Heaven knows I would deserve it. It was completely unreasonable of me to even consider having a mistress at the same time as having a wife, let alone asking you to fulfil the position of the former. If you want me to leave, then I will turn around and go and you can forget me forever. But I would like for you to be able to make an informed choice, a genuine choice on the understanding that if you say yes, you would become the rightful Countess of Weatherby."

"I have no dowry, you must understand," Georgina said.

"Miss Hartley, I am aware and it does not bother me one iota. I can assure you that you will always be taken care of for as long as you live, dowry or no. And my earldom has more than enough funds to be concerned about what money a countess might or might not bring to it on her marriage."

Georgina nodded. Then she said, "I still want you. I've never stopped wanting you if I'm honest."

"But?" Edgar asked.

"But we need to be realistic. What if that's not enough. I'm not one of the ton."

"It's more than enough. You are more than enough, Miss Hartley, and please don't ever think you are not because you are the world in my eyes. You're worth twice as much as the whole damn ton put together! And before you say anything, because I know you have ten retorts already locked and loaded in your brain ready to fire at the first opportunity, you would be marrying me and not the ton," he said.

The earnest glean in Edgar's eyes was unmistakable.

For so long, she had been terrified of letting herself feel any emotional pleasure. Certainly, she was happy to feel physical pleasure, sexual pleasure, artistic pleasure and intellectual pleasure. But sheer delight and enjoyment on an emotional level were sensations she had long refused to let herself experience.

She decided all that was going to change. Today.

She gave Edgar a firm nod. "Your good opinion is the more important consideration."

Edgar's heart leapt.

He got down on one knee. Then he looked up to meet her gaze and took her left hand between both of his.

Beloved Georgina's mouth was slightly open in joyful anticipation.

"Miss Georgina Harriett Hartley, will you do me the honour of consenting to become my lawful wedded wife?" Edgar asked.

"Yes, Edgar, a thousand times yes!"

CHAPTER TWENTY-THREE

"How did you find me?" Georgina enquired.

"Well, Jean Cookson told me you'd gone to stay with the Renoirs -" Edgar began.

Her eyes widened and then she laughed. "Jean? *Jean* told you? Heavens she -"

"Hates me, I know," he chuckled wryly. "But she was the only person I could think of in England who might have had information about where you had gone. Believe me, she was reluctant at first but she understood when I told her of my intentions to propose."

"Well that's a turn out for the books if ever there was one," she said.

Edgar pulled out a small black box from his jacket pocket and opened it. Georgina gasped. Inside the box sat a delicate gold ring topped off by a pristine diamond.

"Edgar, I couldn't possibly -" began Georgina.

"It's only befitting for the future Countess of Weatherby, that you shall have this ring as a token of my affections and a sign of our engagement," Edgar said.

Taking Georgina's left hand in his own, he removed the ring from its box and placed it gently on her ring finger.

The diamond cast a beautiful array of rainbow shimmers on the wall beside the happy couple. Gorgina marvelled at this light effect and moved her hand this way and that to try to create a specific effect with the ring. "It's beautiful, thank you Edgar!"

"Anything for you, my darling Miss Hartley, anything!" he replied. Then he brought her hand to his lips and kissed it, before rubbing each knuckle in gentle circles.

Georgina moaned in pleasure at Edgar's administrations on her hand.

⁂

"The thing is, I'm contracted to finish out this singing engagement in a month," Georgina explained.

Edgar smiled kindly. "And you want to see out the engagement before we wed?"

"Yes."

"That makes sense," Edgar said. "I'll court you for that month."

"Court me?" Edgar was full of surprises today, thought Georgina.

"Yes, court you properly like you deserve."

"But that means -" Georgina's eyes widened.

Edgar nodded. "I don't want to have you or anyone else outside of wedlock ever again, Miss Hartley. Ever."

Georgina's heart soared.

⁂

They had been talking so long that the sun had drawn lower in the sky and dusk would soon be on the way.

"Where are you staying? Have you got somewhere safe to go?" An undercurrent of concern ran through Edgar's voice.

"Yes, Edgar. I've got rooms at the Colazzo for the remainder of the singing contract," Georgina said.

"Alright, but if you ever feel unsafe there let me know and I'll make other arrangements for you," Edgar said.

"Don't worry, I will," she said with a smile.

And, dear reader, as for that missing pianist, he never did turn up.

⁂

Her fiance, and didn't it seem unbelievable to say but it was true all true, took her by the hand and led her down the steps of the bridge across to the other side of the canal.

They walked through the winding alleyways, Edgar running his thumb in gentle circles around the back of her dainty hand. All too soon, they were in front of the apartment building where Georgina was staying.

"This is it, Edgar," she said, with a regret in her voice. For the first time ever since she had known him, Edgar would not be coming upstairs to join her and see where the night took them. Instead, he would be returning to his own accommodations and leaving her to her solitude.

"Goodnight sweetheart," Edgar said, holding her hands gently in his own. "I love you so so much!"

"I love you too," Georgina said.

Then he kissed her on the forehead and turned to head off into the night.

Georgina turned her key in the lock on the maroon wooden door and made her way up the marble stairs, her heels making a soft clicking sound as she went. Not long now until they were united in Holy Matrimony as man and wife! She had longed for this far more than she had been willing to admit to herself, but now the wheels of reality were in motion she was able to let the excitement within her build about her impending nuptials and married life.

⁂

After checking into one of the city's most salubrious hotels, Edgar decided to go for a walk.

He strolled happily through the twilight Venetian streets. All his efforts had not been in vain after all! Georgina had agreed to become his fiancee and soon she would be his lawful wedded wife and the Countess of Weatherby no less.

The lamplights bathed the city in a peaceful tangerine glow that alluded to Venice's darker undertone of sinful, hedonistic pleasures. Once upon a time, Edgar would have leapt at the chance to partake in that scene, but now his love for Georgina had quelled his interest in anyone else. He desired to be with her and only ever her.

Reaching the hotel, he entered the lobby and nodded to the concierge before making his way to his room that overlooked the canal.

Removing his shoes and light jacket, made his way towards the desk. He picked up his box of cigars and removed one from the box. Then he walked towards the window and pushed the shutters open. He sat on the window ledge and lit his cigar, bringing it to his lips and savouring the earthy flavour.

The view outside was impressive and stirred a romantic passion within him. Across the canal he could see Venice's splendour with her distinctly Italianate buildings in the foreground and in the background the top of the Basilica di Santa Maria Gloriosa dei Frari itself. A few gondoliers made their way along the canal below, their lanterns shimmering in the mild night air and the rich tones of their vocals carrying in the wind.

The air itself had a sweetly spiced tinge, the kind that's common around the Mediterranean but is practically unheard of in England.

His heart was full of love for Miss Georgina Hartley and he could not quite believe that his plan had worked. He had journeyed halfway across Europe on the distant hope that he would be able to find her and tell her how he felt and that maybe, just maybe, she would return his feelings and accept his proposal. And she had! She had! Oh, she had! He was the happiest man on earth tonight. He knew she was only a short walk away but he had sworn to himself he was going to court her properly and that meant no more late night séjours with Georgina until they were wed.

He finished his cigar. He went to pour himself a glass of brandy and then sat at the desk. He picked up a quill and some paper and began to write a letter to Xavier to let him know the latest development that would change the destiny of the Weatherby line for the better.

That night, Georgina lay in her bed and thought of Edgar's handsome face with his hawklike brown eyes and dark hair. It had been so long since she had been touched, the last time was by Edgar back in London a couple of days before she wrote her infamous note to him. How it had shattered her heart to write that note to him. But she had seen no other choice at the time. However, the events of the past week had completely turned all of that around. Now, she was due to be married to Edgar in only four weeks.

Thinking of Edgar's strong hands, she moved her own right one between her legs and spread them wide. She began to explore around her bush and then oh so slowly into her folds. She was absolutely soaking and unapologetic about it. Teasing her folds with one finger and then two, she recalled how Edgar had done this so many times in all sorts of different places. His London bachelor pad. The house he provided for her in Fitzrovia. By the lake at Renfregh. In the wildflower woods on his estate. Then when she could resist it no longer, she stroked her pleasure pearl with a delicate finger. Round and round at first before she changed direction and moved up and down, up and down. Thoughts of Edgar exploded in her mind.

"Come with me," she imagined him murmuring commandingly in her ear, just as he had done many times before!

And it was all she could do but to obey his every command, as she would when she was his wife. She felt the pleasure build up within her core and then the delicious relief as she rode out her orgasm on only a single finger.

Contented, she rolled over onto her side and drifted off to sleep.

Chapter Twenty-Four

"So, Edgar, I may have done something last night," she said coquettishly.

Edgar raised an eyebrow. "What was that, darling?"

"I touched myself to thoughts of you."

Edgar's mouth widened in shock and both of his eyebrows shot up above his head. "Miss Hartley! I'm surprised at you."

She giggled.

Edgar continued, "Well, actually I'm not that surprised at all. And I do think it's rather delectable." His voice grew softer, more dangerous like a rich velvet covering encasing a secret cabinet of hitherto unknown pleasures. "That you are so needy for me that you will see to yourself when the desire becomes too great to bear. That you are overcome by your passion for me."

He reached for her hand and kissed it tenderly. "You can touch yourself again at night if you like. In fact, I encourage you to if the desire strikes you. It's good for you, you know, and it's supposed to help you sleep better and get a better rest."

Georgina felt her cheeks burn. Trust Edgar to be so matter of fact yet simultaneously so sensual.

The couple strolled together through the square and into the lobby of the restaurant. They made their way through to the courtyard and sat down at a table.

"I'm not frightened of Christian marriage, Edgar. Nervous maybe, as any bride would be, but not frightened," she said.

"But do you disagree with it, the whole rites?"

"Oh no, not at all! Remember, I spent ten years living in a vicarage. When I was with the Wilsons, we lived and breathed the scriptures and the *Book of Common Prayer* every day. Not everyone may agree with the rites, but I believe they are what will give our marriage structure and a system so we both know where we stand."

Edgar hung on her every word.

She took a sip of her beverage and smiled, before continuing, "Do you disagree with the marriage rites?"

"No, they tie into duty for me, with all the other duties in my life, so they make perfect sense to me. But I still don't want to let you down," he said.

"Edgar, you won't let me down. I know you won't. I believe in you, I wouldn't have said *yes* otherwise," she said.

The pair sat outside the gelato shop.

"So, about those dinners and dances and balls," began Georgina.

"Oh, what about them?" Edgar said.

"Well, you said before they've not been held for some time by your family."

"That's correct. There's no expectation from my side for them to take place, and if anyone else asks why then the simple answer for them is that I don't wish them to." Edgar reached across the table and took Georgina's hand in his own. "But if you do want to get involved in running those events, you have my full support." Edgar kissed Georgina's hand. "You have my full support, whatever you decide darling."

"And attending them, the ones that other families run?"

"We could turn down any invitations as much as we wanted," Edgar sais with a twinkle in his eyes.

Georgina stroked her forearm in a gesture of tentativeness.

Edgar noticed and the mirth left his eyes. "But seriously, Miss Hartley, I'll be there to protect you every step of the way. Whatever social events we may attend, I'll be there right by your side if you want me there."

"And the protocols?"

"Those too, my darling. I'll teach you those, and my sister, the duchess, has offered to as well."

She took a bite of her gelato and then said, "Alright, so my frame of reference is essentially middle class dinner parties at the vicarage. That's what the vicar's wife trained me for, to be a middle class hostess. Have you been to any of those?"

"I've been to some over the years, mostly with the vicar's family in the village near Renfregh. And my Uncle William, my father's second brother, holds a curacy in Suffolk. But you'd still know a lot more than I would about those dinner parties though."

"Let's compare notes then," she said.

"Indeed, my darling," he said with a smile.

***

Georgina sat on the sofa in her small Venice apartment and took the news pamphlet between her hands.

She frowned at the first few pages. They spoke of tides of war rising around the major European powers, with that French general Bonaparte at the helm of all the chaos.

Certainly, France and England were traditional enemies but she herself held her French friends in great affection and she had happy memories of her time in that nation over the course of her career. She was loathe to think of the prospect of war, of yet more bloodshed filling the fields of Europe and the waters of the Mediterranean and the Atlantic.

***

Later that day, the couple met in St Mark's Square and began their promenade arm-in-arm. They were the picture of devoted lovers. Though very few people in Venice knew who they were, to any observer it was immediately evident that they held each other in deep and secure affection.

Edgar liked the protecting way he walked with Georgina. It felt good to offer his beloved his protection and, better still, for her to accept it with joyous relish.

Protection. Now that was a misleading word, thought Edgar. On the one hand, the type of relationship he had with Georgina back when he was her protector was a place where she could gain protection in a sense. Yet on the other hand, the protection he would offer her as her husband would be so much deeper and richer. As the Countess of Weatherby, Georgina could expect protection from her husband on every level.

Georgina's voice pulled Edgar away from his musings. "Have you heard the news?" she said. "They say there's likely going to be another war with France."

He nodded. "Yes, there have been some rumblings."

"And just when we'd signed a peace treaty over the last war as well!" exclaimed Georgina in outrage. "It's simply appalling. What a waste of lives it will be. It makes me feel sick in my stomach to think of all the bloodshed on the horizon."

Edgar rubbed her hand in a gesture of comfort. "You're right. These are turbulent times. But please know that I will do whatever it takes to keep you safe."

The pair shared a gentle smile.

Then Georgina let forth a sigh of resignation. "I don't imagine we'll be back on the continent at any point soon once we cross the Channel though."

"You're right, I fear. Very right indeed," he said.

Edgar bit his lip briefly. Georgina was an intelligent woman, he could not play her for a fool, and her concerns were naturally his concerns as well. He rubbed her hand again. This time around, she wasn't the only person he was attempting to comfort.

CHAPTER TWENTY-FIVE

Georgina put on the gorgeous new blush pink dress Edgar had bought for her. Then she put on the matching pink satin elbow-length gloves and dark maroon velvet hooded cape that went down to her knees and swished as she walked. Then it was time for the piece de resistance. The ornate white full face mask with beautiful pink and gold shimmering swirls. She tied the mask round the back of her head and then drew her cape hood over the top.

Looking at herself in the mirror, she was astonished. She could barely recognise herself. To observers who did not know her, she could have been anyone. A lady of the ton, an opera singer, a courtesan, anyone!

Making her final clothing adjustments, she walked out of the door and made her way through the rear entrance of the building where a gondola was waiting for her.

Georgina enjoyed the sensation of being totally anonymous. She reclined in the gondola seat and enjoyed seeing the scenery of Venice go by as the vessel made its slow progression along the canal.

After ten minutes or so, the gondola pilot docked in front of a grand house.

The pilot helped Georgina disembark onto the shore and then went on his way.

Georgina patted down her skirts and then walked through the ornate wrought iron doors into the entrance hall of the house. Footmen bowed and maids curtsied to her as she made her way along the hall and turned left into the ballroom. Exquisite chandeliers loomed overhead with their bright shining candles casting an invigorating glow around the room.

As she was getting her bearings, a figure dressed entirely in black, from his tricorn hat to his bauta mask to his leather gloves to his waistcoat and breeches came up to her and bowed profusely.

"Good evening, Signorina," he said. "May I have the pleasure of the next dance with you?"

"Why yes, you may." Georgina smiled behind her mask. It was a new sensation to be in the company of a man where he was unable to see her reactions and instead could only infer what she meant by listening to what she said.

The pair began to dance together. From the other end of the room, a string quartet played a vibrant, bright piece that set the tone for frivolity.

"So, Signorina, what brings you to the ball this evening?" The man in black asked as they walked towards one another.

The pair then stepped backwards from one another and turned around, as per the dance routine.

Walking again towards the man, Georgina replied, "I am here to enjoy the music and the dancing."

"And nothing else?" her dancing partner said.

"Nothing else," Georgina said.

Again the pair stepped backwards from each other, turned around and walked towards each other.

"Are you sure there's no other reason?" His voice become softer and dangerous. "I think you're lying, Signorina. Lying to me and lying to yourself about why you're really here tonight."

Georgina felt herself wetten at the man's words. He couldn't see her face and she couldn't see his, but it was as though he had peered into the depths of her soul and was examining her innermost secrets as though she were a specimen in a laboratory.

"You are a complete and utter bastard," she laughed. "A very intelligent one. There's no hiding anything from you. I came here tonight to enjoy the company of a man."

"And which man would that be?" her dancing partner said.

"That's none of your concern," Georgina replied.

"I'll figure it out by the end of the night." His voice was like honey. "You can't hide from me forever."

❧❧❧❧❧ ❦❦❦❦❦

Georgina decided she liked this whole mask scenario. It gave her a new sensation of power, no longer was she an object existing for the pleasure of high class men, constantly on view for them to choose how she would be the object in *their* story. Instead, she was the subject and those men would only learn and see exactly what *she* wanted them to.

The music slowed down and the string quartet began to play a waltz. Georgina and the man in black moved closer to one another and began to waltz together.

"Signorina, has anyone ever told you how beautifully you dance?" he said.

"Maybe once or twice," she replied.

"Well, people should tell you it more often." He leaned in to murmur into her ear. "Because you are an absolutely enchanting lady, I can tell. The way you move, you are so scrumptious. What I wouldn't give to whisk you away right now and have my way with you."

Georgina giggled coquettishly. "Oh, why don't you?"

His voice became sterner. "Because it wouldn't be within the bounds of propriety, Signorina. No man will do that until you are married."

Georgina realised she liked the sternness of the man in black. "But what about after I'm married?"

"Then your husband will do that to you as often as you desire," he whispered seductively. "And we both know that you will be an insatiable harlot of a wife, don't we Signorina?"

Georgina's cheeks turned crimson behind her mask. She was very glad to be wearing it right now, such was her present struggle to control herself in the company of this dashing man.

"I asked you a question, so I expect you to answer," he said.

"Oh, yes, I will be a complete and utter harlot once I am married," she breathed.

He nodded sagely. "That's very good, your husband will be pleased to know that."

As the dance ended, he pulled her into an embrace and stroked the back of her neck gently with his leather-clad hand. She purred to herself at the relaxing sensation. Then the hand increased the intensity of its massage on her neck and she closed her eyes and let herself simply feel the bliss.

The man in black offered Georgina his hand. "Signorina, would you like to take refreshments on the terrace?"

"Why yes," she said.

She took his hand and together they walked through the ballroom and out onto the terrace. There, a sizeable group of attendees mingled on the red bricks that were surrounded by white baroque pillars.

The man in black procured two glasses of white wine from the refreshments table at the side of the terrace and handed one to Georgina.

She took a small sip and savoured the light taste.

Georgina and the man in black walked arm in arm down the hall and exited through the wrought iron gates. Once on the wharf, they removed their respective masks. Georgina smiled at Edgar as he stood in front of her.

"That was incredible," Georgina beamed. "I loved every second."

"As did I," Edgar said. He pulled her into an embrace, tilting her face up towards his with his strong, leather-clad hands. He kissed her with a burning passion and claimed her mouth with his talented tongue.

Georgina ran her hands gently around Edgar's back and he moaned softly into her mouth.

"It's getting late, I should walk you back to your apartment," Edgar said ruefully.

Georgina whimpered. "Ah please, just a few minutes more. The night is still young!"

Edgar chuckled at her bright enthusiasm, but he knew he had to be responsible. It did not sit right with him for the pair to be out so late together unaccompanied. They were technically courting, after all. Even in this libertine city, it would still be scandalous for a lady to be seen out in public in the small hours in the company of a man who was not her husband. Even in a libertine city like Venice, there was too much reputational risk for a woman if she was spotted at this late hour in the embrace of a man who was not her husband.

"Oh you tempt me, sweetheart!" Edgar leaned into Georgina and kissed her once more with ferocious intensity.

She gripped his collar and pulled him tight towards her, desperate for his touch.

Walking down the wharf arm in arm, they stopped to admire the duomo as it was festooned by an altarpiece of stars.

"Do you ever want to stop time?" she asked, turning her face to look up at him.

"Quite frequently, yes," he said. "Especially when I'm with you." He kissed her on the forehead.

"I feel the same way," she said. "I often wish we could stop the whole universe and it would just be you and I."

Sitting at her dressing table and taking down her hair, Georgina felt overjoyed. Tonight had been wonderful. The anonymity the mask afforded her had been unexpectedly liberating and Edgar had been an absolute dream. He had planned the evening meticulously and made it a delectably sensual experience, one she would remember for the rest of her life. It was surprising how sensual it had been considering they had not even kissed until after leaving the masquerade ball. Even with all her life experience, Edgar still surprised her. She was beginning to realise there was still so much she had to learn.

Her nighttime ablutions complete, she climbed into bed and had some very pleasant dreams involving a certain man in black.

Across town, Edgar turned the lock in his hotel room door and entered into his temporary private sanctuary.

What a night it had been! Georgina, his wife-to-be, had been outstanding and he was so proud of her. Over the past few months, he had come to realise the value and importance of having clear conversations on many levels. And that included the sensual side of life. He had had several intricate discussions with Georgina to gain a solid understanding of what exactly it was that appealed to her about masquerade balls and what she wanted to get out of the experience. He had synthesised her thoughts, wishes and desires into a game plan that had played out perfectly tonight.

He removed the leather gloves Georgina adored so much. Then, shedding his waistcoat as he went, he rolled up his shirtsleeves and kicked off his boots.

He smiled as he recalled her enthusiasm for continuing the night for longer. And he wanted that too. Badly. But he knew the most responsible thing to do would be to wait until he and Georgina were united in Holy Matrimony before taking anything further. Once they were wed, all boundaries would be loosened and he would be able to be seen with his sweet Georgina at any time, day or night, without even the slightest, most miniscule hint of scandal.

Edgar poured himself a glass of water and lapped it up quickly. Then he readied himself for bed and before long, he had joined his fiance in the land of pleasant dreams.

His subconscious envisioned her in that pink dress, maroon cloak and delicate mask as she ran joyously through the orchard at Renfregh. She swang around the trunks of several of the trees, always a few paces ahead of him as he followed behind.

Then he caught up with her and pressed her against a tree.

She took her mask off and gazed into his eyes.

"Kiss me, Edgar," the dream version of Georgina said.

Chapter Twenty-Six

The big day had arrived. In so many ways this felt unbelievable to Georgina but this was the choice she was making. She would be giving up her independent life as a singer, as an entertainer of men on more than one level, in return for being the wife of a member of the peerage. Yet even as a singer, as a mistress of rich men, she was not truly independent she mused. Every penny required her to please the appetites of men in one way or another. She had never been able to make a truly independent decision. So her new role as the wife of an earl was not such a drastically restricting state of affairs, she reflected. And in her new life she would have one thing she had never had before: genuine committed love.

Walking up the aisle, Georgina felt completely content. She was radiant in her ivory satin gown and matching stole. Atop her head she wore a golden bridal tiara adorned with shimmering pearls. A delicate lace veil completed the outfit.

At the end of the aisle awaited Edgar, who as per English tradition stood with his back turned from her. He would not lay eyes on her until she reached the end of the aisle when he would turn around to face her.

Georgina admired him in his sleek obsidian tail coat, waistcoat and breeches. He cut a most debonair figure indeed!

She reached the altar. This was it. The big moment.

Edgar turned towards his bride with total love in his eyes. Then they both turned towards the vicar who began the service.

"Dearly beloved, we are gathered together here in the sight of God, and in the face of this Congregation, to join together this man and this woman in holy Matrimony; which is an honourable estate, instituted of God in the time of man's innocency, signifying unto us the mystical union that is betwixt Christ and his Church..." the jolly vicar intoned.

The vicar continued, laying out the reasons for marriage according to the Church.

"It was ordained for the creation of children...It was ordained for a remedy against sin, and to avoid fornication...It was ordained for the mutual society, help, and comfort, that the one ought to have of the other, both in prosperity and adversity..."

The vicar continued with his intonations and then asked, "Edgar, wilt thou have this woman to thy wedded wife, to live together after God's ordinance in the holy estate of Matrimony? Wilt thou love her, comfort her, honour, and keep her, in sickness and in health; and, forsaking all other, keep thee only unto her, so long as ye both shall live?"

"I will," Edgar said with conviction.

Then the vicar said, "Georgina, wilt thou have this man to thy wedded husband, to live together after God's ordinance in the holy estate of Matrimony? Wilt thou obey him, and serve him, love, honour, and keep him, in sickness and in health; and, forsaking all other, keep thee only unto him, so long as ye both shall live?"

"I will," she replied.

The vicar continued with the liturgy and then it was time for Edgar and Georgina to recite the vows.

"I Edgar take thee Georgina to my wedded wife, to have and to hold from this day forward, for better for worse, for richer for poorer, in sickness and in health, to love and to cherish, till death us do part, according to God's holy ordinance; and thereto I plight thee my troth," Edgar said.

"I Georgina take thee Edgar to my wedded husband, to have and to hold from this day forward, for better for worse, for richer for poorer, in sickness and in health, to love, cherish, and to obey, till death us do part, according to God's holy ordinance; and thereto I give thee my troth," Georgina said.

And then Edgar placed a beautiful gold band on Georgina's left ring finger, saying as he did so, "With this ring I thee wed, with my body I thee worship, and with all my worldly goods I thee endow: In the Name of the Father, and of the Son, and of the Holy Ghost. Amen."

Then the vicar continued with the liturgy.

"Those whom God hath joined together let no man put asunder."

Those were heavy words indeed. But they were true. Now Edgar and Georgina were married, no force on earth other than death would be able to separate them.

And then the vicar pronounced them man and wife and they were united in matrimony for life. Edgar's heart swelled! Georgina was his forever and she was now his Countess of Weatherby. He had never been happier.

Then they went to sign the registry book and afterwards left the chapel and entered back into the main hall of the consulate.

As they stepped out onto the street arm in arm, Edgar beamed at his new bride.

"I love you so so much darling," he said.

She placed a delicate kiss on his cheek. "I love you too, Edgar."

They made their way towards the canal and Edgar hired a gondola for the pair.

He assisted her into the gleaming obsidian vessel. Around the top of the gondola's sides was a band of ornate gold filigree that encircled the entire vessel.

She sat down first on the scarlet velvet bench. She spread her satin skirts out to her left side.

Then Edgar joined her, taking the place on the right hand side of the bench. He took Georgina's hand in his own and began to rub her knuckles with tender affection.

"My beautiful darling," he said.

"I love you, husband," she replied with smile.

Behind them, the gondolier dipped his paddle into the turquoise waters and the vessel began to move away from the shore.

With summer's final days, the sweltering temperatures of Venice had started to subside and with each passing sunrise the waters of the lagoon took on an ever more slightly matte appearance.

The gondolier began to sing in a strong tenor voice. It was one of the barcarolle arias that could be heard up and down the city's canals. Some of the barcarolles were long-standing, already decades old, while others were pieces that the gondoliers freshly invented and evolved after a night at the opera. As Georgina did not recognise the piece, and she had taken many gondolas during her time in Venice, she supposed it was a recent creation. Potentially even a composition of the gondolier himself.

She turned to her husband and admired the handsomeness of his visage in the afternoon light. It was good to see him at ease.

He turned to her and smiled. "What are you thinking of, sweetheart?"

"Oh," she blushed, "how handsome you are, dear husband. You really do have the most beautiful face. I hope you know how happy I am to be with you."

"And I you. You make me so happy." He brought her hand to his lips and kissed it reverently.

Past rows of stately pastel houses and mansions they sailed. All the while, they admired the scenery and whispered sweet statements of their mutual adoration.

A quarter of an hour went by and then they were docking outside Edgar's hotel.

Edgar assisted Georgina from the vessel before turning to pay and thank the cheery gondolier. The Weatherbys then made their way through the wrought iron doors of the hotel and into the cool marble of the lobby.

Arm-in-arm they climbed the stairs to Edgar's suites. Edgar delighted in the sensation of her warmth so close to his. Yet even more, he found joy in the knowledge that they would be together always and forever. No power on earth could ever tear them asunder.

Entering his opulent rooms, Edgar carried Georgina across the threshold and gently set her on her feet. He closed the door and took both her hands in his.

"Georgina, I want you to know that I will do anything for you. Anything. Forever and always. You are the most precious person in the world to me."

"Do I have your consent?" he asked in full sincerity.

"Yes, dear husband." She took his face between her hands and kissed him greedily.

"Come my darling, let me worship you," he said.

Then he picked her up again and walked towards the bed with her in his strong arms.

He placed her in the centre of the bed and she spread her legs wide.

Her bridal veil spread out behind her like a luminescent halo. Her lace petticoats and ivory satin skirts bunched up lasciviously around her hips, making her an even more tempting sight for her new husband.

Edgar's eyes widened with desire. "You must surely taste delicious," he said.

"I believe so, why don't you have a try?"

He chuckled. "Yes, I shall do that. But only once you are good and ready."

"Oh you tease! You love to say that," she sighed.

"Ah, but you know the waiting makes it all the sweeter," he said before he took her right foot between his hands and rubbed on the sole. At first his strokes were gentle circles before he pressed harder and harder with his knuckles.

Georgina moaned in pleasure and looked at Edgar through hooded eyes. Her cherry red cheeks were fine evidence that she was well on her way to becoming a woman undone.

After he had paid ample attention to her right foot, and not a moment too soon, Edgar switched his attentions to the left.

His voice reverberated around Georgina's ears. "Every inch of you is perfectly formed, Georgina, from your toes to the hairs on your head and everything in between. And I don't ever want you to forget that, you understand?"

"Yes, I understand, Edgar," she said shakily. She felt herself begin to wetten. She just knew she was going to be a soppen mess by the end of the evening. How wickedly delicious!

Next, Edgar worked his hands up along Georgina's calves. He marvelled at their feminine strength. "You have such beautifully formed calves," he said.

He rubbed his hands further up Georgina's legs until he reached her knees. He tickled behind them with his tantalising fingers.

Georgina writhed up from the bed and she could not help but let a giggle escape from her lips.

Edgar let forth a satisfied chuckle. "That's it, darling, let yourself feel *everything*."

Then, Edgar's strong hands made their merry way further and further up Georgina's legs and onto her soft, womanly thighs. Edgar rolled her silken stockings down and, with real deftness, removed them from her legs one at a time. He rubbed his hands on the inside of Georgina's legs and slowly, oh so slowly, made his way up to the point where her legs met her crotch. He ran his fingers through her ample hair and glided his hands around her crotch.

He enjoyed the wetness that had formed. "Heavens, Georgina, you are absolutely soaking, I am so so proud of all that you are," he said in wonderment. "I can't wait to taste you."

"Don't deny yourself, Edgar," she breathed. Her pulse sped up faster and faster and she was more alert to his presence than she had ever been before. This, waiting for him to make a move and focus on her most special place, was exquisite teasing of the most delectable kind.

"I shall not," he murmured. "Whatever happens, sweetheart, just let yourself feel the pleasure and don't hold back,"

Then he nuzzled his nose between her legs and inhaled her musky scent. Heavens, how he had missed this in the many months since he and Georgina had last been together! This, worshipping her beautiful cunny and relishing her heavenly aroma, this was something he never wanted to go without again as long as they both on earth should live. He *craved* it like a man lost in the Sahara craves water. He swore he would never go so long without worshipping Georgina in this way ever again, not if he had any say in the matter. God had truly made her most fearfully and wonderfully, after all.

Round and round went his tongue on her plump, engorged clit.

Oh how she ached for him! She had not thought it possible but she was getting even wetter still.

Edgar's tongue continued with its delicious motions.

Georgina felt that wonderful tension building within her and, soon enough, she was dancing on the precipice of pleasure. Remembering Edgar's command, she let herself give into it and then she was falling into that oh so exquisite realm of ecstasy. Wave after wave of pleasure rolled through her and she lost track of time and space.

She was reliant fully on Edgar to decide when she had had her fill.

And after giving his new bride many wondrous orgasms, that is exactly what he did.

He helped her prop herself up on the mountain of pillows at the head of the bed. "Come up here," he said.

She did as she was bid and, soon enough, she was kneeling on all fours with her petticoats and skirts forming a creamy pool around her back and knees. Her veil remained in place, flipped over to meet her back, and her shining gold tiara completed the regal vision.

Edgar was awestruck. "My sweet wife, you are absolutely beautiful," he said.

He squeezed the flesh of her buttocks with his firm hands.

"What a delectable rump you have," he growled. He gave a medium strength smack to each cheek of her rear.

She mewed with contentment. "More, please," she said.

"It would not do for me to deny my bride." He brought his hand down again and again in firm smacks against her rump. "Whatever you wish, you need only ask."

"May I have your cock please?" she moaned.

Feigning ignorance, he replied, "My cock? Where would you like my cock? You need to be more specific, wife."

"In my cunny, Edgar. May I have your cock in my cunny, please?"

"Well, when you put it like that darling, it would be wrong for me to deny you," he said.

Georgina mewed in anticipation.

Edgar removed his cock from his breeches and thrust into Georgina.

She let out a yelp of delight.

Then he pulled back until he had almost completely withdrawn from Georgina, before entering into her again with vigour.

In and out, in and out, he moved like that. Each time, Georgina relished the power of his thrust followed by his teasing backwards motion. It was all she could do but to moan in pleasure.

Edgar growled. "That's it, let me take care of you sweetheart."

A strong, masculine hand reached around to Georgina's clit and stroked in teasing, featherlike motions.

Georgina felt a wave of ecstasy build within her. The blend of Edgar's cock inside of her and his fingers against her clit was simply too much to resist.

"Take all the pleasure you need, all the pleasure you deserve," said Edgar.

With that, Georgina let herself fall off the precipice of pleasure and down into an ocean of raptures.

Edgar thrust faster and faster.

Georgina fell into that familiar palace of wonders again and again and again.

After Georgina had had her fill, and not a moment too soon, Edgar released into her with a delighted moan.

His hips slowed down and he pulled out of her completely.

Then he took Georgina in his arms and claimed her mouth in a ferocious kiss.

He panted with flushed cheeks. "You are most fantastic, darling Georgina. I love you so so much."

She slowly opened her hooded eyes so she could take in the glorious sight before her. She had done this, she had made Edgar scarlet with desire for her and her womanly body.

She bit her lip before saying, "And you, dearest Edgar, are truly the most wonderful husband I could ever wish for."

"Come and lay with me, my beautiful wife," he said.

And so they lay together against the mountain of pillows and enjoyed each other's very being.

A little while later, Georgina went to get up to clean the seed from between her legs, as she had always done before she was married. But this time, Edgar reached out to her. "No darling, you stay here with me and rest."

"But Edgar..." Georgina whimpered coquettishly. "I have to clean myself up, or else -"

"Or else nature will take its course and you might bear my heir?" Edgar raised an eyebrow.

Georgina blushed in realisation.

Edgar's voice was gentle and soothing. "Georgina darling, you are my wife now and it is my intention to fuck as many offspring into you as possible, to keep your womb full with my heirs. I will always provide for you, always protect you. I took a sacred vow as your husband, as you took your own vows as my wife."

"Oh yes, that makes sense," Georgina said sleepily. The gloriously hard fucking she had just received had really worn her out. Yet she felt herself wetten at Edgar's words. She could get used to this life and was looking forward to bearing his offspring.

"Now, have a rest and then after we'll have some food," Edgar said.

And with those words, Georgina drifted off to sleep, enwrapped in her husband's arms and feeling the greatest bliss she had ever felt in her entire existence.

A couple of days after her wedding, Georgina sat at the desk and smoothed her silk skirts underneath herself.

She took the quill in her hand and began to write three letters to inform some very important people about her happy news.

The first was to Jean Cookson.

The second was to the Renoirs.

But the third was the most surreal of all. To the vicar and his wife with whom she had lived all those years ago back in Gloucestershire.

CHAPTER TWENTY-SEVEN

"The morning post, my lord," said a footman.

Xavier turned towards the man and took the letters from the silver tray. He thanked the footman, who then bowed and exited the entrance hall.

Xavier took the letters in hand and made his way to his office. Making deft work with the letter opener, he made his way through a dull collection of financial documents and petty social correspondence before stopping at the sight of familiar handwriting on the outside of the bottommost letter. Edgar's hand.

The second son cautiously opened the letter, praying it was not bad news, and read it quickly. First once. Then twice. Then a third time. The words that met his eyes at first seemed unbelievable, as they would have to any member of the ton, but with each reading they sunk in and a smile erupted on Xavier's face.

Dear Xavier,

Well, the matter that we spoke of is under way. After an arduous journey through France, I arrived in Venice. Through Parisienne connections of a certain lady, I was able to locate the object of my affections in Venice. And I am delighted to tell you that has she accepted my proposal of marriage. We are to be wed in one month. By the time you will likely receive this letter, that waiting period will have elapsed and so, as you read this, we now have a new Countess of Weatherby. After our nuptials we will return to England and I will send a note ahead of our arrival time once I am in a position to advise further.

With my most sincere regards,
Edgar

Philomena sat in the drawing room with her nose buried in a book of Wollstonecraft's writings. Several of her younger siblings sat at the other end of the room playing a card game.

Just as she was getting to the part about the necessity of education, Xavier rapped at the door and strode into the room.

"Philomena, can you come to Edgar's office?" he asked.

"Alright." She placed the book on the coffee table, being careful to save her place with a bookmark, and followed Xavier through the door.

As they made their way down the corridor, she turned to her brother and said, "What's all this about?"

"Ah, I've received some important news that you should know," he replied.

Now they were outside Edgar's office door. He held it open for her. "After you."

She entered and he followed, shutting the door behind him. Then he turned to her. "It's news from Edgar. What I'm about to tell you may seem most bizarre. But other than myself, you are going to be the first to know within our family."

"Go on," she said.

"Edgar is married -"

"*Married*? Edgar?"

"Yes, he is a married man. Or will be by now, assuming the circumstances have not changed."

She quirked an eyebrow. "What do you mean, 'assuming the circumstances have not changed'? That's rather cryptic."

"Well, all of this happened in Venice. I received a letter from him this morning saying he would be married in a month's time. Given it takes about a month for the post to arrive here from Venice, unless there has been a drastic change of plans then our brother is now a married man."

"I see. But why Venice? And who has he married? A Venetian?"

"The lady I spoke to you about once in Renfregh, she ended up leaving England earlier in the year to move to Venice. Edgar tracked her down, that's where he's been these past few months," said Xavier.

"Oh the opera singer!" Philomena exclaimed.

"Wait, how do you know about the opera singer?" Xavier said as bemusement flew across his features.

"I overhear the gossip, you know. None of you gentlemen are quite as discrete as you think you are," she replied.

"Who are you and what have you done with my sister?" laughed Xavier before his voice grew serious. "Never mind that now I suppose. Yes, he has married the opera singer. She was Miss Georgina Hartley, though I gather you have probably already acquired that information from one of your underhanded spiders webs of information."

Philomena grasped her hands together in glee.

"I thought you would be more shocked about this," Xavier said.

"It's certainly a surprise, but not an unwelcome one. She must be quite mad though, wanting to become a countess. Oh what fun it will be, she can take me when I am presented at court next year!"

"Philomena!" Xavier growled. "This isn't some kind of joke."

"And I'm not joking. It will be fun to shake up the ton a bit."

"I am not sure the new countess will feel the same way. She's coming in as an outsider so will probably be reluctant to rock the boat," Xavier said.

"Oh rats!" Philomena exclaimed. "When are they coming back?"

"I don't know the exact date at this stage. I understand they will do some sightseeing on the way back, a honeymoon if you will, and come up through France. Edgar said he'd write to me again once their return date is firmer."

The butler addressed the assembled crowd of several dozen household staff after tea in the servants hall of the Weatherby's London home.

"Thank you everyone, I trust that you will make the new countess very welcome indeed," he said as he wrapped up his speech.

Mrs Goodwin, the middle aged housekeeper who had been in the Weatherby family's employ since the days of Edgar's grandfather, followed the butler through the door.

Sheer bemusement filled the servants hall.

"Did I hear that right?" said a young footman named Tibbetts.

"Surely they cannot be serious?" cried a housemaid.

"Miss Hartley, the opera singer, is to be the new countess?" asked a third servant.

Voices cut across the dining table in a canopy of confusion.

The remnants of tea lay forgotten as every member of the Weatherby household staff had their say.

After about twenty minutes, the volume level began to die down as each argument had been expressed and the employees had ruminated on their own individual points of view.

"Well a wage is a wage I suppose," said a valet.

"And his lordship has always been a decent employer," Tibbetts added.

A lady's maid nodded. "And what difference does it make really, it's all the same to me whose clothes I look after so long as I get paid and they treat me decently."

"Plus," said a redheaded maid, "It will be good to have someone who isn't from the hoi poli as one of the aristocracy for a change."

Her friend laughed. "Yes, is this going to be the start of some sort of infiltration? The children of the agricultural labourers beginning their inevitable rise to the top?"

"Oh, I should hope so!" the redheaded maid replied.

CHAPTER TWENTY-EIGHT

Dusk was falling. The married couple walked hand in hand along the shoreline of Venice. They would be leaving in a few days and before they left, were going to do something they had never before been able to do in public as themselves and not as anyone else. Attend a ball.

They stopped outside a three story building, home to a long-established family of Venetian nobility. Ornate brass filigree lanterns hung from the balconies and illuminated the blush pink walls of the house.

Georgina and Edgar climbed the steps to the main doors and entered a marble hallway. Around them were throngs of people making their way to the ballroom. The Weatherbys joined the masses and soon enough they were on the dance floor taking their places.

On a raised podium in the centre of the ballroom sat a small orchestra. They began to play a lively piece by Bach.

"I remember this one!" Georgina exclaimed.

Edgar's eyes lit up with joy to see his wife so happy and at ease. "You are truly a lady of refined taste," he said.

As Edgar twirled Georgina around the room, all eyes were on the enigmatic couple. She in a deep emerald silken gown and golden satin slippers adorned with shimmering jewels. And he looking most dashing in an immaculately tailored black waistcoat and pantaloons with matching jacket and cravat. Members of the assembled crowd around the edges of the room chattered to each other about who exactly they might be.

"I heard he's a Count and she's his Contessa," said one Venetian lady to another as she sipped on her sparkling wine. "From that wet and grey land called Inghilterra."

"Whoever they are, you can tell from the way they look at one another that it's true love," her friend replied.

"Oh, if only I could find love like that one day," a third onlooking lady chimed.

The musicians concluded the piece and smatterings of applause filled the room.

Edgar drew Georgina close and placed a kiss on her hand. "You are so, so beautiful," he said.

Then, the musicians struck up another tune.

"Shall we have another dance, my handsome husband?" Georgina asked.

He nodded. "Yes, let's! Nothing would please me more in this moment than to see you enjoying yourself so."

Georgina and Edgar joined hands and formed part of the lively gallop around the room.

Georgina laughed with sheer delight.

Edgar looked at his wife and drank in her happiness. After everything they had been through, at last they were together and united as one in matrimony. His heart swelled. At last, at last they could be together openly and publicly with nothing to hide and nothing to fear.

The wooden ferry bobbed gently in its moorings awaiting its passengers. The azure waters of the Venetian lagoon sparkled in the sunlight.

Georgina and Edgar walked arm in arm along the foreshore and down the gangplank.

Burly porters followed behind with their luggage.

One trunk, then two trunks, then three, four, five.

Georgina cringed when she realised how much they were bringing with them on the long journey north to England.

"How can we have so many things? I don't understand it," she said in bemusement.

"It seems a reasonable amount to me," Edgar replied. "It's about the amount two of my siblings would take between them when they go down to Renfregh."

"Such is the life of the aristocracy I suppose," Georgina said with a light smile.

"Well you're part of it now, my darling." Edgar kissed his wife.

Throughout the journey through Northern Italy, the pair stayed at each other's side almost constantly. So inseparable were they that barely an activity took place without the pair of them together.

In Verona, they enjoyed the arena with its ancient Roman construction. They also paid a visit to Juliet's Balcony, though fortunately their love would not end in the same tragic way as that of the landmark's namesake.

Then, in Milan, they marvelled at the Duomo and Da Vinci's 'The Last Supper'. Both shining examples of the heights of humanity's potential for artistic achievement. They also took in a few operas at La Scala, a venue where Georgina herself had performed several times over the years. More lavish than any London theatre, La Scala was highly ornate with hundreds of oil lamps lighting the stage and balconies. Georgina, as a married woman, was now retired from the stage. Nonetheless, she found great joy in visiting La Scala.

Upon leaving Milan, the couple travelled northwards towards the Swiss Alps. The going was easy enough at first as the horses trotted through the cypress-lined lanes of Lombardy. But as the carriage drew nearer to the Swiss border, the roads began to grow steeper. With every mile the going became ever more arduous and the horses slowed to a steady plod. One reward, however, was the spectacular mountain views that Switzerland afforded. Both Georgina and Edgar had passed through mountains before but, like so many of their compatriots, they had not previously laid eyes upon this remote corner of Europe. To be able to do so was a true privilege and they knew it.

The couple walked through the village of Adelboden. It was so beautiful here, thought Georgina.

Returning to their secluded chalet, they went to sit on the veranda for tea. It was not the most common drink in this part of the world, but as Edgar was a British earl he was able to get hold of the leaves.

Edgar felt at peace here. He had his beloved wife at his side. The magnificent snowy peak of the Jungfrau towered overhead and a glistening pale azure ribbon of water cut through the valley.

"I'm going to fuck an heir into you, you know," Edgar said matter of factly as Georgina sipped on her tea.

She really shouldn't have been surprised, but to hear Edgar talk so bluntly made her feel warm inside.

"I look forward to that," Georgina replied with a smile.

And, in the light of the late afternoon in the cosy chalet bedroom, they put plans in motion to try exactly that.

Stepping across the Renoir's threshold as a married woman was not something Georgina ever expected to do. Yet here she was, the Countess of Weatherby paying a visit to some of her longest standing friends with her husband at her side.

After the couples exchanged greetings, Monsieur Renoir directed the party into the drawing room.

"Please, have a seat," he said jovially.

Together, they took refreshment from a blue and white willow tea set and a selection of fruit tarts.

Georgina bit into one such pear flavoured delicacy and enjoyed the sweet sensation in her mouth.

Madame Renoir said, "Tell me all about your honeymoon. Where have you been thus far?"

Georgina went into a detailed description of the places and sights the newlyweds had seen. Venice. The Great Lakes. The Swiss Alps. Burgundy.

Here and there, Monsieur Renoir interjected to give his own memories of the places Georgina listed.

But it was the voice of the countess that had the lion's share of airtime.

Edgar looked towards his wife as she held court and admired her with great fervour. She was truly a shining jewel of the most rare kind. Such a thrilling blend of candour, tact and wit.

He sipped his tea and met Madame Renoir's line of sight.

The lady of the house gave a gracious nod of approval in his direction. Her warm eyes evidenced the easy comfort she felt at Georgina's choice of husband.

Edgar felt a wave of relief wash over him. He let out a breath he had not realised he had been holding.

The Renoirs were the first people from Georgina's pre-Venice life whom the Weatherbys had met after their marriage. Moreover, the Renoirs were two of the people who cared most for Georgina in all the world, who were very dear longstanding friends to her and who had helped her during one of her darkest moments.

Obtaining the good opinion of the French couple was a high imperative for Edgar.

He did not care so much about what the snobs of the ton thought of his marriage and his new bride but the Renoirs were not of the ton. They were the common people and they knew the real Georgina.

Edgar always wanted to please those who had known Georgina the longest. The Renoirs mattered to her so naturally they mattered to him too.

❧ ❧

The next day, the streets of Paris were alive with throngs of people going about their daily business. In spite of the bloody revolution of a decade before and the horrendous destruction it at wrought, normal life seemed to continue for many thousands.

Yet beneath the surface lurked a growing tension and one day it would seep out from the earth where it currently lay in wait.

But such tensions were far from the minds of the honeymooners.

"Some might call it uxoriousness, but they can think what they like. And I would ask anyone who criticises, what is so bad about loving one's wife?" Edgar took Georgina's hand in his as they walked down the boulevard. "Now, which modiste would you like to pay a visit to first?"

Georgina surveyed the options nearby and then pointed at a shop with large green windows and an array of evening gowns on display. "That one looks a good place to start."

CHAPTER TWENTY-NINE

This was it, thought Georgina to herself. Her first steps on English soil as a bona fide countess. Certainly, she had been a countess ever since the moment the vicar had declared them man and wife all those weeks ago in Venice. Yet being abroad had put the fact that she was now a member of the peerage mostly on the back of her mind.

Edgar seemed to recognise her apprehension, try as she might to hide it. "It's alright, darling, you're doing so well." He rubbed her arm comfortingly.

She looked every inch the countess that she was. She was in a new blush pink dress with lace trim that she had had made by one of Mrs Renoir's favourite modistes in Paris. On her head she wore a maroon bonnet and around her shoulders she wore the maroon velvet cape she wore all those weeks ago at the masked ball in Venice.

As a married woman of the ton, she had stopped wearing any make up in public apart from a very thin layer of pomade on her lips. Anything else would now be strictly for the boudoir only.

Not wearing discernable make up made her look a lot more innocent and fresh faced, something she had been trying to run away from ever since her first season in Bath. Back in her days as a courtesan, she had tried to look coy yet knowing. That was what almost all her protectors wanted. However, as the Countess of Weatherby she needed to present the very picture of propriety at all times in public. In private with Edgar, it would be a different story though.

A black carriage pulled up, operated by coachmen in the Weatherby livery, They loaded the trunk and then opened the door. Edgar assisted his new bride into the carriage before getting in himself.

The carriage pulled into the outskirts of Sittingbourne as rain drove down in big splashes onto the road. A storm was brewing.

"We'll stop here for the night, darling," Edgar said.

Trotting down the street, the horses neighed as they made their last push for the day. Soon they would be enjoying the relief of a warm, dry stable and bags of hay. They drew to a halt outside a coaching inn. Georgina recognised it because she had stayed here herself a few times over the years.

A coachman opened the door and Edgar stepped down onto the stone steps. Then he held out his hand for Georgina and helped her disembark. They walked together under the archway of the main entrance tower. The area underneath the tower was lit by burning torches, casting a warm glow over the cobblestones and on the inn's sturdy stone walls on this damp and chilly night.

They entered a heavy wooden door on the left hand side of the tower and then they were in the entrance hall. The innkeeper quickly entered the room and bowed.

Edgar spoke with the innkeeper and within minutes the couple were climbing a generous wooden staircase and were being shown into a Jacobean style suite. Rich tapestries adorned much of the walls on three sides of the room. The rest of the room consisted of wood panelled walls, a dining suite, a settee, two armchairs, an imposing stone fireplace replete with roaring fire, and large latticework windows surrounded by sumptuous velvet curtains. Then of course there was the grand four poster bed with its red drapes.

Georgina, not used to staying in such luxurious rooms when travelling, breathed an internal cry of surprise. Of course, she reminded herself, it only made sense that an earl like Edgar would stay in what was very likely the best room in the whole inn.

Edgar spoke with the innkeeper, who nodded and said, "Of course, my lord."

Then Edgar shut the door and turned to Georgina. "You are so beautiful, my darling. Here, let me take your cloak for you."

As they had no maid travelling with them, Edgar was the commensurate gentleman and assisted Georgina out of her cloak. He took it and hung it up in the wardrobe.

She turned to her husband and smiled.

An hour or so went by and a maid from the inn arrived with dinner. Beef cheeks, potatoes, roast vegetables and gravy.

Georgina and Edgar chatted and laughed as they ate.

In between bites of beef, Edgar asked, "What was your favourite place we visited on the continent?"

"Oh, I enjoyed them all," she replied. "But if I had to pick one, I'd say Adelboden. Those Swiss Alps and the views of the Jungfrau are something else."

She took a sip of wine.

"What about you? What was your favourite place?" she asked.

"Like you, Adelboden takes the biscuit for me. Such wonderful scenery. And also," he added, "such wonderful memories with my darling wife."

Georgina blushed in happy reminiscence at Edgar's insinuation. Even after all they had been through together, he still had the ability to make her feel so new and alive.

⁕⁕⁕

The couple finished their meal and a maid came to clear it away.

A short while later, a footman appeared with a large metal bathtub, which he placed in the bathroom. Other footmen came in carrying pails of steaming water which they emptied into the tub and before long it was full.

"Come on sweetheart, bathtime." Edgar offered Georgina his hand and led her into the bathroom. "Let me undress you."

She smiled. "It's not fair that every time we bathe together, I don't get to see you properly. Let *me* undress *you* this time."

He bit his lip briefly before trying to maintain his composure as the calm, self assured earl he normally was. "You're right, it's not fair. I will rectify that tonight. I hope what you see will please you."

"Oh, Edgar," she purred, "I believe it will please me very much indeed. I wish to enjoy my husband's body, to savour how God made you."

She walked around him and encircled him like he was her prey. Then she untied his cravat and kissed his neck hungrily.

He let out a wanton moan and then bit his lip, all thoughts of maintaining his composure flying out the window.

Dainty hands began to unbutton his blue silk waistcoat and then they moved to his shirt buttons. He held out his arms and she undid his cufflinks, rubbing the interior of each of his wrists as she did so.

Next it was on to his breeches. She cupped his arse through the fabric, relishing the sensation of his thinly covered flesh, before she moved to the buttons at the front. She helped him step out of his breeches.

"That's it," she cooed. "Now you are totally bare for me. Exactly the way I like it."

His cock stood proud and erect. "You have such a beautiful cock, Edgar," said Georgina. "And I love that it's all mine mine mine."

She grabbed his buttocks and massaged them with her hands. "And your arse is absolutely delectable, my darling husband. Oh, you are perfectly formed!"

Edgar closed his hawkish brown eyes in wild abandon to the joy he was feeling at the hands of his wife. Before he was wed, back when he spent his nights with mistresses, he was not one to take a truly submissive role during sexual encounters. Though secretly in his own head he had long had an interest in submitting to a woman, he had never before allowed himself to make it a reality because he had always felt the need to be in command in every situation. It was what an earl was supposed to do, he had repeatedly told himself. Be in command of his woman, be in command of his family, be in command of his estates. But now he was united in Holy Matrimony with Georgina, he felt safe enough to express this deeply hidden side of himself and let her take charge.

❧❧❧ ❧❧❧

The next morning, Edgar awoke with a sleepy smile on his face. He yawned and stretched and turned to where his sweet Georgina lay next to him. He propped himself up on one elbow and looked down at her sleeping form in admiration. Heavens, she was so beautiful. He was truly the luckiest man alive!

He reflected on the events of last night, how the tables had turned by mutual consent and Georgina had taken charge. He had found it relaxing and a fantastic way to find his centre again. But today he knew Georgina needed him to, nay she expected him to, take command of the situation. Because today was the day they would arrive at his family's London home and she would truly begin life as a member of British high society.

Edgar was drawn from his thoughts by Georgina snuffling as she awoke.

"Good morning, Edgar," she said.

He kissed her forehead and smiled. Their new life together was only just beginning.

❧ · ◆ · ☙

CHAPTER THIRTY

With every mile that the carriage drew closer to London, the reality of the situation sunk in. Georgina was a countess now, heading straight for the belly of the beast of the British Empire. Georgina felt a pang of nervousness grow within her stomach. She had never met any of Edgar's family before and today she would be coming face to face with nearly all his siblings.

As the carriage pulled into the streets of Mayfair, Edgar sensed her nervous energy and rubbed her hand gently. "You have nothing to fear, sweetheart. You're a Weatherby now."

"Intellectually, I know you're right, but I still can't stop my heart from worrying though," Georgina said.

Edgar looked at his wife with stern, hawkish eyes. "Would it help you if I took control of the situation, to remind you of your place?"

"What do you mean?"

"Some of those gloves you love over your mouth and then I read some reminders to you," he said matter of factly.

"Yes, please."

"Very well, then." Edgar reached over to where his great coat lay on the seat and rummaged in the pockets for his gloves and a small book. He placed the small book on the seat between himself and the carriage door. Then he put the gloves on his fingers and waggled them in Georgina's face as though he were about to perform a magic trick.

Georgina giggled.

Edgar smiled back and took Georgina's chin between his thumb and forefinger. "If at any point you wish to stop, simply bang your fist three times on the seat, like so." Edgar demonstrated the motion. "Understand?"

"Yes, Edgar."

"Then we shall begin."

With that, Edgar placed one hand behind Georgina's head and back around the front of her face to cover her mouth. He picked up the small book in his other hand and opened it to a well worn page.

Georgina looked down at the book Edgar was holding and realised it was a New Testament. Edgar's personal copy! Though she did not know him as a particularly religious man, and she herself was not a woman of strong piety, this revelation did not come as much of a surprise to her when she thought of how Edgar had behaved towards her during their marriage thus far.

"A reading from Ephesians, Chapter Five," began Edgar. "Wives, submit yourselves unto your own husbands as unto the Lord. For the husband is the head of the wife even as Christ is the head of the church: and he is the saviour of the body..."

Georgina felt herself relax as Edgar made his way through the familiar verses.

"Husbands, love your wives even as Christ also loved the church, and gave himself for it," read Edgar.

Georgina's breathing slowed to a steady rhythm through Edgar's leather clad fingers. He felt this change and smiled to himself as he continued to read from the bible. His beloved Georgina was responding in exactly the way he had hoped!

"So ought men to love their wives as their own bodies. He that loveth his wife loveth himself. For no man ever hated his flesh but nourisheth it and cherisheth it..."

By the time Edgar read the final verse of the chapter, "Nevertheless let every one of you in particular so love his wife even as himself; and the wife *see* that she reverence *her* husband," Georgina's breathing was even and deep. If Edgar continued with another chapter, he knew there was a good chance she would be asleep by the end of it, such was her newfound level of relaxation and calm.

Edgar closed the book. "Feel better, darling?"

Georgina nodded and looked at Edgar with a genuine smile in her eyes.

"Good." Edgar kissed her forehead. "I love you so, so much darling."

He removed his hand from her mouth and she found the words to speak. "Thank you Edgar, that was wonderful. Exactly what I needed. One question though."

"Oh, what's that?"

"That Ephesians 5 page, it looks like it's about the most well thumbed page in that New Testament of yours. You've never struck me as an exceptionally religious man, so why that page?"

Edgar kissed her hand. "Because it's been a source of great strength for me this last year. It's something I take very seriously, protecting you and providing for you. Those months after you'd gone to the continent and I was still so up in my own head here in England, and then when I was trying to find you, I used to read that passage every day. Apart from when I was in that village in France, with Madame Toussaint. I've not told anyone that before, about how I came to realise the most important responsibility of a husband is to love. And that's something I swear to you I will do every day of our lives together."

The carriage drew to a halt in the grounds of the house outside the main doors. A footman opened the door and Edgar disembarked. Then he turned to offer his hand to Georgina. She took his hand and set her first feet on Weatherby soil as the countess. Once she had got her bearings, she lifted her head and saw the entire household staff lined up outside the front of the house. Edgar then directed her along a long line of staff all the way from the butler and housekeeper through to the scullery maids and page boys, making introductions as he went. Georgina's head swam, how could she remember all those names?

"And your lady's maid, Miss Felicity Hopkins," said Edgar.

A mousey woman, perhaps ten years older than Georgina, curtsied and smiled.

With that final introduction, Edgar took Georgina by the arm and led her into the house.

Once they were alone in the hallway, he rubbed a comforting arm across her back and said, "I know it's a lot, but you're doing so so well my darling."

⁕⁕⁕

After freshening up, the couple took luncheon in the dining room. Georgina admired the splendour of the room with its plethora of landscapes hanging on the walls.

"I'll give you the full tour of the house after this, and then there are some people I'd like for you to meet," Edgar said with a smile.

⁕⁕⁕

"These are the countess' chambers," Edgar said. "First, the sitting room."

The pair entered a pale peach sitting room with a white marble fireplace. In the centre sat a dark peach settee.

"I know they're rather spartan at the moment, no one has used them since my mother, but decorate them as you see fit," he said and cast his hand around the room.

Then he led Georgina over to a wooden door, opened it and gestured for her to walk through.

"And this is your office," Edgar said.

Georgina found herself in a white panelled room overlooking the garden. There were several bookshelves around the room and a white Rococo desk and chair.

"And finally, your bedroom." Edgar opened another wooden door and led Georgina through it.

Another pale peach room.

Georgina turned to Edgar. "I take it your mother had a big thing for peach?"

"That she did," Edgar nodded with a smile in his eyes.

***

"This is my sister, Philomena," said Edgar before he stepped out of the door and left the two ladies to their own devices.

Philomena gave a small smile, which Georgina returned.

If Georgina had not known any better, she would have thought her new sister-in-law was a little starstruck. It would not have been the first time for a young lady of good breeding to find herself swept up in the glamour of the ladies of the stage, after all.

"How do you do?" the Weatherby sister said.

The two exchanged pleasantries, before Georgina said. "I know I am not what was expected for your brother."

"I'm glad about that. Our brother was out of sorts for months over you, you know," Philomena said.

Georgina kept her face steady and even. She had never met Philomena before, though from what she had heard from Edgar she seemed to be a typical adolescent experiencing great discomfort with her place in the world, and

Georgina wanted nothing less than to start off on the wrong foot with a new in-law.

"He did it to himself though," Philomena continued and then gave a small smirk. "I'm just glad he came to his senses after all that time."

⁂

"What is it like in Venice?" Philomena asked suddenly.

"Different to London in a lot of ways," Georgina said. "Not only the heat, but the whole atmosphere is different. It's a less rigid society than here in some ways and very decadent. The scenery is beautiful, especially the canals and the lagoon. And St Mark's Square too."

"I'll probably never get to go, never even get to leave Britain," Philomena grumbled.

"You might one day," Georgina said. "Where in Britain have you been so far?"

The Weatherby sister's eyes lit up in happy reminiscence. "Bath, I love it when we go there. And Brighton, I've been there sometimes in the summer. Oh and Oxford, the Bodelian library is gorgeous. I wish I could study there."

"In Oxford?"

Philomena nodded and then said sadly, "It seems unlikely though."

Being well aware of the constraints of English society during the reign of George III, the countess was loathe to give Philomena false hope, But she still did not want to dampen her spirits entirely. "Maybe so. Though things are changing slowly, and I daresay your granddaughters will stand a good chance to. Do you study much at home?"

"Oh yes," Philomena said. "We have a most excellent library, has Edgar shown it to you yet? It is fantastic, we get new books all the time."

"And pamphlets?"

Philomena raised a hand to her mouth in an effort to conceal her glee. "How do you know about the pamphlets? Did Edgar tell you."

"Yes, he did. I like reading them myself sometimes. I used to get them from Chancery Lane back before I went to the continent. And the French ones whenever I was in Paris, too."

"Ooh, who do you recommend?" Philomena was pleased to have found a kindred spirit.

And so they spent the next half an hour discussing all the best pamphlets and books.

Philomena simply just knew they were going to get along splendidly.

⁂

Later in the day, Xavier and Georgina sat side by side on the swings in the garden of Weatherby House.

"You know, part of me has long thought Edgar would end up with a lady like you," Xavier said. "He was just so damn stubborn for months. But I'm glad he saw sense in the end. I'm really glad you're here, I can see already that you being with him is doing wonders."

"That's very kind of you to say," she remarked.

"I genuinely mean it though. My brother, well you know him yourself, he isn't one to listen to others much and he's got a sense of duty ten furlongs wide."

"Did he not listen to you then?" Georgina asked.

Xavier bit his lip and nodded. "Yes, there may have been several conversations between the pair of us."

"Oh really? What kind of conversations?"

"Conversations of the kind about how he ought to see sense. Ought to see who he really should be with, rather than focusing on spectres and assumptions about the ton." Xavier gave Georgina a knowing smile, which she returned.

The wind rustled gently through the leaves of the bushes dotted in terracotta pots around the garden.

Georgina kicked her feet a little underneath the seat of her swing. "Then I am glad those spectres and assumptions are of no more import. So, Edgar tells me you studied for the cloth. Are you looking for a curacy?"

"At some point I will. It's inevitable really," he said.

"But not right now?"

"Not right now, no. There's too much of life to experience first."

Georgina nodded. "No need to be in any rush."

They sat in companionable silence for a minute or so, until loud barks cut through the air behind them.

Xavier flicked his head towards where the family basset hound was trotting on the lawn. "Here, Brydon!" Xavier called.

Brydon bounded over to the swings.

Xavier turned back to Georgina. "Yet another Weatherby for you to meet. Brydon, he's a -"

The basset hound chose that precise moment to start howling.

Georgina laughed. "He has excellent timing, I can tell that already."

"That he does indeed," Xavier said.

Brydon barked again and wagged his tail.

Georgina reached out and gave him a pat. She knew right down to the marrow of her bones that she was going to be very happy here, as part of the Weatherby family.

❧ ☙

Three days after her arrival in London, Georgina made her way on foot to Jean Cookson's house. Carrying a small wicker basket in her arms, she looked like the picture of confidence.

She knocked at Jean's door and shortly thereafter it opened to reveal her old friend.

"The Countess of Weatherby," Jean said flatly, yet with a twinkle in her eye. "What brings you to these parts?"

"Jean, come on, you know it's me!"

"I know, I know, I jest my lady," Jean said with a smile. "Come in."

Georgina entered the hallway and Jean shut the door behind her friend.

"I still can't believe this," Jean said.

"Nor can I," Georgina replied. She looked across at the stairs where Edgar had tried to win her back all those months ago, and she had taken him back for a short while before leaving for the continent. So much had changed since, and all for the better, she mused.

The pair entered Jean's kitchen and the modiste began to prepare tea with Georgina boiling the water.

Once the tea was ready, Georgina took her familiar seat at the table with Jean sitting next to her.

"You know, I couldn't believe it when your now husband came into my shop that day asking of your whereabouts. I had half a mind to turn him away with no answer at all, but he was so earnest," the modiste said.

Georgina sipped her tea as her friend continued to speak.

"And then he left London that evening, headed for Dover. Didn't tell a soul outside his family where he was going. It was a good lark running the shop during those first few weeks. So much speculation about where Lord Weatherby had gone and why. There was everything from running off to Brazil to hiding out in the Scottish Highlands. But no one had the truth of it at all."

Georgina burst out laughing. "Running off to Brazil? Whatever for?"

"Your guess is as good as mine." Jean gave a wry smile. "The truth is more incredible though."

Georgina nodded. "When I saw him walk into that theatre in Venice, I thought I was hallucinating, that I'd gone quite mad from the heat. But there he was."

Jean sighed. "How romantic! Your husband, he really is something special. He proved me wrong, that's for sure."

"He proved me wrong too," Georgina said. "When I left him that night, I never thought he'd come to find me."

"But he did," Jean said. "He's a keeper that one."

"And don't I know it!"

The pair chatted amiably about Georgina and Edgar's nuptials.

"So where did you actually wed, since neither of you are Catholic?" Jean said.

"The chapel at the British Consulate," Georgina said. "It's about the only presence of the Church of England for miles and miles. The only presence that takes place openly anyway."

"Kind of like a reverse of -" Jean broke herself off and took a sip of her tea.

Georgina nodded gently. "Yes, a reverse in a sense of your situation here." She rubbed her forearm and then continued. "It's such a stupid state of affairs, the whole business, there and here. I thought Pitt the Younger was going to sort it out on the British side the other year."

"Ha! Never in a month of Sundays," Jean laughed. "Pitt!"

"Ah yes, well now I realise that in hindsight," Georgina said.

"Oh that reminds me," Georgina said as she reached across the table to where the wicker basket she had brought over was located. "I've got some things in here for you." She handed her friend the basket and watched for her reaction with bated breath.

Jean pulled back the covering from the basket and gasped. "Oh Georgina, you shouldn't have!" The modiste pulled out a selection of fine fabric samples, the latest releases from Venice and Paris and ordinarily pieces which would not arrive on English shores for another year or two.

CHAPTER THIRTY-ONE

Mr Payne blinked at the vision that materialised before him. The earl and a lady in a pale blush dress exited the carriage. The new countess. He recognised her from somewhere, but at first could not quite put his finger on it. Then memories came to the forefront of his mind and it struck him who she was! The mistress the earl used to bring with him to Renfregh when the rest of the Weatherby clan were away. Mr Payne was not a man who kept up with the goings on of fashionable society or the news from London, being as he was much more focused on country pursuits and the need to feed his family through selling his labour to Weatherby. Yet, he remembered the mistress as a lady who came from a rural background somewhat like his own. She was very discrete and kept largely to herself, yet had an aspect of her demeanour that indicated someone who carried themselves with a certain confidence.

Casting his mind back to the meeting with the earl last year where his employer gave instructions to renovate the village, Mr Payne reflected that Edgar's original explanation about concerns of revolution likely was not the full story. Certainly, he had heard tales of aristocrats falling in love with their working class mistresses. Yet he could not recall an aristocrat ever going so far as to *marry* their mistress, their courtesan, a lady of the stage. Still, there was a first time for everything and he could not hand on heart say he was opposed to the notion.

❧❧❧❧❧❧ ❦❦❦❦❦❦

"Come this way," Edgar said. Holding out his hand to Georgina, he had a rakish smile on his face that she couldn't resist. This was only Georgina's first day at Renfregh as the Countess of Weatherby and he still had much to show her about the delights of her new country home.

Opening a side door normally hidden in the library wall, Edgar led Georgina through into a room she'd never seen before. A secret room with plush furniture around the edges and a Persian rug in the middle of the floor.

"So dear husband, what's this room used for?"

"Whatever we want it to," Edgar replied wolfishly.

Georgina arched an eyebrow. "Is that so? Then I have an idea for how we can put it to good use." She took Edgar's handsome face between her dainty hands and claimed his mouth with her own. She savoured the now familiar taste of bergamot and molasses.

They broke apart for air.

Edgar let forth a low chuckle. "Pray tell me more, my lady."

Georgina gestured to the chaise longue a few steps away. Its sumptuous covering of maroon velvet belied its sturdy structure. "That is the most perfect place for a fucking.

But first, I would like for you to worship my cunny with that wondrously talented tongue of yours," she said with a coquettish smile.

Edgar grinned like the cat who had the cream. "That, my lady, can most certainly be arranged."

He ran his hands along her shapely buttocks through the silks of her skirts and petticoats. Then he lifted her in the air and carried her towards the chaise longue. He deposited her reverently on the velvet seat. He bent down and removed her satin shoes.

Then he massaged the soles of her feet with his strong, masculine hands.

She moaned in delight.

He laughed. "Oh you like that, do you, my lady?"

"Don't you just know it," she breathed.

He moved his hands upwards, brushing aside her skirts and petticoats along the way, and massaged her calves and those sensitive spots at the backs of her knees.

Then, he plunged his head into the place where her legs met and found her slick and glistening. She was wet, oh so wet, and only ever for him!

He lapped greedily, first along her plump labia and then around and around her clit.

She looked down at him through hooded eyes. "You are so good at doing that."

He chuckled deeply into her and relished the strawberry-like taste of her juices. Around and around, up and down he swirled his talented tongue.

Georgina felt a crescendo building within herself, starting at the point where Edgar was suckling and teasing before blooming out towards her belly and chest and then throughout her whole body. Sometimes it was fire and sometimes it was ice and sometimes it was electricity. Again and again she climaxed, letting out breathy moans and mews of pleasure as she did so.

After she had had her fill of Edgar's wonderful tongue, and not a moment before, she said lustily, "I think now is the time for you to fuck me, Edgar."

Edgar pulled his head back and crawled up the chaise longue until Georgina's face was level with his own. Then he intertwined his fingers with hers and kissed her deeply and intensely on the mouth. "As my lady wishes, so she shall have," he said.

He placed a kiss on her left hand and then got up from the chaise longue. He removed his waistcoat and cravat before undoing his white shirt and dropping them all to the floor.

Georgina propped herself up on one elbow and looked across to where her husband stood. She watched the sight before her with total relish. Edgar's toned chest and athletic arms were most enticing and a delight to her eyes. What a handsome husband she had!

Edgar bent down to remove his boots, but before he could complete the task, Georgina's lascivious voice filled his ears.

"You should leave your boots on," she said.

He smirked. "And the pantaloons? Would you like me to leave those on too?"

"No, just the boots," she replied.

"Very well." He took off his pantaloons and drawers, leaving him already hard in only his black leather riding boots. Exactly how Georgina liked him. He took a step towards her. "Is this what my lady wants?" he asked, though really he already knew full well the answer.

She bit her lip. "Exactly what I want."

He joined her on the chaise longue and placed a fearsome kiss on her mouth. Then he sat with his feet on the ground and pulled her on top of him so that her back was facing his chest. "Ride me, my lady," he said with pure desire in his voice.

It was all she could do to comply. She ground up and down, up and down and it was so so wonderful to be full of him. Though they had fucked many times before, being with Edgar like this was always as exciting as the first time back in her dressing room all those moons ago.

Edgar's voice rumbled low in her ear. "That's it, take what you need my darling."

In and out she rode him and then that deliciously familiar sensation built within her until she could contain it no more and wave after wave of pleasure rolled through her body.

They fucked like that for a while until Georgina said, "Edgar, oh -"

She broke off as another climax overtook her. Then she stilled on top of him.

Edgar chuckled. "You were saying, my darling?"

"How about you bend me over the chaise and keep on fucking me?"

"I like that idea. I like it a lot."

Georgina turned her head to face Edgar and claimed his mouth in a passionate kiss.

The pair rose to their feet and Georgina bent over the arm of the chaise longue.

Edgar lifted her skirts and petticoats and wrapped an arm around her waist. He entered her and thrusted with deep power.

Georgina let forth a mew of delight.

Then, oh so slowly, Edgar withdrew from her almost completely.

"Don't be a tease," she breathed.

"I'm not teasing," Edgar laughed. "I'm only giving you what you require. Remember, as your husband it is my duty to keep you satisfied in every single way."

He reentered her rapidly.

She made a yelp of pleased surprise.

Edgar pumped in and out of her with vigour. "In. Every, Single. Way." He punctuated each word with another powerful thrust.

Georgina felt another climax building within her and, before she knew it, she was riding out a wave of pleasure on Edgar's cock.

Earlier, she had thought to herself that being with Edgar like this was just as exciting as that first time together. Yet, on reflection, she realised that being with Edgar like this as husband and wife was better than anything that had gone before.

❧ ─ ◆ ─ ◆ ─ ❧

CHAPTER THIRTY-TWO

The driving rain lashed against the windows of Georgina's Renfregh bedroom. Thunder roared in the distance.

Inside, Georgina and Edgar lay in her four poster bed.

Edgar was already fast asleep on his stomach, dwelling in the domain of dreams.

Georgina stared through the wide opening in the damask bed curtains and looked across to the uncovered lead lattice windows that faced the foot of the bed.

The world outside was perilous tonight. The rain. The thunder. The storm.

She turned her head towards where Edgar lay and admired his fine form. He was so beautiful. When he was awake, he so often wore the weight of his responsibilities on his shoulders. Yet, she was pleased to observe, he had more frequently relaxed moments now that they were wed. Marriage had been good for him. It had been good for the both of them.

Her life before had been one of ups and downs, achievement yet also regular insecurity. For a decade she had continued down the best path she knew of, and she would never ever be ashamed of that path or apologise for it, but it had been a lonely unforgiving road. Now, with Edgar at her side, she had security, safety and genuine committed love. She had someone on whom she could rely wholly and completely, and someone who could rely on her in turn.

Glad she was not outside or in one of the wooden shacks she had grown up in, Georgina snuggled down, wrapped her arms around her slumbering husband and let herself drift off to sleep.

A week later, Georgina sat sidesaddle on her horse. It had been many years since she had ridden, but after a few sessions trotting gently round the grounds with Edgar at her side, she felt more comfortable. Today she was going up to the village to see this part of the estate up close and to meet with the vicar.

As she rode up the lawn, the air was brisk but the ground underfoot was still firm after the balmy summer that had just passed.

After a while she came to St Anne's Church. She dismounted her horse and tied it to the wooden archway out the front of the churchyard. Looking around the village she could see some renovation works under way. She resolved to ask the vicar about them.

"Reverend, I couldn't help but notice there are a lot of renovations under way in the village," Georgina said.

Across her, in the parlour at the vicarage, sat Reverend Miller. He was a thin man with greying hair. Georgina guessed he was around fifty years of age.

"You are correct, my lady, and we have his lordship to thank for that," Reverend Miller said.

Georgina sipped her tea before asking, "I see. How long ago did they start?"

"It would have been about eight or nine months ago, yes, shortly before advent last. We were all so pleased when they began."

She smiled gently. "Oh yes, I can see how they're making change for the better here. Are there often renovations in the village?"

"Well, no, my lady. These are the first renovations in living memory." There was a note of awkwardness in the vicar's tone.

Georgina felt herself begin to wrinkle her nose as if on autopilot, before she quickly recovered her composure.

⁕⁕⁕⁕⁕ ⁕⁕⁕⁕⁕

As she rode back to the house, Georgina's head was spinning. The first renovations in living memory? Why and how had that been allowed to happen? How had Edgar and his father and grandfather before him been running the estates? She had to confront him. As soon as possible.

Approaching the stables, she slowed her horse to a trot as the stablehands appeared to meet her. She dismounted from the mare and made her way into the house. A maid appeared from across the hall and helped her to remove her riding gear.

Georgina could feel her heart beating faster and faster. She had to find Edgar and find out the truth of what had gone on. She made her way to Edgar's main office and sure enough he was in there with the door slightly ajar, sitting at his writing desk and lost in the process of examining a ledger.

"Oh husband mine," she began coyly.

He looked up at her and smiled.

"I've been up to the village where I had a nice meeting with the vicar. He told me about the renovations that are going on, only I was surprised to hear him say that they're the first renovations in living memory. Is that true, husband?"

Edgar dropped his quill and stood up out of his seat. He walked towards his wife and laid a gentle hand on her shoulder. "Yes, that's correct. And I'm not proud to admit it."

"But how could things have gone so long with no restorations, no updates to the village?"

"It's how I'd done things ever since I became the earl, and how my father had done things before me." Edgar rubbed the back of his neck. "To be honest, it never occurred to me that renovations had much importance and, what little I know of how my father ran the earldom, I don't think he saw the value in them either."

She raised an eyebrow. "Then why the change of heart late last year?"

"I had my eyes opened to some things. It wasn't right the way I was running things, almost neglecting the tenants."

"Only almost neglecting them?"

Edgar closed his eyes briefly and gulped, before opening them and encountering his wife's questioning eyes. "You're right, you're completely right. I was neglecting them. I can try to make excuses and say I didn't know any better but someone in my position absolutely should have known better."

"That's true. Though I'll wager you weren't doing much worse than most lords in this country."

"Still," Edgar said.

"Still," she agreed. "What are you going to do moving forward?"

"After these renovations on the church and the cottages, I'm planning to sort out the main street."

Georgina nodded.

Edgar continued, "But there's something I should ask you, and now's as good a time as any. What do you think I should do?"

"Edgar, you're the earl not me. These decisions lie with you. It's your estate at the end of the day."

"I know. And I don't want to put you on the spot, but well, you understand the realities of living in a village like that in a way I never will. You know better than I could ever hope to if I lived this life a thousand times what people in those villages want and need."

Georgina blinked and then came to a decision, taking Edgar's hands in her own. "Very well, after the main street you need to sort out the water supply. And then once you've done that, you need to set up a school for the children, for the girls as well as the boys."

"A school? But you were taught at a vicarage."

"That's right. But most children won't get that opportunity. They're better off if you set up something more formal, have the children go for a couple of days a week when their families don't need them in the fields."

Edgar pondered what his wife had recommended. On the one hand, some of his fellow lords believed providing schooling to all children merely provided a breeding ground for sedition. It's much harder to start a revolution when you've got no way of disseminating your message in writing and when your desired audience cannot read. Yet the pamphlets were coming thick and fast from London, Paris and the rest and he had no way of stopping them. If he left schooling provision to someone else, he risked someone else eventually coming in and providing it, someone who may not have any reason to support the traditional life of duty the Weatherbys espoused. If he himself took the initiative to provide schooling for those on his estates, then was he not merely fulfilling a duty of noblesse oblige? Did not he, with all the privilege he was born into and the authority of his position as Earl of Weatherby, have a duty and responsibility to look after his tenants and all vulnerable people as best he could? Part of that duty and responsibility therefore surely extended to giving his tenants an opportunity to learn to read and write. What they did with those skills would then be up to them, but if he were the one to provide the schooling in the first place then the Weatherby line stood a better chance of survival than its French equivalents.

A few days later, in the secret room that had now become one of her favourite places at Renfregh, Georgina spread her legs wide open and reclined back on the chaise lounge.

Edgar moved towards the space between her legs and placed delicate kisses on the inside of her thighs. Then slowly, oh so slowly, he made his way up to her most secret place and nuzzled his nose in her folds. He savoured her musky scent and breathed it in deeply. Oh how he loved this! She was all woman woman woman and he was so so proud to call her his wife!

"Oh, husband," she moaned. "You know what to do, so do it!"

He chuckled deeply into her and began to run his tongue about, savouring her sweet strawberry taste.

They were destined for another most pleasant afternoon.

The Weatherby carriage made its way up the hill towards the village.

Georgina sat opposite her lady's maid, Miss Hopkins.

"I remember these harvest festivals from our village growing up," Georgina said. "Did you have them as well?"

"Yes my lady, every year," Miss Hopkins replied. "Mis-shapen vegetable competition and all."

Georgina giggled. "Oh heavens, I remember those! Grotesque twisted marrows and a carrot that looks like old father time's face and all the rest of it. Tasted just as good in the end though."

"That's true," Miss Hopkins nodded. "And I loved the corn dollies."

"Me too! Making them was such fun. What were the ones like in Cambridgeshire?"

"These small handbells, my lady. The top part formed a handle, then the middle was a spiral formation of the corn into the main body of the bell and then we'd put two or three stalks of corn poking out the bottom, to form the clappers." The lady's maid gestured with her hands at each step. "What did you have in your village?"

"We used to make knotted wreaths, a circle to form the main part and then two halves of a heart in the centre of the circle and we'd weave the two halves together to form a heart," Georgina explained.

***

The footman opened the carriage door and assisted Georgina down the step. Miss Hopkins followed closely behind. A round of applause broke out among the crowd and then a band struck up.

Rum tiddly um pum pum pum, went the band. There was someone playing the trumpet, another on a bass drum and a third person playing a fiddle. Georgina did not recognise the tune, probably one of the band's own composition, but she could tell they were competent musicians.

The band finished their piece to hearty applause from the assembled crowd. Then the vicar took to a makeshift podium and gave a speech, ending with, "And it gives me great pleasure to introduce to you the Right Honourable Countess of Weatherby!"

Then he stepped off the podium and Georgina took his place. In her fashionable pale pink dress, maroon velvet cape and pink silk bonnet with maroon bow, she cut a striking figure among the crowd.

Towards the front of the audience, a child tugged at her mother's skirts and exclaimed, "Look, mama! A princess!"

"Not quite, my love, not quite, but pretty close indeed," the mother said.

From her many years on the stage, Georgina had developed a confidence commensurate with being a seasoned performer. Countless nights had she spent singing for the great and the good, and let's be honest the not so good too. Yet she had so rarely ever performed for her people so to speak. Certainly, the people of this village were not the ones she had grown up with but they were the closest it was possible to get without travelling back to the village of her birth. And even though they were her people and she was of them, she could never truly be in them. She had lived too much of a life elsewhere for that to be a possibility.

Opening her mouth, Georgina delivered her pre-prepared speech and as she spoke she could see the crowd jostle first at the ever so slightly familiar rural lilt to her voice that was barely perceptible to most outside South West England.

She had lost most of her accent years ago, it was true, trained out of it as she had been by her tutors and the vicar's wife. But there would always be the occasional strain that would shine through and she was not interested in hiding it. She would never have the cut glass accent of Edgar and the other Weatherbys, but did she really want to sound like that all the time? No!

Through her speech, Georgina said nothing profound but she would remember it all the rest of her days.

Polite applause followed her speech and then it was time to judge the fattest marrow, heaviest chicken and all the rest of it.

A girl, who Georgina guessed was not much older than seven or eight, walked up to Georgina, corn dolly in hand. "Here, my lady, this is for you."

Georgina took the corn dolly from the girl. "Thank you, Miss - what was your name, poppet?"

"Emma Durbin, my lady," the girl said.

"Well, thank you Miss Emma, this is a very pretty corn dolly." Georgina examined the straw construction in her hands, impressed by the quality of the handiwork. A round circle of intricately weaved straw surrounded a portcullis-like structure in the centre. "Did you make it yourself?"

"Oh yes, my lady," Emma said with pride.

CHAPTER THIRTY-THREE

The Wilsons were spending a couple of months in Bath to enjoy the benefits of the spa and the rheumatic treatments. Through their correspondence, Georgina had arranged to meet with them.

Edgar and Georgina made their way through the door of their family home in the Circus and strode out onto the street.

They walked arm in arm along the imposing pavements towards where the Wilsons were staying close to the Roman Baths.

"How are you feeling about seeing the Wilsons, darling?" Edgar asked.

"Mostly good. The dowry issue was all-consuming at the time, but that's in the past," she replied.

Edgar's obsidian walking cane made a thumping sound on the paving stones with each step the couple took.

After walking for just under a quarter of an hour, the pair arrived at the Wilson's rented Bath apartments.

A jovial maid showed them into the apricot drawing room. Then she gave the Weatherbys a curtsey and left.

"Reverend Wilson, Mrs Wilson," began Georgina.

"Georgina Hartley, as I live and breathe!" exclaimed Mrs Wilson from where she sat alongside her husband on a yellow pouffe sofa. "And the Earl of Weatherby! Welcome, welcome."

Though he had retained his curacy, Reverend Wilson was struggling with his eyesight and hearing in his old age. "Who is that?"

"Georgina Hartley, dear," shouted Mrs Wilson. "And her new husband, the Earl of -"

The Reverend smiled in recognition. "Oh, Georgina! How lovely you are here. I hear you are married now. Who is the lucky man?"

"The Earl of Weatherby," supplied Mrs Wilson.

The Reverend scoffed. "Be sensible now, my dear. I'd already know if an earl and a countess were coming to visit us."

Mrs Wilson and Georgina shared a look of amusement, while Edgar did his best to keep a straight face.

"Well come closer, come closer whoever you are," the Reverend bellowed.

Edgar and Georgina made their way to the sofa opposite the Wilsons.

The Reverend peered closely at Edgar. "You say you are the Earl of Weatherby? Ah yes, now I see the resemblance, you look a lot like your late father you know."

Mrs Wilson smirked with a 'told you so' expression and then called to her maid, "Miss Smithers, some tea in the drawing room please!"

⁕⁕⁕

After a couple of pots of tea, the Reverend pulled Edgar aside. "I know you are a gentleman. Do you love Georgina?"

"Yes," Edgar said.

"Promise me you will not hurt her."

"I swear to you that I will not hurt her. You have my word."

"Very good," nodded the Reverend. "Because if you ever do, you'll have to answer for it on Judgement Day."

⁕⁕⁕

Then, once Edgar and the Reverend Wilson had returned to the group and there had been another pot of tea shared amongst them all, the Reverend and Mrs Wilson shared a significant look with each other.

Mrs Wilson turned to Edgar and said loudly, "So, my lord, how do you find Bath at this time of year?"

At the same time as his wife was speaking, Reverend Wilson looked across at Georgina and said, "Georgina, may we go and talk somewhere else please?"

"Yes, of course," she replied.

The Reverend rose from the settee in a juddering way. He led Georgina through the doors, out across the narrow corridor and into an adjacent pokey little study.

He gestured to one of the two walnut-carved chairs, relics of the middle of the last century. "Please, have a seat, Georgina," he said.

She duly did so and watched as the Reverend lowered himself with shaking feet into the chair facing hers.

The pendulum of the grandfather clock plodded away in the otherwise silent room.

Georgina and the Reverend sat like that for nigh on a minute until, eventually, the Reverend began to speak. "Georgina, it has been absolutely lovely to see you again, and to see you doing so well. But I could not let you go today without telling you how truly sorry I am that I failed you all those years ago -"

"Reverend," she interjected softly. "There is no need for this. The past is the past."

"That is most forgiving of you, Georgina. But I fear my trespasses against you are too grave to be put aside so rapidly." His gaze was weary with the guilt of so many years.

Georgina sighed and did not speak for a good few seconds.

The grandfather clock plodded on.

Then Georgina opened her mouth and said, "I understand why you did it, Reverend. There was no other real choice with the lack of money for the dowries."

"But that is exactly it. That is how I failed you. I must humbly apologise for not providing you with the dowry you so desperately needed." Revered Wilson lowered his gaze to the floor for several seconds, before returning his eyes to meet hers. "If it had not been for me sticking my oar in all those years ago and plucking you from your family, none of this would ever have happened."

Georgina said with ferocious alacrity, "Reverend, your moving me into the vicarage and giving me singing lessons, educating me like one of your daughters, that was about the best thing that has ever happened to me. Apart from Edgar." She gestured towards the drawing room where, sure enough, her husband would currently be sitting with Mrs Wilson enjoying Bohea tea and sweet little pastries. "It didn't turn out how any of us had hoped, what with the dowry falling through though, but still I would not have changed it for all the world. It made me who I am today. How else could I have become an opera singer without those years of preparation and training at the vicarage."

"I left you in an unconscionable position though. I failed you. I let you fall into the hands of Briar, for heaven's sake," cried Reverend Wilson.

"Ah now," Georgina quirked her lip. "Mr Briar was not so bad. He helped me out with a decent gentleman when I first went on the stage."

A tear rolled down the old man's cheek. He hastily brushed it away. "I should have done more. I could have done more to save you from all that."

"Reverend," she replied softly, "I don't think there was much you could have done. The financial situation was so parlous and without a dowry I had very limited options. Service wouldn't have suited me, I would've flitted around from place to place never getting anywhere."

"But you could have stayed with us, for as long as you wanted," the Reverend tried through his tears.

Georgina smiled ruefully. "I would have only been an extra mouth to feed."

Reverend Wilson choked back a sob. "I still failed you, Georgina. I should have provided for you -" He broke off and let out another heavy sob.

"Reverend Wilson," she said gently, "It all turned out alright in the end. Granted, the road to get here was not easy but I have had many wondrous experiences. My own sort of Grand Tour, I've been to Paris and Venice several times over. And now, perhaps the most unexpected thing of all, I find myself a countess. Now, who could've predicted that all those years ago when you spotted me singing in church?"

Reverend Wilson made a small smile, his eyes still red but his spirits beginning to rally thanks to Georgina's impassioned speech. "Georgina, I can't say I will ever truly understand. But what I do know is that I don't even need to understand. You were born with so few advantages and dealt some bad hands. Some really bad hands. So far beyond the realm of my experience. In any case, what I do know is that you are a daughter of God who is loved by her creator and who was born for such a time as this."

Georgina smiled softly. "Reverend, you are as wise as ever." She took one his hands in her own. It was more frail than she remembered, the skin grown taut with the turning of the years. "Now, shall we sing together for old time's sake," she said with genuine brightness.

And together they sang *Light Shining out of Darkness*, his ageing tenor's voice still hitting the right notes as he did with the psalms in the days of his youth when he first became a deacon. As for Georgina, well dear reader, her voice was still as sweet and as honeyed as when she had first taken to the stage as an eighteen-year-old in Bath. An echo of the girl the Reverend once knew. And of the woman she was now and of the matriarch she would most surely become. She had come back into the Wilson's lives and would not truly leave it again.

God moves in a mysterious way,
His wonders to perform;
He plants his footsteps in the sea,
And rides upon the storm.

Deep in unfathomable mines
Of never-failing skill,
He treasures up his bright designs,
And works his sov'reign will.

Arm-in-arm, the Weatherbys strolled up Union Street past the array of milliners and dressmakers.

"Heavens," Edgar said. "That really was -"

"Something?" Georgina laughed.

"They genuinely do care about you, you know," Edgar said. "Reverend Wilson pulled me aside and gave me the old father's warning."

"I can't say I'm that surprised."

"He's clearly a good sort. Eccentric on the surface but he genuinely cares about you."

"That's true," Georgina nodded. "That's true indeed."

Edgar took Georgina's free hand in his own and rubbed her knuckles affectionately.

Today had been a bizarre one for Edgar. But it had given him a better understanding of Georgina and the world she grew up in. In fact, he saw her now in a new, brighter light.

Several weeks had passed and the dying days of winter had given way to the first signs of spring. Buds began to form on the beech trees and with each sunrise, the frost on the grass grew ever thinner. Soon the lambing season would begin and new life would be all around at Renfregh.

Walking arm in arm around the landscape gardens at the Wiltshire estate, the happy couple made for a fine pair.

Georgina turned to her husband. "Darling, I've got some good news."

Edgar raised a hawklike eyebrow. "What, pray tell, is your news?"

"Well, I haven't had my courses for two months now," she said with a smile.

The pair stopped along the path and turned to face one another.

Edgar was open mouthed in wonderment. "You mean to say you are -"

"I am with child, yes. The doctor has confirmed it."

"Oh my sweet Georgina, that is truly a blessing." Edgar smiled, before his face turned serious. "But how are you feeling? Are you well?"

"So far."

"If you need anything, at any time, like always, just say the word and you shall have it." Edgar took his wife's hand in his and brought it to his lips, kissing her knuckles with great affection and tenderness.

⁕ ⁕ ⁕

"Congratulations, my lady," said Miss Hopkins when she heard the countess' happy news.

"Thank you Miss Hopkins," Georgina said with a smile. "Now, I intend to have my confinement at our London home, and move up there in a month, so we'll need to make arrangements."

"Of course, my lady."

Georgina then set about explaining to her lady's maid the plans to set in motion for the remainder of her pregnancy.

Chapter Thirty-Four

Georgina sat at her desk at Weatherby House with her quill in hand. She was working on plans for the new school at the Renfregh village. Buried deep in her thoughts, she jolted at the knocking on the door. She got up and went to open it, revealing the second Weatherby daughter.

"May I come in please?" Philomena asked.

"Of course," Georgina said.

Philomena walked into the countess' office and stood wringing her hands.

Georgina took pity on her and shut the door.

"Were you scared?" Philomena asked suddenly.

"Scared, how? When?" Georgina replied.

"Of marriage, of being a wife."

"Not especially, it's a natural state."

"But you were independent for so long! Why give that up?" Philomena asked.

"I had my own career, yes, but I was never truly independent. The lot of opera singers and actresses means you are always reliant on the patronage and the protection of powerful men.”

Philomena sucked in her lips before mumbling, “But at least then you did not have to vow to obey anyone.”

“That's true, but I would have been foolish to think that the patrons and the protectors did not still expect obedience nonetheless.” Georgina looked at her sister-in-law and took a breath before continuing. “Philomena, that is what this is about, no? Marriage as a potential loss of freedom?”

Philomena nodded.

“It's not always a loss of freedom,” Georgina said. “In fact, with a decent husband it can be a way to gain a lot of freedom.”

“That doesn't make sense,” Philomena grumbled.

“Well, sometimes if a woman is in a situation where she is beholden to someone else, like a family member, there's not much she can expect in return. You can't choose your family, after all.”

Philomena smiled wryly at Georgina's last remark.

“So,” Georgina continued, “at least with a husband a woman can choose her own way. And that can be more freeing than having to rely on the good will of family members. It's true, however, some women never marry and make their way through running businesses or working for someone else.”

“But that's not really done in the ton,” Philomena said.

“No, it's not. But it's not a total impossibility for you to decide never to marry at all,” Georgina said.

“Maybe,” Philomena pondered. “But say, hypothetically, if I were to marry -”

Philomena tailed off, trying to find the right words for what she wanted to say.

Georgina held her tongue and gave her sister in law the space to consider her next utterance.

After a pause of about thirty seconds, Philomena began to speak again. "If, hypothetically, I were to marry, what if I end up with a cruel man?" The fear in her voice was real.

"Philomena, I swear to you I will do everything in my power to make sure you don't. And Edgar, I'm confident, will do the same."

"Everything's moving so fast, though."

"Things don't have to go that fast," Georgina said gently. "If you'd rather wait a few more years before trying to find a husband, I anticipate we can do that."

That evening, Georgina and Edgar sat on the settee in his chambers.

"Edgar, I should talk with you about Philomena," said Georgina.

"What's happened?" he asked.

"She came to me today and started asking me about marriage and saying she feels things are moving too fast with the marriage mart. She should wait a few more years before going out into society," she said.

Edgar took his wife's hand between his and brought it to his lips in a tender kiss. "Whatever you think is best, my sweet."

As the months wore on, Georgina grew more and more frustrated at the constraints her pregnancy was placing on her body. She had struggled to get used to the change in her centre of gravity and though Edgar offered to help her all the time, she wanted to retain as much independence as she could. Which was how she found herself nursing at a cut on her left ankle as she sat on the garden steps.

"Oww, oww," she seethed to herself in pain.

At precisely that moment, Edgar came through the french doors onto the patio.

Georgina tried to silence her whimpering in an attempt to prevent her husband from undue concern. But it was in vain.

"My sweet Georgina, what's happened?" Edgar said.

She turned her head back towards him and tried to maintain her composure. "It's nothing, nothing."

He cast his eyes over his wife, scanning from head to toe. "Then why is your ankle bleeding?"

"It's nothing to worry about, just a slight scratch is all."

"Well, let me take a proper look -"

"Edgar, there's no need."

"You're bleeding. Of course there's a need," he replied sternly. He bent down and knelt on the step beneath where Georgina sat. Taking her left foot in his hand, he peered at her ankle and examined it. "Heavens, Georgina! There's a lot of blood here. More than you realise, I'd wager. What happened?"

Georgina sighed. "I managed to cut the back of my ankle on the ledge of these stairs walking down them."

"Confound it all!" he exclaimed, before his voice softened. "Are you injured anywhere else?"

She shook her head. "Just this ankle."

"My darling," he cooed. Then he shouted towards the house. "Tibbetts! Tibbetts!"

A beat later and a reedy young footman appeared from the french doors. "Yes, my lord?"

"The countess has injured her ankle. Bring the medical box and call for the doctor, please," Edgar said.

"At once, my lord." Tibbetts gave a bow and hurried back into the house to carry out the earl's commands.

Edgar shook the doctor's hand before the older man left the Weatherby couple alone in their garden.

"I don't want to be a burden to you," Georgina said.

Edgar raised his eyebrows. "A burden? Whatever do you mean?"

"Well, you've got so many duties to attend to, I don't want to add to them, with you protecting me in situations like this."

"Protecting you isn't just a duty, Georgina. It's a privilege," Edgar said. His ordinarily hawklike eyes instead shone with an earnest glow.

Her ankle long since healed, Georgina reclined lazily on the settee with one hand stroking her heavily pregnant belly. She was fat with the first of what she hoped would be a growing Weatherby brood and would be due next month. If someone had asked her a year ago if she ever imagined she would be in this position as the rightful Countess of Weatherby, she would have laughed a thousand ways of Sunday! But here she was. The last year was all true, it was going to be her and Edgar forever and ever, joined in Holy Matrimony in front of Almighty God!

Edgar entered the room, fresh from his ride around Hyde Park. He walked over towards Georgina, kissed her head and bulging belly. "Hello, darling wife, would you like some relief?"

"Oh, yes please," Georgina said.

"Very well." Edgar took a seat at the end of the settee next to her feet and took them in his leather-gloved hands. Rubbing hard, he enjoyed the moans of delight his wife emitted.

"Oh Edgar, that feels so good," she cried.

"I know something else that will feel even better," he chuckled wickedly. With that, he slid his hands up Georgina's shapely legs and placed one hand between her folds. Moving his hand between her folds, he reached her pleasure pearl and stroked with feather-light touches. He was delighted to find that his sweet Georgina was soaking wet.

Then he placed both protective hands on her pregnant belly and nestled his head between his wife's legs. He lapped gently at her entrance, enjoying the taste of her juices. What a woman, he thought! He nuzzled his nose up into her folds and focused his tongue's attentions on her pleasure pearl.

She writhed with pleasure as leather-clad hands soothingly rubbed her ginormous bump. She felt a wave of pleasure begin to build in her core and spread up into her belly and breasts. Given her pregnant state, everything was heightened and she was needier than ever. Only Edgar could satisfy her properly. Only ever Edgar!

CHAPTER THIRTY-FIVE

At about two in the morning, Georgina awoke feeling an unfamiliar dampness beneath her. She realised it was her waters.

She patted Edgar on the arm. "Edgar, wake up, wake up!"

He groggily came to consciousness. "What is it?"

"My waters, they've broken."

Edgar got up with a jolt. "I'll send for the midwives and your maids."

He rose from the bed and pulled on a pair of breeches and shirt. Then he leant over to where Georgina sat and kissed her on the forehead. "I won't be long, darling. I love you so so much."

Then he left the bedroom and Georgina was alone.

A short while later, her lady's maid Miss Hopkins entered the room followed by two housemaids carrying bowls of water and towels.

The midwives Mrs Shaw and Mrs Pemberton entered the room, women whom Georgina had met with on numerous occasions throughout her confinement. Edgar followed behind.

Georgina got up off the bed and began to pace slowly around the room.

"That's it, my lady, you walk it out, you walk it out," Mrs Pemberton encouraged.

With Edgar supporting her on one side and Mrs Shaw on the other, Georgina knelt astride on her knees and bore down. As she gave a final push, her baby entered the world and made a hearty cry.

"Congratulations, my lady, you have a son," Mrs Pemberton said as she passed the cleaned-up baby to Georgina.

The countess kissed the child's head and, at that very moment, she felt pure happiness.

As Georgina settled down into her innermost confinement chamber, she reflected back on the momentous events of the past twenty-four hours. She had survived what would probably prove to be the most dangerous endeavour of her life. And she was now mother to a beautiful baby boy. She smiled to herself as she lay on the bed and sleep soon claimed her.

After Georgina had been in her confinement chambers for a week, her first cake and caudle party took place. Jean and several of the old opera crowd came happily through the door.

"Congratulations, our lady!" they whooped.

Georgina could not help but laugh at their frivolity and the shout of 'our lady'. She had not felt like much of a lady after giving birth, but the week of rest had set her on the road to feeling more like herself again.

The next day was another cake and caudle party, this time around with the Countess of Solihull, the Viscountess Bournemouth and several friends from the ton. A much more restrained affair than the joyous whoops of the day before, Georgina nonetheless enjoyed spending the afternoon with a group of ladies who wanted to dote on her. She could get used to being the centre of attention, she thought.

❧❧❧❧❧ ❧❧❧❧❧

On the morning of her first foray outside the Weatherby property after giving birth a month before, Georgina stepped happily onto the gravel and, with Edgar's assistance, into the carriage.

Though ordinarily they might walk directly to the church, Georgina's postpartum state meant no one wanted to take any risks. For today was Georgina's Churching ceremony.

"How are you feeling, darling?" Edgar said as the two took their seats in the carriage.

"Excited," she said with a smile. "It's good to be out of the house for a bit."

Edgar squeezed her hand. "I'm glad to hear it. Say, there's a production of *Much Ado About Nothing* on at Drury Lane on Saturday. Do you want to go?"

"Yes! How could I turn that down!"

"I thought you'd say that. I'll organise our box then."

❧❧❧❧❧ ❧❧❧❧❧

A short ride down Grosvenor Street and the carriage pulled up outside St George's, Hannover Square. A footman opened the door and Edgar disembarked, before turning back to assist Georgina.

Xavier, Philomena and various other members of the ton were already inside the church. The earl and countess made their way up the steps, through the doors and shortly thereafter the service began.

Georgina knelt down at the altar rail and the priest intoned, "Forasmuch as it hath pleased almighty God of his goodness to give you safe deliverance, and hath preserved you in the great danger of child-birth..."

❧❧❧❧❧❧ ❦❦❦❦❦❦

On Saturday, two figures who had not been seen at the Theatre Royal on Drury Lane in many months made their way through the doors and up the red carpets of the stairs to their box.

As they arrived on the balcony, the Baroness Chevalier crossed their path and stopped in front of them.

"Good evening, my lord, my lady," she said, casting a smile in Georgina's direction.

Georgina returned the smile, trying to wrack her brains about who the woman was. She knew most of the top tiers of the ton on sight by now but not this woman.

"Good evening, Baroness Chevalier," Edgar said with a bow in the direction of the baroness.

Georgina breathed a sigh of relief. So that's who this mysterious woman was! Chevalier. Chevalier. Chevalier. She vowed to commit her name to memory.

"May I congratulate you on the birth of your heir," the baroness said. "Everyone in the Chevalier household was most delighted to hear the news."

"Thank you, my lady," Georgina said.

"Yes, that's kind of you to say, thank you," Edgar said.

The three then concluded their conversation with cordial greetings and Edgar put his arm around Georgina's waist, directing her towards their box.

⁂

The house lights went down, the curtain rose and applause filled the theatre.

The actors took to the stage and Edgar and Georgina laughed along as Benedick ranted about the traits he sought in a perfect woman and Beatrice displayed her sharp wit.

During the masquerade ball scene, Georgina rubbed her dainty hand up and down Edgar's thigh.

He leaned towards her and whispered in her ear. "Brings back memories for you, my lady?"

"Perhaps, my Lord." A coquettish smile overtook her lips. She took his face between her hands and claimed his mouth with her ravenous tongue.

All too soon, the final scene was playing out upon the stage. As Benedick said the immortal line of "get thee a wife", Edgar rubbed gentle circles on his wife's hand and placed a kiss on her cheek.

⁂

Tobias, Baron Pewsey and heir to the Weatherby earldom, would not remember his christening. He slept through most of the ceremony, only waking up with a shriek when the vicar dipped him lightly into the font. After that brief interruption, Tobias quickly returned to the land of sleep and the ceremony continued without the conscious aware-ness of its star. The Duke of Faversham and the Earl of Mowbrow stood as his godfathers while Belinda became his godmother.

As they walked up the aisle, the group made for a peculiar assortment at first glance. At the head were the Earl and Countess of Weatherby, with young Tobias in the earl's arms. Then behind were the duke and duchess, chatting amiably with Miss Cookson. The Earl of Mowbrow, some ladies of the stage and the rest of the Weatherbys followed behind. And yet, as the party made their way down the stairs of the church and out onto St George Street, no on-looker would have been able to deny the true contentment of the Earl and Countess of Weatherby nor the unified support of their family and friends. For though in theory a marriage between the patriarch of one of Britain's most distinguished noble families and a former opera singer born into rural destitution could never work out, in practice the reality was rather different. High society would have no choice but to take notice. In fact, you might say that the ton would never be the same.

AUTHOR'S NOTE

While neither Georgina nor Edgar nor even the Weatherby earldom ever existed, there are historical instances of lords marrying their mistresses, including former ladies of the stage and courtesans. Just as Lord Redditch notes in the prologue, the third Earl of Bolton is one such example. In 1751 he married his mistress, the actress Lavinia Fenton, and she became his second wife. In part, it was to shine a light on these historical examples that this book was written.

I also wanted to explore the role of the Church of England during marriage of the period. Regardless of how much an individual person did or did not believe in the Church's doctrines, the Church touched the lives of everyone in the entire country. As they do today, Church of England bishops sat in the House of Lords and participated in debates and votes on legislation. In the first decade of the nineteenth century, the only marriages legally able to be performed in England were those according to Jewish and Quaker traditions as well as those performed according to the rites of the Church of England. The overwhelming majority of marriages at the time took place in the Church of England.

Enclosure was another issue I wanted to cover because it has shaped the past millennium of English history more than many other events. Its impacts still matter today and in Georgina's and Edgar's time would have been very rawly felt. Families like Edgar's, a very small minority of the overall population, benefited enormously from enclosure. However, millions like Georgina's family suffered the consequences and spent the nineteenth century in rural poverty or relocating to urban areas to work in often gruelling industries.

One area where I took some historical liberties for artistic purposes was how the economies of the stage worked in Venice during the early nineteenth century. I do hope readers will forgive me for this indulgence.

ACKNOWLEDGEMENTS

First off, thank you to you the reader of this book. I hope that you enjoyed it and that you got something out of Georgina and Edgar's story.

To the team at Miblart, thank you for your excellent work on the cover art, graphic design and branding.

And thank you to MD for everything.

Discussion Questions

1. Enclosure was a process in England over several centuries whereby commoners were deprived of their access to common land. How did the social consequences of this policy influence Georgina's life?

2. Marriage in Regency England was the main form of security for women. Yet it also represented a loss of independence. What did freedom mean for women in that time and place?

3. Edgar was born to inherit the Earldom of Weatherby. Being an earl in Regency England meant holding a position of great power and authority. What use are power and authority if one does not use them to good? And should anyone be in such a position of power in the first place?

4. Until late in the nineteenth century, dowries were expected for English brides from many sections of the class spectrum. Not having a dowry was a real

problem for women. What might you have done if you were a woman in Regency England with little or no dowry?

5. Georgina makes a decision to become a courtesan because she believed she had no other realistic option if she was to survive. In your opinion, did she have any other genuine options?

6. Edgar is highly focused on doing what he thinks the ton views to be correct behaviour. How did the tragedy of his parents' deaths influence his beliefs? Would he take a different perspective if he had not become the earl at a relatively young age?

7. Edgar places a great deal of value on the concept of duty and what duty means to him changes over the course of the book. What does duty mean to you, and do you think it is important?

8. Georgina's friend Jean is a consistent presence throughout her adult life. What can their friendship tell us about the importance of women supporting each other?

9. Until Georgina enters Edgar's life he doesn't really consider the need to make changes in the lives of his tenants or through parliamentary legislation. Learning about Georgina's background spurs him to make changes on his estates. What other changes do you think might happen in the

future? Will there even be an Earl of Weatherby in several generations' time?

10. The performing arts scene around Covent Garden was closely intertwined with sex work. In what ways have attitudes towards sex work changed since the Regency era? In what ways haven't they?

11. Which *A Question of Duty* character is your favourite and why?

About the Author

Chloe Willowfield adores all things historical romance. Ever since she was very young, she has been fascinated by how people lived in the past.

When she's not writing, you'll find her enjoying musicals, visiting local cafes or maybe even going on a hike.

You can connect with Chloe on Instagram, TikTok or Pinterest. You can also keep up-to-date by signing up for her newsletter.

Chloe can be reached via email at chloe@chloewillowfield.com. She'd love to hear from you!

SUBSCRIBE TO CHLOE'S NEWSLETTER

Scan the QR code below to subscribe to Chloe's newsletter and stay updated on the latest releases.

VISIT CHLOE'S WEBSITE

Scan the QR code below or head to
www.chloewillowfield.com

VISIT CHLOE'S WEBSITE

Head to www.chloewillowfield.com

www.ingramcontent.com/pod-product-compliance
Lightning Source LLC
Chambersburg PA
CBHW050855210726
48290CB00004B/1241